Praise for Cres

'One of our favourit
F

'Hopeful and hopelessly
sweep-you-off-your-feet slice of escapism'
Red

'A warm and wonderful read'
Woman's Own

'We couldn't put this down!'
Bella

'You'll devour this'
Woman's Weekly

'Cressida's characters are wonderful!'
Sarah Morgan

'Evocative and gorgeous'
Phillipa Ashley

'Uplifting, heartwarming and brimming with romance'
Cathy Bramley

'Gorgeously romantic . . . forced me to go to bed early
so I could read it'
Sophie Cousens

'I just LOVED this story. All the characters are wonderful'
Isabelle Broom

'Real heart and soul'
Sarra Manning

'The most gorgeously romantic, utterly perfect book'
Rachael Lucas

'A triumph. Breathlessly romantic, it sparkles with wit
and genuine warmth'
Miranda Dickinson

'So many perfect romantic moments that made me melt. Just gorgeous'
Jules Wake

'A wonderful ray of reading sunshine'
Heidi Swain

'I fell completely and utterly in love . . . it had me glued to the pages'
Holly Martin

'A total hands-down treat. A book you'll want to
cancel plans and stay in with'
Pernille Hughes

'Sizzlingly romantic and utterly compelling, I couldn't put it down'
Alex Brown

'Bursting with warmth and wit'
Kirsty Greenwood

'Funny, sexy and sweep-you-off-your-feet-romantic'
Zara Stoneley

'Perfectly pitched between funny, sexy, tender and
downright heartbreaking. I loved it'
Jane Casey

'As hot & steamy as a freshly made hot chocolate, and as sweet
& comforting as the whipped cream & sprinkles that go on top'
Helen Fields

'Just brilliant. Sweet, sexy and sizzzzling. It was a pure joy to read'
Lisa Hall

'A little slice of a Cornish cream tea but without the calories'
Bella Osborne

'Perfect escapism, deliciously romantic. I was utterly transported'
Emily Kerr

'Utter perfection . . . a total gem'
Katy Colins

'Sexy, sweet and simmering with sunshine'
Lynsey James

The Secret Christmas Bookshop

Cressy grew up in South-East London surrounded by books and with a cat named after Lawrence of Arabia. She studied English at the University of East Anglia and now lives in Norwich with her husband David. *The Secret Christmas Bookshop* is her sixteenth novel and her books have sold a million copies worldwide. When she isn't writing, Cressy spends her spare time reading, returning to London, or exploring the beautiful Norfolk coastline.

If you'd like to find out more about Cressy, visit her on her social media channels. She'd love to hear from you!

📷 @cressmclaughlin
f /CressidaMcLaughlinAuthor
𝕏 @CressMcLaughlin

Also by Cressida McLaughlin

A Christmas Tail
The Canal Boat Café
The Canal Boat Café Christmas
The Once in a Blue Moon Guesthouse
The House of Birds and Butterflies
The Staycation
The Happy Hour

The Cornish Cream Tea series
The Cornish Cream Tea Bus
The Cornish Cream Tea Summer
The Cornish Cream Tea Christmas
The Cornish Cream Tea Wedding
Christmas Carols and a Cornish Cream Tea
The Cornish Cream Tea Holiday
The Cornish Cream Tea Bookshop
From Cornwall With Love

The Secret Christmas Bookshop

Cressida McLaughlin

HarperCollins*Publishers*

HarperCollins*Publishers* Ltd
1 London Bridge Street,
London SE1 9GF

www.harpercollins.co.uk

HarperCollins*Publishers*
Macken House, 39/40 Mayor Street Upper
Dublin 1, D01 C9W8

First published by HarperCollins*Publishers* 2024
1

A catalogue record for this book is available from the British Library

ISBN: 978-0-00-862380-7 (PB)

Typeset in Birka by Palimpsest Book Production Limited, Falkirk, Stirlingshire

Printed and bound in the UK using 100% Renewable Electricity by CPI Group (UK) Ltd

MIX
Paper | Supporting
responsible forestry
FSC™ C007454

This book contains FSC™ certified paper and other controlled sources
to ensure responsible forest management.

For more information visit: www.harpercollins.co.uk/green

For Alice

Chapter One

It wasn't even dark when Sophie Stevens heard the first firework, but she knew, then, that it was time to move on. She stood behind her narrow counter in Hartley Country Apparel, twirling a silver biro between her fingers, and listened to the staccato, celebratory pops that sounded too close by.

'Probably some lads from the school.' Fiona didn't look up from her crossword, her brows creased in concentration. She was wearing a tweed jacket, always a living mannequin for the high-end items they sold, her golden hair falling in layered waves that framed her face. 'From now until Christmas they'll be bubbling over with mischief. This is only the beginning.'

'At least they're having fun,' Sophie said.

Fiona looked up. 'Do you want to abandon your notebooks, go and set off some illicit bangers? Have you been hiding a reckless streak from me this entire time?'

'I might have some hidden features you don't know about.' She raised an eyebrow.

'You sound like a smartphone.' Fiona paused, then added, 'Everything's OK, though? You've seemed restless these last few days.'

Sophie tried to hide her surprise. Firework night was her catalyst; the time when she always started to think about leaving. Except that if Fiona had noticed she was restless, her subconscious must have begun priming her for her short-notice disappearing act already. This time she was considering Cornwall, which was almost as far as she could get from where she was now: the sleepy, beautiful village of Mistingham, on the north Norfolk coast. She found that the further she went, the easier it was to start again.

'I'm fine,' she said to Fiona. 'Just gearing up for Christmas, working out which materials I need to reorder, how many more notebooks I need to make to keep my shelves filled.'

'They're very beautiful shelves,' Fiona said.

That was one thing Sophie would miss: the notebook concession she had in Fiona and her husband Ermin's country clothes store. The shop drew in a lot of customers, and unique, luxury notebooks were just the kind of indulgent treat that tourists and visitors let themselves buy on holiday or days out. She always had a range of styles, sizes and price points: clothbound notebooks with ribbon ties; card-covered jotters with hand-painted designs and long-stitch binding; leather, casebound journals that took her the longest to make but were cooed over on a daily basis, the ultimate treasure.

She made them with plain pages for doodling, thick- and thin-lined for to-do lists and general scribbling, dotted for people who were serious about their bullet journals. Her corner of the shop was a cornucopia of colour and texture, offering the endless possibility of hundreds of blank pages.

And at Christmastime, her notebooks shimmied into the limelight. They were bought as presents, of course, because it was easy to be that little bit more lavish when you were buying for someone else. But December was also a month of list-making: lists of presents you needed to buy, who to send Christmas cards to, your shopping list for the Big Lunch. Recipes copied from books and amended to suit your guest list, mindful of any allergies or intolerances. There were secret lists of the gifts you wanted for yourself, or the Christmas wishes you were going to make, because – if you were like Sophie – you still believed in that festive magic at thirty-seven, as well as the power of a fresh, sparkling New Year, even if you would never admit it to anyone.

This was Sophie's time to shine, and every year she leaned into it. She expanded her notebook range, honed her craft, surrounded the workstation in whatever rented flat she was living in with piles of new materials. She had fallen into a pattern of having a frenetic, successful festive season, then packing up all her things, what was left of her stock, and starting again somewhere else.

'Everyone in Mistingham will have at least one new notebook by the end of December, if I have anything to do with it,' she said. There was no reason to change that pattern this year, even if she had found a static home for her business here in Mistingham.

'Why stop at one?' Fiona said. 'Why not aim for a trio of notebooks for every resident? You could put together little packs.'

'I *could*.' Sophie turned to her current to-do list, because she didn't just advocate the power of notebooks, she was a true believer. She always had several on the go, all with different purposes, in the same way Fiona was always wearing at least one item of Hartley Country Apparel stock. 'You're like me,' Fiona had said to her ten months ago, on the day Sophie had arrived in the village with her suitcase and her craft supplies. 'You live it, rather than just selling it.'

Before Mistingham, Sophie had sold her creations at country fairs and festivals, craft and farmers' markets, her online shop receiving a trickle of orders rather than a rush. She supplemented her income working in cafés or pubs, and she hadn't expected to be able to afford shop space, but Fiona and Ermin were big on supporting local businesses, and when the owner of their last concession – a woman who made soy candles – moved away, Fiona had offered the cosy corner of Hartley Country Apparel to her.

Sophie had been able to expand her stock, working in the evenings at the sun-drenched workstation in her living room and, over the last ten months, she'd built up a busy, popular business with lots of tourist sales and repeat customers, a momentum she hadn't experienced before.

Nothing had gone wrong so far – everything was going better than it had done in a long while – but Sophie couldn't ignore the slow simmer of unease in her gut: the knowledge that if she *did* stay much longer, then things would turn sour, as they always did. Restricting herself to a year in each place meant it was easy to break what few ties she'd allowed herself to knot.

The ping of the shop door announced a new customer, and Sophie smiled as Dexter appeared. He owned

Mistingham Bakery, and was a dark-haired hulk of a man. Today he was wearing a green corduroy jacket that looked too light for the weather, and a thick navy scarf.

Beyond the glass, a whisper-soft mist coated everything with a silver tinge, adding to the November chill.

'Afternoon Fiona, Sophie,' Dexter said, rubbing his hands together.

'Have you come in for some gloves?' Fiona turned pointedly to the stand next to her counter. Sophie knew, because it was hard not to stroke them, that the gloves were made of the softest leather and suede. Who wouldn't want to slide their fingers into them? If she'd had a boyfriend to buy a present for – the thought was simultaneously laughable and tinged with sadness – then she would have bought him a pair in buttery, caramel-coloured suede.

'One day,' Dexter said, his smile warm and amused. 'Except that my hands are always covered in flour, so I'd ruin them in a heartbeat. I came to see if you'd got any new scarves in. You had some really colourful ones last year.'

'Is Lucy excited about Christmas?' Fiona asked.

Lucy was Dexter's nine-year-old daughter, and the two of them came as a pair. Dexter's wife – Lucy's mum – had died a few years ago, but Lucy was as high-spirited as her dad, who always had a smile for everyone.

'We're not allowed to be excited about Christmas yet,' Dexter told them. 'Lucy's got it all worked out. We had to focus first on Halloween, then it's Bonfire Night, then Christmas. If she knew I was getting in early with the present buying, I'd get a proper telling off.'

'Why *are* you getting in so early?' Sophie couldn't help asking. She was fascinated by how different families worked because, growing up in so many foster homes, the range of traditions, rules and outlooks of her temporary parents had left her in a constant state of whiplash.

'It's pure panic.' Dexter leaned an elbow on the varnished wood of Fiona's counter, sounding as far from panicked as it was possible to get.

'Panic?'

'Don't you get that?' he asked. 'There's always a sense, round about now, that you should really start buying gifts, but then you get caught up in other day-to-day stuff, and suddenly it's the twentieth of December and you've done none of it. I'm trying to respond to that original instinct before it disappears.'

'I don't usually . . .' *have anyone to buy for*, Sophie could have finished. 'I don't get that panic.'

'I do a big trip to Norwich the last weekend of November,' Fiona said. 'I have a list, and I get everything I need then – whatever I can't get in Mistingham, of course.'

'That's far too organized,' Dexter said. 'Anyway. If I get Luce something now, then I'll at least have *one* thing sorted for her. She's angling for a Kindle, which I can get online – actually, I could do that today.'

Sophie grinned. 'She'll be furious with you if she finds out.'

'Don't think that gets you out of buying a scarf,' Fiona scolded, and Dexter's cheeks turned pink. 'Anyway, what's with this Kindle nonsense? When did a bit of plastic replace a gorgeous hardback with that perfect book smell and a cover you could hang on your wall?'

Sophie absent-mindedly stroked the turquoise leather notebook she had on the counter. The cover was soft, dyed leather, and she'd stitched it together with pink thread and added a pink elastic band closure. It was the perfect place to write thoughts and secrets.

'She's into this YA Romantasy stuff,' Dexter said. 'They're huge books, so she says it would be easier to read them on a Kindle. But she'll want the special editions as well, won't she?' He rubbed at his jacket cuff, suddenly looking anxious, and Sophie felt a pang of sympathy. She couldn't imagine how hard it was for him to do all the parenting, make all those decisions, by himself.

'I get it,' she said gently. 'Sometimes I type notes on my phone for convenience, but if I want a proper list, if I want the satisfaction of ticking off items I've completed, or it's something I want to spend my time writing out, I use a notebook. You don't have to commit to one or the other.'

'You're right, you don't.' Dexter's smile flickered back into place. 'Thanks, Sophie.'

'If The Book Ends was still open, you'd be able to get all Lucy's special editions there,' Fiona said. 'Christmas presents would be easier for everyone; Mistingham would be an entirely different village.'

'It's been closed for a couple of years now, hasn't it?' Sophie asked.

You couldn't live in Mistingham and not know about the fabled bookshop, though Fiona's suggestion that its loss had completely changed the village had to be pushing it. The shop still stood empty, a little way from Hartley Country Apparel on Perpendicular Street, the road that ran up from the seafront through the middle of the village. It was next to the much smaller, but also empty Ye Olde Sweete Shoppe. The Book Ends shop name was still visible in faded yellow script above, with the suggestion 'So Buy Another One' in a smaller font below.

'Nearly three years now,' Fiona said. 'When Bernie Anderly's mind deserted him, and he had to move into a care home. Such a shame – an entirely avoidable one.' She shook her head. 'Anyone want a cuppa?'

'I'd love one,' Sophie said.

Dexter glanced at his watch. 'Me too. If I'm included in that?'

'Of course you are,' Fiona said. 'The longer you stay, the more likely you are to buy something.' She disappeared amongst the stands of cashmere and Fair Isle jumpers, moleskin trousers and suede gilets.

'She's still angry that Bernie's son didn't take over the bookshop,' Dexter said. 'As if she can move the people in this village about like armies on a Risk board.'

Sophie didn't want to dwell on how Fiona might react when she told her she was leaving Mistingham. But she prized her independence more than anything, and Fiona would soon get over it: she'd find someone else to fill her concession corner, and Sophie would be a lost Risk counter that would soon be forgotten about.

'That's Harry Anderly, isn't it?' she asked, pushing her unease away. 'Harry Anderly of Mistingham Manor.' Spoken like that it sounded grand, much grander than the reality, which was that Bernie Anderly's son had moved back to Mistingham from London only in the final months of his father's life, that the manor was more horror film chic than Jane Austen adaptation, and that Harry was hardly ever seen in the village, and seemed to avoid human interaction at all costs.

Sophie had got to know May – who was Harry's house-mate and, most people thought, his girlfriend – a little bit during her time in the village, but she had always been tight-lipped about him, saying only that he was in a difficult position, that he was doggedly focused on repairing the manor rather than purposefully unfriendly. But to Sophie he felt like a fairy-tale villain, someone talked about but rarely seen. May could say all the generous things she liked about him, but he was never around to prove them for himself.

'The least likely person to ever run a bookshop,' Dexter said. 'He'd send customers away with his scowls and mono-syllabic answers. It's bad enough that he's making us move the Christmas festival, that we have to have the fireworks on the beach instead of the green, all because of that bloody oak tree.' He shook his head. 'The modern world is becoming so much more impersonal: Kindles rather than hardbacks; online shopping instead of places like this; watching the fireworks from miles away instead of getting together on the village green. Fiona's holding onto a dream that has already died.'

'And yet you leave genuine wicker baskets, full of bread and cakes and milk, on your customers' doorsteps,' Fiona pointed out, returning with three mismatched mugs full of steaming tea.

'Yeah, well.' Dexter shrugged. 'That's how I choose to run my business, and there's still demand for it in Mistingham, so why should I stop?'

'Why should I give up on my dream that someone will open up that bookshop again?' Fiona parried. 'And as for the supposed *Oak Fest*.' She tutted, tapping her finger on the counter. 'That green has been the site of village events for centuries. The moment Harry's back, he stops *everything*. I know the land is part of the Mistingham Manor estate, but Bernie encouraged all of it, and that upstart's vetoing it. He should go back to London – if he's even wanted there.'

'Come on,' Dexter said gently. 'I agree with you that not being able to use the green is frustrating, but we don't really know Harry, or what he's been through. At the very least his dad died and – well, losing someone close is never easy.'

Sophie gave him a gentle smile: Dexter knew that more than anyone.

Fiona put her mug down with a heavy *thunk*. 'He should talk to us, instead of ripping the heart out of the village.'

Sophie hid her grin at her friend's emotive language. She didn't add that she would have loved the bookshop to be open, that she would have spent a good chunk of her profits on dark thrillers and sparkling romances that held endless wonder in their pages; historical novels that whisked her away to another time.

Books and notebooks: one with the pages already full of magic; the other waiting for you to create some of your own. She couldn't do without either, and she was already looking forward to getting back to *Beach Read* by Emily Henry that evening. And then, maybe she'd start a Christmas book, to get her in the festive spirit.

'Have you got time to show me these scarves, then?' Dexter asked, when he'd drained his tea.

'Of course,' Fiona said smugly. 'This way.'

Once they were hidden behind a rail of expensive jeans, their voices muffled, Sophie opened her notebook to the middle pages and wrote 'Cornwall 2025' at the top. She pushed her ponytail, long and reddish-brown, over her shoulder, and waited for the familiar buzz of energy she usually got when she set out the next chapter in her story, crafted a new life plan. This time, it was distinctly muted. She doodled a flower-shaped bullet point, waited for inspiration to strike, and was distracted by a clatter from outside.

She saw through the window that their A-board, advertising chunky winter knits and luxury leather journals, had fallen over in the wind. She slipped out from behind her counter, pushed open the door and headed for the sign, which was lying on its side on the pavement. Her shoulder connected with something and she jolted back, just as someone said 'Jesus! What the . . .?'

Sophie looked to her right, where a man was staring down at his grey jacket, the unhelpful angle of his takeaway coffee cup, and a dark stain spreading across the fabric. With his gaze elsewhere, Sophie had time to examine him, and felt a spark of recognition. Thick, mid-brown hair that had been tousled by the wind; square jaw brushed with stubble; long, straight nose; thick brows.

Then he looked up, and she added to her cataloguing: eyes that were neither dark nor pale, but that bore into her with an intensity she wasn't used to. This, she realized, was Harry Anderly – as if talking about him had conjured him here, perhaps to admonish them all.

'I didn't see you,' Sophie said.

'Clearly.' His voice was tight.

'I'm sorry,' she went on, 'but you might have noticed me, too. You were walking towards me: I was right in front of you.'

'I was distracted.' He glanced away from her, towards the shop window, as if that had been the cause.

'Right,' she said, when he didn't add anything else. She gestured to his jacket. 'If it's black coffee, it won't leave a mark.'

He looked back at her and their gazes held. She saw that his eyes were hazel, greens and browns mingling together.

'Good to know,' he said after a beat, then cleared his throat.

The silence stretched, and Sophie decided that Dexter's sympathy for him was misplaced. She reached out towards the A-board, but before she could pick it up Harry grabbed hold of it. He slammed it on the ground with almost enough force to crack the paving stones and then, without even glancing at her, strode off up Perpendicular Street.

Sophie stared at him. 'I was *right* in front of you,' she said again, this time to nobody. It was a good job the fireworks were being let off from the beach rather than his land. She couldn't imagine how bad things would get for everyone if he gave into the village's requests and something went wrong. She tapped the top of the A-board, checking Harry had put it back on even ground, then went inside.

Fiona and Dexter were still by the accessories, so she returned to her notebook and her plans for next year. There was a part of her that knew it made no sense, that questioned why, when things were going well, she felt the need to start again. But the memories of Bristol were still stubbornly fresh in her mind. She'd been there for three years, let herself get complacent with a job she loved, a man she believed was in it for the long haul, and it had all fallen apart.

She was happiest when she wasn't tied down, felt lighter when there was nothing holding her to a place or a person.

Everyone was different, and this was how she chose to live her life: there was nothing wrong with it.

Fiona and Dexter were laughing somewhere behind her, and she could see people in heavy coats and thick hats walking past outside, cheeks pink from a bracing walk along the seafront. Sophie decided that she would throw everything into the next two months, make sure her Christmas was as profitable as possible, so she'd have everything she needed to start afresh at the beginning of next year. The buzz of energy and excitement would come as soon as she had something concrete written down, as soon as she firmed up some of her ideas. She was sure of it.

Chapter Two

Mistingham was like a relic from a different time, a village taken straight out of a period drama, if you ignored all the modern cars and people wearing Nikes and Hunter wellies. It was nestled along Norfolk's northern coastline, with a soft, sandy beach and a wide promenade, the North Sea glittering blue, steel grey or close to black, depending on the weather and its mood, the wind farm like a cluster of white garden windmills on the horizon.

Seagulls were a constant presence, cawing or swooping or stalking along the tops of walls, surveying unsuspecting tourists emerging from the establishments on Perpendicular Street: the ice-cream shop Two Scoops; Batter Days – which sold incredible fish and chips right below Sophie's flat; the old-fashioned arcade Penny For Them, and of course, Hartley Country Apparel.

The village pub, the Blossom Bough, had a traditional Norfolk flint exterior and sash windows that emitted a soft, alluring glow on winter nights, the dark wood bar and panelling inside offset by modern lighting, gleaming optics and cream walls. Dexter's bakery was at the top of Perpendicular Street, its delicious smells settling like snow across the village when the wind was blowing in the right direction, and the Mistingham Hotel – run by sisters Mary and Winnie – sat at the top of the gently sloping hill and overlooked Mistingham Green, with its ancient oak tree – the subject of so much consternation – and the low-slung village hall.

The post office had been run from the hotel since before Sophie had moved there, the sisters agreeing to take on the role on top of their already busy schedules rather than lose it altogether, to ensure that the residents – a lot of whom were elderly – didn't have to travel for such a vital service.

On Monday morning, Sophie stepped into Mistingham Hotel's calming foyer. There were no Christmas decorations up yet, but an autumn garland of red and gold leaves trailed along the mantel above the fireplace, a couple of miniature pumpkins left over from Halloween nestled amongst the foliage.

The post office was at the front of the hotel, next to the kitchen, and she breathed in the aromas of butter and roasting meat, her stomach rumbling even though she'd just had breakfast. She made this trip at least twice a week, sending out orders from her online shop, sometimes collecting parcels of paper, leather or board when she had missed the postman trying to deliver them to her flat.

The queue was already long, two women in front of her talking about the fireworks that had gone off without a hitch on the beach on Saturday night.

'They spent more money on it this year judging by how

long it went on,' one woman said, her arms full of packages. 'Probably to placate us.'

'We all had sparklers on the prom,' her friend replied. 'It was a bit windier, but I didn't mind.'

'What's the village green for, if not community events?' The first woman sounded plaintive.

'Ducks?' her friend suggested.

'It doesn't have a pond.'

Sophie hid her smile behind her own parcels, just as Winnie called 'Next!' and Indigo, the teenage son of the Blossom Bough's landlady, Natasha, took his place at the counter, holding a large cardboard box. The women in front of Sophie shuffled forwards, and she did the same.

Winnie got Indigo to put his box on the scales, and they exchanged a joke Sophie couldn't hear, Indigo's chuckle low and soft. She stared out of the window, at three jackdaws tussling over something on the dewy grass, as a shiny black Mercedes pulled into one of the parking spaces in front of the hotel. The sky was a washed-out blue, the sea Sophie had greeted through her kitchen window that morning slate grey and gently rippling.

Footsteps and voices echoed behind her as more people joined the queue, and she couldn't help listening in.

'There has to be some way of doing it.' The woman spoke in a low voice, so although Sophie thought it was vaguely familiar, she couldn't tell who it was without turning around. 'Some way you can—'

'There *isn't*.' The man's reply was sharp, and Sophie knew exactly who *this* was, because two days before he'd bumped into her outside the shop, then given her gruff, tight-lipped responses when she'd been gracious enough to apologise. 'It's hundreds of years old,' Harry Anderly went on. 'It's fragile, already compromised, and there is no possibility—'

'There is always a possibility,' the woman said, and Sophie realized it was May. They lived together at the crumbling manor, had apparently been friends since they were children, and were, according to all the rumours – though Sophie had never asked her outright – a couple. 'At least go to the meeting,' May continued. 'That way you could see—'

'I don't have your rose-tinted view,' Harry cut in. 'The world isn't full of perfect solutions just waiting to be found. Sometimes things simply aren't possible, and all you can do is accept that and move on.'

'You're not trying hard enough,' May said breezily, and Sophie grinned to herself. In their limited interactions, May had always sounded upbeat, as if she was convinced something good was just around the corner if you only believed in it. But Sophie was with Harry on this one: you couldn't simply wish something into existence, no matter how passionately you wanted it. Growing up in foster care, where – for her, at least – the wishing had always outweighed the getting, had put optimism quite a long way behind hard work and practicality in terms of go-to responses.

Harry's reply was a deep, world-weary sigh, and Sophie risked turning her head so she could look at them.

May was a good few inches shorter than Harry – a couple of inches shorter than Sophie – and her long dark hair was pulled up into a messy bun, her dark, intelligent eyes taking in the space around her. She was holding three boxes of the Christmas cards Sophie had seen on a display just inside the door. Harry's hair was still ruffled, his jaw still set tight, and he was wearing the same grey jacket as when she'd last seen him.

'I told you.' She pointed at it. 'Black coffee doesn't stain. Hi, May.'

'Sophie!' May's smile was warm. 'Are you sending off Christmas presents already? You're even earlier than me – I'm only just buying my cards.'

Sophie laughed. 'I'm not, I'm afraid. These are notebooks – online orders from customers. They're probably Christmas presents, but not mine: I'm nowhere near that organized. You're ahead of the game thinking about your cards already.'

'She's the annoying, efficient angel on everyone's shoulder,' Harry said. 'Far too organized and positive. She makes the rest of us look bad.' There was affection there, along with gruffness, and Sophie decided they were the ultimate case of opposites attract.

'Harry won't send anyone a Christmas card,' May said.

'It's a waste of time,' he replied. 'You look at them for two seconds, try to decipher the handwriting, then chuck them in the bin.'

'That's what *you* do,' May corrected. 'Most people aren't like you.'

'I'll take that as a compliment.'

'Don't,' May said brightly.

Harry caught Sophie's eye, and she felt a spark of electricity. He had such a stern, penetrating gaze, it was as if she'd done something wrong just by meeting it. 'You have an online shop as well as your stand in Fiona's?' he asked.

'That's right.' She was surprised he knew even that much about her. 'I couldn't survive solely on what I sell in Hartley's.' Though she couldn't deny that the momentum of the last few months had started to change things, given her business more solid foundations than it had ever had before.

'And you're in the flat above Batter Days?' Harry asked stiffly. 'It's good fish and chips.'

'The curry sauce is to *die* for!' May added, glancing from Harry to Sophie.

Sophie imagined the two of them standing at the Batter Days counter, bundled up in their winter coats, ordering wrapped cod and chips and taking them back to Mistingham Manor, sitting at a polished table in a huge, gleaming kitchen with floor-to-ceiling windows and an Aga. Harry, wide-shouldered and stoically silent, eating his dinner methodically, one chip at a time; May, dainty and dark-haired, covering everything with vinegar, peas slipping off the edge of her plate.

She felt a stab of envy. Whatever shape their relationship took, it was clear they were close, able to be bitingly, teasingly honest with each other, living together in the grand house on the edge of the village. The one-bed flat above Batter Days that she shared with her scruffy dog Clifton couldn't be more different.

'I bet the manor will look so pretty once you've decorated it for Christmas,' she said, then immediately wished she could take it back. At least she hadn't also voiced her fantasy of their cosy fish and chip dinner.

May's eyes lit up. 'Oh, when we do—'

'Decorations won't cover up the cracks,' Harry said, folding his arms tightly. 'It'd be like putting glitter on a grave, so I doubt we'll bother this year. Not when there are so many more important things to get done.' Dismissiveness radiated off him like a glacial chill.

May offered Sophie an apologetic glance, but she was undeterred. 'On the other hand, it would bring some brightness to your home, give you a reason to smile when things feel particularly bleak. A few glitzy baubles, some paper chains.'

He didn't respond immediately, and she resisted the urge to say sorry. It wasn't her fault that she liked daydreaming about families at Christmas, houses decked out in festive finery. She hadn't meant to press on a sore spot.

'Sophie,' Harry said eventually, his voice rough.

'Yes?' She hated sounding hopeful, but she was glad he was going to apologize for being sharp with her.

Instead, he pointed past her. 'It's your turn.'

'Oh!' She spun round, and saw that the two women who had been in front of her had been served. Winnie was waiting for her with a smile, her grey hair a mane of curls. 'Hi, Winnie.' She hurried up to the counter with her parcels, her cheeks warming.

'How are you, Sophie, love?' Winnie asked. 'Got more packages to send out to eager customers?'

'Just a few.' Sophie imagined she could feel Harry's impatience as an oppressive force behind her, and rushed through her interaction with Winnie, wanting to get out of there and back into the cold, fresh air. It was no wonder that even Fiona, with all her powers of persuasion, hadn't been able to change Harry's mind about the business with Mistingham Green and the oak tree. If *she* was in charge, she would probably have moved the events to another village altogether, simply to avoid his wrath.

But then, running away was her modus operandi, so it wasn't a huge surprise Harry Anderly inspired that reaction in her. She took her receipt and thanked Winnie, then set her sights firmly on the doorway.

'Bye, Sophie,' May said.

'Bye.' She gave the other woman a warm smile, then risked a last glance at Harry. He was rubbing his forehead, a pained expression crumpling his features. As she escaped into the November chill, she realized she knew exactly how he felt.

Chapter Three

Sophie was buttoning her coat at the end of the working day when Ermin, Fiona's husband, came in with Sophie's pride and joy on his harness.

'He's been a delight, as always.' Ermin ran a hand through his thick hair, blond with a liberal seasoning of salt and pepper, and handed Sophie the lead.

'That's a relief,' Sophie said with a laugh, though her dog was mostly well behaved. 'Thank you, Ermin.'

'Not a problem,' Ermin assured her. 'I'm always happy to have him.'

She had no idea what mix of breeds Clifton was, but he was the size of a Cairn terrier, with black, curly fur and a fringe that fell into his eyes no matter how often Sophie got it trimmed. He was good-natured, and friendly with other dogs and people. Small children were his favourites, and cats were his enemies.

Sometimes he accompanied Sophie to work, curling up in a basket behind her counter, an added benefit for customers who loved to fuss him, and sometimes – especially if Ermin was visiting wholesalers in his van, or working in his and Fiona's sprawling garden – Clifton spent the day with him. It had been her biggest relief when they offered her the shop space, because she refused to leave him alone for long stretches.

'Have a good evening,' she said now, pushing open the door.

'See you tomorrow!' Fiona called after her as she swapped the warm fug for the cold November afternoon, the daylight already starting to fade, the wind biting. The shortest day of the year wasn't far away now, and Mistingham was, understandably, significantly quieter now than during the summer. The village had its fair share of second homes, as did many places in north Norfolk, but Sophie had never thought of it as bleak or desolate – even when she'd arrived in January. The independent shops, the picturesque green, the hotel with its flint exterior and large, lit windows gave it a friendly atmosphere that was cemented by the people, the majority of whom would say hello when you passed them in the street.

With Clifton at her side and her collar turned up, Sophie walked down Perpendicular Street towards the sea. If she kept her pace up, they could get a good way along the cliff path before they had to turn around.

The North Sea spread out ahead of her, silvery and boisterous, and when she was almost at the promenade she turned left, cutting through an alley that led onto a narrow road flanked by several town houses, then squat holiday homes, a few with pots of hardy grasses beneath their windowsills. They had no room for gardens, but there was no need either, when this was your view.

Sophie passed old Mr Carsdale's house, a flickering gas fire visible through the living-room window. She waved, unsure whether he'd noticed her and then, bunching her scarf more tightly against her neck, powered on, with Clifton padding happily alongside her.

At the end of the narrow street the buildings fell away and the land opened up, a wooden signpost pointing behind her for the village centre, right for the seafront, and straight ahead for the coastal path. In front and to the left of the path, there was an expanse of parkland surrounded by a sturdy-looking, waist-high fence. The public pathway was uneven, edged by unkempt grass that stretched for several feet to the right, before the drop down to the promenade and then the beach. Here it was only a low, gentle slope, but further on the land rose, and so the cliff got steeper and more perilous.

Sophie couldn't help glancing at the parkland as she walked. Harry Anderly owned some of the land in the middle of the village, including Mistingham Green and a couple of the shops on Perpendicular Street, but this was the edge of the Mistingham Manor estate; the grass running down to the sea, clusters of mature trees further inland that mostly shielded the house from view. But she could see glimpses of it through the foliage, grey stone and the flash of the evening sun reflecting off the windows.

'If it was me,' she said to her dog, 'I would have cut some of those trees down.' Clifton looked up at her, inquisitive. 'What's the point of having your grand house so close to the sea, then obscuring the view of it behind a mini forest?'

She didn't expect a reply, so when a loud bleat cut through the background rush of wind and waves, Sophie jumped.

'Shitting shit!' She pressed a hand to her chest as Clifton barked excitedly.

Her dog loved goats, and Felix the pygmy goat was a Mistingham celebrity: much better tempered than his owner, and with more advanced social skills.

'Felix,' Sophie cooed. She stopped so Clifton could put his front paws on a fence rung, then stick his nose through the gap. The goat trotted over to say hello. Today, Felix – who was white with black patches – was wearing a pastel paisley jumper, teal teardrops against a yellow and pink background.

'Maybe I should get Birdie to knit you some jumpers too,' she said to Clifton.

Birdie was Mistingham's well-loved grandmother figure. She grew vegetables and flowers in her cottage garden, and gave them out liberally to residents, sometimes in the form of suspicious concoctions that intrigued and alarmed Sophie in equal measure. She also knitted jumpers for Felix.

'If Harry's such a cold fish,' Sophie said to Felix, 'how come he dresses you in these adorable pullovers? Fiona would give her right hand to have a range of these in the shop; Birdie could be making a fortune.'

Felix accepted a vigorous stroke behind the ears, his bleats gentle and constant, then Sophie stepped away, taking her dog with her. 'Sorry, guys. The light's already fading, and we don't want to be out here in the dark.'

She decided they would go as far as the lookout point, where a bench was precariously positioned on top of the cliff, alongside a fixed telescope, then turn around. The sea was no longer reflecting the sun in silver fragments, and the temperature was dropping sharply.

She was feet away from her turning point, her eyes on the uneven ground, when a loud *thump* made her jump for a second time. 'Bloody hell!' she shrieked, then tried not to full-on scream when a low voice said, 'Sorry, I didn't see you there.'

She spun towards the parkland and saw a shadowy figure, a glowing spotlight trained on one of the fence posts. 'I didn't see you either,' she said, peering through the gloom. For a moment, she thought it was a gardener or workman, but she'd seen him twice recently and she recognized his broad shoulders and his voice. They'd had a very similar interaction outside the shop.

'Obviously you didn't see me.' His reply was slightly breathless. 'Recent experience has taught me that *bloody hell* isn't your standard greeting. Though who am I to judge? Greet people however you like.' He whacked the fence post again, arms raised high above his head before he swung the hammer down with power. Sophie felt the vibration through her boots.

'Is that a good idea, particularly?' she asked. 'Considering it's nearly dark.'

'About as good an idea as walking along an unfenced clifftop in the same conditions.'

Sophie bristled.

'Also, if I don't fix this now, then Felix will get out, and probably Ter . . . my dogs, too. Does your walk have such an urgent purpose?'

Sophie shook her head, though she doubted he'd seen it. 'Clifton needed his evening walk, and it's got dark a lot more quickly than I expected.'

'Winter does that,' Harry said, still not looking up. He

brought the hammer down on the post with another deci-
sive thwack, and Sophie was surprised the wood didn't
splinter in two. He stared at his fence post. 'That should
stop any escape artists.'

'You said you had dogs?'

'Two retrievers. They're around here somewhere.'

Sophie lifted her own dog into her arms and said, 'This
is Clifton.'

Harry stood up straight and, to Sophie's surprise, ruffled
the dog's fur. It was the first time she'd seen him anything
other than irritated. Clifton, of course, decided Harry was
his new best friend, and pushed his wet nose, then his
tongue, into Harry's palm. Sophie wished she could see his
face properly, see if her pet had made him lose that chink
of ice in his eyes.

'Why Clifton?' Harry asked.

'Because I found him, bedraggled and abandoned,
under the Clifton Suspension Bridge when I was living
in Bristol.'

'You rescued him.'

Sophie nodded. They were two strays; two lost souls
finding each other. 'What about your dogs?'

'What about them?' Harry turned his head, as if something had caught his attention behind her. Was it a sea
monster? Something horrendous coming up out of the
waves? It was disconcerting, the gathering gloom, and
Sophie realized she had been foolish to attempt this walk
so late in the afternoon.

'What are they called, to start with?' she asked. This man
was patently incapable of making small talk.

Harry dropped his hand from Clifton's head and glanced

behind him, as if hoping someone would step out of the shadows and save him from this line of questioning.

'Harry?' Sophie prompted. 'That is . . . can I call you – would you prefer Mr Anderly?'

'Definitely not,' Harry said sharply. He picked up his torch. 'My dogs are called Darkness and Terror.'

Sophie leaned forward, almost upending herself over the fence. 'I'm sorry?' She could feel laughter bubbling up in her chest, the ridiculousness of the names combined with shock that he'd admitted it to her.

Harry huffed out a breath. 'Darkness and Terror,' he said again. 'Darkness is a black retriever, Terror is golden. May suggested the names when I got them – as a joke, obviously. She said I should give them names that were appropriate for the Dark Demon Lord of Mistingham that I was clearly trying to become, so – out of spite – I did. At first I refused to back down, and then, by the time I was ready to give them proper names, the dogs had got used to Darkness and Terror, so . . .' He raised the torch in a one-armed shrug. 'Serves me right.'

Sophie had held in her laughter, and now she felt a twist of unexpected empathy for him, because she knew what it was like to feel like an outcast. But it was a story that deserved a comeback, so she said, 'The *Dark Demon Lord of Mistingham*? I'm going to slip that name into conversation with Fiona, see how long it takes for it to get round the village.'

'Please don't,' Harry said in a pained voice. 'Look, it's basically dark now, and you've ended up on the cliffs with no light source whatsoever. Didn't you bring a torch?'

'I've got my phone.' Sophie squared her shoulders. She didn't like the insinuation that she couldn't look after herself.

28

'That's no good,' Harry said. 'Have my torch.'

'No thanks. How will you get back to your country house?'

'A damn sight more easily than you will along that path. How could you let this happen?'

'Oh, I don't know,' Sophie said, 'maybe because somebody engaged me in conversation? I would have been home by now if it wasn't for you.'

'Then take my torch.' He waggled it at her. '*Take* it.'

Sophie should take it. She had decided to leave Mistingham, but she was aiming for Cornwall, not plunging to her death off the north Norfolk cliffs. She put Clifton down, and was about to take his torch when Harry pulled his arm back.

'Fine,' he said.

'What? I was going to take it!'

'You've missed your chance, and I'm not confident a torch is good enough anyway.'

'Oh *you're not confident*. So I have to do what you say?'

'Do you and Clifton want to make it home safely, or not?' He held his free hand out.

'What's that? Your other, invisible torch?'

'Take my hand, and I'll help you over the fence.'

'Why?'

'Because then I can drive you home. In a car. With head-lights.'

'This is just . . .' Sophie shook her head. 'No.'

'Got a better plan?' Harry's frustration was thinly veiled.

Sophie turned away from him, towards the sea, and suddenly felt dizzy. It wasn't quite dark yet, the sky the colour of a smudged bruise, but all the sharp edges had gone. She pulled her phone out of her pocket and put the torch on. The light it cast was brighter than she'd expected, and she felt a sudden surge of confidence, of relief, that she wouldn't have to rely on this abrasive man for help.

'I'll be fine,' she told him.

'You're being ridiculous,' he said sternly. 'You can't possibly—'

'Stop telling me what to do!' She took a deep breath. 'My life, my safety, has nothing to do with you. You've held me up for long enough, so now I need to hurry so I can get home before it's completely dark.'

He put his hand on her arm, wrapping his fingers round her wrist. 'It's not safe.'

'I'll be *fine*,' Sophie said. 'Let me go.'

She watched Harry's brows lower, could just make out the clench of his jaw in the light from her torch. 'It will take five minutes to get back to the manor,' he said. 'We can do it in silence if you'd prefer.'

'I walked out here by myself, and I'm perfectly capable of getting home again.'

He was quiet for a long moment, then he let go of her arm. 'Be careful.'

Sophie barked a laugh. 'Believe me, I have no intention of ending up in the sea. I'm leaving now.'

Harry took a step back, and Sophie waited for him to say something else – a parting shot – but instead he nodded once, then turned around and strode away. He whistled once, loudly, and then there was Felix, a ghostly goat in a paisley jumper, trotting at his side.

'Right,' Sophie said. 'That's that, then. Come on, Clifton.'

She took a first, tentative step, and then, with her phone

torch guiding her, she made her way carefully back along the cliff path, trying to ignore the dark void to her left, the crashing, thrumming beat of the waves. Her pulse refused to settle until she was safely back under the signpost, with concrete beneath her feet and the row of neat holiday homes ahead of her. She let out a long, slow breath, into a night that was, now, completely dark, and decided that she'd never been so pleased to see streetlights in her life.

For a second, she let herself imagine what would have happened if she'd taken Harry's hand; if she'd let him lift her over the fence and drive her home. But the way he had extended the offer – he hadn't even attempted to be polite, so if he was feeling guilty, and maybe a little bit worried about her; well, that was good. She'd survived by herself long enough: she didn't need to start relying on a man – and a rude one at that – to keep her safe.

Chapter Four

Sophie was woken on Thursday morning by Clifton snuffling on the pillow next to her head. She had long given up trying to keep him out of the bedroom, but he was an intelligent dog, and she knew he'd sensed her unease at their precarious walk home along the clifftop path the night before.

'OK, buddy?'

He crawled towards her and pressed his damp nose against her cheek, then followed it with a lick.

It was still early, and while Fiona let her keep her own hours at the shop, she liked to be there from opening until close whenever possible, to maximize her selling opportunities. But instead of pulling the duvet off, Sophie stared at the ceiling. There was hardly any light filtering under her soft blue curtains, suggesting another grey November day where the sea, clouds and sky merged into one.

Once she'd got safely home last night, she had cooked stir fry veg and chicken for dinner, ignoring the tantalizing smells from Batter Days. She'd found *Pretty Woman* on the TV, a film she loved, but she'd been distracted; she hadn't been able to stop thinking about her strange encounter with Harry Anderly. He was a puzzle, mostly cold and disinterested, but desperate to drive her home. He'd admitted naming his dogs Darkness and Terror, and told her about being labelled the Dark Demon Lord of Mistingham, so he was aware of his reputation in the village, but he didn't seem bothered by it, certainly not to the extent of trying to change it. And yet he dressed his pet goat in knitted jumpers, and he'd been almost aggressively concerned for her safety. It was confusing, to say the least.

He shunned the village and its inhabitants, wasn't even trying to meet them halfway when it came to using Mistingham Green for their traditional events. He didn't seem particularly close to anyone except for May, and from what she'd heard he was working single-handedly to make repairs on his estate. Why had he come back to the village when everything about it seemed like such hard work: the state of the manor, interacting with the locals? He could sell up and move anywhere he wanted to.

These thoughts were still pinging around in her head as she got up and made breakfast for herself and Clifton, as she stood at her kitchen window, eating toast and Marmite and gazing at the sea. It was a flat grey tableau, the only spark of interest a tanker moving slowly across the horizon.

Fiona greeted them warmly when they arrived at Hartley Country Apparel, Clifton bustling over to his padded bed at the base of Sophie's display shelves. 'Did you have a nice evening?' she asked.

'It was fine, thanks.' Sophie logged into her till and gave her display a critical once-over. She liked having the brightest notebooks at eye level, the cloth- or leatherbound ones just below, so customers could take them down and feel how smooth and soft they were. Once they were holding them, they didn't usually want to give them back.

She realized Fiona was watching her, and wondered if news of her encounter with Harry had somehow made its way round the village, even though there had been nobody else there. The current of gossip in Mistingham was strong and constant, and she wouldn't have been entirely surprised if someone had found out somehow.

'Is everything OK?' she asked.

Fiona held her gaze for another moment, then said, 'Fancy a coffee?'

'I'd love one.' She breathed a sigh of relief when Fiona went to the back of the shop and the kettle burbled to life.

'I was thinking,' she said, returning minutes later with Sophie's milky coffee, 'we could put up the Christmas lights sooner rather than later.'

'Inside the shop?' Sophie thanked her and sipped her drink, the caffeine perking her up instantly.

'Our twinkly gold lights aren't too over the top, and if the days are going to carry on like this, with no hint of sunshine, we need to add our own sparkle.'

'Sounds good to me.' Sophie loved that the huge cherry tree outside the Blossom Bough was wound through with lights that Natasha kept on all year round, their silver-white bulbs spotlighting the delicate flowers in spring, brightening bare branches in winter, but she wasn't sure they'd have such a romantic effect interspersed with waxed jackets and deerstalkers.

'Is something wrong?' Fiona asked.

Sophie looked up from the pot of jewelled ballpoints she was rearranging. 'Why would you say that?'

'You're awfully distracted. And the other day I noticed you were looking up rental places in Cornwall on your phone.'

Sophie felt as if she'd had a bucket of seawater thrown over her. 'You saw that?'

'You left the screen unlocked when you helped Sian bring her buggy over the step,' Fiona explained. 'Your cup of tea was too close to the edge so I went to rescue it, and there they were. Tiny flats; nothing more enticing than your current place over Batter Days. Cornwall is ridiculously expensive.'

'They were holiday homes,' Sophie rasped out.

Fiona scoffed. 'They were not. Are you seriously thinking about leaving?' She sounded like she was trying to keep her outrage in check, as if Sophie's decision was equal to setting the entire village on fire.

'I don't . . .' she started, but what could she say? This was why she preferred to leave without warning – so people couldn't try and change her mind. She didn't often have a problem – excluding Bristol, which had been nothing *but* a problem – but that was because she stayed in places for such a short amount of time that usually nobody cared. Fiona, it seemed, was going to be the exception.

'Are you unhappy here?' Her friend sounded pained.

'I'm not unhappy,' Sophie rushed out. Fiona had been a good friend from the moment she'd arrived, but it was too complicated – inexplicable to anyone but her – why she had to do this. She thought of their conversation with Dexter the other day, about the importance of physical shops, how they were dying out. 'It's just that I need more space.'

Fiona frowned.

'You have been so kind,' she went on, the words tumbling out of her. 'I couldn't have imagined having all this room for my business a year ago. But because I've been able to expand here, and word-of-mouth has done wonders, it's growing steadily – online orders too – so I just . . . I need more space for it.'

'You need your own shop,' Fiona clarified.

Sophie sighed in relief. It was such a plausible reason. 'I really do.'

'That's easy,' Fiona said. 'I don't suppose you're big enough yet for the old bookshop, but there's Ye Olde Sweete Shoppe, and that's been empty since Delores moved away two summers ago. Such a dinky space.'

Sophie cursed silently. 'I'm not sure . . .'

'I'll give you a tour,' Fiona went on. 'It smells like diabetes, but other than that I think it'll suit you perfectly.'

'Maybe,' Sophie replied, hoping she hadn't just created a brand-new problem for herself. The door opened and a young family came in, a Dalmatian on a lead sniffing curiously at the mat. She could have kissed them all for such a well-timed interruption.

Sophie's chat with Fiona set off a simmering anxiety that stayed with her all morning. She couldn't backtrack on her declaration that she needed more space and hope Fiona would forget about it, because Fiona never forgot about anything. She should have denied that she was moving, then carried on with her plans in secret the way she'd always done. One moment of panic had complicated everything, and in a small, unfair way she blamed Harry Anderly for scattering her thoughts.

She went to Dexter's bakery at lunchtime and came back with two chicken sandwiches bursting with freshly cooked breast meat, juicy tomatoes and mayonnaise. She pushed open the door with her shoulder, realized Fiona wasn't behind the counter, and assumed she was making tea in the back. She left her friend's lunch next to her till, and then saw that, sitting in the middle of her own counter, there was a parcel, wrapped in brown paper and tied up with string.

Sophie put her sandwich down and ran her hands over the smooth, thick paper. Most people used Jiffy bags these days: brown paper and string seemed very old-fashioned.

'Here's your tea.' Fiona put the mug down. 'Oooh, what's that?'

'I don't know,' Sophie said. 'Who dropped it off?'

'It wasn't here when I went to make the drinks, and I didn't hear the door open. But the kettle was loud, so . . . I haven't got the foggiest.'

'There's no name or address on it,' Sophie said, 'so it's probably for you.' But she was reluctant to hand it over. She wanted to be the one to loosen the string, to gently peel off the paper and discover what was beneath.

'It's on your counter,' Fiona pointed out. 'Everyone in Mistingham knows how this shop's set up.'

'Maybe it's from the postman?'

'Without an address label? Are you going to open it, or stand there exfoliating your hands with it?'

'The paper's smooth,' Sophie protested, but she pulled

at the string, the bow loosening easily. She turned the package over, finding the neat folds secured with Sellotape, and slid her finger under the edge. She could feel that the object inside was slightly rough, and for a second she thought she was the most stupid person on the planet: it was clearly the book boards she'd ordered. She had a couple of orders outstanding, so that must be it.

But as she removed the paper she realized she wasn't being stupid, because inside was a single, thick book. It had a cloth cover, the scarlet material slightly scratchy to touch, with gold foil details: a wind-blown tree, some leaves still attached, some scattering to the bottom edge of the cover. Written on the front, also in gold, it said:

Jane Eyre
by
Charlotte Brontë

'That's gorgeous,' Fiona murmured. 'I've never seen that edition before.'

Sophie turned it over. There was no summary on the back, just more falling gold leaves. She tipped it to look at the spine, which had the title, and then a logo at the bottom. It looked like a tiny house, with a pointed roof and a chimney either side: it wasn't a publisher's logo she recognized. That, too, was gold, and so was the ribboned bookmark peeking out at the bottom.

Sophie leafed gently through the pages, and found they were incredibly thin, like the dusty hymn books she'd had to sing from when she'd lived with a foster family in Surrey who never missed the Sunday service. In places, some of the ink was so dark it seemed smudged, and the pages were yellowing at the edges.

Inside, it looked and felt like an old book: good quality but around for a long time, exposed to wear and tear and the elements. But the binding – the cover and the foil detailing – was pristine. She could tell it had been expertly bound, and imagined the meticulous steps that had been taken: carefully extracting the old pages that were split into sections – signatures – from the original cover, putting on new tape, then cotton mull over the top to reinforce the adhesive, before adding the book board and then the fabric.

She was about to say all this to Fiona, to tell her about the discrepancies, when a card slipped out of the book and slid onto the counter. Sophie put *Jane Eyre* down and picked it up.

It was a cheerful scene of Mistingham Beach in summer, the sand dotted with brightly coloured parasols and wind-breakers, tiny figures in the sea, the offshore wind farm a silvery smudge against the bright blue sky. It was incongruous, this shiny, modern postcard next to the classically bound book.

'Come on then,' Fiona said. 'What does it say?'

Sophie turned it over. The handwriting was small and neat, written in biro. 'It *is* for me,' she said. 'Or, at least, it's for someone called Sophie.'

It read:

Dear Sophie, sometimes you have to look closer to home to find what you've been missing. Please accept this gift as an early Christmas present – love from The Secret Bookshop.

'Goodness!' Gleeful curiosity dripped from Fiona's voice.

'What the hell?' Sophie murmured. The message brought her anxiety back in full force. Who in Mistingham would send her something like this, and how could they possibly know that she was looking for something new? It was unsettling and disarming and, although she wanted to think of it like a message inside a fortune cookie, applicable to any situation if you only put your mind to it, someone had left it for *her* along with one of the most beautiful books she'd ever seen: a novel about a woman who had no family, who struggled to find somewhere she belonged. She glanced around the shop, as if she might see a pair of eyes peering at her through the rows of winter jackets, watching her reaction.

'That settles it, then.' Fiona bent to stroke Clifton, who had woken up from a long nap and was blinking sleepily.

'Settles what?' Sophie picked up *Jane Eyre* and looked for pen or pencil marks, scribbled annotations, any hint of who it had belonged to or where it might have come from.

'You can't leave Mistingham now,' Fiona said. 'Not until you've discovered who's behind your gift . . . *The Secret Bookshop*,' she repeated with relish. 'What a wonderful mystery to have, just before Christmas.'

Chapter Five

Sophie couldn't stop thinking about the book, and had given it pride of place on her coffee table before she'd left for the village hall that evening. Fiona had said she couldn't leave Mistingham until she'd discovered who had sent it to her, and Sophie got her point: it was an intriguing present, along with a scarily relevant message, and all the more so for being anonymous.

But Sophie's circle of friends in the village was small, so her immediate – and obvious – thought was that Fiona was behind it. Perhaps it was a copy that had been collecting dust at home, and she'd concocted the ruse as a reason to keep Sophie here? But then, Fiona had already come up with a reason for her to stay – helping her move her notebook business into the old sweet shop. Sophie hadn't told her why she was really going, and why would she think giving her a classic book and a conundrum to solve would make a difference?

No, Sophie dismissed Fiona as her secret book Santa

almost instantly. Besides, she didn't imagine it would take her longer than a few days to find out who it was. It wasn't lost on her that *Jane Eyre* resonated with her own history. She had only read it once, a long time ago, and couldn't remember the intricacies of the plot, but she knew Jane was an orphan who was unhappy and unloved, moving from place to place until she found Mr Rochester – though that wasn't exactly smooth sailing either.

Mr Rochester sent her thoughts skittering to Harry Anderly. He was reclusive, lived in a crumbling mansion, and some of the more outlandish rumours about him in the village were straight out of the book that had ended up on her shop counter. But it took Sophie a nanosecond to decide that practical, distant Harry would be the last person in the whole of Norfolk to send her a thoughtful gift. He was barely civil enough to give her the time of day, and their recent meetings had been decidedly uncomfortable. It made no sense whatsoever.

Mistingham village hall was stuffy, even on this cold, rainy night, the fug created by wet jackets and damp dog hair. A garland of fake summer blossoms hung dejectedly from the ceiling, forgotten after an earlier event, and the mood was one of general disgruntlement. It was clear some of the villagers didn't want to be here but felt they couldn't relinquish their community duties. Sophie wondered if they were also worried that, in their absence, they would be assigned a task, and it was better to come here and actively excuse themselves.

'Right then, everyone.' Ermin tapped the wooden podium on the low stage with the corner of his iPhone, and the chatter faded to muttering as people broke off conversations about Christmas plans and fireworks found in gardens and the temperamental water main down by the stables, and turned their attention to the front of the hall.

'The Mistingham Festive Oak Fest,' Ermin said proudly. 'Our famous Christmas event, always well-attended by locals and visitors alike, will have to be different this year, just as it was last year.'

A groan rippled through the hall, and Sophie cast her gaze around the room. She hadn't been here for last year's event, but she had heard about it. For decades, the festival had taken place on the green, beneath the spreading boughs of the beautifully decorated oak tree. Since Harry's return to the village last spring, he had prevented the planning team holding any events close to the tree and, even though they had still called it the Festive Oak Fest, last year's celebration had been a street festival, taking over the whole of Perpendicular Street.

There had been mulled wine, chips and candy floss, traditional games like Hook the Duck and Splat the Rat, and a motley crew of carol singers that, Fiona had told her, always stuck to the same set list: the same carols, in the same order, for at least the last decade.

'Different?' a silver-haired woman in the second row called out. 'How do you mean, different?'

Next to Sophie, Annie and Jim Devlin exchanged a glance. They ran the amusement arcade, Penny For Them, had two young children, and had always seemed friendly. She thought that, given half the chance, they would help the organizers come up with entertainment a bit less Eighties than Splat the Rat.

'Why different?' old Mr Carsdale echoed from beneath his green felt hat. He sounded curious rather than annoyed.

'Because, along with our necessary change of venue,' Ermin said, 'Winnie can't organize it this year. With the post office moving to the hotel, she doesn't have the capacity to do it.'

'Sorry everyone,' Winnie called from the back of the room. 'I don't want to do a bad job because I'm stretched too thinly.'

'Don't see how processing parcels and passport applications can take up much time,' said a gruff voice Sophie didn't recognize. 'The festival's a tradition, isn't it?'

'There's no need to get into the nitty-gritty.' Ermin flapped his hands, trying to quiet the mutterings that had started up. 'The point is, we have a festival to put on in less than two months, and nobody at the helm. The purpose of this meeting is to assign a new organizer.'

The mutterings fell to a deadly silence. Clifton whimpered and Sophie stroked him. The last thing she wanted was to be volunteered to organize a street festival by her dog. In the quiet, the rain and wind made itself known, battering against the outside of the fogged-up windows, reminding them what a filthy night it was. Sophie thought of the soft pyjamas she would get into after her short walk home, the hot chocolate she would make, her new book waiting for her to open it, using the gold ribbon to keep her place as she lost herself in the story.

Around her, every head was lowered, avoiding meeting Ermin's gaze. Sophie realized that, in all likelihood, the person who had sent her the beautiful book, along with an unsettlingly cryptic message, was in this room right now.

'Does someone really need to organize it, if we're just doing the same as last year?' The bored-sounding teenage voice could only be Indigo, Natasha's son. 'Winnie can give you a list and you can just reorder everything, lights and food and games and stuff, right?'

Ermin shuffled his feet. 'That would, of course, be a sensible starting point. But we did wonder if – ah, I mean, the villagers I've spoken to – if this would be a good chance to   ' He glanced to the back of the room, '   to re-evaluate the plan, slightly. Moving it from the green to Perpendicular Street does come with its own complications.'

'You mean like making sure the council put a proper diversion in place, so you don't end up with furious drivers stuck in the village with nowhere to go?' Natasha suggested. 'The bar truck was next to the cordon, so I got some proper abuse last year.'

'And some of it has got a bit tired,' Simon said carefully. Sophie's landlord and the owner of Batter Days, he was a quiet, generous man with sandy hair and a slim frame.

'I didn't even recognize the rat I splatted last time,' someone agreed. 'Thought it was a hairy cowpat.'

'Right. Yes.' Ermin raised his voice. 'We want a revamp of the Festive Oak Fest, with someone who can really give it some attention, add that extra oomph, and make the most of its new location. Mistingham has so many local producers, people with skills and talents to show off, that I honestly think it could be something rather magnificent, despite the constraints. If we could—'

He was interrupted by a loud *thwack* as the hall door slammed against the indoor wall. A tall figure appeared in the doorway, highlighted by the outdoor light, the rain sparkling in hectic shards behind him.

'Shit,' said the man, and recognition prickled down

Sophie's spine. 'That was the wind, not me,' he announced to the room. 'I wasn't trying to make that sort of entrance.' He stepped inside, shut the door behind him and pulled down his rain-slicked hood, and Sophie was treated to another view of Harry Anderly, with his mess of soft brown hair and his strong features, the tip of his nose pink from the cold.

'Harry!' Ermin's shocked greeting sent nervous titters rippling through the audience. 'I just . . . I didn't—'

'Sorry I'm late,' Harry said. His gaze drifted across the space, and Sophie noticed May sitting at the end of a row. She waved and gave him a full-wattage smile. The look he gave her in return was both affectionate and annoyed. 'It was suggested to me *by a friend* that I should come tonight. I want to reiterate that the oak tree is old and fragile, so Mistingham Green is still out of bounds, but that doesn't mean I don't want the festival to be a success.'

The silence that followed was profound. The villagers stared at him, as if he was a rare creature who'd escaped from a zoo, and Sophie wondered if everyone was thinking what she was – that he'd come to check up on them, make sure they didn't disobey his orders.

It sent up an indignant flare inside her, something he seemed to inspire every time they were close. Then her earlier thought returned: someone in this room had sent her the copy of *Jane Eyre*. Someone here was behind her gift from The Secret Bookshop. If she was involved in the festival, then she would have to speak to a whole lot of villagers: she could look them in the eye, ask questions, and see how they responded.

If she suggested the event had a book-related element,

perhaps a stall promoting Christmas reads like *A Christmas Carol*, *The Polar Express*, *The Night Before Christmas*, could she use that as a reason to ask around, find out about people's relationships with books: what they loved, where they bought or borrowed their reading material from? Could taking an active role in the festival help her solve her mystery?

She slowly raised her hand, stretching her arm above the rows of heads.

'Sophie,' Ermin said warmly. 'What's your question?'

'Oh! No,' she said. 'I thought, maybe—'

'*Sophie*,' Winnie called out. 'Yes! You would do a marvellous job. You have those kind of eyes.'

Sophie blinked as heads swivelled towards her, everyone probably wondering how her unremarkable brown eyes could signify that she'd be great at organizing a festival.

'I don't think I'd do a good job by *myself*,' she said, feeling the blush warm her cheeks as she raised her voice, 'but I'd be happy to be involved. If there were a few of us, perhaps, then it would be—'

'Well!' Ermin said. 'This is grand! And a lot easier than I'd hoped.'

'I can't do it on my own,' she reiterated.

'You won't be on your own.' Ermin clasped his hands in front of him. 'Harry just said he wants the festival to be a success, so—'

'Hang on.' Harry took a step forwards. 'That doesn't mean—'

'Harry knows the village better than *anyone*.' This was Mary, Winnie's sister, her voice rising emphatically above the chattering that had started up again.

'And as he's decided that the oak tree is no-go, he's best

47

placed to organize something that will fit all his rules and regulations,' Jason said. He was Simon's husband, and ran Two Scoops, the ice-cream parlour. Where Simon was quiet and measured, Jason was permanently outspoken, not afraid to say what everyone else was thinking, and right now his hostility was barely concealed.

'It does make a lot of sense.' Fiona's eyes were gleaming with satisfaction.

'Oh no,' Sophie whispered, lifting Clifton onto her lap. 'No, no, no. That's not what I meant at all.'

'One person won't be enough,' Ermin said, 'not with our more ambitious plans, but to have two young, competent people at the helm stands us in great stead for a top-notch Oak Fest. This really is a much better outcome than I'd hoped for.'

'I didn't agree to this,' Harry said loudly. 'I just came to—'

'Check up on us?' Mary asked sweetly.

'Of course that's not why I'm here.'

'Then it stands to reason that you came to offer your help,' Winnie said, continuing the tag team with her sister.

Harry's jaw tightened, and Sophie noticed his hands curl into fists at his sides.

'Harry.' May stood up and went over to him. She rested her hand on his arm, reached up and whispered something into his ear. If it was possible, his jaw clenched even more tightly, but when she stepped away, he gave a jerky nod.

'I could offer some assistance,' he said grimly, as if he'd just agreed to push all the older residents into the sea rather than help put on a sparkly Christmas festival. Sophie found herself empathizing with him all over again. She wanted to melt into a puddle of despair on the floor.

Fiona joined her husband on the stage, sporting a look of such unfettered delight that Sophie wondered if, actually, she should do her midnight flit immediately – *tonight* – and leave Mistingham for good, anonymous book-gifter be damned.

'What a wonderful outcome,' Fiona said. 'To have such a strong team in charge this year. Residents who I know are hugely committed to Mistingham—' she paused long enough for Sophie to glare at her '—who will do everything in their power to make this the best Oak Fest we've had. Please, everyone, give it up for Sophie Stevens and Harry Anderly – and, when they come to talk to you about your contribution, please be as helpful as you can. A successful event benefits us all.'

There was a smattering of applause, a few cheers shot through with relief from people who had dodged bullets, who hadn't opened their big mouths and put themselves forward for entirely stupid reasons. Who hadn't ended up in such an impossible, unenviable position.

While everyone gathered their coats and chatted with their neighbours, Sophie held Clifton against her chest and skimmed her gaze over the crowd. May looked pleased as punch that Harry had shown up and walked straight into Ermin's trap, Fiona was talking animatedly with Birdie, knitter of tiny goat jumpers, and Dexter was laughing with Mary, his arm around his daughter Lucy's narrow shoulders.

Then she looked over at the door. Harry had stepped aside, letting people out into the unforgiving night, and his eyes were trained perfectly on hers. He looked part shocked, part accusatory, as if she had somehow tricked him into organizing the festival with her.

It was the worst possible outcome. Working with the world's grumpiest man, on an event everyone cared deeply about, that he'd forced them to compromise on because he was a prominent landowner who was precious about a *tree*. He would be even less cheery doing this than he was hitting fence posts with a hammer.

It was going to be torturous, and it was all the fault of the mysterious book. If it wasn't for the beautiful hardback of *Jane Eyre* with its fancy gold foil, she would never have considered offering up her time. And now she wasn't just helping to plan the festival, she was 50 per cent of the planning team.

And the other half, standing in his dripping coat with his pink-tipped nose and his hard-as-diamonds gaze, his dogs with stupid names and his baffling indulgence of a goat who had *knitted jumpers*, for God's sake, was not going to make things easy for her. She could tell that already, without a shadow of a doubt.

Chapter Six

The sensible thing would have been to approach Harry then and there, to at the very least arrange to meet up and discuss how it was going to work. But Sophie was flustered, her original plan sent into disarray, and Harry's stare was colder than it was outside, so instead, she wove through the chairs, nodding and smiling as villagers gave her curious looks, and slipped her arm through Fiona's.

'Sophie!' Fiona was jubilant. 'I don't know why I didn't think of it before now – you'll do a wonderful job.'

Sophie glanced over her shoulder, looking for a tall figure with brown hair. 'Do you want to show me the old sweet shop?'

'What, *now*?'

'Now is as good a time as any.' She could have left; slipped out of the door and hot-footed it back to her flat, but she wanted reinforcements in case Harry sought her out, and if she convinced Fiona that she was excited about the possibility of moving into the sweet shop, then her friend wouldn't let anything stand in the way of a late-night tour.

'OK, then,' Fiona said. 'I'll just tell Ermin. Wait here.'

Sophie tucked her chin into her collar, trying to look as unapproachable as possible.

'Here we are.' Fiona held up a large key ring, the keys jostling and clinking together.

When they stepped outside, the cold was like a physical force propelling them backwards, and a mist had rolled in off the sea, draping the green and streets around them in ghostly gossamer. The streetlights emitted a weak golden haze, and Sophie shivered and zipped her coat up to the neck.

She followed Fiona, Clifton quiet alongside her, and resisted the urge to look behind and see if Harry was following: if she'd made him even angrier by leaving without arranging to talk things through. They skirted the edge of the green, the leaves of the giant oak rustling in the wind, as if protesting at being left out of the festivities, and then, once on the pavement, their footsteps echoed in the evening air.

'Give me two minutes,' Sophie said, gesturing to her dog, and Fiona nodded.

Sophie didn't know what the old shop was like inside, particularly the state of the floor, so she hurried back to her flat, only a minute away, settled Clifton inside and raced back to Fiona, who was standing outside Ye Olde Sweete Shoppe, The Book Ends next door to it.

Both shops looked unwelcoming, the interiors dark, the window displays dismantled, the large panes of glass streaked with dust. The sweet shop's door frame and windowsills were still a bright, candy pink, though the paint obviously hadn't been refreshed for a couple of years. The bookshop was more muted, though the glow from the streetlight picked out its cherry-red door.

Fiona tried different keys in the lock of the smaller shop, before she found one that made a satisfying clunk, the door pushing inwards with a groan. Sophie followed her inside. The scent of sugar still lingered in the air, and it made her smile as she turned on her phone torch and panned it across the spartan space. There were fitted shelves on opposite walls, and behind the small counter at the back of the shop. A door in the far wall presumably led to an office or tiny bathroom.

'Delores had it fitted with all mod cons not long before she gave it up,' Fiona said. 'She paid May a fortune to install the latest tech: a snazzy payment system, lighting built into the shelves to show off her jars of sweets. The electricity will be switched off now, but if you decide to take it on, it should only take a bit of elbow grease, a few phone calls and new contracts, to bring it up to muster. Not that you can see much in the dark,' she added pointedly. 'We could come back tomorrow.'

Sophie turned in a circle, the floorboards creaking under her boots. Annoyingly, it was perfect for her. It would take more stock than she currently had, allowing her to be more creative, develop her designs and try new things, but it wasn't so big that it was daunting. It was a cosy space and – while obviously dusty at the moment – elegantly kitted out. She imagined painting the walls teal or lilac, the shelves a glossy white to best display her cloth and leather notebooks with their delicate threads and gilded edges. Then she pushed those thoughts away.

'It's a good space.' She tried to sound matter of fact. This tour was purely a distraction, and she *wasn't* moving in here. After the New Year, she wouldn't be here at all.

'It's ideal for you,' Fiona said. 'Just imagine – notebooks here, books next door.'

'There are no books next door.' Sophie tried not to roll her eyes at the worn conversation. 'Everyone's said that Harry isn't going to resurrect the bookshop.'

'Nobody knows that for certain. Did you expect him to agree to help out tonight? Maybe he's changing his ways.'

'I think *was strong-armed* is more accurate than *agreed*,' Sophie said, her words cut off when a loud bang reverberated through the shop.

'Goodness!' Fiona pressed a hand to her chest.

'Maybe the only thing left in the bookshop is the ghost?'

'You know the story, don't you?' Fiona ran her finger along a shelf, Sophie's torch beam picking out the impressive dust bunny she collected.

'Is it the ghost of the village bibliophiles' unsatisfied needs?' Sophie suggested.

Fiona chuckled. '*Apparently* it's the ghost of a customer who died in the Fifties, before Harry's father took over the shop. He was heartbroken, had lost his love, you know the sort of thing, and he came into the shop and bought a copy of his favourite book, then—'

'What was the book?' Sophie asked.

'I have no idea,' Fiona said. 'Let's say . . . *Great Expectations*, because none of his were met. So, he bought his book, left the shop, turned right and walked down to the beach, straight into the icy water, not stopping until he was lost to the waves.'

Sophie frowned. 'Why did he buy a book if he was about to do that?'

Fiona shrugged. 'As some sort of message?'

'It's a bit far-fetched. I mean, what about—' Another loud bang shook the shelves on the wall between the sweet shop and the bookshop.

Sophie sucked in a breath.

'A bit far-fetched?' Fiona repeated, looking nervously around the space.

'The *story*.' Sophie dropped her voice to a whisper. 'Not that there's not a . . . I mean, I don't believe in ghosts. But what *is* that?'

'A pigeon? A bat? A *badger*?'

'Do you have the bookshop key on that ring?' Sophie asked.

'I do.' Fiona swallowed. 'You can't possibly want to go and check in the dark?'

'Don't you think we should?'

'You're braver than you look, Sophie Stevens. Come on then, let's go and see what horrors we can discover.'

Fiona locked the sweet shop and they stood in front of the bookshop's red door. Further up the hill, the last few stragglers were filtering out of the village hall, saying their goodnights. Sophie had the sudden urge to run back there, into the light and the warm. She wouldn't even mind if Harry was waiting for her.

Instead, she cupped her hands around her eyes and pressed her forehead to the cold glass of the bookshop window. She could see nothing but the vague outlines of empty shelves, the rest in darkness. The banging had stopped. All was still. It was her turn to swallow.

'Are we going in?' Fiona asked.

'Yes,' Sophie said, with more confidence than she felt. She imagined Harry standing beside them – a tall, imposing presence. From what little she knew of him, he seemed to have a no-nonsense attitude, something they could do with right now. For a second, she wished he was here.

'You know,' Fiona said, holding the bunch of keys up to the light, 'he called the shop yesterday.'

'Who did?' She wondered, not for the first time, if Fiona could read her mind.

'Harry Anderly,' her friend clarified. 'We were just talking about him changing his ways, and I forgot to mention that he phoned the shop. All he wanted to know was if you were working; if you were OK.' She found the right key, then turned to Sophie. 'Anything I should know about?'

Sophie stared at Fiona, bemused. And then she remembered: it was only two evenings ago that she'd met him on the cliff path, refused his curt offer of a lift home. He'd really been bothered enough by it to check up on her the following day?

'No,' she said, feeling even more uneasy. 'There's nothing you need to know about.'

'OK then,' Fiona replied. 'You know I'll find out anyway.'

'Of course.'

'Oh, now this isn't a good sign.'

'What isn't?'

Fiona had put the key halfway in the lock, and the door had swung inward.

'It's broken?' Sophie asked.

Fiona nodded. 'Someone – or some*thing* – has broken it.'

'Should we call the police?' Her pulse started to race.

'Let's have a little look first,' Fiona said, stepping inside.

'Now who's braver than they look?' Sophie murmured.

It smelled mustier in here, but then it had been shut longer than the sweet shop, and books *were* musty, though usually in an appealing sort of way. Sophie closed the door and they stood there, listening. Everything was quiet. Everything was dark. There were no sounds from outside, where Mistingham was slowly getting ready for bed, and no sounds in the shop. But the lock was broken, so they hadn't imagined the noises.

'Maybe the lock's been broken for ages?' Sophie whispered.

Fiona hummed. 'Maybe.'

There was another bang from deep inside the building, and they exchanged an anxious look.

'Split up?' Sophie suggested, even though her heart was pounding.

'Good idea. I'll go this way.' Fiona pointed to her right, which was *not* where the sound had come from. Sophie wanted to argue, but she was the one who had insisted they investigate.

'I'll go this way.' She pointlessly gestured in the opposite direction.

They both took cautious, quiet steps, and soon they were out of sight of each other, swallowed by the darkness, the hodgepodge rooms like a cave system leading to treasure, all the nooks now devoid of bookish delights.

Sophie couldn't help wondering how well she'd know this place by now if it had stayed open. She probably would have set up a tab, told whoever owned it to keep her bank card hostage behind the till. She thought of Susan Hill's ghost stories, *The Woman in Black* and *The Small Hand*, and Michelle Paver. She wasn't climbing a mountain, like in *Thin Air,* but she felt as if things were scuttling on the floor, just out of reach of the torch beam, imagined she could feel whisper-soft touches on the back of her neck. She was holding her breath, her ears and eyes straining for anything unusual: a disjointed moan or chink of chains, a see-through, ghostly figure; a wisp of white in the gloom.

Stop it, she told herself. *There is nothing here.*

She stepped through a narrow doorway into another compact space, then walked through that, twisting to her left, aware that she was getting further from the front door and an easy escape. She moved into yet another room, and realized as she swept her phone around that this one was bigger. She had reached the last room: the one that shared its wall with the sweet shop.

She blinked into the light, tried to ignore the total darkness on either side of its beam, swallowing air that felt particularly thick. But there was something else amongst the mustiness, something that smelt like food: bread or cake, a hint of something tangy. Was this where an animal had made its den? She took another step on creaky boards. Was she about to find carcasses? Did they have big cats in north Norfolk? *Big cats that make their homes in abandoned bookshops?* She shook her head and walked forwards. Did they—

A loud squeal filled the space and Sophie froze, terror clawing up her throat as the darkness to her left seemed to change shape, followed by a flash of bright red, a wash of something pallid. She stepped backwards and her heel caught on an uneven board. She felt herself fall, put her hands out behind her to try and lessen the impact, her phone clattering onto the floor before her bum hit it. She cried out as a sharp pain sliced through her wrist and up her arm, but she kept her eyes glued on the shifting shapes until they settled.

Sophie groped for her phone, found that it was undamaged and that the torch was still on, and angled the beam ahead of her. She was staring up at a person: a person with a shock of bright red hair, wrapped in a rough, dark blue blanket, their pale, moon face gazing down at her.

It was a young woman.

'Hello,' Sophie said, trying to ignore the pain in her wrist. She could hear Fiona's fast footsteps, running then stopping, trying to find her way through the night-time maze of the shop. 'Who are you?'

The silence stretched between them, punctuated by shouts from Fiona that got louder as she got closer: 'Are you OK, Sophie? What's happened? Where are you?'

The girl stared down at her, and Sophie tried a smile. 'I'm Sophie,' she said, 'in case you hadn't guessed.'

Still the girl stared. She looked wary and intrigued, wrapped in her blanket cocoon.

'I'm Jazz,' she said eventually, in a voice that was more defiant than Sophie would have expected. 'Do you need me to help you up?'

Fiona burst into the room and took in the sight, her mouth and eyes widening in surprise. 'What's going on?' she said. 'What . . . what is this?'

'I'm Jazz,' the young woman repeated. She let the blanket fall and held her hand out to Sophie. Sophie reached for it, then changed her mind and, letting Fiona's torch light the space, put her phone down and offered up her left hand instead. 'I'm not a ghost,' Jazz added. 'I didn't mean to scare you, but it's hard to get comfortable and every sound echoes in here. I just came for some fish and chips.'

'Excellent.' Fiona sounded completely flustered. She peered at Jazz, then Sophie, her brows hooded with concern. 'This is a somewhat unexpected turn of events,' she said, which Sophie thought all three of them could probably agree on.

Chapter Seven

'The hostel I was staying at in Norwich got full up.' Jazz had her hands curled tightly around a steaming mug of tea, her knees pressed together as she took up as little space as possible on Fiona's cream sofa. It was late, and Fiona had turned on the lamps, casting the room in soft shadow, the French windows looking out onto the night. Poppet, Fiona and Ermin's miniature schnauzer, was sitting patiently at Jazz's feet, and the young woman bent down to stroke her head. 'They can't guarantee you a place every day, and I was late arriving one night, so then I was out.'

'How long were you there?' Fiona asked.

Jazz shrugged. 'A couple of months, on and off. But this time I thought . . . it's so cold, it's going to be cold *every-where*, and at least here I get to see the sea, have fish and chips, so fuck it. I took a bus up here. Longest bus journey ever. I must have been on it for three days.'

Sophie laughed. She surreptitiously rubbed her wrist,

trying to loosen the ache without anyone noticing. 'Where were you before Norwich?'

'Ipswich,' Jazz said. 'Bury St Edmunds before that. Chelmsford. I've been all over, really.' A catalogue of different towns in her recent past. Sophie wondered, if they compared notes, how long their respective lists would be.

'How old are you?' Fiona asked, an edge of steel in her voice. Sophie didn't think it was aimed at Jazz.

The young woman kept her eyes on her tea. Beneath the blanket she'd been wrapped in, she was wearing a dirty purple hoody with holes in the cuffs, jeans, and trainers that looked as if they were falling apart. 'Eighteen,' she said.

'*Eighteen?*' Fiona sounded outraged, as if it should be impossible for this to happen to someone so young, but Sophie – while she agreed it was awful – wasn't surprised. In some of her foster placements she'd met teenagers who had spent time on the streets, some who left the safety of the homes because they clashed with the adults, and ended up sofa-surfing or in hostels. There were too many of them and too few people who had the time, resources or desire to look out for them, so inevitably some slipped through the cracks. There were a couple of times when she had almost been one of them.

'Your family home wasn't a safe place?' she asked gently.

Jazz looked up. 'My mum died when I was fourteen, and my dad remarried. They brought out the worst in each other. Lots of drinking, sometimes drugs. They didn't care what I did, and I decided I'd rather be anywhere else than there, so I made it happen.' She took a chocolate biscuit off the plate that Ermin had produced. 'It's OK when it's warm, but right now it's fucking freezing. That old shop was a good place to hunker down.' She smiled wistfully, as if she missed it.

'We can do better than that,' Fiona said. 'You need a bed and a bowl of porridge in the mornings.'

Jazz sat up straighter. 'I'm not Goldilocks. I can look after myself.'

'As demonstrated by the fact that you're here,' Fiona said, 'and you look incredibly healthy for someone living rough. *Can* doesn't mean *should*, however, and there are enough rumours about the old bookshop being haunted without you adding fuel to the fire.'

'There's a *ghost*?' Jazz's smile was bright and crinkled the edges of her eyes, and Sophie felt a twinge because she'd seen girls and boys who smiled so rarely that it felt like a miracle when they did.

'You probably know more than anyone else,' she said. 'You've been staying there.'

'Only for one night before you found me.' Jazz shook her head. 'But nah – not even rats.'

'Thank God for that!' Fiona picked up a biscuit. 'You don't want them getting next door and nibbling your beautiful notebooks.'

'Fiona, I'm not—'

'You sell notebooks?' Jazz asked.

Sophie nodded. 'I make them. They're great for all sorts – for lists, or making plans, or writing down your worries . . . I always have one with me.'

Jazz chewed her lip.

'I'll give you one,' Sophie continued. 'Tomorrow. Come into the shop and you can pick your favourite.'

She shrugged. 'I wouldn't use it.' She'd brought a rucksack

with her, saggy and far too empty, considering it contained all her worldly possessions. There was definitely room in it for a notebook.

'You could give it a try,' Sophie said softly. 'See if anything comes to mind. The blank pages will wait as long as you need them to. Think of it as a Welcome to Mistingham present.'

'And *I* think you should stay here tonight, rather than the bookshop,' Fiona said. 'You'll have to share your sleeping space with a couple of broken mannequins, but if you're fine with that, then you're very welcome.'

Jazz's mouth fell open. 'You *what*?'

'You probably aren't planning on being here long term,' Fiona went on. 'But we can look at things afresh in the morning.'

Jazz shook her head. 'No way. I never meant—'

'It's just one night,' Fiona said gently. 'To stop you getting hypothermia. We can . . .' she paused. '*You* can look at other options tomorrow.'

'I don't . . . I can't . . . can I use your toilet?' Jazz asked.

'Of course. Go into the hall and turn right, and it's the door on the left, just before you reach the kitchen.'

'Ta.' Jazz got up and hurried out of the room, leaving her mug on the floor next to the snoozing dog.

'That's very generous,' Sophie whispered. 'You don't know anything about her. Are you sure Ermin's going to be OK with it?'

'I'll check in a moment,' Fiona said. 'But I would put money on him agreeing with me. And it's just for tonight: we can't take her back to the bookshop, can we? Return her to fusty, musty floorboards.'

'What about the hotel?' Sophie asked. 'We could chip in to get her a night there.'

'I think she'd benefit from something a little more personal.' Fiona tapped her polished nails against her cup. 'I used to volunteer in a homeless shelter, decades ago. I might not be as sharp as I used to be, but I still have some understanding of the young and chronically unloved. Jazz deserves a chance, and one night can't do any harm.'

'Everyone deserves a chance,' Sophie said. Fiona had taken her under her wing as soon as she'd moved to Mistingham, even though she was thirty-six and perfectly independent. She loved taking care of people. 'Just be careful, OK?'

'Of course.' Fiona nodded. 'There will be ground rules. Now, let me have a look at that wrist.'

'What?' Sophie moved her arm behind her back.

'Don't think I didn't notice.' She tutted. 'You fell on it.' She moved across to Sophie's sofa, and Sophie reluctantly held out her arm. Her skin had turned purple, stark against the cream cuff of her jumper. 'I think you need to get this checked out properly,' Fiona said, as the doorbell echoed through the room.

'Who's that?' Sophie asked, wincing as Fiona took her hand. It was getting late for casual callers.

'The bookshop lock is broken, so I got Ermin to give—'

'Here he is!' Ermin appeared in the living-room doorway, and Sophie sucked in a breath when she saw who *he* was. Harry Anderly, towering over Fiona's husband, wearing the same waterproof coat he had been wearing earlier, as well as the same stony expression.

'Harry,' Fiona said. 'Thank you for coming.'

'You said it was about the bookshop?' He raised an eyebrow.

'I'm afraid the lock is broken.'

Harry stepped awkwardly into the living room. He looked far too handsome, and also slightly mutinous. His jacket was unzipped and his rust-coloured jumper set off the gold flecks in his eyes, which were suddenly focused on where Fiona was still holding Sophie's wrist.

'How did the door get broken?' he asked.

'It was me,' Jazz said, slipping back into the room. She seemed even smaller under Harry's glare. 'I'm really sorry. I-I'm Jazz. I was looking for somewhere dry to sleep, somewhere a bit warmer than a bus shelter, so . . .' Her words trailed away.

Harry's gaze softened a fraction. 'It's good to meet you, Jazz. The door is an easy fix; please don't worry about it.'

'Right.' Jazz sank back onto the sofa.

'She's staying here tonight,' Fiona said, exchanging a look with Ermin, who nodded his assent. 'Thank you for coming, Harry. I didn't want to wait until tomorrow to let you know about the lock. You might want to get it fixed right away.'

'There's nothing in there worth stealing.' His gaze landed on Sophie. 'Are you staying here too?'

'No.' She felt a blush creep into her cheeks. 'No, I'm . . .' She stood up and shoved her phone into her pocket. 'I need to get back to Clifton. I dropped him off at the flat, and—'

'I'll walk you out,' Harry said.

Sophie exchanged a wide-eyed look with her friend, wished them all goodnight, and followed him down the corridor.

Fiona waved them off then gently closed the front door, and then it was just the two of them, standing on the pavement outside Fiona and Ermin's house, a couple of cheery gnomes standing sentry in the slate-covered beds in their garden, a water feature trickling gently.

'That looks sore.' Harry gestured to her wrist.

Sophie resisted the urge to hide it again. 'I'll be OK.'

'How?'

'What do you mean, *how*?'

'How will you be OK, if you don't get it looked at?'

'I'm sure it's just a sprain. I really need to go—'

'Hang on.' He stilled her with a touch on her arm, then gently lifted her injured hand, Sophie's fingers tingling at the contact. 'May I?' he asked, and she realized she was holding her breath. She nodded, transfixed by the way he was touching her, carefully pressing the pads of his fingers into the purpling flesh around her wrist.

'Does that hurt?' he asked.

'A little. It's not too bad.'

'Can you move it? Rotate the joint?'

Sophie did, closing her eyes briefly as pain jolted through her. But she could move it, and that meant it couldn't be too serious. 'I think it's OK,' she whispered.

'Did you fall on it?'

'I put my hand down to break my fall.'

He nodded. 'It probably *is* a sprain. You could do with getting it checked out by the doctor, but I could wrap it up for you in the meantime?'

'Do you have a first-aid kit in your car?' She peered past him to the dark hulk of a Land Rover Defender parked at the kerb.

He shook his head quickly. 'At home.'

'Mistingham Manor?'

'My home,' Harry repeated. 'We could be done in twenty minutes, then I'll drive you to your place.'

Sophie sighed. It seemed like days, rather than hours, since she'd been in the village hall, foolhardily raising her hand to offer her assistance with a project she had no expertise in. 'I need to get home and check Clifton's OK,' she said again.

'You don't like accepting help, do you?'

Sophie laughed. 'I just don't think I need it on this occasion, but thank you for offering.'

She moved to go past him, and he put his hand on her arm again, the touch warm but fleeting. 'We should get together,' he said. Then, after a pause, added, 'To talk about the festival.'

'Sure.' Sophie swallowed. It felt intimate, the two of them standing in the dark, just beyond the gentle glow of Fiona's outdoor light; the quiet, misty village in shadow. 'I'll be in touch.'

She took a step back, and Harry dropped his hand.

'Fine,' he called after her as she walked away. 'Just don't leave it too long, OK?'

As Sophie strode home, her wrist throbbing in time with her footsteps, she decided she'd imagined his concern when he was looking at her bruised skin. He was Harry Anderly, the Dark Demon Lord of Mistingham, and any gestures of kindness or affection were an aberration she would do well to ignore. They could plan this festival together, as efficiently as possible, then get on with their own lives. It didn't have to get complicated, and if there was anyone who was an expert at keeping control of her feelings, then it was her.

Chapter Eight

Norfolk had a reputation for being a flat county, with expanses of farmed fields and heathland, the marshes bleeding into the sea, green turning to gold turning to blue, and the famed big Norfolk sky above. But, along the coast, there were enough hills and dips to make Sophie's runs challenging, and she relished the head space they gave her.

The day after the village hall meeting and finding Jazz, she got up early and went to the local pharmacist, who confirmed her wrist was sprained and expertly bandaged it for her. Then she decided that the best way to work out the tension of the last few days was to go for a long run.

It was a cold but bright day, the blue sky peppered with white clouds, and Sophie took her usual route, running down to the promenade, keeping the deep, entrancing blue of the sea on her right, dodging dog walkers with shoulders hunched against the cold, their scarves flying out behind them. She'd left Clifton at home, wanting to pound her legs and run her lungs ragged.

Even in winter, Mistingham was beautiful, and as Sophie headed inland she found herself smiling at the dinky cottages and elegant town houses, some adorned with Christmas wreaths already, others with trailing winter jasmines or cyclamen in pots, small stone sculptures decorating front gardens. It was a place where people took pride in their homes, where they felt privileged to live. There were some properties with unlit windows and little personalization, a couple of streets that were mostly second homes, but Sophie tended to avoid those.

She was turning onto Perpendicular Street, wondering how many people she'd have to dodge along the edge of the green, when someone appeared right in front of her. She veered away at the last minute, the soft sludge of the damp, grass-covered mud helping to slow her pace.

'Yikes!' A hand grabbed her arm and she was steadied just before she fell.

Sophie tried to catch her breath. 'May,' she puffed out. 'H-hello. I'm so sorry – and thank you – that was a quick reaction.'

'Are you OK?' May asked, as Sophie bent over, putting her good hand on her knee.

'I'm fine. I must have been going faster than I thought.'

'Certainly faster than I could manage,' May said. 'What are you doing now?'

'Sweating,' Sophie said. 'Panting. Thinking about a long, hot shower.' Her cheeks felt raw, windburned, in contrast to the rest of her overheated body.

'What are you doing in two hours?'

'I have the day off,' she said, glancing at her watch. She didn't add that she was trying to work up the courage to speak to Harry, to follow up on her dismissive *I'll be in touch* the day before. If they didn't get together soon, then the Christmas festival would be a paltry singsong comprised of two people – and possibly Harry's goat – along with some fish and chips from Batter Days.

'Do you want to grab a coffee in the hotel?' May asked. 'We could have one of their famous cakes.'

Sophie only thought for a second. 'That sounds great. And two hours should give me long enough to make myself presentable.'

'Wonderful.' May's smile was warm. 'The perks of working for yourself.'

'I thought you worked for the entire village,' Sophie said. 'Aren't you on call twenty-four-seven, sorting out everyone's technical problems?'

'It does feel like that sometimes,' May admitted with a laugh. 'Catch you in a bit.'

Sophie nodded, then willed herself to find a final burst of energy and headed for home at a slow jog.

Mistingham Hotel's lounge managed to be both comfortingly traditional and modern enough to feel classy, the floral patterns of the curtains and cushion covers delicate rather than gaudy, a soft, pistachio-green carpet, and elegant crystal chandeliers hanging from the high ceiling. Its wide windows looked out on the village green, the oak tree and, beyond, thin slivers of the sea in the gaps between buildings.

When Sophie arrived, May was already at a round table in the window. It was covered with a cream cloth, and a bud vase with a pink rose sat in the centre. The room smelt faintly of sugar, making Sophie's stomach rumble as she made her way over, taking the seat opposite the other woman.

'Hello.'

'You made it!' May was wearing an indigo jumper, the sleeves falling over her hands, and her straight dark hair was pulled back in a ponytail. Her features were a lot more delicate than Sophie's, almost elfin. If she didn't already know, Sophie would never in a million years have guessed she was a tech wizard, with a brief spell in Silicon Valley behind her.

'I don't know what you fancy.' May pointed to the menu printed on thick, cream card. 'But I'd like one of everything, and I haven't been on a run.'

'I'm going for the chocolate eclair,' Sophie said, after a brief glance at the menu.

May laughed. 'That was quick.'

'I've seen people eating them, from outside.'

'But you haven't had one before?'

'Not yet,' Sophie said, which felt silly because she'd been here for nearly a year. 'I just haven't got around to it.'

A young man in a white shirt and black pressed trousers took their order, then disappeared as quietly as he'd arrived. Sophie had imagined the lounge would be full of pensioners meeting up for crosswords and gossip, but the customers were a lot more varied than she'd expected. Some were clearly retired, but others looked like they were here on a winter break or conducting low-key business meetings.

'It's lovely here,' she said.

'It's a good place to escape to, when you want to get away from your desk,' May said, 'or your shop counter. I imagine it's fun, working with Fiona.'

'Oh it is,' Sophie said. 'She's generous, easy to talk to, and she knows everything that goes on in Mistingham.'

'She's formidable, too,' May added. 'You know who wears the trousers between her and Ermin.'

Sophie laughed. 'She can seem strict, but mostly she's a softie. Did you hear about Jazz?' She assumed Harry would have told her when he got home last night.

'The poor girl who was sleeping in The Book Ends?'

'Fiona and I thought she was the ghost – except she'd broken the lock to get in.'

'It's awful how some people end up like that.' May's cautious tone told Sophie that, even though they had only talked occasionally, she knew about her background. Sophie had never particularly hidden the fact that she had grown up in foster care, and she wasn't surprised it had made its way around the village. 'But Fiona's taken her in?'

'She did last night,' Sophie said. 'I don't know what the plan is now, whether Jazz will want to move on, or stay here for a while. I don't suppose it's brimming with job opportunities, if that's what she's after, but some places might need seasonal staff.'

'Maybe Mary and Winnie could do with some help,' May suggested. 'I'm sure, if that was what she wanted to do, then Fiona could put in a good word.' She grinned. 'Was she behind your decision to volunteer for the festival?'

Sophie groaned. 'No. That was all my own stupidity.'

'Stupidity?'

'I didn't . . .' She stopped. Did she want to tell May about the book? It had been an anonymous gift, and Sophie had decided she needed to be cautious if she wanted to unearth the culprit. After all, they must have stayed hidden for a reason. 'I wanted to contribute something,' she settled on. 'I thought there would be a team of us, but instead . . .'

'Instead it's just you and Harry,' May finished. Her eyes were twinkling.

'You think that's amusing?' Sophie wondered if May had been teasing him about his predicament.

'You're not looking forward to it?' May parried.

Sophie was glad when the young man brought their lattes and cakes over on a silver tray. Her chocolate eclair was huge, with cream bursting out between the chocolate-covered layers, and May's doughnut – which Sophie had thought might be a conservative choice – had sticky pink jam oozing out of it, and sherbet hearts stuck on its pale pink icing.

'Wow,' she murmured, the conversation momentarily forgotten while they tucked into their cakes, exchanging wide-eyed looks of delight.

'Great, huh?' May said.

'*So* good.' Sophie felt a pang of regret that she'd waited this long to try one.

'So. You and Harry,' May prompted. 'You don't seem thrilled about working with him.'

Sophie took a few beats to reply. She didn't want to be rude about May's boyfriend, even though she was obviously under no illusions about how hostile he could seem – if he was to be believed, it was May who'd given him the 'Dark Demon Lord of Mistingham' title. 'We don't know each other very well,' she said cautiously. 'And it isn't going to be easy, planning an entire street festival between us.'

'I wish he'd relax about the oak tree,' May said with an eye-roll. 'I get that he's protective of his family's land, but

73

that tree has been there for hundreds of years and hasn't shown any signs of falling down.'

'It used to be the focal point of the festival?'

'Of *all* events in the village,' May confirmed. 'But by saying the oak is out of bounds, he's effectively making the entire green a no-go area, which is ridiculous. I've given up trying to make him listen to me, though.' She took a large bite of her doughnut.

'Sometimes you need a fresh voice,' Sophie said with a shrug.

'Exactly! I think there are a whole lot of people holding out hope that you'll be able to talk him round.'

Sophie's eclair was momentarily forgotten. 'I thought I was planning the festival with him.'

'You are. But I wouldn't be surprised if Ermin is *also* hoping you'll get Harry to back down, so it can go back to its original location.'

'But why me?' Sophie tried to keep the panic out of her voice. 'It would make much more sense for you to talk him round.'

'I told you,' May said with a laugh, 'he stopped listening to me ages ago.'

'He didn't seem that approachable after the meeting.' But even as she said it, she felt a stab of guilt, because he might still have been a little bit chilly, but he'd seemed genuinely concerned about her wrist, and *he'd* reminded *her* they needed to get together to start work on the festival.

'He was brooding,' May said. 'Which, to be fair, is one of his favourite states. But he's really lovely when he lets his guard down.'

'How long have you known him?' Sophie asked.

'Oh, decades now,' May said. 'We both grew up here, and even though he's a few years older than me, my brother Avery hung around with him a lot, and I ended up being the annoying little sister hanger-on. But when we were older we became friends in our own right, and stayed in touch when I was in the US and he was in London. We both gravitated back here at roughly the same time, and it was so generous of him to let me move into the manor house when I got back.'

Generous? Sophie frowned. That didn't sound like something you'd say if you were together. Maybe they'd only become a couple fairly recently. 'Are your parents still in the village?' She couldn't remember May mentioning them before.

'They moved to Cornwall about eight years ago, replacing one beautiful, hard-to-get-to part of the country with another.'

Sophie tried not to react at the mention of Cornwall. 'What about your brother?'

'He lives in Norwich, so he's not too far away, and he's a builder, so he gets around a lot of the county, depending on where the work is.'

'It's good that he's close by.'

'What about you?' May took another bite of her doughnut. 'I remember you mentioning that you moved around a bit.'

Sophie nodded. 'That's right. Staying with different foster families.'

'You weren't ever adopted? I hope you don't mind me asking.'

'Not at all.' Sophie had made it a rule to never be ashamed

of her history. It hadn't always been great, but there were plenty of children who had suffered a lot more than her, and it hadn't been her – or any of their – faults. 'I was going to be adopted when I was three, but the whole thing fell through before it could happen. I didn't know about it until I was older, and by then I'd got used to not staying anywhere for very long.' *Just like Jazz*, she thought. 'Before moving here I was in Canterbury, and it was Bristol before that.'

'What made you come to Mistingham?'

The truth was, she'd heard someone on a train talking about their magical family holiday at the Norfolk seaside. She had been living in Canterbury for a year at that point, and she didn't feel settled there. She'd loved the thought of going somewhere a little more remote where she could enjoy the contrasts – the emptiness in the wintertime, the buzz of tourists during spring and summer.

Many people wouldn't understand why someone would uproot their life on such a whim, but she thought May might. 'I heard someone saying how wonderful it was,' she admitted. 'I'd had a day out at the seaside in Kent, and I was on the train home, listening in to the conversations around me – as you do.'

'Of course.' May grinned.

'I was selling my notebooks at fairs and markets, and didn't have anything particularly tying me to Canterbury. So I just decided – Mistingham would be where I'd head next.'

'And now you're here, you've fallen in love and never want to leave.' May said it so easily, and Sophie felt a slow shame creep over her, even though she didn't know what she had to be ashamed of.

'It's a beautiful place,' she said blandly. And then, wanting to change the subject, added, 'Harry told me how you tricked him into naming his dogs Darkness and Terror. They're such ridiculous names.'

'He *admitted* it?' May squeezed her doughnut so hard that jam squirted onto her plate.

'Yep. Well, I had to drag it out of him – it wasn't something he offered up with relish. It makes me a bit worried about us working together,' she admitted, half to herself.

'It'll be good for him,' May said indulgently, and Sophie wondered how much softer he was with her.

'What will be? Having to interact with other villagers, or working with me?'

May sipped her latte. 'Both. He came back here for a reason.'

'What was it?'

May shrugged. 'It's probably best if I let him tell you that. It's one thing to encourage him to attend village meetings, another to give away all his secrets.'

'Secrets?'

'To Harry, *everything* is his business and nobody else's, which is why I was surprised he told you about the dogs. He plays on his isolation. He doesn't have any family left here – his sister, Daisy, moved away when she was eighteen and, according to him, is intent on never coming back. He doesn't do anything to discourage the rumours about him, he isn't prepared to meet Ermin halfway about the oak tree. He could change everyone's opinions about him *so* easily, but he says it's about the principle.'

'So what's my play?' Sophie asked her. 'I told him I'd be in touch, but do you think I should turn up at the manor?

Ask you very nicely for his number, or give you mine to pass on to him? Or should I start planning things without him and see how long it takes him to get mad?'

May laughed. 'If you pick that option, you might end up doing the whole thing on your own. Why don't you give me your number, and I'll get him to call you. Also, this way we can stay in touch and meet up for coffee and cake again, or a drink in the Blossom Bough?'

'That would be great.' May was good fun, and Sophie wondered why they hadn't done this before. They'd got on well, chatting easily if they both happened to be in the pub, and whenever they bumped into each other, but they had never purposefully got together until now. She suspected that May might want to keep an eye on her now she was going to be spending a lot of time with her boyfriend, but she certainly wasn't coming across as possessive.

Sophie couldn't change her outlook now, though. In a couple of months, she would be gone. She would plan the Christmas festival, with or without Harry's help, and she would find out who had sent her the beautiful copy of *Jane Eyre*. Perhaps she would spend more time with May, too, but then she would pack up her things and start the next chapter. It was how she protected herself, and it had worked so far: there was no reason things needed to be different this time around.

Chapter Nine

The book was on Sophie's wooden coffee table, still loosely wrapped in its brown paper. She sat on the sofa, cradling her coffee, while Clifton snoozed in his dog bed, under a patch of winter sun filtering in through the window.

She picked up *Jane Eyre*, held it to her nose and sniffed. It had that familiar, slightly musty scent, with a faint chemical undertone that might have been the glue used to rebind it. She flicked through it, stopping to read a paragraph here, a line there, pausing on a page that caught her eye:

I see no enemy to a fortunate issue but in the brow; and that brow professes to say – 'I can live alone, if self-respect, and circumstances require me so to do. I need not sell my soul to buy bliss. I have an inward treasure born with me, which can keep me alive if all extraneous delights should be withheld, or offered only at a price I cannot afford to give.'

With a lump clogging her throat, she turned back to the first page and slid the gold ribbon in to it.

Next, she reread the postcard:

Dear Sophie, sometimes you have to look closer to home to find what you've been missing. Please accept this gift as an early Christmas present – love from The Secret Bookshop.

She hadn't heard anyone in Mistingham mention a secret bookshop, and Fiona hadn't either. She wished, now, that she'd asked May about it on Saturday, but there had been too many other things to talk about. She still felt indignant that there was someone out there who thought she was missing something in her life, who thought they knew her well enough to tell her that, but indignation was far outweighed by intrigue, and she was desperate to find out who had given it to her.

She put the book and postcard back on her coffee table, finished her drink and went to get ready for work.

'Aunty Sophie! Uncle Clifton!' was the shout that greeted her when she arrived at the bakery at lunch time. As usual, its incredible smells met her even before she'd walked through the open door – a mix of baking bread, frying bacon and melting cheese – and Sophie's taste buds burst into life in anticipation.

'Lucy.' Dexter wearily ran a hand through his hair. 'Not everyone is Aunt and Uncle.'

Lucy had been sitting on the bakery counter swinging her legs, but now she jumped off and wrapped her arms around Sophie, then crouched to stroke her dog while Sophie tied him up outside, next to a large metal water bowl.

Lucy's dark hair was a tangle of glossy curls, and Sophie had always thought of her and Clifton as kindred spirits. She was surprised how long the girl's legs looked in jeans; how much more grown-up she seemed without her school uniform on.

'You said *loads* of people called random friends Aunt and Uncle,' Lucy pointed out, 'so why can't Sophie be Aunty?'

Dexter gave Sophie an exasperated look as she stepped inside. 'Well, if she agrees. But Clifton can't be Uncle. He's a dog.'

'In the book I'm reading there's a horse called Great-Uncle Arthur.'

'Does your book have dragons in, too? Goblins? Unicorns?'

'They're ogres, not goblins,' Lucy said.

'There you go then,' her dad replied. 'It's a completely different world, so it's a different set of rules.'

Sophie shrugged. 'Uncle Clifton sounds pretty cute to me, though.'

'Don't encourage her,' Dexter said with a smile. 'What can I get you?'

'Two of your epic chicken sandwiches please, with mayo and red onion and tomato and mustard – the works.'

'Good choice.' He turned to his preparation counter.

The bakery was at the top of Perpendicular Street but set back slightly from the road, with a small patch of grass in front of it that was constantly flattened by people queuing up for sourdough loaves, croissants and baguettes. Dexter also made a range of savoury pastries – his cheese, onion and bacon had legend status in the village – and fresh sandwiches for the lunch crowd. Sophie tried to make lunch at home and bring it with her, but with the bakery so close, and the greeting so warm, her willpower wasn't always up to it.

'Why aren't you at school?' she asked Lucy.

'Insect day,' Lucy said.

'Inset,' Dexter corrected. 'Your teachers aren't going around hunting for woodlice and spiders.'

'Spiders aren't insects,' Lucy told him. 'They're arachnids.'

'True. But I doubt your teachers are looking for them either. It's some kind of training day.'

'So I'm working here today,' Lucy said to Sophie. 'But I might go and help Birdie with her allotment this afternoon.'

'As long as you wear your hat,' Dexter said. 'It's cold today.'

'Nice to have a bit of sunshine, though.' Except that, when Sophie turned to the window, she saw that the blue sky was fighting a losing battle with a wall of grey cloud. She chewed her lip. She wasn't going to get anywhere if she didn't ask any questions. 'Have either of you heard of The Secret Bookshop?'

Dexter looked up from his chopping board. 'No, what is that? Some kind of experience in London?'

'There's the secret bunker in Essex,' Lucy said, 'but it has brown tourist signs pointing the way, so I don't think it's still a proper secret.' She twirled one of her curls around her finger. 'What's the point of a Secret Bookshop, anyway? How would you find the books?'

'With a magic key?' Dexter suggested. 'You're the one who reads all the Romantasy. There must be a special way of getting in: a handshake, some kind of seal, or a hidden door in a bookcase.'

'Oh I *love* those,' Lucy said, her dark eyes wide with excitement. 'I've never seen one in real life, though.'

'Me neither,' Sophie admitted. 'I don't have any details about The Secret Bookshop, I just . . . I was given a book the other day. It turned up on my counter in the shop, but I don't know who left it there. It's a beautiful copy of *Jane Eyre*, and there was this anonymous note saying it was from The Secret Bookshop. I just . . . I wondered if you'd heard anything about it.'

Dexter turned around, a finished sandwich in one large, plastic-gloved hand. 'No, never, as far as I can recall, and I've lived here all my life.'

'I haven't heard anything about it at school,' Lucy said. 'It sounds *amazing*, though! I bet Uncle Clifton knows, but he can't say anything because he only speaks dog.'

'The shop doesn't have CCTV, does it?' Dexter asked. 'Then you could check to see who left it for you.'

'I don't think Fiona's into all that modern security stuff.' She sighed. 'Thank you, though. It made me think of The Book Ends. From the way everyone talks about it, it sounds as if it was special – the kind of place that might have been involved in mystery book deliveries.'

'Oh it was.' Dexter slid the sandwiches carefully into paper bags. 'It was really unique, and now it's just—'

'Haunted,' Lucy finished. 'It's *definitely* haunted!'

'We sort of debunked the ghost story,' Sophie told her. 'Did you hear?'

'About the young woman who was sleeping in there?' Dexter said. 'Jazz, isn't it?'

'That's right. She's staying with Fiona for a few days.' She didn't think it was her place to say anything more, like the fact that Fiona had turned up in a tizzy that morning, because she'd offered Jazz another week with her and Ermin, and at first Jazz had said she was leaving immediately, that she didn't want their charity, and then, once they had persuaded her to stay for a couple more days, she had shut herself up in her room.

Fiona was being generous, and Sophie sympathized with her frustration, but she could have told her at the beginning that offering her home to someone like Jazz, who'd had such a difficult, turbulent life, was unlikely to be plain sailing.

'Hopefully having somewhere safe to stay will give her a bit of stability,' she said to Dexter. 'A pushing-off point for whatever she wants to do next.'

'Sometimes all anyone needs is a breather,' Dexter said. 'A break from the full-time struggle to survive. Do you need a sandwich for her, too?'

'No thanks – she's at Fiona's today, not the shop. Anyway, she didn't see any ghosts while she was in The Book Ends.'

'I expect she missed it,' Lucy said authoritatively. 'It probably went somewhere else for the night. That big old house has ghosts, too.'

'Mistingham Manor?' Sophie wondered what Harry thought of that particular rumour, then answered her own question. He wouldn't give it the time of day.

'Everywhere in this place is haunted if you listen to the older residents,' Dexter said.

'Not our bakery.' Lucy folded her arms. 'But the bookshop, and that crumbly old house, and my friend Alice's mum said she saw this old man in the village hall when a minute before it had been empty. She was taking down the balloons after Alice's baby brother's party, and he was just *sitting* there!'

'It was probably a relative in a sugar coma,' Dexter said with a chuckle.

'No it wasn't, Dad. It was someone she'd never even *seen* before!'

'Right. Ghosts everywhere.' Dexter gave Sophie a wry smile. 'But none of that helps you with your secret bookshop, or your strange gift.' He put the wrapped sandwiches into a larger paper bag, which had *Mistingham Bakery* written on the side in a purple roundel. 'There's nobody you've got close to recently? Nobody you might expect a gift from, out of the blue?'

'Dad means a boyfriend,' Lucy said.

'Oh.' Sophie felt herself flush. 'Nobody like that, no. Not on the horizon or . . . or anything.'

'Right.' Dexter nodded, then looked away.

'God.' Lucy sighed. 'Adults are *so awkward*.'

'Just wait until you're a teenager,' Dexter said, then gave Sophie a horrified look. 'My daughter is going to be a teenager.'

'Not for four years.' Sophie didn't point out that she was already acting like one.

'You're so cringe, Dad,' Lucy said. 'Can I go outside and play with Clifton on the grass?'

'Uncle Clifton would love that,' Sophie told her. Lucy grinned and hurried out of the door. 'She's a happy handful,' she said to Dexter once they were alone.

'Yeah, she's amazing.' Dexter rolled his shoulders. 'She keeps me on my toes, which I need. And she's happy, which is the main thing I care about.'

'She's very lucky to have you.'

'Right.' Dexter looked pensive all of a sudden, so she took the initiative to stop him from having to ask.

'I can't exactly speak with much authority, but I think having one stable, loving parent is a gift. Of course, Lucy will miss some things not having her mum in her life, but you're doing an amazing job of being all the parent she needs.'

'I worry about it,' Dexter said. 'But I always make her my priority – or I try to.'

'It shows.'

'*Jane Eyre* was the book you were given by this mysterious, secret bookshop?'

'I know.' Sophie laughed. 'One of the most famous orphans in literature. But I'm creeping up on forty, so I don't really think of myself as an orphan any more.'

'It was someone who knows you well enough, though,' Dexter said. 'To know that about you, I mean.'

'But we live in Mistingham,' Sophie pointed out, remembering how May had mentioned her upbringing the other day, too. 'It only takes one person to have that nugget of information, then the entire village does.'

Dexter returned her smile. 'One of the curses of living here.'

'How many curses can one place have?'

Sophie jumped at the deep voice behind her, and Dexter's easy smile morphed into shock.

She turned to find Harry Anderly in the doorway. He was wearing jeans and a grey and black checked shirt, the sleeves rolled up, showing off forearms that were tanned despite it being November. His brown hair was unkempt, and stubble covered his jaw. It was obvious that he didn't care a whole lot about his appearance, and yet he was tall and broad-shouldered, his features classically handsome, then with all the edges roughened in a way that should have dulled the effect but somehow enhanced it.

His glance flitted between her and Dexter while they both stared at him. Then he shrugged and said, 'It was a rhetorical question anyway. What specific curse were you talking about?'

Sophie found her voice first. 'The curse of everyone here knowing your business after you've told a single person.'

'Ah. That one. It's why I tend not to share details too widely.'

'Except about your dogs—'

'Could I have a seeded sourdough please, Dexter?' Harry spoke over Sophie, then gave her a stern look.

She felt a pleasant shiver run through her, but she set her expression to mild indifference and murmured, 'You can't keep it quiet for ever.'

'I can try,' he said, leaning towards her. 'I see it was a mistake to trust you with it.'

Was he *teasing* her? She mimed zipping her lips closed.

'How are you, Dex?' Harry asked.

Dexter took a few seconds to reply. 'Great, thanks. Yeah, I'm . . . I'm good.'

'And Lucy? I saw her outside playing with a black mop. Strange toy for a nine-year-old.'

'That's my *dog*.' Sophie was incredulous. It seemed Harry Anderly *was* capable of teasing.

'I know,' he said. 'I met Clifton, remember?'

'Lucy's really well too.' Dexter sounded cautiously bewildered, like he was waiting for the trick to be revealed. 'How are you, Harry?'

'I'm OK, thanks. Dealing with the consequences of listening to other people, rather than trusting my own instincts.'

'You mean volunteering for festival planning?' Sophie asked him.

'I *got* volunteered,' Harry pointed out. 'And it makes no sense. I'm enemy number one because I want to protect the oak, so why anyone's keen for me to get involved in their precious festival, I don't know.'

'Maybe it's an olive branch?' Dexter suggested.

'Or it's punishment,' Harry said. 'Not sure how getting me to do community service is an olive branch.'

Sophie folded her arms. 'You think working with me is a punishment?'

Harry opened his mouth, and she had a delicious moment of seeing him lost for words.

'Anyone would be lucky to work with you, Sophie,' Dexter said sincerely, and she blew him a kiss.

'We need to get together,' Harry said abruptly. 'Meet up to start planning it. The sooner we start, the sooner it'll be over.'

'That's the spirit,' Sophie said brightly. The look she got in return could have frozen her eyelashes.

'Anything else for you, Harry?' Dexter put his wrapped loaf on top of the glass cabinet.

'Um.' Harry released Sophie from his glare and looked at the display of pastries. He was closer to her now, and she remembered how he'd taken her hand, pressing gently, turning it over as if it was something precious. He smelled of fresh air and grass, something darker and spicier underneath. 'A steak slice, please,' he said, oblivious to Sophie's scattering thoughts.

'Good choice.' Dexter got his tongs.

'What shall we do first, then?' Sophie forced herself to ask. 'I wasn't here last year, so I don't know what it's supposed

88

to be like. But Winnie could be our starting point. I'm sure she'd help.'

'She'd make it torturous,' Harry said.

'Why?'

'Have you met Winnie?'

'Of course! She's nice – she runs the post office as well as the hotel. She's clearly efficient.'

'She's also a menace.'

'A menace whose hotel sells the best chocolate eclairs in Norfolk?'

'May said you loved the eclair.'

'What else did she say?'

Harry shrugged. 'You're right: we should speak to Winnie first. Otherwise we'll be floundering in the dark.'

'Great. When?'

'What about when you finish work tomorrow, unless you have other plans?'

'That's fine,' Sophie said. 'We're usually done at five on a Tuesday.'

Harry nodded. 'I'll speak to Winnie after this, let you know if it's on.'

'Thank you,' Sophie said. 'That's kind.'

Harry accepted his bread and the steak slice, and took out his wallet to pay for them. 'Good to see you,' he said to Dexter, then glanced at Sophie and added, 'I'll be in touch.' She didn't think it was a coincidence that he was echoing her words from the other night.

'Looking forward to it,' she said.

She was so tempted to call after him, to ask him to say hello to Darkness and Terror for her, but he'd offered her a glimpse of his softer side, had made her think they might be able to work together without killing each other, and she didn't want to lose that so soon.

Dexter rested his arms on the counter. 'That wasn't on my Bingo card for today.'

'We've got to plan the Christmas festival together,' Sophie said with a shrug. 'He's going to have to interact with people, so maybe he's getting some practice in?'

'He behaved like a normal human being.'

'It seems some things *are* possible.'

'Wow.' Lucy burst into the bakery with Clifton under her arm. 'That was Uncle Harry, right?'

Dexter sighed. 'Not *everyone's* Uncle or Aunty, Luce.'

'He didn't mind when I called him Uncle Harry,' Lucy said, and Dexter winced.

Sophie burst out laughing. She couldn't remember enjoying a lunch break so much, even if she'd spent the whole time talking, and Fiona would be wondering where her sandwich was.

'He *did* say Uncle Clifton looked like a mop, though,' Lucy added thoughtfully, and Sophie's laughter faded. Right. Next time, she was definitely going to out Harry's stupid dog names. If he was going to give it out, then she was more than prepared to dish it right back.

She paid for her sandwiches, took her reluctant dog back from Lucy and said goodbye to her and Dexter. As she turned in the direction of Hartley Country Apparel, she saw Harry walking up to the hotel's main entrance. His stride had some bounce in it, and she might have been imagining it, because he was quite a way away, but it looked very much like the Dark Demon Lord of Mistingham was actually smiling.

Chapter Ten

As the clock ticked round to five o'clock on Tuesday, Sophie found herself getting flustered. For the most part she was calm and collected – in the face of disgruntled or disparaging customers; when it came to decisions about her future; when she happened upon an angry bull in a field on one of her runs. Growing up with constant uncertainty and some volatile characters, being moved on at short notice or missing out on something she'd been promised, she had learnt that getting worked up never solved anything.

But now, despite a successful day in the shop, with good sales and a commission for four notebooks from a regular customer who lived in Wells-next-the-Sea, her pulse was thudding and her hands were prickling with sweat. In half an hour she would meet Harry and, together, they would get the details about last year's festival from Winnie. It wasn't a scary task, so why was she so nervous?

'OK, Sophie?' Fiona asked.

'Of course.' Sophie cleared her throat.

'Any progress with that book of yours?'

'Not so far,' she admitted. 'But it's only been a few days, and so much has happened since then. The festival . . . Jazz.' She looked pointedly at her friend.

Fiona sighed. 'She came down for dinner last night, but she hardly said a word. I'm worried we've offended her in some way.'

'This whole thing must be a huge adjustment for her,' Sophie said gently. 'She's been living on the streets, not knowing where she's going to sleep or get a decent meal, and then suddenly she's got you and Ermin looking after her, checking on her, asking what she needs. I think that . . .' She swallowed. 'A big part of it, for someone who hasn't had a whole lot of good things happen to them, is that they start telling themselves they don't deserve them. Somehow, this is where they *should* be, and anything positive seems too good to be true. You can't expect Jazz to be a smiling, grateful open book right away. She's probably finding it hard to trust you – trust the situation.'

Fiona nodded. 'I wonder if she'd feel more at home in a hostel, but I don't want to give her the impression we don't want her here.'

'The best thing you can do is sit down and talk about it. What *she* wants, and what you want and are prepared to do. I would maybe give it a few more days, but don't leave it too long to find out what she's thinking.'

Fiona gave her a weak smile. 'You're wise beyond your years.'

'I've had to be.' Sophie said it with a grin, so it didn't come across as bitter. 'Anyway, now I need to focus on this blinking festival, work out how I'm going to organize it with someone who rations himself to roughly five words an hour.'

'That man.' Fiona shook her head.

'Ermin was more than happy to let him be involved.'

'Ermin had a lapse of judgement. Harry doesn't care about this village at all.'

Sophie thought of their meeting at the bakery. 'I don't know if that's entirely true,' she said carefully, 'but I'll find out soon enough.'

'Just see if you can bring it into the twenty-first century,' Fiona said. 'Winnie is one of my favourite people in the world, but Hook the Duck is a little bit outdated.'

'What makes you think we'll do any better?' Sophie glanced at the clock. 'Hook the Duck might be Harry's favourite game.'

'I'd imagine he's more of a "playing chess by himself, brooding over a glass of whisky" type man.' Fiona sounded accusatory, but Sophie didn't mind the image it conjured up: his features lit by the soft glow of a crackling fire, the leather of the chair creaking as he shifted position. She pushed the image away, remembering May's quiet indulgence as she'd spoken about him. No good could come of mooning over someone who was so completely unavailable. She reminded herself that Harry infuriated her every time they met, and went back to watching the hands of the clock tick slowly round towards her fate.

Harry was waiting for her next to the steps leading up to Mistingham Hotel's welcoming front door. The temperature had fallen with the sun, and an icy twilight made the village feel crisp and clean, the first stars visible in the deep blue sky. Under the hotel's generous porch light, Sophie could see her fellow planner was wearing jeans and a forest green jumper, his waxed jacket open over the top. His hair looked a little less like he'd run through a hedge than usual.

'Hey.' He raised a hand as she approached.

'Hey yourself. How are Darkness and Terror?'

His jaw tightened. 'They're fine. How's the mop?'

'He's with Ermin; I'm picking him up later. What jumper is Felix wearing today?'

Harry narrowed his eyes. She thought he wasn't going to answer, then he said, 'It's red with white pompoms.'

'Oh my God! Do you have a photo?'

'No. Shall we go in?'

'Winnie was happy for us to grill her?'

'Of course she was.' Harry sounded eternally put upon, and Sophie's curiosity grew.

'Lead the way,' she said.

He did.

'Good to see the prodigal son is getting back into the thick of things.' Winnie settled herself in her chair at their chosen table, in a cosy corner of the hotel's lounge. 'Henry Anderly in the flesh, sitting right here, opposite me.'

Harry gave a gentle sigh. 'It's Harry, Winnie. It has been since I was small. And I've been back in Mistingham for over a year and a half.'

'Nobody would know it, though, would they?' Winnie had tried to clip her wayward hair back from her face, but a good portion of it had come free and was haloed around her head. She was wearing an apron with something gold and sticky-looking – possibly honey – smeared across it.

Sophie knew the older woman was outspoken, but she almost laughed when Winnie leaned over the table and prodded Harry in the chest. 'You've been hiding. Are you ashamed at how you left Bernie to struggle on his own?'

'That's not how it was.' He'd dropped his voice, as if he didn't want anyone, least of all Sophie, to hear the words he was grinding out. 'Not that I have to explain myself to you. It's all in the past now, anyway.'

'You think anything's ever really in the past?' Winnie said. 'The Book Ends is standing empty, and that's a testament to how wrong things went.'

'We didn't come here to talk about this,' Harry said firmly, 'and Sophie doesn't want to be caught up in it. If you want to chew me out for my life decisions, let's schedule a different meeting, OK?'

Winnie gave him a steely-eyed stare, but Harry didn't look away. 'Fine,' she said eventually. 'But know that it's not right. None of this is.'

'Oh, I know,' Harry said with a tinge of bitterness. 'Now, what can you tell us about the festival? Do you have notes? Lists of suppliers you've used in the past? I assume we want to keep everything as local as possible.'

'I can tell you that it would be much better on the green, with that beautiful tree decorated like a fir, than as some chaotic street festival.'

'You've made your point. What else?'

'Don't take that tone with me, young man,' Winnie snapped. 'I remember when you were running around on the beach with your shorts falling down.'

'What would you say the spirit of the festival is?' Sophie rushed out. 'Ermin is keen for us to update some of the elements, but we want to do your legacy – and Mistingham – justice, so what do you suggest we focus on?'

Winnie turned a beaming smile on her, and Sophie saw Harry's shoulders slump. 'It's all about community,' she said. 'Celebrating what makes Mistingham unique. This village is unlike any other: we're not a ghost town in the winter, we've held on to our identity because a lot of folk still live here all year round, and we have independent shops and suppliers. You need to balance putting on a traditional show for the locals, and not alienating any winter visitors. We welcome everyone.' She shot a look at Harry. 'Even if they've betrayed the foundations of this place.'

Sophie held her breath, waiting for his reply. She was desperate to know the full story, but she'd only ever heard snippets about why everyone was so against him. He'd abandoned his father, and the bookshop, supposedly, but there had to be more to it; there had to be a side of the story that he had yet to tell. She didn't know how anyone could have his self-control, stay in a place where he was so frowned upon. Perhaps that was a small part of why he was here with her right now; perhaps he wanted things to change. After all, he could have point-blank refused when Ermin had asked him to be involved, but he hadn't.

Harry ran a finger over the soft cream tablecloth and said, gently, 'I'm trying my best, Winnie.'

Sophie felt a pang of sympathy. There was a lot going on beneath his granite persona, and she wondered if she'd get a chance to see some of it over the next few weeks.

Harry's almost-apology seemed to mollify Winnie some-what, and Sophie got her notebook out. It was a deep purple, covered in silver foil snowflakes, the lines on the pages wide and faint. She had made it a couple of months ago, a practice run for new winter designs for the shop, and it had since become one of her bestsellers.

She opened it to the next blank page and smoothed the pages. 'Can you tell us a few of the things you've organized in the past? Your favourite suppliers or attractions – especially from last year, when it was a street festival.'

'I'd be glad to.' Winnie leaned over the table towards her. 'Let's start with the games. Hook the Duck, I know for a fact, never gets old.'

When they left the hotel, some of the evening traffic had died away and the roads were quiet, a thin layer of frost dusting the grass and the roof of the village hall. It added to the sense of cold, and Sophie shivered.

'Do you need to pick up Clifton?' Harry sounded dejected, as if he'd exhausted his hostility and had nothing left. For once Sophie couldn't blame him – not after the dressing-down he'd got from Winnie.

'Why do you ask?'

'We've got some basic information, but don't you think we should work out what *we're* going to do? The longer we leave it, the harder and more stressful it'll be.'

'Sounds good to me.'

'So come back to mine?' He gestured to his mud-splattered Defender.

For a moment, Sophie was so surprised she couldn't speak. He was inviting her to the impressively mysterious, supposedly haunted Mistingham Manor? She fumbled with her phone. 'Let me check in with Ermin.'

'Sure.'

She fired off a text, and Ermin's reply was almost instant. 'I can get Clifton any time.'

'Great. So you'll come?'

'Let's do this!' Sophie knew her reaction was cringingly over-the-top, but Harry didn't comment on it.

It was only a few minutes' drive to the manor, but Sophie appreciated the car, because it would have been a cold, dark walk. As Harry indicated and turned off the main road, down a wide, tree-lined avenue that looked terrifying even in the glow of the headlights, she kept all her thoughts to herself, because she didn't want to ask a question he'd be able to ignore when they arrived at their destination.

She got a fleeting glimpse of the house as they drove past it, then he parked down the side, opened the passenger door for her and led her round to the front.

Mistingham Manor wasn't as large as she had imagined, but it was still impressive. It was made of grey stone, solid and imposing, and the main entrance was double-height, with two arched wooden doors. A series of evenly spaced spotlights were angled up at the building, highlighting window frames that needed a fresh coat of paint.

There were four front-facing windows on the ground floor and five on the first: the middle one was arched, echoing the shape of the doors below. Five of the nine windows were glowing, as if the manor was inhabited by a large, sprawling family instead of two adults and two dogs.

Taking in as many details as possible, Sophie followed Harry up the wide stone steps, and was surprised to see a beautiful Christmas wreath hanging on one of the doors. It was a glossy mix of holly and pine leaves, gold-sprayed pine cones nestled alongside dried orange slices and cinnamon sticks tied with twine. An elaborate, silver-blue ribbon sat in a big, shimmering bow at the bottom.

'I thought you weren't doing decorations, let alone getting in early?' Sophie leaned in and sniffed: it smelt like mulled wine, like cosy December nights tucked up under snug blankets. 'Did May do it?'

'No, I did,' Harry said.

'You *made* it?'

He shrugged, and she thought he had to be remembering their conversation in the post office, how adamant he'd been that decorating for Christmas was a waste of time. 'There are healthy holly trees in the driveway, and Birdie had dried orange and cinnamon made up ready. It's just a wreath,' he added defensively, when he saw her grin. 'Come on.'

He pushed open the door and Sophie stepped into an entrance hall that was bigger than her flat. She'd been expecting something dark and draughty, but instead the space had soft cream walls and polished pine floorboards. The stairs rose up on the left, then turned ninety degrees onto a landing. At the end of that they turned another ninety degrees, rising up and disappearing on the right side of the hall. The banister uprights were threaded through with a silver and purple garland, frosted leaves and tinsel and shiny baubles. *Just a wreath?* It was on the tip of her tongue, but he was looking studiously away from her.

'This is lovely,' she said instead. 'And it's so *warm.*' There was a gargantuan fireplace along the right-hand wall, a fire crackling and spitting inside it. 'Is May home?'

'She's probably upstairs,' he said, juggling his car keys. 'She must have lit it earlier. The rest of the house is not

99

like this, believe me. But I'm pleased with the entrance – first impressions matter, that's what everyone says.' He took a breath. 'Sophie—'

There was a skittering noise, a single, joyous bark, and then Darkness and Terror appeared. They gave their owner a cursory greeting, then raced up to Sophie, their noses up, jostling against her legs so she was forced to bend and lavish them with attention. Terror whined happily, and Darkness put a paw on her knee, his dark, liquid eyes beseeching.

Sophie laughed. 'They're so affectionate.'

'Sickening, isn't it? They've completely failed to live up to their names.' She looked up in time to see a brief flicker of a smile, there and then gone. 'Let me take your coat.'

Sophie slipped out of her coat and Harry hung it on the tall coat stand that, she couldn't fail to notice, was electric blue. She loved how the hall had its original features alongside splashes of creativity, of colour and energy, and wondered if he was planning the same style for the rest of the house.

'Do you want anything to eat or drink?' he asked. 'It didn't escape my attention that Winnie didn't even offer us a cup of tea.'

'What are *you* offering?' Sophie was expecting a glass of water, maybe a mug of PG tips.

He shrugged. 'Beer and a cheese toastie?'

'That would be perfect.' She hoped she didn't sound too surprised, and decided to try her luck in the face of his sudden hospitality. 'And a tour?'

'Not a chance,' Harry said. 'Not right now, anyway. You can wait in my study: the kitchen's a total shitshow, but it's clean enough to cook in. I'm not about to poison you.'

'Good to know.'

Harry led her to the door on the left of the hallway, then pushed it open. 'Make yourself at home. I'll be back soon.'

'OK.' Darkness and Terror stayed with her, pawing and sniffing, not letting her forget their presence as she took in her surroundings and tried to make sense of Harry's sudden about-turn. Had May told him to play nice, or had he reasoned that everything would be a whole lot harder if he wasn't at least cordial with her while they worked together?

His study had floor-to-ceiling bookshelves that took up two of the walls and were filled with a jumble of hardbacks and paperbacks. Some were organized in neat rows, others stacked vertically as if they'd been put down in a rush. They all looked fairly modern, with none of the old-fashioned, leather- or clothbound tomes like the one she'd received.

A large pine desk stood under the window, the pale wood gleaming in the light of a second fire that May must have lit in the fireplace on the opposite wall. The desk chair was modern, and a shiny MacBook was partly hidden beneath untidy piles of papers.

The window behind the desk was framed by heavy curtains, but they'd been left open, exposing the room to the night, and a frayed rug lay over old carpet in front of the hearth, where two leather chairs faced each other over a low coffee table. Sophie flushed when she noticed a chess set on a separate table in the corner of the room – it looked as if Fiona's musings had been fairly accurate – but it was a large, elaborate set with pieces shaped like characters that must have been from a book or a film. She didn't recognize them, and she was desperate to ask him, to discover a little piece of Harry Anderly geekiness.

The armchairs by the fire felt too intimate, so she sat in the fabric chair on the other side of his desk, facing the window, and – as if needing to demonstrate how focused she was – cleared a space amongst the papers and got her notebook out.

The dogs got up before she heard Harry's footsteps, and when he shouldered the door open carrying a tray, they were quicker to reach him.

'Down,' he said firmly, as they angled their noses up. Sophie couldn't blame them; her mouth was watering at the delicious smells of grilled cheese and toast.

'Shall I . . .?' She stared at his desk, unsure what to do.

'Just move it all to the windowsill.'

'Just . . .' She mimed picking it all up, and he nodded.

She scooped up as many bits of paper as she could and, purposely not looking at them, slid them onto the wide windowsill, then moved his sleek laptop to the side. She wondered what he did, now he was back in Mistingham. Had his London job allowed him to work from home? He was clearly modernizing the manor, but was he doing that full time? The amount of paperwork suggested otherwise – unless these were all documents to do with the running of the estate. Every new question that was answered seemed to raise at least five more in its place.

'Thanks.' He put the tray down, then moved the plates and bottles of beer onto the desk, settling himself in the chair opposite her as he ordered the dogs over to the rug in front of the fireplace.

'This room isn't finished,' he told her, gesturing vaguely at the bookshelves.

'It's cosy, though,' she said. 'Even in its unfinished state.'

'A bit gloomy. There's too much dark furniture.'

'Was it your dad's?'

His shoulders rose and fell in a silent sigh, and he nodded. 'He spent a lot of time in here when he wasn't at the bookshop. The view from the window looks down to the sea – I mean, you must have realized: it's at the front of the house.'

'But your desk chair faces away.'

Harry rubbed his jaw, his stubble rasping. 'I wouldn't get much work done if I faced the window. I've always found the sea a bit too mesmerizing . . . Anyway, dig in.' He picked up one half of his sandwich, and Sophie did the same. It was so good, the bread golden-brown, the Cheddar thick and strong and gooey, still bubbling as it oozed out of the sides.

'I didn't put in any onion or chutney. I didn't know what you liked, or if you were allergic to anything.'

'Nothing, as far as I know.' Sophie pulled a cheese string off her lower lip. 'This is amazing.'

'Good.' Harry gave her a quick smile. 'I wasn't sure. You get your sandwiches from Dexter, and that's a high bar.'

'Oh, you've definitely met that standard,' Sophie said, enthusiastically.

They munched away in contented silence, and then, when Harry had finished, he pointed at her notebook. 'You're a proper fan, then. You don't just sell them.'

'Of course not. I make them, too.'

Harry's eyes widened. 'You made this?'

Sophie nodded, savouring the last bite of her sandwich, regretting its loss as soon as it was gone. 'I've always loved notebooks – everyone should have at least one good one – and after I finished art college, I realized it was what I wanted to do: making things that were beautiful and practical, being able to sell them too. I wanted to be busy, but not stuck in a studio every day, only showing my pasty face for exhibitions.'

'You learnt how to bind them?' He sounded incredulous, as if it was impossible for an individual without high-powered machinery to be able to bind books to a high standard.

'There are a lot of different techniques,' she explained. 'I'm limited to which ones I can do, because I only have a tiny workspace in my flat.' She thought of the old sweet shop, the room behind the shop floor that she hadn't investigated yet. Would it be big enough to allow her to expand her designs? 'But there are a few I've got good at: stitched, casebound, spiral-bound. You're acting like you don't believe it.'

'No, I . . . no! Not at all! It's – I'm surprised, that's all.' He laughed, but it sounded awkward, as if he was unpractised. He tapped his laptop. 'I'm afraid I don't use notebooks.'

'Writing is a completely different thing to typing,' Sophie said. 'There's something about scribbling on a page that's cathartic and illuminating. It fires your thoughts in different ways. Even if it's just a to-do list, or a note to someone else – I'm not just talking about journalling.'

'But you do? Keep a journal, I mean?'

'Most days,' Sophie admitted. 'I like to get my thoughts out of my head. Sometimes it feels like there isn't enough room for them, and when I've written them down, I feel lighter.' She flushed at the confession, and at the way Harry was watching her, his gaze steady. It was disconcerting to be sitting opposite him. He was a big presence even when he was silent.

'What sort of thoughts?' he asked gently, and Sophie was, once again, at a loss. He'd barely been able to say hello to her a few days ago, and now . . . this?

'All sorts,' she said vaguely. 'Outlines for new notebook designs, marketing strategies. Plans for my future.' She cleared her throat. 'What do you do, then?'

'About what?'

'What helps you clear your head? You obviously have a lot to deal with.' She gestured to the paperwork on the windowsill. 'You face questions and challenges whenever you leave this place.'

He puffed out a sigh. 'I like working outside, being practical. That helps me sort through anything I need to – fresh air and physical exertion.'

'I run too,' Sophie said.

'Not along cliffs in the dark, I hope? Or at least, not that often.' He gave her a half-smile.

Sophie grinned. 'Not *that* often. Winnie was hard on you,' she added. 'I can see why you were reluctant to meet with her.'

'There aren't many people here who approve of the way I've dealt with things over the last few years – and please don't mention the oak tree.'

'Fiona thinks you should have taken over the bookshop from your dad, rather than let it close down.'

Harry groaned. 'My other favourite subject.' He picked at the label on his beer bottle. 'She's not the only one who thinks that, and I don't know how much you know – how many rumours you've heard – but I couldn't come back here when Dad first got ill. Also, he was much better off in the care home than he would have been here, with me looking after him. I would have been a hopeless carer.'

Sophie sipped her beer, letting the bubbles invade her mouth. 'I bet you would have done a better job than you imagine,' she said quietly. 'But only you can make the right decision for you and the people you love. Anyone can look in from the outside and have an opinion, but nobody knows all the variables except you.'

He stared at her. 'Thank you. May's the only other person who gets it, but she's known me a long time.'

'You both grew up here?'

Harry nodded. 'With my shorts falling down most of the time, according to Winnie.'

Sophie laughed. 'And are you . . .?' It was on the tip of her tongue to ask. Were they actually together? Would it be strange for them to live here, just the two of them, if they were nothing more than friends, or was she being old-fashioned?

'Am I what?' Harry's brows drew together, the side of his face turned golden by the fire. Sophie felt a flutter of something, but pushed it away before she could examine it too closely. He'd been nice to her for an hour, and her affection-starved brain was making too much of it. 'Sophie?' he prompted.

'Nothing!' she said brightly. 'We'd better get going on this festival, hadn't we?'

'You think we can do it, then?' He gestured to the notebook. 'Plan the entire thing, just the two of us?'

Sophie sat back in her chair. 'Of course we can. We can give it a good go, anyway. And just *imagine* if we do a genuinely great job – the village's black sheep and its temporary outcast, putting on the best Christmas event Mistingham's ever seen.' She laughed, expecting Harry to at least muster up a smile.

Instead, he said, 'Temporary?' and she cursed herself for using that description.

'I've not been here a year yet.'

'That's not what temporary means.'

'You have a lot of books,' she said, clunkily changing the subject.

'I like reading,' he said with a shrug. 'Not entirely surprising considering Dad ran a bookshop. When this room is finished, they'll be a lot more organized.'

'It's snug in here. I like it – and I love the books.'

'What do you read?'

'Oh, all sorts. Good thrillers, juicy romances, historical fiction sometimes. I like going back to the classics, too.' She watched him carefully, wanting to see his response, but he was looking at the shelves.

'Well, you can borrow anything from here – if you want to. It's not exactly a library, but . . .'

'That's really kind,' Sophie said. She was genuinely touched by the offer, even if he seemed embarrassed about having such a wealth of stories to share. 'I'd love to have a look. Afterwards.' She put her hand on her open notebook. 'Otherwise we'll never get anywhere.'

Harry leaned forward and took a long, slow sip of beer. 'Where should we start?'

Sophie tapped her lips, pretending to think. 'Oh, I know.' Her insides skipped, but she decided to say it anyway. 'Why don't we move the festival from Perpendicular Street to the village green? There's a lot more room there, and we could put some lights up in that rickety old oak tree.' She grinned, her heart thudding.

When Harry's scowl came – a scowl she had absolutely

expected – she was surprised, because his eyes shimmered with amusement, and he didn't point to the door or tell her to leave. Instead, he said, 'Are you going to be trouble, Sophie Stevens?' in a way that, if she'd trusted her instincts at that moment, she would have said was flirtatious. But it wasn't – it *couldn't* be for so many reasons, especially because of May . . . At least she'd teased him without him shutting down completely, though. More than anything else that evening, she counted that as a solid win.

Chapter Eleven

Nestled in the cosy study, Harry and Sophie worked their way methodically through every element of the festival – food, drink, decorations and entertainment, logistics and practicalities. She had read out the notes she'd written during their chat with Winnie, and he had offered up more suggestions.

He knew someone in Norwich who could supply them with as many sets of lights as they wanted, and a choir a couple of villages along who would be able to sing carols if the usual group weren't available. He even suggested they hire a real reindeer, which Sophie thought would be fun but potentially problematic. He wasn't arrogant or pushy, just calm and considered, as if, now he'd accepted his involvement in the festival, the most painless approach was simply to get on with it.

They would use Mistingham businesses wherever possible, especially as the festival was going to be on Perpendicular Street. Batter Days could provide festival-sized portions of fish and chips, and Jim and Annie in Penny For Them could hire some Christmassy amusements to have in pride of place in their arcade. It was a relief to have some concrete ideas written down, even if all they had achieved was a list of people to approach.

Once they'd done all they could without picking up the phone, Harry had driven her home. 'Thank you for tonight,' he said, idling the Land Rover outside her flat. It was late, and Sophie could see Simon clearing down inside Batter Days, the sign on the door turned to Closed.

They'd picked Clifton up from Fiona and Ermin's house, Harry waiting in the car while Sophie went to get him. 'Good night?' Fiona had asked, eyes sparkling with curiosity, and Sophie had smiled and nodded and thanked her for dog-sitting, without offering any other details.

Now she turned in the passenger seat so she could look at him. 'Why are you thanking me? We were at your house, eating your food and drinking your beer, and you organized the meeting with Winnie. *I* should be thanking *you*.'

He shook his head. 'It was easy. And we've made progress.'

Sophie laughed. 'You thought I would make it difficult?'

'After our last few meetings, I wasn't sure.' He shrugged. 'I wouldn't have blamed you, either.'

'Well.' It came out more primly than she'd intended. 'You made it easy, too. We've got a plan, and it was . . . fun. I had a good time.' She cleared her throat. 'Shall we check in when we've both got somewhere?'

'Of course. Night, Sophie.' He ruffled Clifton's head. 'Goodnight, mop.'

Clifton clearly didn't mind the nickname, because he crawled into Harry's lap. Harry gave him a more effusive goodbye, then Sophie took her dog and got out of the car. She heard the Land Rover lingering on the roadside until she'd shut the front door and climbed the narrow flight of stairs to her flat.

'It's going well, then?' Fiona said the next day, when Sophie had given her a brief rundown of their meeting.

'It was better than I'd expected,' she admitted. She was reorganizing her display, filling in gaps after a welcome flurry of sales. 'It's early days, but we're actually talking, which is good.' She wrinkled her nose, thinking how much Harry had changed. When it was just the two of them, he was a different person.

'Talking civilly?' Fiona asked.

'Being friendly, even.'

'Goodness.' Fiona sounded as surprised as she felt.

'How's Jazz?' Sophie asked.

'Eating me out of biscuits,' Fiona said morosely.

Sophie gave her a warm smile. 'I know you want her to be OK, but it's not going to be a quick fix.'

'I'm not sure she wants to stay here.'

Sophie laid out her most recent creations on the counter in front of her. They were thin, card-covered notebooks with a holographic Christmas tree design; threadbound, with wide lines inside. 'That's up to Jazz,' she said evenly. 'If she's used to moving around, if that's how she feels safe, then you need to let her.'

Fiona scoffed. 'I wouldn't *stop* her.'

'It would be hard for you to let her go, though,' Sophie said. 'Have you had a proper chat with her?'

'She's not inclined to come out of her room. I persuaded

111

her down for some lasagne, but she kept her eyes on her plate, gave monosyllabic answers. I'm sure she could have a job at the hotel, at least until after Christmas.'

'If that's what she wants.'

There was a spark of frustration in Fiona's eyes. 'I don't want her heading back out into the wilderness, sleeping in deserted shops, risking hypothermia and not eating properly. She's letting me take her for a check-up at the doctor's, but nothing else.'

'I'm sorry,' Sophie said softly. 'You're being so generous, but I guess . . .' She thought of how she had been at eighteen: free of the foster system, her new, thrilling independence mingling with panic at having to make all her own decisions. She had her art course and the confidence that Mrs Fairweather, her favourite foster parent, had instilled in her, but that was about it. 'I guess she's using the time you're giving her to think through her options. That's as scary as hostel-hopping in its own way.'

'I understand,' Fiona said quietly. 'It doesn't make it easy, though.'

'I know. Shall I go and make us some tea?'

'Thanks, Sophie. Tea is exactly what I need right now.'

When she came back with two steaming mugs of Earl Grey, Dexter was leaning on Fiona's counter, the two of them laughing about something.

'Oh Dexter, hello! Do you want one?'

He waved her away. 'I can't stay long, just came to give you a heads-up.'

'For what?' Sophie asked.

'Lucy wants to get her three best friends gift bags for Christmas. The four of them have decided to do that, rather than buy each other more expensive gifts. Sweets, hair decorations, that sort of thing.'

'It's a great idea,' Fiona said. 'It's always fun finding those little bits, and exactly what girls want at that age.'

'And it's less pressure, because she can get most of it herself.' Dexter stood up straight. 'Except that, obviously, she's asked *me* to scout out notebooks. She wants three original Sophie Stevens designs, but she's got football practice after school today, then a sleepover on Friday and – well, basically, I have been instructed by my nine-year-old daughter to take photos of your top picks, then show them to her so she can decide.'

Fiona chuckled. 'It's a good thing she doesn't have you under her thumb.'

Dexter's eye-roll was pure affection.

'Come over here, then.' Sophie took her tea behind her counter. 'I can show you what I've got – are you thinking sparkly, feminine colours, or would that offend her?'

'Depends on the day of the week, to be honest. Sometimes she's in full-on princess mode, sometimes pink is an assault to her eyes. I can take photos of the shelves, then a few of your top designs.'

'OK.' Sophie took her favourite notebooks off the display and laid them out on the counter. Clifton raised his head to give her a bleary look, then went back to his snooze.

Dexter took his time, picking each notebook up, examining it carefully before setting it back down and taking a photo. Sophie thought Lucy would likely go for the sparklier options, perhaps the ones she'd used foil on, and her thoughts skipped to her copy of *Jane Eyre*. She had got precisely nowhere with finding out who had given it to her.

'This one's great,' Dexter said. It had a navy leather cover and an elastic closure, and suited him perfectly.

Sophie leaned over the counter. 'I'm not sure it's Lucy's style,' she said. 'What about this one, with little books all over it?' She placed her selection on top of his.

'Fair point,' he said, grinning at her, just as the shop door swung open and let in a blast of cool seaside air, followed by Harry.

Sophie stood up straight, though she didn't quite know why.

'Hey,' Harry said. 'Hi, Fiona. Dexter.' He gave the other man a curt nod. He looked as if he had already run out of patience, and Sophie's spirits sank.

'Hi, Harry,' Dexter said, oblivious to the atmosphere. 'Come to buy some notebooks?'

Harry's eyes roamed over Sophie's display, and she realized she was holding her breath.

'No,' he said, after a beat. 'Though I can see that they would make good Christmas presents. Did you make all of these?'

'I did. I'd like to have a bigger selection, but I don't have enough time or space to—'

'We've come up with a solution for that,' Fiona cut in. 'Ye Olde Sweete Shoppe.'

'Too many e's,' Dexter and Harry said in unison, and Sophie grinned.

'This one,' she said to Dexter, before either of them could ask precisely *how* the old sweet shop was a solution. She tapped his hand where it rested on top of the notebook she'd suggested. 'I've done it in three colour-ways, so she could give a different one to each of her friends.'

'That sounds perfect.' He smiled. 'Thanks, Sophie. I knew I could count on you.'

She did a mock curtsey. 'Always happy to help with people's blank-page-related queries. Let me lay them all out, so you can take photos.'

Harry cleared his throat and gestured to the door. 'I'll come back later.'

'Oh no,' Sophie said. 'Give me two minutes.'

Dexter snapped the photos, then put his phone away. 'I'm done. I'll check in with Lucy, let you know what she says. Good to see you Fiona, Harry. Thanks again, Sophie – I can tick this off my to-do list.'

'I hope you've written it in a notebook,' Sophie called after him, and he turned and grinned, then opened the door and stepped outside.

'I've got a few things to catch you up on,' Harry said, 'if now's a good time?'

'Now is perfect,' she told him. 'I'll get my coat.'

They walked down to the seafront, where the wind was blustering and the waves crunched rhythmically along the sand, like someone constantly trying to clear a frog from their throat.

'What have you got to catch me up on since last night?' Sophie asked. Harry was like a wall at her side, sheltering her from the worst of the icy gusts.

'What do you think about having a Father Christmas grotto at the festival?'

Sophie stopped trying to work out whether a dark, bobbing shape in the waves was a seal, and turned to face him. Harry did the same, so they were both leaning on the promenade wall, looking at each other, their hair being tangled by the wind.

'The world's grumpiest Santa,' Sophie said.

Harry rolled his eyes. 'I do have other settings.'

She grinned. 'I'm just starting to discover that. You're offering to do it, though? Not get old Mr Carsdale togged up in a red suit and beard? Or Ermin?'

'I don't know.' His gaze drifted out to the horizon. 'I haven't thought beyond the fact that it was missing last year. I'm not sure if they had it before that, when it was . . .'

'On the village green?'

He ignored her pointed words. 'I know it's a kid's thing, but—'

'It takes pressure off the parents, too,' Sophie finished.

She remembered Santa coming to Mrs Fairweather's house, how at first she'd decided she was too old, but had enjoyed the excitement of the other children. And then, later, her foster carer handing her the slim, beautifully wrapped package; her delight when she'd unwrapped the pale green notebook inside, along with a slim, maroon hardback of *A Christmas Carol* by Charles Dickens. There was something magical about Santa Claus, even if you were an adult and knew it was someone wearing an itchy suit and a beard.

'It's a brilliant idea,' she told Harry. 'Whoever we get to do it.'

'Good.' He exhaled. 'And I thought we could get Dexter to make mince pies.'

'I'm sure he'd be happy to. I've set up a meeting with Annie.'

'Maybe we could run a Whack-A-Crab tournament?' Harry suggested.

'You love Whack-A-Crab?' It was Penny For Them's version of Whack-A-Mole, but with a distinctly Norfolk theme.

He frowned. 'Don't you?'

'Of course I do! It's the best thing in there.'

'What's your highest score?'

'Thirty-six,' she said proudly.

His eyes widened. 'In a *minute*?'

She nodded, gleeful.

Harry rubbed his jaw. 'Shit. I'm going to have to practise.'

'Come on then. What's yours?'

'Twenty-nine,' he admitted. 'But I don't get to the arcade very often.'

'So ready with the excuses.' Sophie folded her arms, shivering slightly in the wind.

'Do you want to go back?' he asked. 'Anything else we need to discuss that you don't want Fiona to overhear?'

'She wants to know *everything*,' Sophie said with a groan. 'She's like a hawk, watching my every move.'

'She likes being in control,' Harry said, more kindly than Sophie would have expected. 'She and Ermin do a lot for the village, and maybe it's harder than they thought: they're used to Winnie being in charge, knowing exactly what she's doing.' He frowned. 'The last couple of years, it can't have been easy . . .' His words trailed away, and Sophie wondered if he was beginning to realize what his sanctions had cost them.

'And now they've given responsibility to a couple of unknowns,' she said.

'Right. The black sheep and the . . . what did you call yourself? Temporary outcast?' He emphasized *temporary*, and Sophie winced.

'Do you like *Jane Eyre?*' she blurted.

'I do,' he said, after a moment. 'It's very, um . . . romantic. The relationship between Jane and Rochester. Gnarly and intense and a bit desperate in places, but ultimately, very romantic. Why?'

Sophie stared at the wind turbines rotating on the horizon. 'No real reason. Just . . . you know, thinking about Christmas presents.' She hoped he wouldn't ask her who she was buying for.

'It's not easy to get present-worthy editions locally any more,' Harry said, and Sophie watched a series of emotions play across his face. She couldn't help it: she squeezed his arm. His gaze shot to hers, surprised.

'Hey,' she said gently. 'You're helping with the festival now. People can't talk nonsense about you for ever.'

He raised an eyebrow, and it was such a haughty, attractive expression that Sophie squeezed him tighter. 'Are you sure about that?' he murmured. 'Or will they just come up with new rumours, perhaps about who I'm spending my time with? Why I'm finally talking to people, instead of being—'

'The Dark Demon Lord of Mistingham?' Sophie finished.

He nodded and swallowed. He didn't release her gaze or pull his arm away, and Sophie felt the charge between them. But it was just surprise, wasn't it? That he'd started to warm up, to tease and joke; that they actually seemed to be getting along with each other. That would make anyone feel off-kilter, especially after their less than positive start.

A seagull let out a plaintive cry, startling them both. Harry blinked and cleared his throat, and Sophie dropped her hand.

'I'd better get back,' she said.

'Yes, me too. Too much daylight and I might turn to dust.'

She laughed. 'You can't be a demon, a vampire *and* Santa Claus.'

'Can't I?' He sounded amused. 'What a shame.'

They walked back to the clothes shop in a silence that felt almost comfortable, and Sophie couldn't help wondering what he was thinking. Why *had* he agreed to help with the festival – a festival most of the villagers thought he had already ruined – instead of refusing Ermin's request? Had May given him an ultimatum: *stop being such an angry recluse and make peace with Mistingham*, or was there another reason? It felt like another mystery she needed to unpack, along with uncovering who was behind The Secret Bookshop. She hoped spending more time with him would help her find at least one of her answers.

Chapter Twelve

Annie Devlin was five foot nothing but had a laugh twice as big as she was. Did it come from working in an amusement arcade? Being surrounded by people playing games, winning cuddly toys and bits of plastic that, while not the best quality, would remind them of a day out or holiday they loved?

'Sophie, come, come!' She waved expansively, and Sophie followed her into Penny For Them where, at lunchtime on a Friday in November, the customers were sparse but the jingling, doo-wop sounds of the games filled her head like audio candy. 'How are you?'

'I'm really good, thanks.'

'Got a haul of change you want to use up?'

'Not exactly.' But she automatically felt in her pockets to see what was there. Was there anyone in the world who didn't love a two-pence machine: a little cardboard cup filled with dirty bronze coins offering up all that possibility? 'I wanted to talk to you about the festival, actually.'

'Oooh. Let's talk in here for a sec, where it's quieter.' Annie pushed open the door into a tiny office. There was a plain wooden table being used as a desk, two tatty office chairs, and a plethora of colourful children's drawings on the walls, along with some framed family photos. 'We've run out of space on the fridge at home,' she said, when she saw Sophie looking. 'Now, the festival. I saw how thrilled you were when Ermin teamed you up with that chap from the manor house.'

'Harry Anderly,' Sophie confirmed. 'It's actually going better than I hoped, and I wanted to check in with you. As it's going to be a street festival again this year, I wondered if you would be happy to hire some festive games to have here?'

'Of course. We've got a few different suppliers, so I'll talk to Jim and let you know what's available.'

'That's great,' Sophie said. 'Thank you, that was easy.' There was a cacophony from the arcade floor, a series of dings and bells that were louder than the rest.

'The pinball machine's paid out,' Annie explained. 'Someone has won the grand sum of ten pounds.'

'Woah. That's a fortune for a day at the seaside.'

Annie laughed. 'I know what you mean. You only need enough for an ice cream, a game of pool or duster hockey, then fish and chips before you go home. The beach is free.'

'Although it's a bit cold for paddling today.'

'But never too cold for ice cream,' Annie said, as they walked out of the office.

Sophie almost didn't ask her next question, but this was the reason she'd accepted this role, and she couldn't keep backing out. 'On an unrelated note, I was thinking about starting a book club.'

'You were?'

'It's the perfect activity for winter evenings, when you can't always get outside. Would you like to be involved? Are you a big reader? What kind of books do you like?' She forced herself to take a breath.

Annie folded her arms, the picture of practicality in her thick grey fleece, her blonde hair scraped back into a ponytail. 'I read true crime, mostly. I can't get enough of them: how the police and FBI track down serial killers. It's fascinating.'

'No . . . romances? Classics?'

'Oh no, I don't have time for all that. I need something fast paced, that grabs me and holds on tight. Jim likes Charles Dickens.'

'Really?' Sophie perked up, then thought how awkward it would be if Annie's husband had given her the copy of *Jane Eyre*. And why would he? That was what would get her to the truth: finding someone who had a motive, who cared about what she was looking for in life, or else wanted to confound her. It should have been easy; her social circle in Mistingham wasn't exactly large. 'I'll let you know when I've firmed up the details, anyway,' she said. 'Then you can decided if you want to come along.' She was already pretty sure that Annie and her husband had nothing to do with The Secret Bookshop.

As they walked through the brightly coloured arcade, Sophie's gaze fell on Whack-A-Crab. It was painted like a beach, with a glittering blue sea and yellow sand, the tops of the bright orange crabs visible inside their shallow holes. The large foam hammer was purple, attached to the game by a woven cord.

She was about to ask what the top score was now – it had

been a while since she'd played, but Harry mentioning it had unearthed a dormant competitiveness – when Fiona appeared in the doorway, her cheeks flushed, her breaths coming in short, sharp bursts.

'Quick,' she said. 'Quick, Sophie!'

'What's wrong?' Sophie had never seen her friend so panicked.

'It's Felix,' Fiona huffed out. 'Felix is on the rampage.'

'Felix . . .' It took a moment for her brain to kick into gear. Harry's goat. The sweetest thing she'd ever seen, who loved paisley knitted jumpers. 'On the *rampage*?'

'He's in Birdie's garden,' Fiona explained, as Sophie wished Annie a hurried goodbye and they raced up Perpendicular Street. 'I don't think there's going to be anything left if we don't get him out of there soon.'

Birdie's house was one road back from the green, an ancient flint cottage surrounded by gardens that looked like a fairy grotto. There were mature, twisting trees, grasses that added shades of green, blue and yellow throughout the year, a vegetable plot that changed with the seasons. Right now a winter jasmine was lush with delicate yellow flowers, and Sophie remembered how dreamlike her garden had looked in summer, the burst of colour and scent, the myriad flowers the old woman had nurtured to perfection. On first glance it gave the impression of being wildly over-grown, until you looked closer and saw order in the chaos.

As Sophie and Fiona reached the cottage, they could hear voices coming from the back garden, Felix's name being called, the high screech of a young girl. Lucy, Sophie thought, as they pushed open the gate and took the cobbled path round the side of the house.

Birdie was standing on her back doorstep, her arms folded over her chest. Her silver dress was covered in tiny, twinkling beads, her long grey hair pulled into a bun. Sophie was surprised to see Jazz standing next to her. She hadn't seen her since the night they'd found her, and she looked better – less tired, less unkempt – but still had a restless energy about her that Sophie understood all too well.

'Hey, Sophie.' Jazz gave her a quick smile then turned back to the drama.

'It's good to see you, Jazz.'

'You too,' Jazz said distractedly. 'Get a load of this.'

This was Dexter, standing with his feet gingerly planted between two rows of winter vegetables, his arms outstretched, while Lucy hopped up and down on one of the meandering, paved walkways. Felix, wearing a purple jumper with a pattern Sophie couldn't make out, was standing on the roof of the shed, munching on something.

'I told you, Sophie!' Fiona pressed her hands to her cheeks.

'How did he get up there?' Sophie asked.

'He's a goat,' Dexter called. 'Goats love jumping, and they love making mischief.'

'It's a rather ungrateful move, considering I've made him all those jumpers.' Birdie turned her twinkling eyes on Sophie and Fiona. 'It's lovely to see you both.'

'Are you OK?' Fiona asked. 'He's destroying all your hard work.'

'He's a very small goat,' Birdie said. 'He's trampled one of the grasses, stolen a couple of carrots and unearthed a sprout tree, but that was ready to harvest anyway.'

'This is like a proper community garden,' Jazz said, sounding awed. 'There's so much here.'

'It's wonderful, isn't it?' Sophie said. 'You're not angry, Birdie?'

'I would rather he got down from the roof,' Birdie mused, 'and I don't want to have the *entire* vegetable plot uprooted, but I do like seeing how well he is. It's Dexter and Lucy who are making a big deal of it.'

As if to prove her point, Lucy squealed when Felix took a step closer to the edge of the roof.

'He'll be OK, Lucy!' Dexter inched closer, as if there was an unexploded bomb up there rather than an adorable goat. 'We just need to get him down.'

'What if he falls?' Lucy shouted.

'He won't, darling,' Birdie said. 'Goats are incredibly agile.'

Jazz put her hand over her mouth, probably to hide a grin.

It was, Sophie had to admit, a funny situation, but Lucy looked on the verge of tears.

Fiona went over and wrapped her arms around the girl. 'Your dad will get him down,' she said soothingly.

'Someone needs to call Harry,' Dexter shouted. 'I have no fu— flipping clue how to get this goat to come down.' He turned his head. 'Sophie, can you do it? You know him better than I do.'

'Yes, Sophie,' Fiona said. 'Get Harry to come and retrieve his rampaging goat.'

Sophie looked at the sweetly dressed animal chewing happily on his carrot, and stifled a laugh as she took out her phone and found Harry's number.

He picked up on the third ring. 'Sophie!' He sounded out of breath.

'Um, Felix is on Birdie's shed roof,' she said. 'Hello, by the way.'

'Fuck,' Harry said emphatically. 'He's chewed through the fence again. I was searching for him, but I didn't know where . . .' He exhaled. 'Birdie's shed is a whole lot better than I thought it would be, but still.'

'Fuck?' Sophie tried.

'Exactly that. Give me five minutes.'

'See you soon.' They hung up, and Sophie realized everyone was watching her. 'He'll be here in five minutes,' she announced, and Dexter's shoulders sagged with relief.

'Have you got Harry Anderly at your beck and call?' Fiona asked, amused. She still had her arms wrapped around Lucy, who was looking worriedly up at Felix.

'He's hardly at my beck and call,' Sophie scoffed. 'He's only coming because his goat has escaped.'

'He dotes on little Felix,' Birdie said. 'After Oliver, Felix's brother, died so young, I think he let him live in the house.'

'Felix had a brother?' Sophie glanced at the goat. 'Poor thing.'

'I was only going to make one jumper, but Harry likes to indulge him and I love to knit, and—'

'And now he's repaying you by eating your veg,' Dexter said, joining them on the patio.

Felix had lain down and was looking serene, like a fluffy white king on his shed throne.

'A tiny proportion of my veg,' Birdie said. 'He's done no harm, really. It's good to see my harvest being appreciated.'

'Your harvest is always appreciated,' Fiona said.

'Do you want a stall at the street festival?' Sophie asked.

Birdie peered at her. 'You mean I can sell my chutneys and jams?'

'Anything you want,' Sophie said.

'Not your herb . . . concoctions,' Fiona cut in. 'Not unless they're harmless.'

'All my concoctions heal,' Birdie said. 'None of them are harmful. But I will stick to the jams and chutneys. Thank you for asking me – Winnie never let me.'

'Winnie thinks you're a practising witch,' Dexter said matter of factly, then his face fell as Lucy, who was supposedly still agonizing over Felix, gave the older woman a curious look.

'A *witch*?' Her voice was breathless with excitement.

'No, Luce—' Dexter started.

'Do you want me to show you my book of magic?' Birdie asked.

'Ohmygod yes please!' Lucy squealed. Her dad tipped his head back and groaned.

'All harmless.' Birdie patted Dexter's arm, and he shot her a look that was half irritated, half amused.

Birdie held her hand out and Lucy abandoned Fiona, and her distress about Felix, to go inside with her.

'I don't think Birdie's as worried about Felix being here as we are,' Fiona said, once they'd disappeared.

'That goat's just hanging out, doing goaty things.' Jazz shrugged. 'Hey, why are you having a street festival when there's the village green out there?'

'You can ask Harry when he turns up,' Dexter said.

'It's a sore point,' Fiona added, her expression softening as she spoke to Jazz. 'But this village wouldn't be what it is without some drama here and there.'

Sophie folded her arms. 'You've changed your tune. I thought you were as angry with Harry as anyone.'

'It's like *Midsomer Murders*,' Jazz said, leaning against

Birdie's wall, 'but without all the death. Everyone knows everyone else, you all chip in where you can.' She shook her head. 'Five people turning up to get a goat off an old woman's roof, even though you've actually done fuck-all.' She gestured at Felix, still happily munching.

'Jazz,' Fiona chided with a chuckle.

'It's nice,' Jazz went on, sounding wistful. 'The way this place is. None of you living in silos, being friendly and getting in each other's business.'

'It can be a bit claustrophobic at times,' Sophie said, and got looks from Fiona and Dexter that made her wonder if she should have kept that thought to herself. 'Just . . . you know. It's so small. Everyone knows *everything*.'

'It's nicer than people being lonely, though,' Jazz pointed out. 'I bet your events are more like giant house parties. Everyone bringing a dish, Scrabble tournaments.' She smiled indulgently, then quickly flattened her expression. 'You know – old people stuff. Book clubs, singsongs, all that rubbish.'

A flicker of something ignited in Sophie's brain, but she had no time to grab hold of it because the unmistakable, throaty sound of Harry's Land Rover cut through the quiet, and a moment later he appeared round the side of the house.

His jeans and shirt were covered in mud, his hair was more askew than usual and he had a smudge of grime mingling with the sweat on his forehead. He looked wild, angry and worried, and Sophie felt an unexpected twist of concern for this man she barely knew.

'He's OK,' she said, hurrying over to him.

Harry glanced at her, then his gaze followed her outstretched arm to the shed, where Felix was lying, the carrot-top sticking out of his mouth, looking like a cute farmyard poster.

'Thank fuck,' Harry murmured. 'And I'm so sorry . . .' He looked around. 'Where's Birdie?'

'Inside,' Dexter said grimly. 'Teaching my daughter how to become a witch.'

Harry stared at him, agog, then winced. 'Shit. Sorry, Dex. Seems like you might come off worse than me from this little . . . escapade.'

Dexter folded his arms, but his lips were twitching. 'We followed your goat in here, trying to be good citizens, and now look what's happened.' He glanced at the house, then back at Harry. 'Want help getting your pet down from there?'

'Thanks.'

Sophie, Jazz and Fiona watched as the two men approached the shed. Felix eyed them curiously and made no move to get up.

'Come on, Felix,' Harry coaxed, stretching his arms up. 'Playtime's over.'

Felix gave a long, high bleat, dropping his carrot top in the process.

'Felix,' Harry said wearily. He glanced at Dexter, then caught Sophie's eye before turning back to his goat. 'If you don't get down from there now, Birdie won't knit you any more jumpers.'

Felix bleated again.

'I mean it.' There was more steel in his voice this time.

Sophie didn't know if the goat actually understood what he was saying, or if it was the change in Harry's tone, but Felix stood up, came to the edge of the shed and then, without any warning, jumped down into his owner's arms.

Harry caught him easily, holding him against his chest and, as he turned, Sophie saw him give Felix a quick kiss on the head. At that moment, she thought that *she* would be the one who came off worst from this whole situation. It was so overwhelming: Harry, ruffled and muddy and handsome, holding the fluffy goat he clearly adored, which was wearing a purple knitted jumper.

'This is too much,' she said, then flushed. She had *not* meant to say it out loud.

'The peculiarities of Mistingham.' Fiona sounded amused. 'I'd better get back to the shop now the excitement is over. Jazz, do you want to help me this afternoon? I'll pay you.'

Sophie bit her lip, waiting while Jazz considered her options. 'Yeah, all right,' she said eventually.

'Excellent.' Fiona beamed. 'Coming, Sophie?'

'In a minute. I need to update Harry on my chat with Annie.'

'Of course. See you soon.' Fiona and Jazz went back round the side of the house, and Sophie resisted the urge to call a thank you to the young woman, because her words had sparked an idea, something possibly ridiculous but potentially brilliant.

Dexter went inside to rescue Lucy before she became a fully fledged witch, and then it was just Sophie, Harry and his goat.

'I'll have to make it up to Birdie somehow,' Harry said. 'After I've reinforced the entire perimeter fence, fixed the dodgy plumbing in the manor, replaced the draughty windows and got Felix some kind of escape alarm.'

Felix bleated, looking up at Harry.

'Yes, I am talking about you,' he said. The goat batted his head against Harry's chin.

Sophie's pulse was fluttering unnaturally. She wanted to wipe the mud off Harry's forehead. 'Are you OK?' she asked instead. 'That sounds like a long to-do list.'

'My life is one long to-do list,' Harry told her. 'I'm used to it though. Sort of.'

'Are you working, as well as fixing the house?'

'I still do some financial consultancy for the firms I worked with in London. I don't have to go down there more than once a month, though, and it pays well. The manor is turning into a money pit, so every bit is welcome, even if the work itself isn't that stimulating.' He sighed. 'How are you?'

Sophie resisted asking more questions. What *would* he do, if he could do anything? 'I'm good,' she said. 'Annie's going to look into festive games for the arcade, and Birdie's delighted that she can sell her chutneys and jams this year.'

'Don't let her bring packets of mushrooms to sell.'

Sophie's mouth fell open. 'Seriously?'

'Seriously. But chutney and jam should be fine: we'll make her give us an ingredient list. We'll need that for all food and drink, anyway, in case anyone has allergies or intolerances, but the suppliers should be used to that. And we need to check what regulations there are; any permits we need.'

'Winnie didn't mention anything about that.'

'Winnie is used to it, running the hotel – she would have done it without a second thought – but we need to look into it. It's better to be safe than sorry.'

'Of course,' Sophie said, just as Harry winced. 'What is it?' she asked. 'Do you need to put Felix down?'

'It's not that,' he said, as they walked through Birdie's garden towards his Defender. 'I just realized that I sounded like the most boring person on the planet.'

Sophie laughed. 'Since when do you care what people think of you?'

She thought Harry must not have heard. He was busy securing his goat in the back of the Land Rover.

Once his arms were empty, he leaned against the driver's door. 'Thanks for sorting those things out.'

'No problem.'

He rubbed a hand over his eyes. He smelled of grass and mud and a hint of the clean sea air. Sophie's insides were a jangle of knots and confusion. She took a step towards him.

'You know,' she said, 'if you need help with things at Mistingham Manor, then you can always ask me. You're helping me with the festival, so it's only fair.'

He dropped his hand. 'It's not fair. We both got volunteered for this thing. It doesn't stand to reason that you should fix all my problems too.'

'But the village, the community . . .' Sophie thought of what Jazz had said. 'We help each other out, don't we? I don't like to think of you struggling by yourself.'

'I'm not,' he said gently. 'I've got May, at the house, not to mention Darkness and Terror.' His mouth curved. 'And Felix.'

'A goat and two dogs can't help you repair draughty windows,' she said, but his mention of May was like a bucket of cold water. She was overstepping, and she needed to back off.

'I'm fine, honestly. But thank you for checking in.'

'You look . . .' She bit her lip.

'I look what?'

She thought about it for an agonising, protracted moment, but she couldn't help herself. She reached up and wiped her thumb along his muddy forehead. It did hardly anything, made the smear worse, maybe, but it meant her fingers could brush against his hair, feel how soft it was, in all its messy disarray.

Harry went completely still. He stared at her, his lips slightly parted. His eyes were a chaos of green and brown, his pupils inky black. She wasn't that much shorter than him, and she knew if she tipped forwards, even slightly, they would be close enough for their breaths to mingle.

'That's better,' she said, pulling her hand away. *So much for backing off.*

'Thanks.' He cleared his throat. 'And thank you, for letting me know about Felix.'

'Of course.' Sophie felt silly, and guilty, and like a total fool. 'I'd better . . .'

She turned away, and warm fingers wrapped around hers.

Harry tugged her back to face him. 'I mean it,' he said. 'Thank you, Sophie. I just – I'm lucky to have May, and Felix and the dogs are great, but they aren't always . . .' He shook his head. 'I'm glad we're doing this together.'

Sophie waited. She wanted more from him, something more explicit, but she didn't know what, exactly, so instead she said, 'Me too,' and they stayed like that, looking down at their intertwined fingers for one heartbeat, two, before she let go. Then he said goodbye, got in his car, and drove his rampaging goat back to Mistingham Manor, while Sophie tried to get her head in gear for an afternoon of avoiding all Fiona's questions.

Chapter Thirteen

Sophie had made a list in the very middle of her snow-flake-covered notebook, because the middle always felt like the safest place to write things you didn't want other people to discover. So far, it read:

Fiona
Ermin
Harry
May
Birdie
Dexter
Lucy
Annie
Winnie

She was sure Annie hadn't given her the book, and she'd discounted Harry and May from the beginning, because until a few weeks ago she hadn't known either of them that well, so they had no reason to give her anything, let alone a cryptic message about finding what she was looking for.

She had put a circle around Fiona, who was still her most likely suspect, even though that felt weak. Fiona was her closest friend in Mistingham, and it made sense that she would want Sophie to stick around, but it didn't seem like her style: she was straight down the middle, not one for subterfuge or subtle hints.

Sophie turned to the page where the gold bookmark rested and read a couple of pages of *Jane Eyre*, as she had started doing whenever she was home and had a spare minute. She found Rochester's description of Thornfield Hall, and couldn't help thinking of how Harry saw Mistingham Manor.

. . . you see it through a charmed medium: you cannot discern that the gilding is slime and the silk draperies cobwebs; that the marble is sordid slate, and the polished woods mere refuse chips and scaly bark.

'What do you think, Clifton?' Her dog was standing on the arm of the sofa, looking out at the horizon. The sun was setting, the sky a pale peach, and Sophie was glad she had plans that evening. Fiona and Ermin had invited her to the pub, and she was going to make the most of it: the socializing, of course, but also being in the heart of the village, surrounded by people who might have a motive to secretly give her a book. She was going to do some drinking, some talking, and some investigating.

Stepping from the cold, dark night into the Blossom Bough was like walking into a warm, welcoming hug. The lighting was soft, with twinkly white bulbs running along the back of the bar, providing sparkle all year round and, no doubt, soon to be joined by some more festive adornments. The walls were cream, the tables and chairs walnut, the booths and benches covered in a velvety cherry red fabric. There was no music playing in the background, no television mounted on the wall, but tea lights glimmered on all the tables, to the soft chink of glasses and hum of people enjoying a Saturday night with friends.

The one, incongruous object was a life-sized cardboard cutout of Elvis Presley wearing a garland of fake cherry blossoms. The landlady Natasha was a huge fan, though Sophie couldn't remember the story about where the cutout had come from.

She pushed her way to the back of the pub, and found Fiona and Ermin at their favourite table, their mini schnauzer Poppet sitting underneath. Sophie set Clifton down and he greeted the other dog, his playmate on the days Ermin looked after him.

'Hello.' She shrugged off her coat and gestured to their half-full glasses. 'Top-up?'

'If you're offering,' Ermin said. 'I'm having the local IPA.'

'And I've got Merlot,' Fiona added.

'Sure.' Sophie went to the bar, sliding between two old men sitting on stools, their Norfolk accents thick as they spoke in low voices. 'Sorry.'

'Not at all, lass,' one of them said. 'You take your time.'

'All right?' Natasha asked when she'd finished serving at the other end of the bar. 'Need a break from the street festival?'

She was, Sophie guessed, in her mid-forties, a natural blonde with blue eyes, and only a couple of inches shorter than Sophie. She'd been running the pub for over a decade, since she'd broken up with her husband and moved from North Walsham to the coast. Her nineteen-year-old son Indigo worked here when he wasn't with his friends or at art college in Norwich.

'We're just getting started,' Sophie admitted, 'but I do want to talk to you about running the bar stand.'

'I'm always glad to help out. Any chance I'll get to do more than bog-standard mulled wine this year? I've got some other winter warmers I'm keen to sell.'

'Let's talk about it, but I can't see how having some variety would be a bad thing.'

'You're breaking out of the mould, then?'

Sophie laughed. 'Mostly because Harry and I don't know what we're doing.' Except that the idea she'd had in Birdie's garden was taking shape, and she needed to speak to Harry about it. If they were going to make changes, they needed to make them soon.

'So Harry's real then, not made of stone like one of the creepy old statues in the manor grounds?'

'Oh, he's definitely real,' Sophie said, then worried she'd sounded salacious. 'Anyway, let's get together and decide what we're doing.'

'You're on. Now, what can I get you? I'll have a mob on my hands if I stand here chatting too much longer.'

Sophie gave the other woman her order, then carried the drinks to her friends, navigating around tables, extended feet and dogs slumped happily near their owners. It was a beautiful pub, popular with tourists but unmistakably a country haunt, and Sophie had been in here more than once when a shooting party came in for a quick snifter on their way back to a six-course lunch at a country estate, crowing about the number of pheasants they'd shot.

'Grand, thank you,' Ermin said, as Sophie set the drinks down.

'You're welcome.' The three of them clinked glasses, the red wine sloshing in Sophie's glass.

'How are you getting on with the book?' Fiona asked, once Sophie was settled.

She shot a glance at Ermin, who leaned forward. 'Fi told me,' he said in a loud whisper. 'There are no secrets between us, but I have promised to keep my mouth shut. Fi says you're doing some kind of . . . treasure hunt?'

Sophie raised an eyebrow at her friend.

'I'm not sure those were the words I used,' Fiona said. 'I just told him you were investigating, keeping things on the down-low.'

'On the down-low,' Sophie murmured, trying not to laugh. 'I just want to find out who sent me the book, why someone thinks I need instructions about how to live my life. How do they know I'm missing anything? But if I shout about it, or ask everyone en masse at a village meeting, then whoever sent it might go to ground and I'll never find out – otherwise, why didn't they put their name on it to begin with? So, I'm trying to be stealthy.' It sounded ridiculous, bandying about phrases like *go to ground* and *stealthy*. She was as bad as Fiona.

This was a small village and it was a thoughtful gift, but it was the anonymity that was baffling her; the fact that someone had chosen her, but didn't want to reveal themselves.

'Who's in the frame?' Fiona asked. 'I swear on the future of Hartley Country Apparel that it isn't me or Ermin.'

'Scout's honour.' Ermin crossed his finger over his chest in a gesture that Sophie didn't think had anything to do with scouts.

'I did wonder,' Sophie admitted. 'After what we talked about the other day.'

'You mean you waltzing off to Cornwall like some kind of nomad?'

'*Fiona*,' Sophie hiss-whispered.

Ermin held his hands up. 'As I said, there are no secrets between us. But Fiona would sell your car or take Clifton hostage if she thought you were serious. She wouldn't do something so baffling as to send you a book with a cryptic message.'

'Great to know you're looking out for me,' Sophie said, laughing. 'I am going, though.' It was her plan and she wasn't deviating from it. After Christmas, after the festival, after she'd found out who was behind The Secret Bookshop, she'd be off.

'We'll see.' Fiona sipped her wine, not sounding concerned.

'Anyway. Back to *Jane Eyre*.' Sophie took her notebook out of her bag, opening it on the list she'd written. 'This is where I've got to.'

'Blimey.' Ermin rubbed his forehead. 'This looks serious. Let me go and get another round in. Same again?'

'Yes please,' Sophie and Fiona chorused as they leant over the notebook.

'Annie is a serial killer fiend?' Fiona said when Sophie had told her everything she'd found out – who she thought wasn't in the frame and who was still a possibility.

Sophie laughed. 'Is that what you're taking from this?'

'It's surprising, that's all. But you're right, she's an unlikely culprit.'

Everyone, according to Fiona and Ermin, was an unlikely culprit, and Sophie felt as though she hadn't moved from square one. She started scoring neat lines through all the names.

'What's this, then?' said a voice behind her. 'Festival planning?'

Sophie turned and smiled at Jason Brass, who tonight had swapped his ice-cream parlour for the pub. His dark hair was impeccably styled, his cheeks were rosy, and he was holding a full pint glass. He and his husband, Simon, were kind and fair, and Sophie was lucky to have them as her landlords. Still, if Jason got wind of her mystery, she could kiss goodbye to her stealth approach.

'That's right.' She casually leaned her arm over the page. 'How are you, Jason?'

'All good.' He rocked back on his heels. 'I was thinking of doing baked Alaska for the festival. Wintry flavours – cranberry and cinnamon, mince pie, that kind of thing. I reckon something a bit different will go down a treat.'

'That sounds delicious. Let me speak to Harry, and we'll pop by and see you.'

'Harry Anderly.' Jason shook his head. 'Bit hypocritical, helping out with the festival when he's the one who's fucked it up.'

Sophie shrugged. 'The oak tree is really fragile, apparently, so—'

'The oak tree has been there for hundreds of years. It'll take more than a few fairy lights and some music to fell it. His dad always encouraged use of the green, but Harry's the opposite.'

'You've known him a long time?' Sophie asked.

'Yup,' Jason said. 'He was quiet at school, friendly when-ever I spoke to him, but I wasn't surprised he went off to London as soon as he could. There was something about him – a kind of restlessness, like he knew he could achieve big things as long as he wasn't here. I'm more surprised that he's come back.'

'Maybe now Sophie's teamed up with him, he'll reveal his inner workings,' Fiona suggested.

'He's not a grandfather clock,' Ermin said with a chuckle.

'Best leave you to it.' Jason raised his pint and sauntered to his table, joining a man and two women Sophie didn't recognize. Simon would be busy in Batter Days, and she wondered how much they got to see of each other when their businesses had such contrasting opening hours.

'The coast is clear,' Fiona said in a loud whisper, pulling the notebook towards her and tapping the edge of the page. 'What *about* Harry?'

'Are we talking about the festival now?' Sophie tucked her hair behind her ears.

'I'm talking about *Jane Eyre.*'

The pub door opened, admitting an Arctic blast that slunk menacingly around the room.

'Harry didn't send me *Jane Eyre,*' Sophie scoffed, as the door banged closed. She remembered how naturally he'd responded when she'd mentioned the title to him; there'd been no hint of guilt or embarrassment.

'Harry's dad owned the bookshop in town,' Fiona said. 'That place was full of weird and wonderful editions. He didn't just buy in new stock, but had little corners full of hidden gems, pockets of gilt-edged hardbacks, folio editions

141

from decades ago. If anyone could get their hands on a book like that, it's Harry.'

Sophie pictured his study, his shelves full of modern paperbacks and hardbacks. There had been a mix of genres, but nothing that looked old: no sets of leatherbound books with matching spines and debossed lettering.

'No way did he send it,' she reiterated, then sipped her wine.

'You're right.' Fiona sighed. 'A man like that isn't capable of giving someone such a thoughtful gift.'

Sophie bristled. 'I only said that because I didn't know him at all when it turned up on my counter. I still don't know him that well, but I think it's harsh to say he isn't capable of being thoughtful.'

'A man who wouldn't come home when his father had to move into a care home, who treats that manor like it's on a separate island to the rest of us – a *far more exclusive* island, I might add – and destroys decades of tradition by keeping his land cordoned off from the rest of us, even though it's *literally* in the centre of the village, and has been used for events as far back as I can remember?' She nodded decisively, her point made.

'We don't know about him and his dad, love,' Ermin said gently. 'What their relationship was like.'

'Bernard Anderly was one of the nicest men you could ever hope to meet,' Fiona said. 'There was absolutely *no* reason for Harry not to come home and at least *visit* him, even if he couldn't look after him himself.'

'Fiona . . .' Ermin started.

Sophie tried to remember what Harry had said about it, that evening in his study. He'd alluded to things not being easy, had said he *couldn't* come home, but hadn't gone into detail. And why should he?

'He's warmed up a lot since we've been working together.'

She could almost feel Fiona change tack, abandoning her disgruntlement in favour of curiosity. 'Warmed up? In what way?'

'Just . . . that he took the lead with Winnie, even though she was incredibly unforgiving. He's working really hard to repair the manor, doing consulting at the same time, and . . . all those rumours about him being a reclusive ogre, they're nonsense!'

'Reclusive ogre?' Sophie jumped as Jason appeared once more and put his pint glass firmly on their table. 'We're back to Harry, are we?'

'Fiona and Ermin don't believe he's capable of being friendly.'

'He hasn't exactly got involved in village life,' Jason said. 'He's been back . . . nearly two years, I think. Hard not to read something into that.'

'That's true, Jason,' Fiona said.

'I haven't got a clue what he's done in the past,' Sophie said. 'I only know that he's been great with me – recently, anyway.' Her thoughts slid to the day before, when she'd wiped mud off his forehead, and he'd told her he was glad they were working together.

'Harry Anderly being nice sounds like urban legend stuff,' Jason said with a grin.

One of the old men who had been sitting at the bar wandered past on his way to the toilet. Unashamedly listening in, he added, 'Harry Anderly thinks he's above the rest of us, with his fancy London job and his big old house with the sea views. What a tosser.' He shook his head dismissively, and Sophie felt indignation flare, hot and bubbling, in her chest.

'That is *not* true.' It came out much louder than she'd intended.

Jason folded his arms. 'Prove it.'

'What?' She blinked. 'How can I?'

'Call him. Invite him for a pint here, now. See what he says.'

Sophie looked at her watch. It was half past eight. 'Oh, he won't . . .'

'Won't what?' Jason asked. 'No harm in trying, is there?'

Sophie turned to Fiona and Ermin for help, but they stayed quiet, and she knew they were curious too; that they wanted Harry Anderly to step through the door of the Blossom Bough, like some kind of mythical creature, and have a pint with them. But she *had* seen a different side to him, and if everyone else got a chance to see it too . . .

'Fine.' She took her phone out of her bag, then put her notebook securely inside, before it got taken by someone and flicked through.

She found Harry's number, her thumb hovering over the screen for a moment. Then she pressed it, sucking in a breath as she listened to the ringing noise, and—

'Hello? Sophie? Are you OK?'

'Harry, hi. How are you?'

There was a pause, then he said, 'I'm good. You're all right, are you?'

'Yeah. Yes. I'm just . . . I'm in the pub, with Fiona and Ermin and Jason. We wondered if you'd like to come and have a drink with us. If you're free, of course. You might be

144

super busy, or . . . I don't know. Doing things. You could bring May too?' She kept her gaze on the scuffed wood of the table.

The silence might have gone on for a decade, or a second, but Sophie refused to look at the other people around the table. Then she heard Harry say, 'May's working, but I'm free. Give me fifteen minutes, and I'll be there.'

'You *will*?' She looked up, her shock mirrored on the faces of her friends.

'Fifteen minutes,' he said firmly. 'Don't go anywhere, OK?' Then he hung up.

Chapter Fourteen

After Sophie put the phone down, it felt as if the entire pub was holding its breath.

'He's coming, then?' There was laughter in Jason's voice, but also genuine surprise.

'He is.'

'Well I never,' Fiona said. 'A turn-up for the books, that's for sure.'

'Another round then. Dutch courage, and all that.' Jason stood up.

'Why do we need courage?' Sophie asked, but she felt it, too: the curiosity, the anticipation of the others, which was ridiculous because he was just a man, and there was nothing remotely mysterious about him. Or not *that* much, anyway.

'Another wine?' Jason asked her.

She shook her head. 'Water, please.' She'd only had a couple of glasses, but she didn't want any more. 'I never should have called him,' she said, mostly to herself.

'Why not?' Fiona asked.

'If he hadn't wanted to come, he could have just said no,' Ermin added.

'God knows he's said no to things easily enough up until now,' Fiona said tartly.

Jason returned with their drinks and Sophie sipped her water, on high alert while the others chatted around her. How had she allowed them to persuade her into inviting him? She felt all the pressure of having made the call. Then the door opened, letting in a snake of cold air, and the chatter in the pub faded.

Sophie was reminded how well Harry Anderly filled a doorway. His gaze cast about the room and, when he found her, a small smile lit his eyes, then he strode across to join them, murmurs following him like ripples in his wake.

'Hello.' He stood next to the table, as if he wasn't sure what to do next. 'Jason,' he nodded. 'Fiona, Ermin. Sophie, thanks for inviting me.' He sounded stiff, as if he'd just realized he would have to engage in conversation with all of them.

'Here.' Sophie scooted over on her bench. 'Sit next to me.'

Harry shrugged off his coat to reveal a soft-looking grey jumper. His jeans were dark, rucking over the tops of sturdy brown boots, and when he sat down he rolled up his sleeves, revealing tanned forearms dusted with brown hair.

'Let me get you a drink,' Sophie said.

'No, it's my round.' Jason stood up. 'What do you fancy?'

'A pint, please. Whatever you're having. Thanks.' When Jason was gone he turned to Sophie, gesturing to her glass. 'My presence requires you to have a pint of vodka?'

Sophie shook her head. 'It's water.'

'How are you, Harry?' Fiona asked, from across the table.

'I'm good thanks, Fiona. How are you both?'

'Very well,' Ermin said, with his customary chuckle. 'I hear you and Sophie are doing a grand job of organizing our festival.'

'We're just getting started,' Harry admitted. 'There's a lot to do.'

'Will it involve goats?' Jason put a pint in front of Harry.

'Thanks.' He rubbed his forehead. 'We've not planned it that way, but at the moment it's very much up to Felix where he goes. Unless I build a huge brick wall around the entire estate.'

'He just wants to have fun,' Sophie said.

'Goats just want to have fun!' Fiona said delightedly. 'Perfect.'

Sophie glanced at Harry, and saw that he was grinning. It transformed him from dour to carefree, and her breath caught. Under the pub's soft lighting, his hair had blond highlights, and his eyes looked more green than brown. He had weekend stubble, and she couldn't stop her gaze flitting between his face and his forearms resting on the table, one hand wrapped loosely around the glass that Jason had just placed in front of him.

'How's the ice-cream business?' he asked Jason. 'Do you get by OK in the winter?'

'More than I expected to.' Jason leaned back in his chair. 'Obviously we've got Batter Days too, and that has a steadier income stream – it carries Scoops a little – but the good people of Norfolk know that an ice cream on a winter's day is a proper treat, and as long as we keep innovating, we'll be fine.'

'Glad to hear it.' Harry nodded firmly.

'What about you?' Jason asked. 'I expect the upkeep of Mistingham Manor is a full-time job.'

Harry stared into the amber liquid in his glass. 'It's not easy, and I still do some consulting work on the side, because the manor certainly has a habit of gobbling up money.' He caught Sophie's eye, acknowledging that he'd said the same to her the day before.

'What do you consult on?' Ermin asked. 'If you don't mind me probing.'

'Investments,' Harry said. 'For businesses, mostly, rather than individuals. It's pretty dry stuff, but I've got a lot of experience now, and it means I can work when I want to, alongside spending time on the house. It's not where my passions lie.'

'Where *do* they lie?' Fiona asked.

'The manor,' Harry said. 'Felix and the dogs. Mistingham.' He cleared his throat. 'Though I know I haven't exactly been . . .'

'Around much?' Jason finished. 'It's up to you, mate. Live your life how you want, but it's grand to see you here. Grand that Sophie asked you.'

Harry looked at her, and she dropped her gaze to the floor. Clifton was staring up at her, so she pulled him onto her lap. Harry stroked the dog's silky ears, his fingers inches from hers.

'I'm glad she asked me too,' he said. 'I've got into the habit of spending Saturday nights pottering and trying to fix things, which isn't very easy once the daylight's gone.'

'May's working?' Sophie asked. Why hadn't Harry said *she* was one of his passions? It wouldn't hurt, she thought, to find out a little bit more. 'You don't have film nights together or . . . anything?'

149

'Sometimes,' Harry said. 'But she works on a tech helpline, and if she covers calls on Saturday nights she gets paid triple, so . . .' He shrugged and took a sip of his pint.

'I hear your goat had fun in Birdie's vegetable patch yesterday,' Jason said jauntily, as if he was trying to cut through the stilted conversation.

Harry looked up at the ceiling, and Sophie held her breath. Was that it? Had he run out of his capacity for small talk? Was he about to lose patience in the face of a gentle interrogation?

He dropped his gaze and turned towards Jason, his knee nudging against Sophie's. She waited for him to move it, but instead he leaned forward, increasing the contact, and said, 'Felix getting into Birdie's allotment is one of the least outrageous things he's done recently. He's acting out, in his adolescent years. Last week I found him on my bed, muddy hooves rucked into the duvet, eating my copy of *The Secret History*.'

'Oh I *love* that book,' Sophie said, and Harry looked at her, surprised.

'Me too. I must have read it a dozen times. No more, though – or not this copy, anyway.'

'That scene before the funeral.' Sophie winced. 'I thought I was going to be sick, it was so tense.'

'It's horrible.' Harry shook his head. 'When Richard was succumbing to the cold, that lonely winter before Henry rescued him – I could feel it. I had to put on an extra jumper.'

'How did Felix get into your bedroom?' Jason asked, calling a halt to their Donna Tartt love-in.

'I left the front door open,' Harry admitted. 'I was fixing

150

the spotlights at the front of the house, and thought it'd be fine if I left it ajar while I carted tools in and out. Apparently not.'

'How did you get him out?' Fiona asked.

'With quite a bit of difficulty and a lot of swearing.'

Sophie watched a sigh escape his lips, then he smiled, soft and genuine, and her heart contracted.

'The thing you have to understand about Felix,' he went on, 'is that he knows he'll have your whole attention if he's laying waste to things: destruction, antagonism, whatever it is. And he also knows that, without a shadow of a doubt, he'll get away with it.'

'Because he's so cute,' Sophie said.

'Well then,' Fiona said, 'you are somewhat hoist on your own petard.'

'Because of the jumpers?' Harry asked. 'I know. Felix is a disaster of my own making, and my burden to bear.' He was still smiling as his hand returned to Clifton's head. Sophie wondered if he usually had Terror or Darkness by his side, if stroking them was his version of a stress ball: the warm, unconditional love of his dogs. And Felix, of course, who Sophie couldn't think of as anything but mischievously charming.

'What else has he done?' Ermin asked.

'What hasn't he done?' Harry started listing Felix's misadventures, telling each story in a way that had everyone laughing, people looking over from other tables. His delivery was dry, his timing was perfect.

Sophie conjured up a list of all the things she believed about Harry Anderly: that he would be a wonderful Santa Claus; that he was denying Mistingham the pleasure of his company by mostly hiding away in his spooky manor house; that she wouldn't mind his long fingers stroking through *her* hair, if things had been different; that he was warming up here too, enjoying the company; that, even if calling him had been an *I'll show everyone* moment, she was glad she'd done it.

When they'd finished laughing at a story about how Felix had got into the postman's van when he'd been dropping off a couple of parcels, Harry had ended up chasing the van down the driveway, and they'd discovered the goat chewing through a Bravissimo catalogue, Fiona glanced at her watch and said, 'Goodness! It's almost last orders.'

'Shit, seriously?' Jason sank the last of his drink. 'I promised Simon I'd help with clear-up tonight.' He stood and pulled on his coat. 'Great to catch you all. You especially, Harry.'

'I owe you a pint,' Harry said, and the two men shook hands.

'Next time, then? Don't leave it so long.'

'I won't,' Harry assured him.

Fiona and Ermin said their goodbyes, and Fiona even let Harry peck her on the cheek. 'Don't be a stranger,' she said and he nodded warily.

'Good to see you, old chap.' Ermin patted his shoulder as he walked past.

Sophie put on her coat, her arm flailing as she tried to find one of the sleeves.

'Here.' Harry held it for her and then pulled it gently over her shoulders. He turned her around and straightened the collar.

'Thanks.'

'You know, after inviting me here, you've been pretty quiet all evening.'

'You kept the conversation going, though,' she said with a smile.

'I enjoyed myself.' He sounded surprised. 'Jason, Fiona and Ermin – it's been a long time since I spoke to any of them properly.'

'Fiona's been quite unkind about you, though.'

Harry nodded. 'Everyone has opinions, and a lot of people here have strong ones about me and my family, but . . .' He shrugged. 'Can I walk you home?'

'You walked?'

'I didn't know how many pints I'd end up having.'

'You have a torch?' She raised an eyebrow, but he reached into his coat pocket and pulled out a hefty looking Maglite. She laughed. 'Of course you do.'

He opened the door for her and they stepped out into the dark, the stars like pinpricks in a blackout curtain above, the crisp, cold air stroking icy fingertips across her skin.

'Wow.' She tipped her head up. 'I will never, *ever* get over seeing this many stars. It makes you feel so small.'

'It does,' Harry said quietly. He was standing behind her, and when she leaned too far back to follow the line of a constellation, he put his hand gently between her shoulder blades. 'I've got you,' he whispered, and for some reason those three words clogged Sophie's throat.

'We should go,' she said, standing upright. 'It's so cold, and you've got further to walk than me.'

'Lead the way.'

Clifton trotted alongside them, and after a moment Harry held his elbow out, and Sophie slipped her arm through his, until she was anchored to his side. It made her feel safer, more secure, and also – perhaps because it was just the two of them now – she found it easier to speak.

'I'm sorry about your copy of *The Secret History*.'

Harry glanced at her. 'It's OK. I bought another one.'

'You must miss The Book Ends,' she said gently. She didn't know if it was forbidden ground, but he'd been so much more open in the pub.

'I do,' he admitted. 'It was this strange mix of organized and haphazard; you never knew what you were going to find in any of the rooms, but if you wanted something specific, either it would be there or Dad would order it in.'

'You didn't want to take it over?'

'I couldn't,' he said simply. 'I had to be in London.'

He looked towards the seafront, and Sophie followed his gaze. The water was a black hole, except for the silver pathway cast across it by the moon, picking out the white of the foam-topped waves.

'Everyone loved my dad,' he said. 'He was always ready with a kind word or a joke, and he had an immense knowledge of books. He ordered whatever people wanted immediately, so they had it in days. He came across as generous and competent, but . . .' Harry shook his head. 'In the last few years he'd run the bookshop into the ground, he was in so much debt he was about to lose the shop *and* the manor, and I didn't have a choice. People say there's always a choice, that you can make anything work if you really want to, but willpower – just *wanting* something – won't win over real life and all the barriers you're faced with.'

Sophie knew about barriers. She knew that wanting to be part of a family didn't make it happen, that you couldn't just wish it into existence, just as you couldn't make somewhere your home if it didn't feel right, and you couldn't hold on to love if the other person didn't want it as much as you. 'What are your barriers?' she asked quietly.

'Money, expectation, reputation, rules. Desire can't overrule all those things.' His voice was gruff, as if he was holding in his emotions, and Sophie thought how hard it must have been, to deal with the financial mess his father had left, while everyone in Mistingham thought his dad was the good guy and Harry the villain. And, although she knew he was talking about desire in general terms, she could only think of one kind: a kind that was totally inappropriate because of May. But, being this close to him in the dark, his body warm against hers, the laughter from his goat stories echoing in her head, she couldn't help it.

'But you still love books,' she said, dragging herself onto safer ground.

'I'll always love books.'

'Me too,' she murmured. 'Have you heard of The Secret Bookshop?'

'The *Secret* Bookshop? No, what is that?'

'I've had this . . . this book given to me, and I have no idea who did it. It's a random, anonymous gift.'

'What do you mean? Which book?' He sounded so perplexed that Sophie knew Fiona was wrong: there was no way Harry was behind her copy of *Jane Eyre*.

So, instead of pursuing her mystery, she decided to be bold. 'Why can't we hold the Christmas festival close to the oak tree?'

Harry looked away, his breath puffing a cloud into the night air. 'Dad was so cavalier with everything,' he said.

'The shop, the estate, money. Me and my sister Daisy, even. He did whatever he wanted to, believed everything would just *work out* somehow, even when it started falling apart. I think it was how he dealt with his grief, after my mum died. Denial was his default, but . . .' He turned to face her. 'I had a survey done on the oak when I moved back here, and they said it was unstable: that it could be compromised if it's messed about with too much.'

Sophie gave him a gentle smile. 'So you'd rather nobody went near it? Looked at it, enjoyed it, but from a distance? Preserve the tree, but stop everyone using the green that surrounds it?'

'Soph—'

'Do you really think a few fairy lights strung through its branches are going to bring it tumbling down? That people walking near it will make it collapse?'

He shut his eyes. 'It's over four-hundred years old. It's sheltered people from the rain, been home for countless insects and birds.'

Sophie squeezed his arm. 'My very favourite foster mum, Mrs Fairweather, once told me that it was better to enjoy things and make use of them, rather than keep them carefully shut up and save them for the perfect moment. She said that the perfect moment might never come and, by waiting for it, you end up missing out instead.'

'She sounds wise,' Harry said. 'How long did you live with her?'

'Only a couple of years. She retired when I was seventeen, after a long, exhausting career of making lost kids feel cherished. I owe her so much, and I trust the things she told me.' She looked up at Harry. 'Your dad may have

156

managed his finances badly, and caused you a whole load of grief in the process, but that doesn't mean he was wrong about everything. Jazz was saying how important community is, how it's better for people to be too close than distant, and I thought we could incorporate that into the festival: bring the community into it as much as possible.'

Now she'd said it aloud, she knew it made sense. 'The best way to do that would be to use the green and the village hall, have indoor and outdoor activities: pot-luck food, some kind of games tournament, an open-mic night.'

'An open-*mic* night?'

'What's more community-spirited than that? Then everyone who wants to be part of the performance *can* be. It would be so good, Harry. Come on.' She was bouncing on her feet now. 'The oak tree would love to be at the heart of it. Think how many village events it must have presided over. You can't take that away from it.'

Harry started walking again. 'And *you* can't anthropomorphize a tree and expect me to change my mind.'

'You think it's a great idea – admit it.' She grinned at him, then couldn't stop a huge yawn escaping. She turned her head away and covered her mouth.

'Right,' Harry said decisively. 'Time for bed.'

Her gaze shot to his. But he hadn't meant that. Of *course* he hadn't.

He cleared his throat. 'I mean . . .'

'I'm just here.' She gestured to her front door, wondering if her cheeks were as pink as his.

'I know that,' Harry murmured. Batter Days was in darkness, but Sophie could see a faint glow in the back, could make out the shadowy figures of Simon and Jason moving about in the far room.

'Thank you,' she said, 'for coming tonight, and for walking me home. And will you at least think about what I've said?'

'I'll think about it, but . . .' He turned away, looking in the direction of the darkened sea.

'What is it?' She touched his chin gently, bringing him back to face her. 'I'm right here, in front of you. You can tell me anything you want to.'

'I'm trying not to.'

'Why not?'

He reached up and tucked a chunk of her hair behind her ear. 'Because if I do, this whole situation might run away with us.'

'Run away?' Sophie whispered.

He was closer now, his eyes like miniature galaxies, black holes in the middle, swallowing the light. 'I'm going to go now.'

'Probably wise,' she murmured, every bit of her wishing he would stay. She could take hold of his collar or his belt or his arms, slide her hands behind his neck. 'It wouldn't be fair.'

'Fair to who?' he whispered, frowning.

She shook her head. 'Night, Harry. Thanks for coming to the pub.'

'Thanks for inviting me.' He turned away from her, shoving one hand in his pocket as he strode away, the other wielding the torch, ready to turn it on when he was beyond the reach of the streetlights. Then he stopped, turned abruptly, and called out to her: 'I've thought about it, and you're right.'

'About what?'

'The festival. The green. The bloody oak tree!'

Sophie's heart thudded. Had she misheard? Was she going mad? Had that been vodka in her glass, after all? 'You mean we can do the festival on the green, instead of the street?'

'Yes! Let's do it – let's not wait for the perfect moment, but enjoy it all right now.' He grinned, then waved and turned away, leaving her stunned and confounded and – after a moment – elated, on her doorstep.

She had changed Harry's mind. She'd invited him to the pub, got him to open up and now, *now*, the villagers could have the festival they really wanted. It would be a fitting end to her time in Mistingham – she could disappear to Cornwall, leaving them all on a high.

With a grin mirroring Harry's, Sophie unlocked the door of her flat and went inside.

Chapter Fifteen

When Sophie climbed into Harry's Land Rover on Monday afternoon, the heater was blowing gently through the vents and the leather seat hugged her perfectly, and she knew that if she wasn't careful she would fall asleep. She had messaged him yesterday, still on a high from Saturday night, and wanting to get the ball rolling before he got cold feet. Buying lights to thread through the oak tree's branches was a good first step, and Harry said he knew exactly where they could go.

'OK?' he asked. He was wearing a cotton shirt, navy with a thin red check, and his usual dark jeans. Sophie shifted in her seat and got a waft of aftershave, something surprisingly vanilla-ish, even if there was a darker, woody scent beneath.

'I'm fine,' she said. 'Good, even.'

'Good, even?' Harry repeated, amused. 'Something to be celebrated, then.'

'I'm excited about the festival – about having it on the green.'

'Yes. Well,' he grumbled.

Sophie grinned. 'You know it's the right decision. I can't wait to tell everyone.'

'You haven't told Fiona and Ermin?'

'Not yet,' she admitted. 'But we need to let them know soon, because it changes the logistics. We'll need games for the green or the hall, rather than at Penny For Them, and whatever refreshments we serve will need to be in food trucks. There's a lot to organize.'

'It almost seems like we're making everything harder by moving it,' Harry said lightly.

'But it'll be more of a community event like this, rather than spread out along Perpendicular Street. We want everyone to be together.'

'You sound like that old Prudential advert, but I get your point.'

'Good.' She smiled at him. 'And the first easy win is lights. Where's your person?'

'On one of the business parks on the outskirts of Norwich. It'll take about forty-five minutes.' He switched on the radio, so low it was barely audible, but Sophie recognized the melody of 'Last Christmas' and was surprised all over again.

'You don't listen to farming radio?'

'One goat doesn't make me a farmer,' he pointed out. 'Felix is a boy, so he's no good for milk and he's not going in a stew anytime soon. I don't farm anything.'

'Birdie mentioned that he had a brother, Oliver.'

Harry swallowed, the bob of his Adam's apple distinct in profile. 'He died when he was a few months old.'

'I'm sorry,' Sophie said. 'Where did they come from?'

Harry glanced at her, then turned back to the road. 'Not soon after I'd moved back here, I went to buy cement from a builder's yard about ten miles away. There was this scruffy farm next door – I only noticed because I could hear the goats. They were bleating constantly, so I followed the sound, and . . . they were so small, stuck in this cramped pen, squalid conditions. It was clear they were distressed.'

'How awful,' Sophie murmured.

'I went and found the farmer – if you could call him that. He said male goats had no value, that he was waiting to take them to the abattoir, and I-I couldn't let that happen.' He shook his head. 'I offered to buy them – *demanded* is probably more like it, actually – and the farmer was overjoyed, because he would have had to pay to have them killed. Instead, Felix and Oliver came back to Mistingham Manor with me.'

'You named them?'

'A bit different to Darkness and Terror,' he said with a smile. 'But Oliver was already ill, because of the conditions he'd been kept in. I took him to the vets, we tried everything, but he didn't make it.'

'I'm sorry.'

Harry shrugged. 'I still have Felix. I was worried, after he lost his brother, because they're such sociable animals, but he's a resilient little bugger and I suppose . . . that's why I indulge him. The jumpers, the sentimentality – it must seem like madness.'

'It doesn't exactly fit your Dark Demon Lord persona.'

Harry laughed. 'No. Felix is my weakness. I can't help it.'

'I doubt many people could,' Sophie said.

'You're humouring me.' He flipped the indicator and they turned onto a wide road with stark, grey-brown fields on either side, the sky a liquid blue haze, mist hanging in clumps above the pared-back land. It was beautiful and wild, and it made Sophie's breath catch. She wondered how different Cornwall would be.

'I'm not humouring you,' she told him. 'It's perfectly acceptable for a man who's . . . how old *are* you?' She'd guessed he was about her own age.

'Forty-two,' he admitted, his brows knitting together. 'Forty-two years old, and I hardly have my life together.'

'Hey,' she said. 'You have your own house, which has to count for something.'

'I inherited that, I very nearly lost it altogether, and it's basically falling down.'

'You *didn't* lose it, and you're fixing it.'

'Trying to.'

'Succeeding. Rome wasn't built in a day.'

'Starting from scratch might be less hassle.'

'I doubt that,' Sophie said. 'Anyway, I'm not much younger than you, and I have a rented flat above a chippy, a forgotten corner of another person's shop to sell my handmade note-books in, and the only being who relies on me is a scruffy dog I rescued from under a bridge. My list of life achievements is short.'

'I don't agree,' Harry said. 'You're proudly independent, and you know what you want out of life. You're not bowing to pressure from friends or villagers, or society. You do what you want, not what's expected of you.'

Sophie hid her surprise. 'You don't think I'm in the position I'm in because I haven't had much choice?'

'Not at all. You're determined. I think if you wanted something different, you'd find a way to get it.'

Sophie nodded, thinking about Cornwall. She *was* determined to have the life she wanted, and sometimes that meant starting again somewhere new. It was the best way she knew of feeling in control: keeping people at arm's length was better than caring too much, giving them control of you. That wasn't something she was about to admit to Harry, so she stared out of the window as the flat, winter-sparse fields were broken up by quaint villages, cottages decorated with wreaths, outdoor trees draped with golden lights that twinkled even though it was morning. Christmas was coming, and Sophie and Harry were responsible for bringing it to Mistingham. She hoped they could pull it off.

Harry swung onto the large car park and Sophie looked up at the building they were about to enter. Called the Seasonal Superstore, it clearly changed with the time of year, and right now, over halfway through November, it was all about Christmas. It was also an assault for the senses.

In the window, a slightly wonky tree was draped with various different light strings, some static, some winking; they were gold and frosty white, blue and multicoloured. There was a forest scene of two plastic reindeer, a snowman and, inexplicably, a giant hedgehog, all of them lit from within, like the figures Sophie had sometimes seen decorating front lawns during December. An inflatable Santa was stuck halfway up the window, a sack with illuminated presents spilling out of it, the disaster frozen in time. Two gold angels stood discreetly in the corner. Sophie imagined they were cowering.

'This is . . . classy,' she said, as they walked up to the door.

'We're not decorating Sandringham,' Harry replied. 'Now we've committed to this, the first thing we need to do is bling up our oak tree.'

'*Bling it up?*' Sophie spluttered out a laugh. 'Can you say that again so I can record it?'

'No,' Harry said, but she thought he was fighting a smile as he held the door open for her.

She stepped into a space that, despite the warning in the windows, she wasn't prepared for. 'Holy shit.'

'It's . . . a lot,' Harry agreed. That was, possibly, an under-statement. Displays of ornaments, lights and baubles, trees and statues and garlands shimmered, twinkled and flashed in every colour imaginable, while speakers blared out 'Fairytale of New York'.

'Harry, my dude!' A man appeared from somewhere, dressed in a red shirt that was at least two sizes too big for him, his brown hair straggling over his shoulders, a scruffy goatee on his narrow face. 'It's been an age.'

'It's good to see you, Scratch.' Harry sounded slightly embarrassed. 'This is Sophie – Sophie, meet Scratch. We knew each other at school.'

'Yeah, but I hightailed it out of Mistingham as soon as I could, in search of the bright lights.' He laughed at his own joke, and Sophie tried to join in. 'You need my assis-tance.'

'We need to decorate the oak tree for our festival,' Harry said. Sophie might have been imagining it, but she thought he sounded relieved, as if a part of him had been wanting to give in to the villagers' requests all along.

'Ah, the Mistingham Oak. For sure.' Scratch nodded. 'Come this way, and I'll show you all the possibilities.'

'*All* of them?' Sophie whispered, horrified, as she followed the two men to the back of the shop.

An hour later, her head ached and she felt as if dust had worked its way into all her cracks and crevices, but they had their lights.

They'd chosen a string of simple globe bulbs in bright colours and one of little illuminated books, which Sophie had secretly picked in tribute to her copy of *Jane Eyre*. Scratch had insisted on them having a whimsical string of acorns as well, because it was an oak tree. Sophie was surprised at how good quality the lights seemed, how robust they were, and she was feeling a lot more confident than she had when they'd come in.

They were on their way back to the till, when she spotted something that made her gasp.

'OK?' Harry asked.

'Look!' She pointed.

'Sophie.' His deep tone held a warning, and a shiver ran down her spine. She realized how much she loved his voice, an entirely unhelpful thought that she quickly dismissed.

'We have to get it,' she said. 'For the green.'

'No, we don't.'

'Felix would *love* it.'

His sigh was harsh. 'I have no idea how Felix would react, but luckily we're not going to find out.'

'We are.' She hurried over and picked it up. 'Look how adorable it is.'

Harry rolled his eyes.

It was another of the glowing animals, but this one was

a goat, its tiny horns and large ears giving it a distinct personality, despite it not having eyes. It was so Felix-like, she couldn't imagine leaving without it.

'This as well, please,' she said to Scratch, who was carefully boxing up their lights.

'Oh, the goat. Sure.' He began rootling around beneath the counter.

She could feel Harry's stare on the side of her face. 'Sophie,' he said calmly, 'what are you doing?'

'I'm buying us the goat.'

'Us? Or the good people of Mistingham?'

'The good people of Mistingham,' she said. 'But also us.' She could *not* think about there being an *us*.

Harry shook his head. 'If you're that enamoured, you can borrow Felix. He'd love a couple of nights in your flat: he'd only destroy about 90 per cent of it.'

'This way, he'll have a little friend.' When she glanced at Harry, he was rubbing his eyes, looking put-upon and frustrated and utterly, deliciously grumpy. Sophie grinned. She decided that low-key riling Harry Anderly was one of her new favourite pastimes. When Scratch had boxed up their lights, they paid for them with the festival funds they'd been assigned by Ermin, raised at various fundraising events throughout the year. Sophie paid for the goat herself. She carried it out to the car, while Harry carried the boxes of lights. She had an extra spring in her step, and she realized her headache had gone. She couldn't help thinking of a line from *Jane Eyre*, one that had stuck with her when she'd come across it:

I laughed and made my escape, still laughing as I ran upstairs. 'A good idea!' I thought with glee. 'I see I have the means of fretting him out of his melancholy for some time to come.'

They drove back to Mistingham and went straight to Vea's Crafts, which was tucked away down a narrow road behind the seafront, a hidden jewel of a shop with a colourful window display that promised soft textures and delicate projects to while away a few, satisfying hours. Sophie had used Vea for as many of her notebook supplies as possible, and she'd always been helpful when Sophie had wanted to order in anything specific. After the assault of the seasonal superstore, it felt like a balm.

Inside, the shop smelled of cinnamon. The front room was tiny, much of the space reserved for large rolls of fabric at the back, and Sophie could feel how close Harry was behind her.

Vea wafted through the white muslin curtain that cordoned off the fabric room from the rest of the shop, her smile on seeing Sophie turning to surprise when her gaze landed on Harry.

'Goodness!' She pressed a hand to her chest. 'I thought I'd stepped into the past for a moment, though you've filled out a bit since you were a teenager.'

Vea was Jamaican, in her sixties, Sophie thought, though she seemed a lot more youthful, the grey in her corkscrew curls looking more like silver dye, the frames of her glasses pink and studded with jewels.

'Hi, Vea.' Harry cleared his throat. 'How have you been keeping?'

'Oh well, well, thank you! And you? How's the patch-up job on the manor going? What about all those books?'

Harry shoved his hands deep in his jeans pockets. 'The books went when Dad closed the shop.'

Vea fiddled with the gold chain round her neck. 'Is that the case?'

'Are you a big reader, then?' Sophie cut in. She could add another name to her anonymous gifter list.

'I wouldn't say *big* reader,' Vea said, her focus still on Harry. 'It's mostly cookbooks and crafting manuals, more practical than recreational. Harry reads, though.'

'I know.' Sophie deflated a little. Crossing someone off the list wasn't as good as circling their name.

'Such a shame,' Vea said heavily, 'that the leftover stock from The Book Ends was sold or given away.'

'What else was I supposed to do with it?' Harry's voice was tight. 'The shop had to close, and I had no use for a lorry-load of books. I sent what I could back to the wholesalers, some went to other bookshops in the area, I took a few boxes to Dad's care home, for their library. Of course a few came back to the manor with me, but . . . it was all I could do.'

'You could have kept them,' Vea said, in a way that managed to be both soft and steely.

'We've come to talk to you about bunting,' Sophie said desperately. 'We want a whole lot of Christmas bunting for the Oak Festival.'

Vea finally gave Sophie her attention. 'Do you want to make it, or do you want me to?'

'Oooh.' Sophie turned wide eyes on Harry. 'What do you think?'

He stared at her as if she'd sprouted three heads. 'No. Sophie—'

'What does making bunting involve?' she asked Vea.

'I sell you whichever fabrics you like, give you a pattern for the pennants and the edging, and you put it all together. It'll be simple – especially considering how skilled you are at your notebooks.'

'Would we need a sewing machine?'

'We?' Harry echoed.

'It would make quicker work of it, especially if you're making a lot. I can lend you one.'

'Amazing!' Sophie felt a flutter of excitement. She wanted this festival to be about community, about getting involved, and they needed to set a good example for the rest of Mistingham.

'Sophie, we don't have the time or money—'

'Sure we do.' She flapped a dismissive hand at Harry. 'I don't mind paying for a few extra crafting bits, and this is a great plan. Vea, can you show us your fabrics?'

'I absolutely can. This way, please. Come and pick your Christmas materials.'

Harry carried the sewing machine to his Land Rover.

'We're making bunting.' He sounded incredulous, as if he couldn't quite believe he'd been talked into it. 'With a sewing machine.'

'It's going to take us a whole lot longer if we hand-stitch it. And think how much money we're saving as opposed to buying the ready-made stuff. It sounds pretty simple, doesn't it?'

'What if I said I might not have been listening fully to Vea's instructions?'

'Then *I'd* say it's doubly good that we've got the pattern. Anyway, crafting is good for you.'

'So is kale, but I'm not going to start eating it. Are we taking this to your flat?'

'There's more room at the manor.'

Harry was in the process of putting the machine in his boot, but he paused and looked up at her. They were organizing this together, but Sophie knew that just inviting herself to his house, invading his space and getting him to do crafting with her – of all things – was perhaps a step too far.

'You're taking the lead on it, though,' he said after a moment.

Her heart thudded. Maybe *not* a step too far, then. 'Of course,' she said. 'It'll be worth it, I promise. When we see that bunting flying, knowing that we made it? It'll feel great. Doing things with your hands is really satisfying.'

Harry's gaze was steady, somehow both hard and soft, and it was turning her insides into a hot, liquid puddle.

'It can be,' he said, deadpan, then he got into the Land Rover, leaving Sophie to scramble into the passenger side and play back their exchange, then consider all the ways it could be interpreted that had absolutely nothing to do with bunting.

As the silence between them stretched, and she fought the urge to cross her legs because she was 100 per cent sure that he would notice, she realized that Harry had grown on her, slowly and stealthily, like a jaguar approaching its prey, and that she had to put a stop to her feelings before someone ended up getting hurt.

Chapter Sixteen

'One month and three days until Christmas.' Sophie spoke the words into the quiet of Harry's study, the fire crackling in the background. Darkness, Terror and Clifton were asleep on the rug in front of the flames, the wind whispering through the trees in the darkness outside, beyond the cosy barrier of the curtains.

Harry didn't reply immediately, just as he'd so far ignored his beer, whereas Sophie was nearly at the bottom of her bottle. But she didn't say anything else, because there was a lot of pleasure in watching him work, his head bent over the ancient sewing machine Vea had lent them, creating the bunting that, at the beginning of the week, he'd had no interest in making. Now, he was focusing on it as if his life depended on producing a hundred perfect pennants.

'You are *great* at this.' She couldn't hide her wonder, because she hadn't expected such delicate dexterity from a man who was adept at knocking fence posts into the ground. 'There I was extolling the virtues of working with your hands, and you're the one who should be teaching me.'

'I could certainly teach you some things, if you wanted me to.'

Sophie's breath hitched.

Harry looked up, his lips parted. 'Sorry,' he said. 'Sophie, I'm sorry, I—'

'It's OK.' She grinned to cover her fluttering heart and racing thoughts. How immersed in his work must he have been to let those words slip out? She didn't think he'd been joking – or not entirely.

His eyes were back on the sewing machine, perhaps out of embarrassment, and with the overhead light above him – they'd turned it on so they could see well enough to work – his long eyelashes made feathery shadows on his cheeks.

'This is a lot of bunting,' he said gruffly, after a few minutes of awkward silence.

'I know,' Sophie said. 'But it'll be worth it. We're supposed to be doing it together, though.'

Technically, they still were. Sophie was tidying up the pennants Harry had sewn together using the thick, glittery ribbon they'd chosen, snipping off loose threads and generally neatening up where necessary. Except he really had it under control, and now they had a long trail of Christmas pudding bunting, another with gambolling reindeer on, and a third that was a frenzied delight of triangles in glittering red, green, gold and silver, which made Sophie's eyes hurt.

'We *are* doing it together,' Harry murmured, his focus on the fabric and ribbon he was easing beneath the needle. 'Anyway, I'm going to get to the end of this row, then we're downing tools.'

'We are?' Sophie hid her disappointment. She thought of her flat, homely but with few distractions on a Friday night in November.

'I thought I could cook something, if you wanted?' Harry said. 'Unless you have other plans.'

'Oh! No, I don't. I'd love that.' She pointed at the sewing machine. 'Hurry up, then. I'm starving.'

'Yes, boss.' He flashed her a smile that felt more dangerous than she cared to admit.

He refused to let her help him in the kitchen, which left her stuck in the study, unwilling to take herself on an illicit tour of his house while he was otherwise occupied. She got out her notebook, looked at her paltry list of Secret Bookshop candidates, then put it away again. At least getting involved in the festival had done the village some good, even if it hadn't yet solved her book-shaped mystery.

Fiona and Ermin had been delighted when she'd cornered them both in the shop and told them the festival was moving to the village green, and they'd embraced her ideas about involving the community: the pot-luck buffet, the open-mic night, everyone making decorations for the tree and some kind of games tournament.

'Which game?' Ermin had asked eagerly, Poppet dancing at his feet, impatient for her walk.

'I don't know yet. I need to see what games the village hall has first.'

'And you'll allow anything at the open-mic night?' Fiona asked. 'Any talent at all?'

'I think so,' Sophie said. 'We want everyone to feel comfortable taking part.'

'Jazz mentioned something about singing,' Fiona said. 'She's done some busking in the past, and I was going to suggest she could get involved in the carol choir, but she might want do something on her own.'

'How's she doing?' Sophie saw her whenever she popped into the shop, but she still seemed elusive, almost like the ghost they had believed her to be when they'd heard her in the abandoned bookshop.

'She's still here,' Fiona had said, her smile wavering. 'She says she's grateful for our help, but she doesn't want to be in debt to us. She's going to see Mary about a job at the hotel, because she wants to pay us rent. She said she might stay until Christmas, then move on.'

Sophie had felt a dull ache in her chest. It was all so familiar, that need to be self-sufficient, to not want to rely on other people. 'I'll ask her to coffee,' she'd said, wanting to help in some way.

'Why?' Fiona had asked. 'So you can share your plans about leaving Mistingham behind?'

Sophie hadn't known what to say to that. She hadn't wanted to tell her friend that she'd done nothing more to set her move in motion since looking up Cornwall on her phone. The truth of it was that mysterious books, Christmas festivals and Harry taking up so much of her time meant she hadn't had a chance to plan her getaway in any more detail.

Harry came back into the study carrying two plates piled high with food. There were sausages, mashed potato and gravy, peas spilling across the top, and Yorkshire puddings placed precariously on the side.

'This looks incredible,' Sophie said, moving to his desk.

'The Yorkshires are Aunt Bessie's, but the sausages are local.'

'Do you always eat in here?' she asked, as Harry put a plate in front of her.

'Not always, but the kitchen and dining room are disaster areas right now. I *think* the mash is dust free.'

Sophie scooped some up on her fork and tried it. 'Well, even if it's not, it tastes delicious.'

They tucked into the food, the silence between them so much more comfortable than it had been a couple of weeks ago.

'What will you do when the house is finished?' Sophie asked. 'Find a full-time consulting job?'

He laughed. 'I don't know if the house will ever be finished.'

'You're committed to staying here, then?'

'Of course.' He sounded surprised. 'Did you think I was going to refurbish it, then sell it and move away?'

'I didn't know, honestly.' She shrugged. 'You were in London for a long time, and you don't always seem happy here. You don't enjoy the consultancy work – it's not your long-term plan – so what will you do when the house is exactly as you want it?'

He cut into a sausage, speared a piece on his fork. 'Something more creative,' he said. 'Something to do with the manor, maybe. But I haven't allowed myself to think about that yet. I'm still trying to catch up, after everything that happened with Dad. It's not been the easiest few years.'

'Has it helped, having May close by?'

'Absolutely,' he said. 'She's the most positive person I

know, and it was hard to see her after she came back from America. She was so defeated by it; how the whole thing – the industry, the lifestyle – differed from her expectations. But she's bounced back, we've helped each other, I think, and it's good not to be rattling around here by myself.'

Sophie stabbed peas onto her fork, avoiding his gaze. 'How long have you been together?'

Harry was silent for a long time, and eventually, Sophie looked up.

'May and I aren't together,' he said, but he didn't sound surprised that she'd asked. 'We were, briefly, as teenagers – which feels like a lifetime ago – but it didn't last. We're good friends now, and I honestly don't know what I would have done without her, but there are no romantic feelings there, for either of us.'

'OK,' Sophie said, far too brightly, and went back to her dinner.

'I don't think she's spent any time thinking about what my hands are capable of,' he murmured, and her breath caught. She looked up to find him staring at her, his expression impassive. Was he waiting for her to reply? Was he teasing her? Sometimes she had no idea what was going on behind his hazel eyes.

'Harry—' she started.

'What about you and Dexter?'

'*Dexter?*'

'You're close, aren't you?'

'We're friends,' Sophie said. 'Just friends. It hasn't been that long since his wife died, I have no idea if he's even considering . . .' She shook her head. 'There's never been anything between us.'

'Right,' Harry said. He nodded, then went back to his food.

In the quiet that followed, the crackling, smouldering fire seemed to echo the tension simmering between them, the atmosphere no longer comfortable but instead charged with something that, to Sophie at least, felt as if it could set the entire manor alight if they weren't careful about it.

Once they'd finished eating, they moved to the armchairs in front of the fire.

'Tell me about Mrs Fairweather,' Harry said, cradling his mug of hot chocolate. He'd made it for them after he'd cleared up the plates, had even found some marshmallows in a cupboard that he assured Sophie were still in date. 'You said she did more for you than anyone else?'

Sophie tucked her feet up under her, inhaled the sweetness coming from her mug. The dogs were drowsy and content in front of the flames, and Sophie wished she felt the same. Everything had shifted since she'd asked him about May, the boundary between them suddenly gone, making room for possibility that brought with it an undercurrent of panic. She didn't know what to do with her newfound understanding. Mrs Fairweather was easier ground, and she was glad he'd asked.

'She treated me like a real person,' Sophie said. 'She told me that my hopes were valid, that growing up the way I had shouldn't stop me from pursuing whatever life I wanted. She bought me a beautiful notebook one Christmas, and told me that writing my thoughts down would help me to sort through them. When she saw how much I loved crafts – collages and sewing, I did leatherwork at school – she encouraged me to go to art college.' She smiled at the memories. Mrs Fairweather had been tall and rosy-cheeked, friendly more often than she was stern, though she wouldn't let her kids get away with much.

'And you decided to make notebooks?'

'Not until I'd finished college. My final piece was all about different types of paper – collages and origami, pop-up greeting cards. I made a series of tiny sculptures with pages of old books, newspapers, tissue paper – and it just . . . it made me feel more excited than anything else I'd considered doing. I started small, getting to know the different processes and techniques around bar jobs and waitressing, spending whatever spare wages I had on supplies.'

'You must have been dedicated, to get to where you are now.'

She smiled. 'Partly. I was devastated when Mrs Fairweather retired, but I was seventeen, so I wouldn't have been able to stay with her much longer anyway. We kept in touch, mostly by email, but she died four years ago.'

'I'm sorry.'

'Thank you.' She swallowed. 'I was lucky to have her, and even luckier that she left me some money in her will. It's been a big help, allowed me to focus more on my business. It's never been the most lucrative of livings, but I'm building up a good customer base now, and I wouldn't want to do anything else.'

'Didn't Fiona say something about the old sweet shop?' Harry frowned. 'I'm sure she mentioned it . . . a while ago?'

Sophie's stomach flipped. 'She suggested that I might be able to rent it out, have a permanent home for my note-books, as well as somewhere more suitable to make them. It would be an investment, but I could work on more designs, buy in other stationery lines: pens and letter holders, quirky things that tourists would love.'

'It sounds ideal,' Harry said. 'And I'm sure the owner would be fair with the rent, for something so creatively worthwhile.'

She laughed. 'You're just getting back on your feet; you can't offer mates' rates. Anyway, I'm not sure it's something I want to do right now.'

Harry crossed one knee over the other. 'Mates' rates would be better than the zero rent I'm collecting at the moment. Those shops have been so far down my to-do list that I haven't made finding tenants a priority. And you've just told me all the ways it would help you expand your business. I'd love to rent it out to you.'

Sophie stared into the fire. It sounded promising, but it was also a gamble. She would need to lay out a lot of money – to secure the lease, on shop touch-ups, notebook materials, other stock – before she saw any return. It might not work out, and anyway – *anyway* – she was leaving. None of it mattered.

'I don't know what my plans are, longer term,' she said cautiously. 'They might not involve Mistingham.'

Her words were followed by silence, and she saw the moment they landed, Harry's eyes widening a fraction before he schooled his features into impassivity. 'You're not staying here?'

'I don't know,' she admitted. 'There's this place in Cornwall . . .'

'That's hundreds of miles away. Do you have family there? Friends?'

Sophie shook her head. 'Sometimes it's good to shake things up.' It was hard to put any conviction into her words when she was sitting here, opposite him.

'You're planning on moving to the other side of the country? Leaving this beautiful seaside village behind, leaving everyone – Fiona and Ermin, Dexter – because you want to "shake things up"?' He was quiet, incredulous, and Sophie wished she could explain it to him in a way that would make sense. But was that even possible? Her decisions usually only made sense to her.

'I haven't decided yet,' she said, and realized it was the truth. In the past, excluding Bristol, moving on had always felt right – exciting, full of possibility, not muddied with dread or uncertainty. Over the last few weeks, a tiny voice had been whispering to her, saying that maybe, this time, she was getting it wrong: maybe Mistingham held answers to questions she'd never stayed anywhere long enough to ask.

But Harry didn't seem mollified by her answer. He nodded, his lips pressed into a thin line as he stared into the fire. 'It's getting late,' he said after a moment. 'Do you want me to drive you back?'

'Oh.' Her throat clogged with disappointment. 'That would be great. Thank you.'

He stood up and held his hand out, and Sophie took it. She felt an unmistakable tingle as her warm skin touched his, felt his strength as he easily pulled her to her feet. But there was a bigger distance between them now than there had been earlier, when they were sitting on opposite sides of his desk, when she'd thought he was in a relationship with May and he'd believed she had a thing with Dexter.

Despite the cosiness of Harry's study, the gently burning fire, Sophie suddenly felt cold.

Chapter Seventeen

On Monday morning, Sophie arrived at Hartley Country Apparel earlier even than Fiona. She hadn't slept well, tossing and turning, her thoughts running wild after her conversation with Harry in front of the fire. She'd established that he wasn't with May after all – something she had started to suspect, especially after their walk home from the pub – and in return she had quashed his assumptions about Dexter. So far, so good. Then she'd ruined it by being honest with him about her future. This, *this*, was why she didn't get close to people. It caused too much hurt, led to miscommunications and disappointments, or *unmet expectations* in the case of Trent, her boyfriend in Bristol.

She turned on the shop lights and the twinkling gold fairy lights, and switched the kettle on. She was logging into her till when Fiona arrived with Jazz. The young woman looked relaxed but smart, in navy jeans and a raspberry jumper that matched her hair.

'Morning, Sophie.'

'Jazz! How are you?'

'All right,' she said with a shrug. 'Mary's giving me a trial run at the hotel later.'

'That's brilliant.' Whatever Jazz's long-term plans were, Sophie was relieved that she felt comfortable enough here to get a seasonal job, to make some money and be more prepared for whatever she chose to do next. 'Are you looking forward to it?'

'I am, actually. Fiona says Mary and Winnie are cool, and the hotel's pretty nice. I hope it'll be fun.'

'Of course it will be,' Fiona said bullishly, as if she hadn't had a moment's worry about Jazz or her future. 'You could do a lot worse than putting down roots in Mistingham. Now, Sophie, do you want to update us on the festival? I told Jazz you're planning an open-mic night, and we want to know details.'

'Let me make drinks first. What do you want?'

Once they were settled, Sophie ran through the ideas she and Harry had cobbled together and their purchases so far.

'Pot-luck food?' Fiona raised an eyebrow. 'You're letting everyone make and bring a dish for general consumption? Have you had the misfortune of trying Mrs Elderberry's sweet potato curry?'

'Not so far,' Sophie said, with a laugh. 'But that will only be a small part of it. We'll still have Batter Days and the Blossom Bough offering fish and chips and drinks, but I want all the villagers to have a chance to contribute. You gave me the idea, Jazz.'

'I did?' She stopped slumping on the counter.

'What you said about everyone here looking out for each other. It made me think about how people can be lonely, especially at Christmastime if they don't have friends or family nearby. Not everyone will love the arcade games and bar truck, but if we give them the chance to share their favourite dish, run a Scrabble tournament in the hall, it'll appeal to the residents who might not have come otherwise.'

Jazz's smile was filled with pride. 'I knew there was a reason I came here. Apparently, it was to teach you all a valuable lesson.'

Sophie laughed. 'You might just be right.'

'If you carry this off as well as I think you will,' Fiona said to Sophie, 'Ermin will recruit you as Mistingham's permanent events coordinator.'

'Fiona,' she said, 'I don't think—'

'You'd be great at that,' Jazz cut in.

Sophie sighed. 'I'm not sure what I'm doing next year.'

'Are you off on a round-the-world trip?'

'I'm probably moving to Cornwall,' she admitted.

Fiona scoffed not so discreetly.

'Why?' Jazz looked puzzled. 'Everything here's pretty sweet for you, isn't it? Do you really want to leave?'

Sophie hesitated. Standing in the warm shop, with her notebooks displayed elegantly on the shelves, with Fiona's friendship and Jazz's open curiosity, excitement about the festival bubbling just below the surface and the memory of Harry's hand round hers, and his muted, distant expression when she'd told him about Cornwall, the answer to Jazz's question seemed more elusive than ever.

She was about to offer up something non-committal, when the door of the shop opened and a family bustled inside, the young girl and boy, who looked about eight years old and were possibly twins, staring wide-eyed at the twinkling lights, the colourful displays of clothing and notebooks: a Santa's grotto a month before Christmas.

'Hello,' Fiona said brightly. 'How can I help?'

Sophie stayed busy for the rest of the week, with a flurry of customers seeking out the perfect present and notebook commissions to work on in the evenings. In moments in between, she arranged to talk to villagers about the festival. Everyone knew it had moved back to Mistingham Green, and were adapting their plans accordingly. They'd taken the change in their strides, and Sophie was reminded that, apart from last year when Harry had kept them away from the oak tree, this was what they were used to.

She stayed in touch with him by text, but he hadn't invited her to the manor again, or suggested they meet up for anything else. He was always enthusiastic; he told her he could arrange the speaker system for the open-mic night, the outdoor power they would need to run that and the lights, but every exchange was festival-focused, and Sophie thought he was distancing himself from her.

She should be grateful. It would make leaving a lot easier if their growing closeness was stopped in its tracks, but she felt the loss of him like someone taking a warm, comforting blanket away from her on a frosty night.

On Thursday she visited the hotel, and was greeted by Jazz, dressed in a white shirt and smart black trousers, her red hair styled in a fancy up-do.

'How's it going?' she asked. 'I was hoping to talk to Winnie about permits for the festival. My contact at the council has gone dark, and I need to check that our new location and plans are covered by the one we've already applied for.'

Jazz laughed. 'Nervous, much?'

Sophie sucked in a breath. 'Maybe,' she admitted. 'There's a lot to think about. How have your first couple of days been?'

'Great,' Jazz said. 'It's a steep learning curve, and Mary's had to remind me about not swearing at least five times – which is fucking nuts,' she added in a conspiratorial whisper, making Sophie laugh. 'But everyone's really friendly, even the more hoity-toity customers, and it's so nice to be . . . *busy*, I guess. To be doing something that isn't completely self-centred.' She smiled, but her words pulled Sophie up short.

'What do you mean?'

Jazz's gaze was direct. 'Fiona told me you grew up in foster homes, so you must know what I'm talking about. When you're on your own, and so much is out of your control, you have to look out for yourself, don't you? Where will I get a hot dinner, where am I going to sleep, why does someone else deserve that job more than me?'

'But that's totally understandable,' Sophie said in a rush.

'I know it is,' Jazz replied. 'But Fiona and Ermin have been so kind to me, and now Winnie and Mary, too. Everyone here says hello – Dexter and Lucy, Natasha in the pub. Indigo.' Her smile was fleeting, there and then gone. 'I've got room to breathe, so I can start thinking about them now, too. I want to buy something nice for Fiona and Ermin, take them out to dinner if they won't let me give them rent money. I can do a really good job here, because I know I've got somewhere safe to go to when my shift ends.' She shrugged, suddenly bashful, as if she'd said too much. 'It's nice, being able to think about everyone else. You must feel that too, living here.'

Sophie returned her smile, but her thoughts were racing. She had always put herself first, always been focused on self-preservation. She remembered Trent saying that to her, when she'd told him that she wasn't ready to move in with him. He'd accused her of never considering anyone else's feelings, of being self-centred. She remembered Harry's closed-off expression the other night. Had she ever stopped to think of other people over her own needs? What her decisions might do to them?

'It's great, isn't it?' she said half-heartedly. 'Do you know where Winnie is?'

'Probably in the office, mooning over some book she got given.'

Sophie's pulse skipped. 'A book?'

'Yeah, it's this beautiful edition of a book called . . . *Mrs Palfrey at the Claremont*. It's by Elizabeth Taylor, but not *the* Elizabeth Taylor apparently.'

'Who gave it to her?'

'Beats me,' Jazz said, but then the woman in question appeared behind her, her grey curls untamed.

'It's from somewhere called The Secret Bookshop,' Winnie said with a laugh. 'Though goodness only knows what *that* is. It's one of my favourite books, though – which is not that surprising, considering what I do for a living.'

'How lovely,' Sophie managed, her voice scratchy. 'And did it . . . was there a note with it? Any kind of message?'

Winnie frowned. 'There was a postcard – one of the local ones: Mistingham Green in the morning mist, the sun rising

187

over the sea beyond. It mentioned The Secret Bookshop on the back. Are you OK, Sophie? You look like a stunned mullet. Come to the office, and I'll show you.'

'"Have a very happy hotel Christmas"', Sophie read aloud.

Winnie's office was small and neat, the scents of bacon and cranberry wafting through from the kitchen, a cold November rain splattering the glass. The book Winnie had been given was as beautiful as *Jane Eyre*, the cloth cover pale blue, the title and author added in coral pink. No foil details, but it had the same logo as her book – a tiny house with chimneys – on the spine. But, compared to Sophie's, the message was bland.

'Lovely, no?' Winnie said. 'What a treat to have such a gorgeous edition of this novel.'

'Who left it for you?' Sophie turned the postcard over again, wondering if she would recognize the handwriting. She didn't.

'I've no idea, pet. But my name is on the postcard, and it came wrapped in this lovely brown paper. Left right here on the desk for me: someone must have sneaked in.'

'How will you find out?'

Winnie finished typing something on her computer, then looked up at her. 'I'm not sure I will. If The Secret Bookshop wants to give out Secret Santa gifts like this, then let them – that's what I say.' She chuckled. 'I don't want them taking it back. I'm due a reread, and how lucky that I get to do it with this edition? It might be my favourite Christmas present, and it's not even December.

'Now, Sophie love, what is it you need to know about a permit? Well done for talking Harry Anderly round, by the way. Seems like you've got some Christmas magic all of your own, because that can't have been an easy thing to do.'

Sophie sank into the chair on the other side of Winnie's desk, trying to ignore how much this quick visit to the hotel had upended everything. Jazz's words, Winnie's book. At the moment, the festival was proving to be the most straightforward part of her life, and that was saying something. 'Thanks for helping, Winnie,' she said. 'I promise it won't take long.'

Chapter Eighteen

Sophie couldn't stand it any longer.

Jumbled thoughts ran on a wobbly loop through her head: Jazz's comments about how important it was not to act selfishly; Harry's lack of communication; the fact that The Secret Bookshop had sent Winnie a book and she didn't even care about finding out who was behind it, when Sophie had been acting like some sort of mad private investigator to try and discover the culprit . . .

Had she got *everything* wrong? The one thing that was going right was the festival. Her ideas were coming together; they were accumulating the supplies, suppliers and permits they needed, and it would be a triumph as long as Harry didn't give up on her. She needed to make sure that didn't happen.

The weather was grey and drab, and she could count on the fingers of one hand the number of people who had come into Hartley Country Apparel that morning, even though she'd been making an extra effort promoting her business on social media. After the last few days' flurry of customers, the quiet hours just added to her frustration.

'I'll cover for you this afternoon,' Fiona said. 'If you can cover on Monday morning.'

Sophie looked at her in surprise. 'Are you sure?'

'Absolutely. You're bubbling over with nervous energy, so go and do whatever it is you need to do, and I'll man the notebook stand.'

'Thanks.' She went to get her coat. 'Doing anything fun on Monday?'

'Jazz and I are decorating her room. She's got a day off from the hotel, and last night she mentioned how much she loved the dark blue feature wall in the hotel's dining room.' Fiona smiled. 'I asked if she'd like something like that, and she said she couldn't possibly ask me to change the decor for her, but I told her that of *course* we could. So I think, maybe, she wants to stay for a little while.'

'That's great.' Sophie wondered if Jazz was really serious about staying, but then realized she was just projecting her own insecurities, when Jazz had already proved she was much braver than Sophie had managed to be in thirty-seven years.

'Taking a chance on her was the right thing to do.'

'Giving someone a chance is always the right thing to do,' Sophie said with a smile. 'I'll see you tomorrow.'

'Have a good afternoon.' Fiona waved goodbye, and Sophie collected Clifton, stepped out into the damp, cold air, and began walking in the direction of Mistingham Manor.

The treelined driveway looked sinister and imposing in the gloom, the grey stone manor looming ahead, and Sophie wondered how different it would be when Harry had installed spotlights all the way along here, like he'd told her he was going to. Would it seem more welcoming on winter days like this?

She crunched up the driveway, Clifton scampering at her side, and paused when she was in front of the house. There was no welcoming glow today, the windows like dark, eyeless sockets, and she felt a sudden prickle of foreboding. She walked up to the door and saw that it was open a crack, the Christmas wreath moving gently in the breeze.

'Hello?' she called, and a couple of pigeons flew into the sky from their tree perches nearby. 'Anyone here?'

She was met with silence, so she stepped into the large hall. It was cold since the door had been left open, the fireplace still and dark. 'Harry?' she called. 'May?'

There was no reply, no sound of a door opening deeper within the house.

'Is anyone at home?' she shouted, louder now, her words echoing off the walls.

And then she heard barking, loud and vigorous, from behind her – from outside. She pushed back through the front door, onto the wide step, and surveyed the grounds: the clusters of stark trees, the grass running towards the cliffs, the sea a hazy line on the horizon. She took a couple of steps, and then Darkness appeared through the trees, barking non-stop, followed by Terror. They raced up to her and Clifton, danced in circles around them, and Sophie could tell, from the way they were prancing and pawing at her, that something was wrong.

'What is it?' Her sense of foreboding grew, and when the dogs skittered towards the lawn, looking back at her every couple of seconds, she followed. The grass was squelchy underfoot from the recent rain, and she slid a couple of times as she strode across it. The dogs had reached the far left of the lawn, and Sophie saw, behind a thin copse of young trees, the dull, flat surface of a lake. It was small, clearly man-made, with a low fence around it. She picked up her pace as the dogs wove through the trees.

'Harry?' she called. 'Are you here?'

At first there was nothing, just the rhythmic sound of the far-off waves crunching on the sand, then she heard a distant, shouted, 'Hello?'

Relief sliced through her and she started jogging, following the dogs through the trees, past the crumbling, distorted shapes of what looked like a couple of old statues and out the other side, until she was standing next to the lake, and could take in the scene in front of her.

'Oh my God!' For a moment, she couldn't do anything but stare.

Harry was standing on the steep bank of the lake, one welly-clad foot inches from the water's edge, the other further up, as if he was practising his surfing stance. He was holding tightly onto the fence, his gaze trained on the water. It was baffling, his position too precarious, and Sophie wondered why he didn't just haul himself up the bank, back onto firmer ground. Then she took a couple more steps, and saw what the problem was.

Of course. It was Felix. He was about fifteen feet out into the lake, standing on what looked like a mound of earth – a tiny island protruding from the water, big enough only for him. His jumper – which might once have been blue – was slick with mud, and he had what looked like a thick, slimy rope wrapped around one leg. He was bleating as if his life depended on it which, at this moment, it might well do.

'Sophie,' Harry called, and her name on his lips, a mix of frustration and panic, shook her out of her stupor, and she hurried over to him. The dogs were already there, barking frantically.

'Harry!' She tied Clifton's lead around one of the fence posts. 'Are you OK? Are you stuck?'

This close, she could see how worried he was. There was a sheen of sweat on his forehead, and she didn't know how long he'd been there; how long he'd been standing like that.

'Can you get up the bank?' she asked.

'I could,' he said breathlessly, 'but I can't leave Felix.'

'How did he get out there?' She climbed over the fence so she was on his side of it, holding on to the top rung with both hands.

'He swam,' Harry said. 'He swam out there and got up on that stupid little island, and any moment now he's going to get back down and try to swim back, but he's got weeds wrapped around his leg. If he tries to do that, he's going to get stuck, and then he's going to drown. Honestly. This fucking goat.' His usual tenderness was gone, and Sophie didn't blame him. 'I could wade in, but the bottom is thick with vegetation, and the mud's like quicksand.'

'And it looks cold.'

'Cold is an understatement.' They snagged gazes, and she was the first to look away. His knuckles had gone white where he was gripping the fence.

'We have to do something,' she said, trying to think through her panic.

'I'm going to have to go in.' He loosened his grip.

'No!' She held out her hand. 'No, Harry. You can't.'

Felix bleated plaintively.

'I should just leave you here!' he called, and Felix's bleated reply was so forlorn that, despite the seriousness of the situation, Sophie had the urge to laugh.

'Right.' She took off her coat.

'What are you doing?'

'I'm lighter than you. I've got less chance of getting stuck in the mud.'

'No, Sophie—'

'Besides, you can keep hold of me. I'll wade out and get him, you make sure I don't sink or get tangled up in weeds.'

'This is a really bad idea.'

'You have a better one?' She stepped tentatively along the fence, still holding onto it, until she reached him. 'Is your grip firm?'

'Sort of,' he said, 'but I can't feel my fingers.' He swallowed. 'I really don't want you to do this.'

'If it all goes wrong, use my phone to call for help. It's in my coat pocket.'

Harry's face was pale as she held onto his shoulders, then used him as an anchor while she moved carefully down the bank.

'It's too cold,' he said, when she was nose to nose with him. Their breaths were mingling, but his were harsh, and she didn't know how much longer he could hold on.

'It'll be fine.' She gave him a reassuring smile, then took another step. Icy lake water filled her boot and seeped through her sock. 'Fucking hell!'

'Don't do this,' Harry said. 'Don't—'

'Felix is going to try and swim back. He won't stay out there much longer.'

'I can't hold on much longer,' Harry gritted out.

'We'll be quick, then.' Sophie turned away from the rise and fall of his chest, the stark look in his eyes, his clenched jaw. This, she told herself, was how she could be selfless. She could think about other people: she could help them even when it was uncomfortable for her. Gripping tightly onto Harry's arm, she took another couple of steps into the water, until it was halfway up her shins. She gasped, the soft, oozing mud spreading beneath her feet, threatening to suck her in. Speed, she decided, was a priority.

She waded forward, clutching onto Harry's arm, sucking in short breaths as the freezing water reached her thighs, her hips, her waist.

'Sophie?' Harry asked.

'I'm O-OK,' she stammered. 'Nearly . . .' But she couldn't quite reach Felix and his island. She wasn't going to be able to get him even if she was only anchored to Harry by his fingertips. Their arm spans combined weren't long enough. 'I'm going to have to—'

'No,' Harry said. She could tell every part of him was straining forwards.

'It's not very deep.' She was shuddering now, and she wanted to let go of Harry so he didn't notice.

'The mud, though. The weeds, I—'

'I'm going,' she said defiantly, hoping it wasn't obvious how much her teeth were chattering. Before he could say anything else she let go of him and waded further in, the water sloshing, the mud slurping and sucking around her feet, taking her deeper. Two, three sticky strides, and she was there: next to the island.

'Felix.' She reached out to him. The water was up to her shoulders now, seeping down inside her jumper.

The little goat bleated, and didn't resist when Sophie reached up, pulling at the weed caught around his leg, tugging at it with numb, slippery fingers. It took her a few moments, but then it came away and his leg was free. She lifted him off the island, and Felix burrowed his cold head into her neck, his cries soft and panicked.

Now she had to turn around. She tried to lift her foot, tried to pull it out of the mud, but it was stuck. 'Fuck,' she whispered. Felix was nibbling her hair, and it was comforting, despite the madness of the situation, the intense cold.

'Soph?' Harry called. 'Sophie, are you—?'

'Just a minute!' she shouted. She tried again to get her foot out, but it was fully wedged. 'If I can just get my boot—' She gasped as there was a surge of water behind her, and then arms clamped around her waist and pulled, and she felt her boot come out of the mud with a big *suck*.

Harry dragged them to the edge of the lake, his movements fast and uncoordinated, as if he could beat the weeds and the mud by sheer brute force . . . and maybe he could because a few moments later they had reached the bank, and he was hauling her up with him, trying to find purchase on the slick, steep mud. Sophie tried to help, tried to pull them up with her one free hand, but then Felix wriggled out of her grasp, bounced up to the fence and leapt over it. He turned and watched them, skittering backwards and forwards, bleating.

Sophie flopped against the bank, breathing heavily, her clothes and skin covered in mud. Harry was facing her, his arm still loosely wrapped around her. He was trying to catch his breath, and he looked as muddy and soaked as she was.

'Y-you OK?' he managed, through chattering teeth.

'Fine,' she sighed out, exhaustion and cold making her feel sluggish.

'We need to get you i-into the warm.' From the way he was shuddering, she knew he needed the warmth as much as she did. 'Don't g-go anywhere,' he said forcefully, and she realized he was talking to his goat.

Harry pushed himself onto his knees, crawled the rest of the way up the bank, then turned and held out his hand. Sophie grabbed it gratefully, even though her fingers were numb, and every part of her was rigid with cold. Harry pulled her unceremoniously up the bank, and then, using the fence for support, they both struggled to their feet.

Harry got Sophie's coat and draped it around her shoulders. His gaze was sharp with concern, and in the fading sun – which had decided to show itself at the very last minute – the kiss of amber against his skin made him look otherworldly, like a god who had risen out of the mud, the streaks on his face somehow enhancing his attractiveness.

'I'm going mad,' she murmured.

He frowned. 'You need to get warm.' He pulled her coat tightly around her. It seemed pointless when the clothes beneath were soaked, but she appreciated the gesture.

'How long were you out here, before I arrived?' she asked.

He shook his head, his fingers fumbling with the knot she'd tied in Clifton's lead. 'Fuck,' he muttered, then flexed his fingers and tried again, eventually freeing it. Then he wrapped his arm around Sophie's shoulders and nestled her against him as they strode towards the manor, three dogs and a soaked goat staying close to their heels.

* * *

Harry pushed open the front door, seemingly unconcerned about the unholy mess their muddy, dripping clothes would cause, or the fact that one of their party was a sodden goat.

Sophie hovered on the threshold.

'In,' he said. 'Now. All of you.'

Felix bleated and pranced inside, and Harry dropped to a crouch and took off the ruined jumper.

'Harry . . .' Sophie said.

'I don't care about the mess.' He looked up at her. 'Go to the first floor, the door on the right, next to the window seat. It's my room, and it's got an en suite. Have a bath or shower, whatever you need. Use any of the towels, and I'll find you some clothes. I'll light the fires.'

'Harry, you're as wet as me.'

He shook his head. 'I need to get Felix in the bath – I'll use another bathroom. Go, Soph. I'll come and find you.'

His tone left no room for argument, so she slipped her coat off her shoulders and then, with fizzing, freezing fingers, managed to yank off her boots, gasping at how much mud there was.

'Don't worry about any of this,' Harry said again. 'Please. You need to get warm. This is all my fault, and I—'

'No.' She shook her head. 'You needed to rescue Felix. It's nobody's fault.' With that, she headed for the staircase, deciding that they could argue about it properly when both of them were warm and clean.

The staircase was a mountain, and she had to use the banister to haul herself up. It turned one-hundred-and-eighty degrees, and at the top there was a landing with the large, arched window she had seen from outside. Through it, Sophie had a perfect view of the Mistingham

Manor estate as dusk fell over it, the lawn faded to a soft purple, the cliff path barely visible beyond, and then the sea, a silky pewter slab in the dying light. She could see the lake from here, off to the left behind the trees, a still, innocuous mirror.

Nestled below the window was a wide seat with a cream, cushioned bench that Sophie didn't dare go near. Instead, she turned to the door on her right and pushed it open, stepping into Harry's bedroom.

It was huge, with two windows that looked out on the same, striking view. There was a large bed against the back wall, a dusky blue counterpane over the top. Both bedside tables had stacks of books on them, and were made of the same wood as the wardrobe and chest of drawers. A flat-screen TV was mounted on the wall between the two windows.

It was simple and sparse, as if Harry had done the bare minimum to make it comfortable, and hadn't got round to adding any personal touches. The dark blue carpet was plush beneath her bare, muddy feet, and she winced as she tiptoed across it to the door on the opposite wall.

The bathroom looked like something from a luxury hotel brochure: white subway tiles were interspersed with rows of ocean blue and green, and there was a huge shower with a rainfall shower head to her right, a deep bathtub in front of the glazed glass window on her left.

She peeled off her clothes, which were cold and wet and infused with disgusting lake slime, and put everything in a small, miserable pile. Then she stepped into the shower, fiddling with the dials until the water was hot and powerful, steam rising all around her.

She closed her eyes and let it pummel her limbs, warming them and bringing back sensation. This was Harry's shower, in his *bedroom,* and he was somewhere else in this house, still in his soaked clothes, making sure his goat – who had caused all this trouble – got warm before he did.

She didn't know how long she'd been in there when a knock sounded on the door.

'Sophie?' Harry called. 'I've put some clothes on the bed for you.'

'Are you coming in?' she shouted, unthinking, and wasn't surprised when he didn't answer. She turned off the shower, took a soft, navy towel off the heated towel rail and wrapped it around her, then tiptoed to the door and opened it.

Harry was standing on the other side, in his muddy jeans and a T-shirt that might once have been white. He was holding himself very still, which meant Sophie could see that he was shivering.

'I'll use the other bathroom,' he said hoarsely.

'I bet it's not as nice as this one,' she replied, and watched his gaze drift to her bare shoulders, the hint of cleavage visible above the towel.

'I'll be fine.'

'Get in there.' She pointed behind her. 'Under that massive rainwater shower head with its endless hot water.'

He sighed. 'There are joggers and a jumper on the bed. I messaged May, who's out working, and she said I could lend them to you.'

'Thank you. Now, go. I can hear your teeth chattering.'

Harry glared at her, but there wasn't much heat in it. She stepped aside and he went into the bathroom and shut the door. The clothes were laid out neatly for her, and she pressed her hand into the soft counterpane, found the mattress firm and unyielding. She swallowed.

It all felt so intimate, drying herself in his room, wearing clothes he'd found for her. She reached for the jumper, then realized she wasn't alone. Sitting under the window, in a curious little row, were Darkness, Terror, Clifton, and a very fluffy goat, a butter-wouldn't-melt expression on his adorable little face.

When the bathroom door opened ten minutes later, Sophie was sitting on the edge of Harry's bed. She hadn't known where to go, so she'd stayed put. Of course, now, that meant she was faced with him wearing only a towel. It was wrapped firmly around his waist and left a lot on display.

His torso was firm and slender but not ostentatiously muscled, with a slight brush of brown chest hair fading to a happy trail that ran down his stomach. It was mouth-watering, this glimpse of him: bare chested, his damp hair dark, water rivulets sliding down his neck. It did nothing to quash the feelings that had been slowly growing over the last few weeks.

He stood in the bathroom doorway, his gaze trailing from her, sitting on the edge of the bed, to the animals patiently waiting beneath the window.

'You let a goat in your bedroom,' Sophie said, mostly so she didn't instead say something like, 'Can I lick you?' or, 'We'd both be warmer if we got under your duvet without any clothes on.'

'I didn't *let* him,' Harry said. 'But I didn't want him outside tonight, after his . . . adventure.' He walked towards her, seemingly unconcerned about his lack of clothes, and she

202

stood up, panic – and something else – fluttering in her chest. 'How are you feeling?' he asked. 'Are you warm enough? Have you had enough of me and this madhouse yet?' He reached out and pushed a wave of damp hair off her forehead.

She laughed nervously. 'That is a lot of questions.'

'Sorry,' he said. 'I was worried. You didn't have to go in for Felix: you shouldn't have had to do any of that. It's my fault, and I—'

'Shhhh.' She pressed two fingers against his lips, the action bringing her closer to him; to his warm, bare skin, the heat radiating off him. 'The answer to the last one is no.'

'No?' he murmured against her fingers.

'I haven't had enough of you,' she said. 'I was coming here to tell you that, to find out what was going on. To see if we could maybe . . . work things out.'

'Work things out?' His gaze was fixed to hers, and Sophie felt the opposite of numb. The shower and Harry – mostly Harry – had woken her up, set her alight.

'For the festival,' she clarified.

'For the festival,' he repeated, stepping closer. 'That is important.'

'That's what I thought. We need to be on the same page for that, at the very least.' She was tingling all over. He was so close and warm and tantalizing. *He was right in front of her.*

'Sophie,' he whispered.

'Yes, Harry?' She held her breath, waiting for what came next.

Chapter Nineteen

The silence stretched between them. Sophie wished, with her whole being, that he would close the gap and lean down, find her lips with his. And yet, part of her was clearly intent on sabotaging the moment.

'You stopped talking to me,' she said. 'You didn't want to make bunting together any more.'

She saw his surprise. Then his brows dipped, and she didn't know if it was confusion or irritation.

'It wasn't that I didn't *want* to make it with you,' he said. 'Sophie, I . . .'

'What?' She dropped her fingers. She'd had them on his lips for far too long.

He brought his hands to her shoulders. They were warm through the borrowed jumper, and she sucked in a breath. 'Can I . . .?'

'What?' she said stupidly, and his eyebrow kicked up. 'Oh. I mean, yes. Except you didn't finish the sentence, so I'm not entirely sure what you're asking, but . . .'

'I'd like to kiss you,' he said patiently. 'Is that OK?'

'More than,' she replied, then cursed herself for sounding so prim.

Harry's soft laughter reverberated through her, then he bent his head, tipped her chin up with a finger, and pressed his lips against hers. He was gentle, his movements hesitant, a whisper of a kiss more than a shout, and Sophie felt every part of her get hotter, chasing away the memory of the cold. She ran her hands up his bare stomach, trailed them over his chest, and that was all the encouragement he needed to deepen the kiss, angling his head to get better access to her lips.

It was the best kiss Sophie could remember, Harry's pressure the perfect mix of dogged commitment and restraint, turning her molten and making her desperate for more. She wished she was still wrapped in a towel, then wondered if that was wise – if any of this was wise.

He broke away suddenly, as if he'd read her thoughts, and they stared at each other, chests rising and falling in tandem. 'I should get dressed,' he said roughly. 'Make us some food.'

'You don't have to,' Sophie rushed out. 'I should get back.'

'No, I—'

'You need to deal with your menagerie.' She gestured to the row of animals. 'And I should go home. I need to . . . um, call someone.'

Harry frowned. 'Sophie, I'm sorry. Should I not have—?'

'No, you should have. I loved it.' She winced. 'That was . . . I mean, it's been a strange afternoon. I don't know if we should . . .' She flapped her hand back and forth between them. '. . . Right now, anyway. Maybe if we just—'

'It's OK,' Harry said quietly, rescuing her from her incessant babbling. 'I understand. At least let me drive you home?'

'That would be lovely, thank you. I'll go and find my ruined clothes.'

'They're still in the bathroom. I'll find a bag and bring them down.'

'Right. Great. Thanks.' She backed towards the door. 'I'll leave you to get dressed, then.'

He nodded, and Sophie nodded back, like a marionette. Then she turned and fled the room, choosing the beautiful window seat as her refuge now she was free of lake slime. The darkness had fallen, and the view was nothing but shades of grey and black, apart from the gravel, illuminated by the manor's outside lights. She waited there until Harry opened the door, dressed in jeans and a thick grey jumper, and then all six of them – Felix included – went down to the mud-splattered hall, and Harry found Sophie a pair of May's slipper boots for her to wear on the journey home.

For the next few days, Sophie sold notebooks in the shop, made more at home in the evenings, and went on early morning runs with Clifton that didn't stray too near Mistingham Manor.

She and Harry had parted amicably on Friday evening, Harry giving her a decidedly platonic kiss on the cheek, telling her to eat something hot, get under a blanket, to shroud herself in extra warmth. She'd buried her disappointment deep down, told him to do the same and then, when he'd gone, she'd bought herself fish and chips and settled in for an evening in front of the TV, accompanied by her duvet and her dog. Nobody needed to know that what she'd actually done was replay their kiss over and over in her mind.

Harry had messaged, checking on her, and she'd replied as lightly as possible. They'd fallen back into an easy rhythm, and it was as if he hadn't ever gone cold on her, but also as if she hadn't explored his bare torso with her fingers, as if they hadn't kissed in his bedroom, and she'd thought – was still thinking – about doing so much more.

Jane Eyre somehow kept pace with her, taking her thoughts and mirroring them so perfectly that she almost felt as though it was alive with some of Birdie's magic:

> *Well, he is not a ghost; yet every nerve I have is unstrung: for a moment I am beyond my own mastery. What does it mean? I did not think I should tremble in this way when I saw him, or lose my voice or the power of motion in his presence.*

But, she told herself firmly, they had a festival to put on, and they needed to find some middle ground between staying away from each other and giving into the tension between them if they wanted it to be successful, and the last thing she could do was look to a book for all her answers.

On Thursday, she met May at the hotel, for coffee and cheese scones with crispy tops and warm, fluffy insides, the butter soft and melting. Jazz served them, her red hair adding a shock of colour to the elegant room.

'OK, Sophie?' she asked.

'I'm great thanks. Are you still enjoying it all?'

'Yeah, Mary and Winnie are good as gold. I'm Jazz.' She held her hand out to May, and May shook it.

'Lovely to meet you. I've heard a lot about you.'

Jazz shrugged. 'Not a whole lot to tell.' She smiled and went to serve another table.

'She's made me rethink a few things,' Sophie admitted, when it was just the two of them.

'Has she made you realize that your calling in life is to take over the old sweet shop and become the stationery queen of Mistingham?' May's grin was impish, and Sophie laughed.

'Not exactly. Something she said got me to rethink the festival, see if I could include more of the community, and not just the people who always attend village festivities. A lot of people are lonely, even if they don't admit it.' She spread her butter to the edges of her scone. 'There's old Mr Carsdale, and Birdie – though I know she sells her vegetables and herbal concoctions to a lot of the locals. I'm sure Dexter gets lonely, too, bringing up Lucy on his own, without his wife to share decisions, those memorable moments.'

'There's Harry,' May added, 'knocking about at the manor.'

The mention of his name, when he'd been so much in her thoughts, gave her a jolt. She wondered how much May knew about what had happened the week before. 'Harry has you,' she said, which was a lot easier to admit now she knew their relationship was platonic.

May shrugged. 'I'm there, but I work for a technical helpline quite a bit, then go out on calls. I meet friends in Norwich – I'm meeting you. Until he started working with you on the festival, Harry kept to himself, and he's still doing that too much for my liking: roaming about the estate, getting into scrapes.'

Sophie could feel May's gaze on her as she broke her scone into pieces. 'I was thinking about starting a book club.' She popped a piece in her mouth, the cheese rich and delicious. 'I've been given this book, by something called The Secret Bookshop,' she went on when she'd finished. 'I thought I'd been singled out, but Winnie's had one too, and it made me think about The Book Ends; how popular it was. Do you think people here would be up for a book club?'

May smiled. 'I think it's a lovely idea. I'm intrigued by these book gifts, though: they sound really special. You'd run the club as part of the festival?'

'To start with,' Sophie said. 'We're having events in the hall as well as outside, so I thought we could launch it there, and then – depending how much of a success it is – see about keeping it going.'

'Beyond Christmas?' May lifted her mug to her lips.

Sophie replayed her kiss with Harry for the thousandth time. The air had shimmered with possibility, and she thought he'd wanted more too, even as they'd both held back. She thought of Jazz, telling her that being in Mistingham, having that sense of security, had allowed her to be more generous. Could she change her plans? Let the shallow roots she'd put down here deepen?

'Maybe,' she said carefully. 'I mean, if people were into it.'

'I love it,' May said. 'You'd be at the helm, I'm guessing?'

'I'm up for giving it a go. I haven't got involved in much community stuff before now.'

'Why not?' May sounded genuinely curious.

Sophie spread more butter on her scone. 'I've never stayed

anywhere long enough to be asked, and I haven't taken the initiative myself. Sometimes it's easier to leave before things get too tangled.'

'I can see that,' May said. 'I stayed too long in America, tried to make my situation work when it was beyond saving. But a lot of the time, sticking around is worth the complications. When it's no longer worth the effort, *that's* when you extract yourself, not before you've given it a chance.'

'I guess.'

'Even if,' May went on, 'some of those complications put you in unfathomable situations, like trying to rescue goats from freezing lakes.'

Sophie groaned. 'He told you about that?'

'He phoned me to ask if he could lend you my clothes, and that needed an explanation if nothing else. Then, when I got home, he was polishing the hallway to within an inch of its life, and Felix looked as if he'd had a blow dry.' She shook her head. 'That goat is going to be the death of him.'

'Don't say that,' Sophie urged, but she was grinning. 'I can't remember ever being that cold before.'

'No, Harry said it wasn't pleasant, which is funny, because after it happened he was in a really good mood. Cheerier than I've seen him for a while.'

Heat flooded Sophie's cheeks. 'He must have been relieved that Felix was OK.'

'Yes, that must have been it.' May sounded entirely unconvinced. 'He's a great guy, underneath that grizzled outer layer.'

'I know that,' Sophie said. 'It takes a while for him to warm up, but once he has, once he knows he can trust you . . . he's one of the kindest people I've met.' Now she knew her cheeks were on fire, but she couldn't help it: the memory of his lips on hers was playing on an almost constant loop in her head.

When she glanced up, May was giving her a knowing smile, as if she could tell exactly what Sophie was thinking about. 'What book are you going to start with, for the book group?'

Sophie was grateful for the change of subject. 'I'm not sure,' she said slowly, 'but I was thinking about a classic. Something with a lot of atmosphere, that celebrates the beauty of the countryside, that's romantic and uplifting – in the end, anyway.' She pulled off another piece of scone, put it in her mouth, chewed and swallowed. 'I was thinking about maybe doing *Jane Eyre*.'

Chapter Twenty

On Saturday, Annie phoned Sophie to tell her the festive games they'd hired had arrived, and were in the storeroom at Penny For Them. Sophie arranged to meet Harry there later that afternoon, the fact that it would be the first time she'd seen him since the night they'd rescued Felix uppermost in her mind.

She waited outside the arcade, enjoying the weak winter sun on her face, the hint of warmth after a series of cold, damp days, the soft mist that hung close to the water. Take a photo and it would look like a spring morning, rather than a Saturday at the beginning of December.

She turned away from the sea and saw Harry approaching from the centre of town. He had the collar of his dark jacket turned up, his features set in their usual impassive mask. Had he been thinking about their kiss as much as she had?

'Hello,' he said, when he reached her. 'OK?'

'Good thanks, you?'

'Nothing untoward has happened since we spoke on the

phone.' He frowned, and she wondered if he'd realized how uptight he'd sounded.

'Great.' She grinned. 'Shall we go in? Annie's probably waiting.'

Annie greeted them warmly and led them to the back of the arcade, through a set of double doors and into a space with only a couple of small, high windows, and a distinctly musty smell.

She held her arms out wide, gesturing to the three games that took up most of the space. 'What do you think?'

'Rudolph Hoopla,' Harry said, approaching the first one. Three comedic-looking stuffed reindeer heads, with antlers and large red noses, stuck out of the back panel, and there were stacks of coloured rings on a counter at the front. 'You get different points for the different parts?'

'More for the noses, because they're not as easy to hook onto,' Annie explained. 'And it has a kooky soundtrack and flashing lights, if you've got an external power source.'

'We have,' Sophie confirmed.

'Great! Get a load of this.' She switched it on, and the game came to life with flashing, multicoloured lights racing around the top, and a dance remix of 'Rudolph the Red-Nosed Reindeer'.

'That is hideous.' Harry had to shout to be heard.

'The kids will love it!' Annie grinned.

'Oh my God,' Sophie said. 'The reindeer *move*?' The heads were dipping down and up, moving from side to side.

'That's for added difficulty,' Annie told her. 'You can turn it on or off.'

'I say on.' Harry folded his arms, wincing as the music changed key.

'Harry Anderly,' Sophie said, mock-sternly, 'do you want to make all the Mistingham children cry? How will you ever shake off the Dark Demon Lord of Mistingham title if you behave like this?'

He shot her an irritated glance.

'The dark demon *what?*' Annie said.

'Nothing,' Harry replied quickly. 'What's next?'

Annie switched off the disco reindeer and the room fell into blessed quiet. She showed them the Christmas Tree Carnival Toss, which was a cutout wooden Christmas tree, at least seven feet tall, painted beautifully in dark green with old-fashioned decorations. It had holes cut in it, into which players had to try and throw sponge balls, and no lights or blaring sounds. 'Thank God,' Harry said emphatically.

'This is the last one.' Annie gestured to a large plastic pond, currently without water, but full of little plastic figures all dressed as festive characters – elves and Santas, robins and snowmen. The surround was painted in red, green and gold glitter paint.

'It's Hook the Duck,' Harry said incredulously.

Sophie felt laughter bubble up inside her.

'Hook the *Christmas* Duck,' Annie corrected.

'Right,' he said. 'That's an entirely different kettle of fish, then.'

'Don't you mean an entirely different pond of mallards?' Sophie asked.

The look he gave her could have frozen the surface of the sea.

They agreed on a price with Annie for the hire of all three games, and the task of getting them moved to the green, then stepped into the winter sunshine.

'What's next?' Harry asked.

'I need to go to Vea's and pick up the supplies I ordered for oak-tree decorating.' A cloud slipped in front of the sun, and Sophie tucked her chin into her collar.

'Ah yes, the part where we don't just decorate the "at risk" tree with fancy lights, we allow the villagers to hang decorations on it.'

Sophie stopped walking. 'You *loved* this idea when we talked about it: getting everyone to make a decoration in the village hall in the week leading up to the festival, writing a Christmas wish or something they're grateful for on it, then putting it on the tree. We'll have someone there – you or Dexter or Ermin – to do the actual hanging, because children especially won't be able to reach, but . . .' She huffed out a breath. 'Why have you reverted back to Lord Grump?'

'Reverted?' he echoed.

'Yes,' she said. '*Reverted*. You were pretty blunt when we first met, then we started working together and I saw a whole other side to you. *Then* you effectively ghosted me, hoarding all the bunting at the manor, and then we . . . rescued Felix from the lake.' She cleared her throat. 'Today, you're back to how we were at the beginning of this whole thing. Are you really going to backtrack on all our plans?'

He stared at her, and she could sense he was working out how to respond to her frankness. 'Soph.' He sounded cautious. 'The truth is—'

'Sophie! Harry!' She jumped, her attention dragged away when she saw who was standing outside the village hall, two baguettes under his arms and a Santa hat on his head.

'Dexter,' she said with a laugh. 'I'm tempted to ask what you're doing, but I'm not sure I want to know the answer.'

He grinned. 'I'm making French bread pizzas for Amber's birthday party – one of Lucy's best friends. It's fancy dress, and Lucy said I had to have an outfit even though I'm hired help, but my wardrobe is a bit on the sparse side.'

Sophie winced. 'Not sure she's going to be impressed with just a Santa hat.'

'She can't expect me to make delicious food *and* be a source of ridicule.' Dexter shrugged. 'I'm hoping her and her friends' stomachs will win out on this occasion. How are you, Harry?'

'Great thanks,' Harry said, sounding anything but. 'We're off to Vea's, to immerse ourselves in Wasabi tape, or whatever it is.'

Sophie nudged him in the ribs. 'It's *Washi* tape, and he loves it really,' she told Dexter. 'He's just practising being the Christmas Grinch for the Oak Fest.'

Dexter laughed. 'Looks like you've got it nailed.'

'Doesn't it?' Sophie said, keeping the smile on her face.

Once Dexter had waved a baguette in goodbye and was out of sight, Harry put his lips close to Sophie's ear and murmured, 'I'm going to be Santa at the festival, not the Grinch.'

'Well, then.' She ignored the delicious shiver that his breath on her ear had set free, and turned her head towards his, so their lips were inches apart. 'You'd better buck your ideas up, or you're going to ruin Father Christmas for everyone, for ever.'

His eyes sparked with more than just anger, but before he could say or do anything else, Sophie took a step back.

She could feel him glowering beside her all the way to Vea's craft shop.

Vea had outdone herself, ordering in a range of felts, leathers and cardboard, shimmering threads and sequins, tiny pearls and beads, glitter snowflakes, gossamer fabrics and watery silks. There were also several rolls of festive Washi tape, which Sophie took pleasure in pointing out to Harry.

He stayed quiet while Vea helped Sophie pack everything up, and while she selected the tools she would need – needles and glues, staplers and leather punches. There were indelible, fine-tipped markers for the messages she wanted everyone to write, glitter pens for festive cheer, cinnamon sticks and dried orange for anyone who wanted to add the scents of the season to their decorations.

'This is perfect, Vea, thank you.'

'How did the bunting go?'

'It's done,' Harry said. 'I'll bring the sewing machine back in the next couple of days.'

Vea waved him away. 'You've got it until January. Take it to the hall, if you like – as long as there's someone super-vising the children.'

'Thank you Vea,' Sophie said, hefting up her bags, 'for everything.'

Once they were outside, Sophie turned towards home. She had been looking forward to seeing Harry again, antic-ipation thrumming through her at how it might be between them after their kiss. But instead of it bringing them closer, he'd decided to shut off from her altogether.

'I'd better take these back to the flat,' she said.

Harry stopped, motionless, in front of Vea's window

217

display. There were glittering angels and woolly felt sheep, a wicker manger holding a felt baby Jesus. 'That's it?' he asked.

'I don't know what else to say.' She shrugged, her paper bags crackling with the movement. 'You're clearly not up for this right now, and I'm done trying to get blood out of a stone.'

He closed his eyes. 'Sophie.'

'What?' She stood there, waiting for his answer, and when none was forthcoming she turned away. 'I'm going home.'

'Wait!' He put his hand on her shoulder. 'I'm sorry.'

'What for?' She turned to face him, noticing how his eyes seemed greener in the afternoon light, his skin faintly freckled. He looked unfairly healthy for December, even though there were smudges under his eyes.

'For being an arsehole,' he said. 'I wasn't sure how you felt, after last weekend – if you thought it was a mistake, because of . . . your plans. I didn't know what to do.'

She laughed lightly, feeling a twinge of guilt, of regret, that he'd been put off because she was leaving. But of *course* he had: it was self-preservation, something she knew far too much about. 'So . . . ask me?'

He gave her a rueful smile. 'That's a bit easy, don't you think?' He ran a hand through his hair, leaving some of it sticking up. 'I should have done that, I'm sorry. I don't know what's got into me.'

Sophie could sympathize. She'd felt unlike herself, giddier, since their kiss. She was contemplating changing her future because of him. 'I didn't think it was a mistake,' she said. 'Kissing you was . . .' She shook her head. 'I've been looking forward to seeing you again.'

'Right.' Harry swallowed. 'Good. Me too.'

Relief flooded, warm and vital, through her body. 'Great. So . . . what do you want to do? Do you need to get home?'

He shook his head. 'I think we should . . . go and play Whack-A-Crab.'

'What?' Sophie laughed.

'That is *exactly* what we should do.' His eyes brightened, and the dour, uptight Harry slipped away, replaced by the version she'd started to get used to. 'You've got a higher score than me, and I can't let it stand.'

'OK,' she said.

'Then we should go and get fish and chips; have a proper night out at the seaside.'

'In December?'

'Mistingham is the perfect seaside village. Have you really taken full advantage of it while you've been here?'

'In the summer, I—'

'But it's great all year round. So often, people don't make the most of living somewhere like this, with the sea and the countryside on their doorstep, old-fashioned arcades, fish and chips a stone's throw away—'

'Right below their flat,' Sophie cut in.

'Exactly,' Harry said with a smile. 'Let's indulge ourselves. A Batter Days tea and a Whack-A-Crab face-off. Do you really not want to do this with me?'

'You've gone from grumpy to insane in five minutes,' Sophie said, stalling for time. But the truth was, she was never going to say no. She thought of how Jane Eyre owned her feelings about Rochester: how bold she was in the face of his teasing, his dominance. She always gave as good as she got.

219

'I'm seizing the moment,' Harry said. 'Not waiting for things to be perfect, but making the most of right now. Someone taught me that recently.'

Sophie rolled her eyes, but she was grinning. 'Let me drop these bags off at the flat, then we can go.'

'Deal,' he said.

'Deal,' she echoed, and as the sun sizzled down to the horizon, casting Harry in a golden hue that was far too magical to be real, they held each other's gaze for a beat too long.

Chapter Twenty-One

As they headed in the direction of Sophie's flat, Harry told her the background to the empty sweet shop. 'Delores, who ran it for twenty-five years, ended up running off to Italy with a man thirty years younger than her. I was in London when she absconded, but it was a big enough scandal that I heard about it through Dad's carer, and his care home was five miles outside Mistingham.'

'I wish I'd met Delores,' Sophie said. 'She sounds like a proper character. Fiona said she was thin as a rake – if I worked in a sweet shop, I'd eat at least a pound of sugar a day.'

'She probably got sick of it. I wish she'd got sick of the bloody e's in the name, too.'

'If you were Simon, would you get sick of fish and chips?'

Harry was silent for a moment, then said, 'I don't think that's possible.'

They carried the bags of craft materials up to Sophie's flat, the tension sparking between them once they were inside, just metres from her bedroom. She took a step towards him, saw the moment his breath stalled, but then he grabbed her hand and led her down the stairs, to where Batter Days was waiting.

'Jason told me you were out and about,' Simon said, when they walked into the warm shop, the air thick with the scent of fried chips and the sharp tang of vinegar.

'You make it sound like I've been in a coma,' Harry said with a smile.

Simon laughed nervously. 'I just meant that it's great to see you.'

'I knew what you meant,' Harry grinned. 'It's good to see you too. I'm giving Sophie the full Mistingham experience, and we're starting with your fish and chips.'

Simon looked mystified. 'Haven't you been here nearly a year, Sophie?'

'I have,' she said, smiling.

'And you live right above here.' He pointed to the ceiling.

'Everyone needs an evening at the seaside now and then.' Harry rested his forearms on the glass counter.

'A cold, misty evening in December?' Simon shovelled chips into cardboard trays, selected crispy pieces of cod and placed them on top.

'Mistingham's great all year round,' Harry said mildly. 'You know that, Simon.'

'Of course! I just—'

'Ignore him.' Sophie squeezed Harry's arm. 'He's teasing you, which I know is an unlikely prospect, but—'

'Hey,' Harry said with a laugh. 'Sorry, Simon – she's right. Ignore me.'

'Oh no, that's fine,' Simon said. 'Do you want salt? Vinegar?'

They both answered in the affirmative.

'Shall we eat these in my flat?' Sophie asked, once Harry had paid, they'd thanked a bewildered Simon and were back outside.

'That's not what we'd do if we were visiting Mistingham for a perfect evening out.'

'Where, then? I don't think the village hall is open.'

'The sea wall,' Harry said.

'It'll be freezing!'

'We'll huddle together for warmth.' He was undeterred, and Sophie could do nothing but follow him.

She hadn't seen anything more befitting a ghost story than Mistingham seafront shrouded in fog. The waves beat their steady rhythm against the sand, and through the dense swirls she could see the white foam of the breakers, luminous against the impenetrable black water. Along the promenade, the streetlights were quaintly old-fashioned, like something out of a Dickens novel.

'Here.' Harry patted the concrete wall, then winced.

'Is it as cold as it looks?'

'You can sit on my coat.' He started to take it off, and Sophie put a hand on his shoulder.

'We'll soon warm up.' She sat down, and the cold seeped instantly through her jeans. Harry sat next to her, and she felt, rather than heard, him sigh.

'I have a sneaking suspicion that this was a stupid idea.'

'Not true.' Sophie unwrapped the parcels from Batter Days and handed him one, along with a wooden fork. 'Fish and chips is never a bad idea.' She bit into the first chip, and it was delicious. A slight crunch on the outside, fluffy in the middle, the sharpness of the vinegar that went so well with the salt-fresh air, the heat of the parcel on her knees contrasting with the cold of their chosen pew. 'This is . . . actually perfect.' She laughed.

'It is?'

'It's delicious,' Sophie said. 'And I look out of my window at the nothingness of the sea when it's dark, but it's so different being right next to it.'

'From my bedroom windows, I can see lights on the horizon – fishing trawlers or container ships – and I wonder what it would be like to be out there, in the middle of somewhere so vast and unknowable, so dark. How aren't they terrified?'

'I have no idea,' Sophie said. 'Do you sit on your window seat a lot?'

'The one at the top of the stairs?'

She nodded.

'I only put that in a few weeks ago. The window needed a clean, and it's got such a good view. It was crying out for a bench.'

'What will you do with it?'

'What, the window seat?'

Sophie tore a chunk off her fish and bit into it, delighting in the crunchy batter. 'The manor,' she said once she'd finished chewing. 'When you've fixed it all, made it beautiful again. Are you just going to live in it, you and May and the dogs?'

Harry's laugh sounded tired. 'May can stay as long as she likes, and I'm dedicated now to making it shine again. Too many old buildings fall into ruin, or get turned into fancy hotels with the soul stripped out of them. Dad loved the manor – Mum too, when she was alive – and I'm glad I was able to save it. But I know we're fuelling the rumours: May's a good friend, but everyone thinks it's a strange set-up.'

'So . . . what? You'd like a family?'

Harry didn't say anything for such a long time, Sophie thought she'd gone too far. 'I'd love a family,' he said eventually. 'I'm forty-two now, and I don't necessarily want children. But . . . love.' He shook his head. 'I don't know, Soph.' Her name was a sigh, and she felt a sharp twinge in her gut, remembering how May had counted Harry among the lonely people in the village.

'Did you ever have someone, in London?' she asked.

'I had several someones.' He gave her a small smile. 'There was one, Maya, who I thought, at the time, I would be with for ever, but things didn't work out. What about you?'

'I was with someone – Trent – for two years when I lived in Bristol.'

'Things didn't work out for you, either?'

'They didn't.' Sophie speared another chip. 'But . . .'

'What happened?' Harry asked gently.

She chewed slowly, buying herself time. 'I couldn't commit to him as much as he wanted me to,' she admitted. 'Two years into our relationship, I was still reluctant to move in with him. I had a toothbrush at his, a few clothes, but that was it. I needed my own space.'

'That's understandable, though.' Harry's voice was soft, hesitant, and Sophie wondered if he really believed that.

'He also said my job was . . . weak. Making and selling notebooks wasn't future-proof, wasn't *a solid enough career*. And I know on some level he was right, because until Mistingham and Fiona's concession stand, I've always had to supplement it with other things.'

Harry frowned. 'But you love it: you've made it work, and what's wrong with supplementing your passion so you can keep doing it? It's much better that way, than giving your whole self up to something soulless and abandoning what you care about.'

'I hadn't thought of it like that.' Sophie's whole body warmed as she realized how much he understood her. 'And I *do* want to work harder on building a brand, but . . .' She stopped, because the struggles she'd had were all of her own making: it was hard to build something without stable foundations, and she was the one who kept destroying them. 'Anyway.' She forced a laugh. 'Isn't this supposed to be our perfect night at the seaside? Why are we talking about this stuff?'

'You're right,' Harry said. 'Nearly finished?'

'Nearly.' The fish and chips had gone down easily.

'Excellent. Want to paddle?' He stood up and gestured to the dark sea.

'You're not serious.'

Harry didn't reply, just held out his hand.

It was, without a doubt, a stupid idea, but it was also Harry. And, Sophie realized, as she grabbed the empty wrappers and pushed them into a bin along the wall before running back to join him, she really wanted to be a little bit stupid with Harry.

'Holy shitting shit, that's freezing!' Five minutes later, Harry was in the shallows, his boots off and his jeans rolled up, acting like he was walking on coals. The tide was coming in, and they had picked a section of the beach with solid steps down to the sand, a streetlight providing a weak glimmer of light that, despite the fog, just about reached them. Sophie had made Harry promise not to go in deeper than calf-height, but seeing his reaction she didn't think she needed to worry about them drowning.

'Get out then,' she said with a laugh.

'I can't get out until you've come in.'

Sophie pulled off her boot, hovering on one foot so she didn't put her sock on the damp sand, then pulled that off too. Even the sand was cold, and she grimaced. 'We could just *say* we've done it.'

'Nope.' Harry was adamant. 'Come here.' He held out his hands again, and Sophie caught her breath. He was so commanding, standing in the shadows, with the black gulf of the sea behind him. He was Poseidon luring her into the waves, and the problem was, she would go gladly.

She took her other boot off, pushed the sock inside it then tiptoed towards him, her eyes on the lapping water.

'Here, Soph.' Harry took her hands. His skin was warm and, a second later, her feet were ice. She sucked in a breath at the contrast. 'OK?' he asked.

Sophie met his gaze. 'It's not as bad as your stupid lake,' she said.

Harry laughed, the sound loud on the empty beach, then he pulled her against him, wrapping his arms around her, letting her nestle against his chest. She could feel her feet turning blue, perhaps preparing to drop off, but as for the rest of her – well, she didn't really want to move at all.

'What's your score again?'

The paddling hadn't lasted long, despite Sophie's reluctance to leave Harry's arms, and they had soon pulled their socks back onto damp feet, relaced their boots and left the dark beach behind.

Now they were back in Penny For Them, Sophie relishing the warmth even though the doors remained open, and they were standing next to Whack-A-Crab, Harry hefting the foam hammer like he was about to knock in several hundred fence posts.

'Thirty-six,' she said. 'You think you can beat it, even though all our extremities have been numbed by the North Sea?'

He laughed. 'It's my toes that I can't feel, not my fingers. Ready?'

'Oh, I am *so* ready.' Sophie folded her arms as Harry put a pound coin in the slot and pressed the Start button. A cartoon soundtrack burst into life and, a moment later, one of the beady-eyed crabs popped its plastic head out of its hole, and Harry brought the hammer down with a *whack*. Sophie grinned and settled in to watch.

He was, upsettingly, really good, and nothing like the furious attack dog she'd expected. He was calm and methodical, wielding the toy hammer with precision rather than force. She was tempted to distract him, considered sliding her hand into the back pocket of his jeans, but she wanted a fair fight. The music soon came to an end, and his score flashed up on the display: 33.

'You beat your top score,' Sophie said, as he tipped his head back and groaned.

'I haven't beaten *you*, though. Three behind, still.' He held out the hammer. 'Go on. See if you can do even more damage.'

'I'm a little rusty,' she said, wrapping her fingers around the handle.

'Starting with the excuses already.' His voice was silky, and when she met his gaze, her stomach flipped.

'Don't distract me.'

'I wouldn't dream of it.' He made a big show of stepping back.

But it was too late. As he put in another coin and the music started up again, all she could think about was his low voice and how safe she'd felt tucked up against him on the beach; the moment she'd realized, as he had stood in front of her, chest bared in his bedroom, that he was going to kiss her; the taste of his lips against hers, and how she'd felt the liquid heat of it everywhere. The crabs popped up and she went for them, often a fraction too late, sometimes swinging wide so she didn't get that satisfying squeak as she hit one squarely on the head.

All too soon the music came to an end, and her paltry score flashed up: 18.

'What happened?' Harry sounded mystified rather than smug.

Sophie let the hammer drop. 'You distracted me.'

'I didn't.' He held his hands up.

'You're always distracting me,' she admitted. 'You're a very distracting person, Harry Anderly.'

'Hey.' He grabbed her hand and pulled her towards him, so they were only inches apart. 'You're not exactly forgettable, yourself.' Then he was kissing her, his fingers lightly grazing her jawline, setting off a tingle that sparked through her entire body. He tasted of vinegar, his skin smelled like the dark, unknowable sea, and in this garish place with its flashing lights and victory noises, Sophie lost herself in him.

She trailed her fingers through his hair, feeling how soft the strands were. He anchored her to him with a hand against her lower back, and Sophie almost moaned at the feel of their hips pressed together, how he managed to be firm and gentle all at once. A sound penetrated through her fog of desire, the door banging hard against the wall and then flapping closed, and Harry broke away and looked towards it.

'The wind's getting up.'

'Maybe it's time to call it a night.'

'I'll walk you back to yours.' He took her hand and led her to the exit.

'No,' Sophie said. 'I don't want you walking back to the manor on your own, in the dark.'

'I'm a forty-two-year-old man.'

'Great. What's that got to do with anything?'

'Sophie.' He laughed. 'You really want to come back?'

'I want to see you home safely. And I'm not . . . expecting anything.'

'But you're not walking back to your flat once we've reached the manor.'

Outside, the fog had thickened and the temperature had dropped, and the thought of walking *anywhere* wasn't that appealing. But Clifton was having a sleepover with Poppet and Jazz, and the thought of being alone in her silent, empty flat after such a fun evening made her spirits sink.

'You must have a spare room I can use,' she said. 'Even if it's not been refurbished yet.'

Harry swallowed. 'I do. Right, come on then.' They headed up Perpendicular Street, her arm laced tightly through his.

'Tell me something about Mistingham,' she said. 'Something I wouldn't know already.'

'That's a vague request.'

'You must have hundreds of stories like the one about Delores.'

'OK.' He was quiet as they walked through the village, their footsteps echoing. There weren't that many people out, the weather sending everyone scurrying indoors, and only occasional sets of headlights passed them, picking out whorls of fog. They left the built-up area behind, turning onto the country road that would take them to the long, tree-lined driveway of Mistingham Manor, and Harry took out his phone and put the torch on. He'd obviously forgotten his Maglite, or perhaps he hadn't expected to be out this late.

'When Delores opened the sweet shop,' he said eventually, 'there was an old man here – Mr Trayton, he died about a decade ago – who started a petition to get her to drop the e's at the ends of the words.'

'What?' Sophie laughed. 'No!'

'I'm completely serious. He wanted it to be *the Old Sweet Shop*, no additional e's. He was adamant.'

'But he didn't get his way?'

'Of course not. Everyone liked how country cottage the name was, and Delores would never have backed down. Even if they'd come back 100 per cent in agreement with Mr Trayton, she wouldn't have changed it.'

'You don't love the e's, do you?'

'I do not,' Harry confirmed, as they turned onto his winding driveway. 'But even though we owned the building, it was Delores's shop. People can be as reckless with their vowels as they want.'

'If I was staying, I'd take over the old sweet shop and call it Ye Olde Notebooke Emporiume. E's on the end of everything – maybe two on each word.'

'*If* you were staying. You're definitely leaving, then?'

Sophie swallowed. She didn't know any more. Tonight – so many things, recently – had made her question what she was doing. She wished she hadn't brought it up, made a dent in this fun, carefree evening.

Harry stopped walking, and Sophie thought he was going to turn them around, make her go home. Instead, he slipped his phone into his pocket, the torch shining out a blue-tinged light through the fabric, and took both her hands. 'For what it's worth,' he said quietly, 'I would be fully behind Ye Olde Notebooke Emporiume. You could have as many e's as you wanted, and I wouldn't grumble.'

She smiled. 'You're only saying that because I've told you I'm leaving.'

'I would say exactly the same thing if you told me you were staying. I wish you *would* stay – you must know that, Soph.'

This time when he kissed her, it was gentler, his lips caressing hers, his fingers sliding through her wind-tangled hair. They didn't linger for long, instead hurrying the rest of the way to Mistingham Manor, where the lights were glowing and the Christmas wreath was twinkling, and the fire was crackling in the hearth in the large hall, with two dogs and a goat lying contentedly in front of it.

May must have heard them come in, because she appeared in the doorway, dressed in black joggers and a long red jumper, her dark hair in a messy bun.

'Sophie!' she said. 'It's so lovely to see you. How did the game testing go?'

'It was great,' she said, 'but not as much fun as paddling.'

'You went *paddling?*' May sounded horrified. 'Are you mad?'

232

'Very likely,' Harry admitted. 'We survived though. Fancy a nightcap?'

'Perfect.' May smiled. 'If you're sure it's OK for me to—'

'We'd love you to,' Sophie said, at the same time as Harry said, 'Of course.'

The dogs and Felix followed them into Harry's study, and Sophie wondered if his goat was a permanent indoor resident now.

There was a sideboard over by the chess set, and Harry poured brandy into three glasses. May hurried to the far corner of the room, where the bookshelves reached up to the ceiling, and Sophie heard a loud click. The light in the room softened, as if she'd turned off a lamp hidden amongst the shelves.

'Have the bookshelves got inbuilt lighting?' she asked, as May pulled Harry's desk chair over to join the armchairs by the fire.

'What? Oh no,' May said with a laugh. 'Nothing that fancy. I borrowed one of Harry's books – *The Last Remains* by Elly Griffiths – and wanted to make sure I'd put it back.'

'Not everyone's happy lending out their books so freely,' Sophie said. She got the sense that May looked after Harry in a lot of small, almost invisible ways. She didn't want to feel envious, because Harry had assured her they were just friends, but somehow she couldn't quite get rid of that little green goblin.

'Here we go.' Harry handed out three generous glasses of brandy, then dropped into one of the chairs.

'Thank you.' Sophie stretched her leg out and nudged Felix's fluffy bum. The goat bleated, but stayed focused on the flames. 'That's a strange-looking dog,' she said.

'Oh, he's completely given up,' May said with a grin. 'Harry's not the Dark Demon Lord of Mistingham – Felix is.'

'It's cold outside,' Harry grumbled. 'He doesn't understand why he's not treated the same as Darkness and Terror, so I decided he didn't have to be. He comes outside with us, does his business when they do.'

'I have never met anyone so defensively besotted about a pet goat.'

'He'll be taking Felix to bed with him next,' May said.

'That is *not* the plan.' Harry's gaze was fixed on the fire, and Sophie shivered. It was on the tip of her tongue to ask him what, exactly, the plan was. 'Anyway,' he went on, 'why are you two ganging up on me?'

'Because it's fun,' May said.

'It's like poking a bear who's getting softer by the minute,' Sophie added with a grin.

'Getting softer?' Harry sounded outraged. 'Not a chance.'

Sophie pointed at Felix and raised her eyebrow.

Harry lifted his glass to his mouth, but she saw him smile behind it, and her stomach flipped.

'Right.' May drained her drink. 'I'm pooped after a long shift of remote technical support, telling people to turn their devices off and then on again, so I'm heading to bed. Sophie, it was great to see you.'

'You too.'

'Night both.' She took her empty glass and stepped into the hall, closing the door quietly behind her.

Sophie could feel her cheeks warming, drowsiness creeping over her after the cold night air, the shock of the icy water earlier followed by the ferocious warmth of the fire.

'I should show you to your room,' Harry said quietly.

'What?' She sat up straighter. 'No, I'm fine. I . . .' She noticed how everything about him was softer in the fireside glow; his skin and hair tinged with gold, his posture in the armchair relaxed. The only thing that was sharp was his gaze, his intense focus leaving her no room to hide.

'We should probably go to bed,' he said, his voice impossibly lower.

'We should.' Sophie swallowed.

'The best spare room is opposite mine.' He finished his drink and stood up, not taking his eyes off her. 'It's got an en suite, and there should be fresh towels.'

'OK.' Sophie got to her feet, and they stood, looking at each other while the fire crackled and the silence grew between them.

Then Harry took their glasses and put them on the table. He whistled, and the two dogs and Felix raised their heads. 'I'll take them outside before I go up, then I'll come and check you've got everything you need.'

'Great,' Sophie said. 'Thank you.'

He led the way to the door, his pets at Sophie's feet. In the hall, he pulled on his coat, and she climbed the stairs, able to enjoy the soft carpet now that she wasn't covered in mud.

When she got to the landing, she hesitated. He'd told her where her room was, but was that really what he wanted? She'd suggested the spare room and Harry, being considerate, hadn't questioned it. She went to the beautiful window seat under the arched window and sank onto the soft cushion, the moonlight fractured through the tree branches outside, her heart in her throat while she waited.

Ten minutes later she heard the front door click open,

the sound of clawed feet and hooves tapping on the tiles, Harry's low murmur as he said goodnight to his animals.

Sophie's pulse pounded as she listened to the soft tread of his footsteps, and she wondered if it was too late to escape into the spare room. But . . . no. Harry was here, she was here, and—

'Sophie?' he said, reaching the top of the stairs. 'Is everything OK?'

'Yes, of course. I'm . . . I'm fine.'

'Is there something wrong with the room?'

She stood up. 'There is, actually. One big thing.'

'Oh?' She must have let something slip into her voice, because his concern dissolved, and when he stepped closer, an eyebrow raised, it was pure seduction. 'What might that be?'

She gave him a whisper of a smile. 'It doesn't have you in it.'

He bent his head towards hers. 'I was thinking the same thing about my room,' he murmured. 'That it didn't have you in it. Maybe we can change that.'

'We could certainly try,' she said, and closed the gap.

Sophie let herself sink into the kiss, let him wrap her up in his arms until they were pressed together, tasting and touching each other, Harry's skin still cold from outside. Pulling apart felt impossible, but Harry managed it, only enough to open his bedroom door and lead her inside. He closed it and pressed her up against the wood, continuing their kiss.

He trailed his lips along her jaw and down her throat, and Sophie gasped, the heat at her core unbearable. She slid her leg up, anchoring it around his hip, and he groaned into her mouth.

'Sophie,' he murmured. 'God.'

He leaned back enough to pull her jumper over her head, and she waited for the nerves to overwhelm her, for her thoughts to put a stop to it. But instead they urged her onwards, in tandem with her body, tingling and scorching and desperate. She had been thinking about him, wanting him, for so long, and all she cared about was getting closer.

She slid her hands to the brass button at the waistband of his jeans, and Harry walked backwards, leading her over to the bed. They undressed each other, Sophie's breath catching when his fingertips grazed the soft skin of her stomach, trailed a silky path up her back.

Then his lips were on hers again, and she slid her hands around his waist, pressing her palms against the warm skin of his back, then lower, down inside the waistband of his boxers. She felt herself turn to liquid, warm and pliable. Everything felt so good: all the places where they touched, the bounce as they landed on his bed, the soft weave of the bedspread luxurious against her bare skin.

The room smelled of sea air and the woody, vanilla scent of his aftershave, as Harry kissed his way across her body, taking his time, exploring every inch of her. Sophie closed her eyes so she could do more feeling, so she could catalogue every sizzling, delicious moment. She couldn't help wondering why it had taken them so long to reach this point, when it was clearly what they had been destined for all along.

Chapter Twenty-Two

Sophie woke to a cacophony of bird song unlike anything she heard from her flat, where seagulls provided the overriding chorus. It took her a few seconds to remember where she was, why she felt bone tired but happy, why the duvet was so beautifully weighted, light but warm. Then awareness rippled through her, and she opened her eyes and found she was looking at Harry's peaceful, sleeping face, his eyelashes inky against his skin. His hair was in disarray, reminding her of the night before, and she felt the grin stretch her cheeks.

She rolled onto her back and saw from the clock on the bedside table that it was just after seven. Through the partially closed curtains, the sun was making its glamorous entrance, a fiery pink sunrise spilling into the room. It was breathtaking, and she inexplicably found her eyes burning with the possibility of tears.

She didn't want to wake Harry, and she wasn't sure what the etiquette of Mistingham Manor was, but she didn't think it was beyond her to make coffee and buttery toast in an unusual kitchen, even if it was partly a building site.

She slid out of bed, found her jeans and jumper on the floor where they had been discarded the night before, and pulled them on. She tiptoed downstairs, and found the kitchen easily enough; a large open space at the back of the building, the double-aspect windows looking out onto trees, the birdsong here as loud as if it were being played through stereo speakers.

A small portion of clean worktop was exposed, next to a dated oven and gas hob. The rest was covered in plastic sheeting, cupboards and a dishwasher standing untethered, waiting to be installed. One alcove was pure Seventies nostalgia, with orange, brown and white floral wallpaper, and Sophie wondered how difficult it was for Harry to rip all this out, to essentially plaster over the rooms he'd grown up in, which held memories of his parents, his family.

She went hunting and found a cafetière, and a packet of coffee in the fridge, along with milk and butter. There was half a loaf of bread on the counter, wrapped in one of Dexter's bakery bags. Sophie cut slices, boiled the kettle and assembled her tray, all the while expecting one of the dogs, or Harry or May, to find her.

But the manor was in a deep Sunday slumber, and she tried not to think about *The Haunting of Hill House* by Shirley Jackson, where the house at the centre of the story had a personality, sometimes innocently quiet, sometimes intent on wreaking a creeping, dread-filled havoc on the occupants.

Before Mistingham, Sophie hadn't been in a place this grand for more than dinner or a posh afternoon tea, and she still found it difficult to accept that Harry lived here, that he'd been closeted by these thick stone walls when he was growing up. It made her realize how different they were, how their upbringings had been polar opposites of each other.

When everything was ready, she went as quietly up the stairs as she could with a heavy, crockery-filled tray. The arched window showed off the estate in all its shimmering, winter sunrise glory; wisps of mist covering the frost-dusted lawn, the sea kissed with pearly peach light. Sophie thought about how the different seasons would adorn Mistingham estate and the sea beyond in new and varied ways, no two days the same. She felt an ache in her chest, an unexpected longing for familiarity, for the chance to see each magical new version of the landscape.

She lowered the door handle with her elbow, then tiptoed into the room with her tray. She watched Harry stir, saw him blink and then stare at her, a gruff laugh bursting out of him.

'Breakfast in bed?' he said in a sleep-roughened voice. 'What have I done to deserve this?'

Sophie shrugged, but inside she was a riot of happy butterflies. 'I can think of a few things from last night.' She grinned.

'Come here.' Harry sat up against the pillows, and Sophie couldn't help gazing at his strong chest, at how his hair was the very definition of bedhead after their night together.

'With the breakfast, or . . .?'

'In a bit.' He flung back the duvet in invitation, and Sophie put the tray on the chest of drawers and went to join him.

* * *

Afterwards, they sat up against the pillows, eating cold, spongy toast and drinking lukewarm coffee, Sophie wearing a blue T-shirt Harry had pulled out of a drawer for her.

'It's still good,' he said, breaking off a crust and popping it in his mouth.

'Only because we're ravenous,' Sophie replied. 'It wouldn't win any awards.'

'I would give it an award.'

'You might be biased.'

'Maybe,' Harry said. 'I'm not sure anyone would blame me, though. Last night and this morning have been . . . unexpectedly amazing.'

'Unexpectedly?' Sophie asked.

Harry lifted his mug. 'I was fully prepared for you to stay in the spare room last night. I thought there was a very real chance you didn't want . . . this.'

'You thought I didn't want you?'

'I honestly didn't know. We'd kissed, but I wasn't sure how . . . serious you were about any of it. And if,' he hurried to add, 'this is just a one-off, then of course that's fine – you're in charge, Sophie.' He put his plate on the bedside table.

She could hear all the unspoken thoughts between his words: that she'd told him she was leaving, and hadn't given him a proper answer when he'd asked again last night. But this . . . *this*. All her carefully laid plans, of organizing the festival, discovering who had given her the book, finding somewhere to rent in Cornwall, saying goodbye to Mistingham – it was as if they were a wall of dominoes, set up carefully to fall one by one, each knocking into the next, a clear and logical path. But now Harry had come along and scattered them with a single sweep of his hand, revealing a brand-new game board beneath, full of new possibilities.

Sophie liked to be sure of things, and right now she wasn't sure of anything. She needed to change the subject, so she asked the question that had been on her mind since she'd seen the kitchen.

'Is it hard, going through the manor and updating everything, erasing how it was when your dad was here, when you were growing up?'

Harry sighed. 'It hasn't always been easy, but I've tried to take the common-sense approach. It was all so dated, so dusty and damaged, that I knew if I wanted to live here, it had to be redone. And I have the important things. His desk, some of his books. I was so close to losing all of it, so I'm lucky I have the chance to choose which parts to keep.'

Sophie put her mug down and snuggled into his side. He put his arm around her, bringing her closer. 'I've never had those kinds of issues,' she admitted. 'Never had anything from my past that I wanted to hold on to.'

'Nothing from any of the families you stayed with? Not from Mrs Fairweather?'

'I never stayed anywhere for that long,' Sophie said. 'And with Mrs Fairweather, the things she gave me can't be seen or held. I'm sure I wouldn't still be making notebooks, making money from them, if it wasn't for her. And she was so kind to me – to all the children she looked after. She saw us as individuals, with different skills and aspirations and ambitions, rather than problems she had to deal with.'

'Some of the homes treated you like that?' Harry's voice was deceptively gentle, but his arm tensed around her.

'There are wonderful foster parents, of course, but there are some who think it's their job to fix us: that every child who ends up without a family has done something wrong, not just been a victim of circumstance.'

'Do you know what happened to your parents?'

Sophie nodded. 'My mum gave me up as soon as I was born. She was only young, and she couldn't cope with me. My dad wasn't in the picture, and there was nowhere for me to go except foster care. She chose my name, though. That's all I've brought with me.'

'It's an important thing, your name,' Harry said. 'And Sophie is beautiful.'

She no longer felt a tidal wave of sadness when she talked about her mum. She'd never known her, had no memories of her. From a young age she'd understood that she was on her own, and there was a certain freedom in that: she could go anywhere she wanted, at any time. No obligations to a place or person, just her and Clifton and the things she could fit in her beaten-up old car.

'Are you a Henry?' she asked. 'I remember Winnie calling you Henry when we went to see her.'

'I was christened Henry, but I've been Harry for as long as I can remember. My mum was Harriet.'

'How old were you when she died?'

'Fifteen,' he said. 'She'd been ill for a while, but you can't ever prepare yourself for a parent dying, I don't think. And then Dad . . . he threw himself into the bookshop. He spent all his time there, made it his singular focus, which is why it was so well-loved in the village. And I understand why. I think it was the only way he could contain his grief, but he left me and Daisy, my younger sister, to fend for ourselves.

'The only place he paid us any attention was at the bookshop, as if, away from this house, with all its memories of Mum, he could breathe and give our relationship space. The manor got neglected, and it no longer felt like home.' Harry trailed his hand up Sophie's arm.

'I'm so sorry,' she said. 'So then . . . you went to London as soon as you could?'

'To escape this backwater? Of course.' He laughed, but it sounded sad. 'London was huge and full of possibility. I had a strong head for figures, and ended up managing people's investments, then companies' investments. It felt important – at least at the time. It took me a while to realize how impersonal it all was, how much I'd lost touch with the things that mattered. I found hobbies I cared about, and the plan was to change jobs, to get out of it completely, but then . . .'

'Then?' Sophie prompted, looking up at him.

'Then Dad got in touch, and he was upset; more emotional than I'd heard him in years. He told me things he'd been keeping from me for ages: that the estate was falling apart; that the bookshop, while popular in the village, wasn't making money. That, in fact, he'd put so much into it without getting enough back, built up such a huge debt, that he was close to losing the entire estate, all the land – close to having everything repossessed. Everyone here saw him as their best friend, the kindest man they knew, but he'd let everything crumble at the expense of being well-liked. My only option was to keep earning good money, to work as hard as I could, to save it all.' He gazed down at his hands, as if he was examining the lines across his palms.

Sophie swallowed. 'So you stayed in London because . . .'

'I had to,' he finished. 'I felt guilty for not realizing how bad things were, for staying away for so long. I had to make sure Dad was financially OK again. And then, when the estate was safe, when we'd scraped through by the skin of our teeth, he got sick, and I knew that living here, with me caring for him, wouldn't give him the best chance. It wasn't the healthiest environment; parts of it weren't really safe any more.

'So I found the best place I could for him, and I knew that moving back here and working as a remote consultant wouldn't cut it for the care-home fees, so I stayed in London and worked harder than ever, all the hours I could, paying for Dad's care, building up savings so I could come home and be closer to him when I had a big enough cushion.

'Dad wouldn't let me sell the manor. It was the easiest solution when he was first diagnosed with dementia, to pay for his care home, but when I suggested it he point-blank refused. He told me it had to stay in the family, that it meant so much to him, had meant a lot to Mum, and that I had worked so hard to save it, I couldn't just let it go. So then I had this grand idea that I would restore it when things got easier, when I was able to.'

He stopped talking, and Sophie waited for what came next. She glanced up at him, and he was staring ahead, his expression blank.

'Hey,' she said, but he wouldn't look at her, so she pushed back the duvet and slid her leg over his hips, so she was facing him, straddling his lap, and he couldn't avoid her.

He met her gaze, his distant look replaced by something more intense. His hands came up to her hips and squeezed.

'What made you come back?' she asked.

He gave her a rueful smile. 'A book.'

Sophie sucked in a breath. 'A *book*?'

'Dad had only been in the home a year, but he had already lost so much of himself. When I phoned, and the few times I came back to visit, he didn't recognize me. Then I got this book in the post: an old copy of *North and South* by Elizabeth Gaskell. The inscription said, *To my darling Harry, all my love, Bernie.* It must have been a gift he'd given Mum years ago – it was her favourite novel – and he'd held onto it after she died. I don't know whether he knew he was sending it to me, passing the gift down the line and ensuring it wasn't lost, or if, in his confusion, he somehow thought it was going to Mum.

'He must have had the address of my London flat, told the nurse where to send it. Obviously she knew the truth – that his wife had died over twenty years before – and I'd spoken to her plenty of times, so she knew I was Harry, too. But it didn't matter what Dad had thought he was doing, or who had a role in the book getting to me, because it made me realize . . .' He swallowed. 'I realized that I could earn all the money in the world, but here was my dad, slowly disappearing, and I wasn't even visiting him. Daisy is a career woman, she was busy too, and we'd both convinced ourselves that we were doing the right thing, but I think we were running away.'

'Running away?'

He pressed his nose into her collar bone. 'He effectively abandoned us after Mum died, and I know that, really, we were doing the same to him. Not entirely consciously – probably more out of fear that he wasn't Dad any more, telling ourselves that it was so much easier to get on with our own lives and, in my case, that I was helping by funding his care. But when I got that book, I realized that he was still, somehow, holding on to his love for Mum, even after so much else had deserted him. I knew I had to come back.'

'And you did.' Sophie's throat was thick. She tipped his head back, her finger under his chin. 'You came back to him.'

'I had a few months with him before he died,' Harry said. 'It wasn't really enough.'

'But at least you came.' Sophie's thoughts were whirring, because he'd been sent a book, and it had changed the course of his life. It had made him realize that he needed to uproot everything and come home. But he'd known from the beginning who sent it to him, it hadn't been a mystery. But the coincidence . . .

'Soph?' he asked. 'Are you OK?'

'I'm fine,' she said. 'And I'm so sorry. You've been through so much. You stayed away to help your dad, and everyone thinks you deserted him, that you deserted all of it – the estate, Mistingham.'

'But I was doing that too.' Harry slid his hands up her back, beneath the T-shirt.

'You're making up for it now, though.' She searched his face, looking for a hint of smugness, something that would reveal he'd given her the copy of *Jane Eyre*, and that telling her the story about his dad sending him *North and South* was his way of admitting it. Was the book that Winnie had been given some kind of peace offering from him, after their sparring match? But Sophie was sure she'd told him about her mysterious present from The Secret Bookshop, and he'd seemed as baffled as she was. Except . . . *had* she told him? That night after the pub, when he'd walked her home? She couldn't remember how much she'd said to him.

Harry's hands slid around her waist and his fingers danced a path over her stomach, making her muscles contract.

'*Harry*.' She'd meant it as a protest, but it was half-hearted at best.

'Mmmm?' He leaned up and kissed her, long and slow and sensuous. All thoughts of books went out of Sophie's head as he pulled the T-shirt up, broke the kiss so he could lift it over her head, then dragged the duvet over both of them, sliding them lower in the bed.

'Thank you for telling me,' she said, needing to acknowledge the faith he must have in her to want to tell her about his family, about the things he was ashamed of.

'I'd tell you anything,' Harry said, as he wrapped his arms around her, then moved them until she was on her back, and he was hovering over her. 'Anything you want to know, Soph. I'm an open book when it comes to you.'

Sophie smiled up at him, soft and lazy and full of desire, and she knew, then, that he had nothing to do with her anonymous gift. It was just a coincidence: this place was full of books, full of the memory of them, and they were a good present to get – that's all it was. And besides, she thought, as she closed her eyes and tried to hold back a gasp, Harry was giving her a pretty good gift right that moment.

She would work out who had sent her the book, who Mistingham's secret book Santa was, just as soon as she recovered her senses and escaped the perfect, pleasure-filled haven of Harry's bed. But there was no rush, she told herself. Absolutely no rush at all.

Chapter Twenty-Three

On Monday evening after work, Sophie left Clifton curled up on her sofa, the smell of her cheese and tomato toastie still lingering in the air, the sea a black void beyond her kitchen window, and walked to the village hall.

The days were getting colder, and today the sky had been a cloudless, washed-out blue, so even though it was just gone six o'clock, the darkness was dusted with stars and a layer of glittering frost. Sophie had pulled her woolly hat down over her ears, her gloved hands were shoved deep in her pockets, and her nose tingled with cold.

Mistingham was still bustling, with cars turning into the Blossom Bough car park, the hotel lit up like Norfolk's most welcoming dolls' house: windows aglow, twinkling chandeliers and elaborate Christmas trees visible through the panes.

The lights were on in the hall, and as Sophie walked across the crunchy, frost-hardened grass, she glanced up at the stately oak. Despite what Harry had told her, it looked stronger than ever, its branches waving jauntily in the light wind. She felt a fizz of excitement as she thought how good it would look draped in lights, the lower limbs adorned with handmade decorations.

When she stepped into the musty, dusty hall, Jazz was already there, standing among sleek black equipment: a microphone, amplifier and snakes of cable.

'This is sound kit.' She grinned at Sophie, then pressed a button on the amp so it squealed with feedback.

'Did Harry drop it off?' Sophie asked, disappointment settling in her gut. She took off her hat, then realized it wasn't much warmer in here than it was outside.

'May did,' Jazz said, not looking up. 'Apparently Harry had some kind of issue with Felix – *big* surprise . . .' she rolled her eyes, 'but she said all the equipment should be working, and it does seem to be.'

'Is Felix OK?' Sophie asked.

Jazz glanced up. 'Oh. Yeah, he's fine. He got into somewhere he wasn't supposed to, or something. I wasn't really listening. But he's all right, and Harry is, too: just pissed off.'

Sophie nodded. She would message him later. She'd hardly stopped thinking about him since they'd said goodbye at the manor yesterday lunchtime, Sophie insisting she needed to collect Clifton from Fiona's house. They'd parted with a promise to see each other again soon, to finalize what they needed to for the festival, and Harry hadn't stopped kissing her until she'd physically extricated herself, and even then he'd come onto the gravel driveway in his bare feet, as if he couldn't bear to let her go.

It had been harder to leave him than she'd expected. It wasn't just that she was addicted to his touch – although she most definitely was – but that she wanted to sit with him for hours in front of the fire in his study, listening to him talk about his family and his favourite books, about what he wanted for the future, and the moments that had shaped him.

She wondered why he hadn't told the whole story to Fiona, the other villagers who'd judged him: that he'd had to stay away to save the bookshop and Mistingham estate, then to pay for his dad's care. But she was beginning to understand him, and she thought he'd simply decided it wasn't their business. He wasn't accountable to anyone, wasn't going to make excuses. She realized that was one of the reasons she admired him so much.

He was so certain about what he wanted, and what other people were entitled to when it came to his personal life, and it felt almost magical that he had let her in, told her about his past, about the vulnerabilities that were still there. And his touch had been both strong and tender, sometimes commanding, sometimes hesitant, as if he wasn't entirely sure she was real, and needed to prove it to himself.

She didn't want him to be uncertain about them, but could she really stay here, give up the independence that was so important to her, for a chance to be with Harry? She had done that once before; she had been so sure of Trent's love, then it had ended so suddenly. That was the worst part: she hadn't had an inkling that he was unhappy, had thought he'd accepted that it took her longer to settle into things. It had made her feel weak, and she had decided, then, that she shouldn't be relying on anyone but herself.

Was this thing with Harry, that was still so new and full of promise, any different?

'That's good,' she said, after a gap that was far too long to make sense, but Jazz didn't seem to notice. 'So the open-mic equipment's all set?'

'Yeah, and it's robust stuff.' Jazz was kneeling on the hard floor, checking the settings, her jeans already dusty. 'It should be fine on the outside stage. You're going to have this place as a sort of refuge, during the festival?'

'It'll just be a bit quieter,' Sophie said. 'It's where everyone will come to make their decorations, and we'll have some games and the book club discussion.'

'*Jane Eyre*,' Jazz said.

Sophie nodded. Her beautiful copy had become an anchor for her, something she returned to whenever she got home, every morning when she woke up. She read a few pages whenever she could, and she was a good way through it now.

She still wanted to know who had given it to her, who had written that message – even more so because the note accompanying Winnie's book had been so much more straightforward – but her motives had changed. She didn't want to unearth The Secret Bookshop so she could put the mystery to bed and move on, she wanted to do it so she could ask them why they had chosen her; so she could thank them.

'Have you read it?' she asked Jazz.

'Fiona's given me a copy, and I've started it, but I've never been a big reader. Besides, the hotel is keeping me busy.'

'You're enjoying it?'

Jazz grinned. 'Yeah, I am. I can't quite believe it, you know? That Fiona and Ermin, Winnie and Mary, have given me this chance. I *didn't* believe it for a while.'

252

Sophie remembered how frustrated Fiona had been when Jazz was holed up in her room, refusing to talk or come down for meals. 'It's hard to accept it,' she said, 'when you're always braced for the worst, but then things start to pick up – it's like you're waiting for the other shoe to drop.'

'Exactly.' Jazz swivelled on her bum, ignoring the sound system for a moment. 'When I got here, after that crazy long bus ride, I thought this place would be boring, full of ancient people who followed the same routines every day: that it'd be one of those places where people came to die, you know?'

Sophie laughed. 'I do know.'

'But it's not, is it? The hotel's popular with all sorts of guests, not just doddery old folk, and the pub's definitely got a younger vibe.' A smile slipped onto her lips, and Sophie wondered if Jazz was thinking about Indigo, Natasha's son.

'Not to mention that the older people are still pretty spirited,' Sophie pointed out. 'Have you met Mr Carsdale?'

'Not yet. Fiona's told me about him, though.' Jazz returned to her work, untangling the microphone lead, and Sophie went to see if the pile of tatty board games had any hidden gems they could use for their festival tournament. 'She also told me that you really are leaving,' Jazz called over. 'That you weren't joking when we talked about it before.'

Sophie turned around. 'I was going to leave. In January. I prefer staying nimble, being—'

'Being able to move on at a moment's notice,' Jazz finished. 'When things don't feel good any more.'

Sophie nodded, but the lump in her throat stopped her from replying.

'What about Mistingham doesn't feel good?' Jazz spread her arms wide, her laugh incredulous.

'That's what I mean,' Sophie said haltingly. 'I *was* going to leave.'

'You mean you're not now? You're staying?'

Sophie swallowed. She hadn't said it aloud to anyone yet, had perhaps only decided properly a few minutes ago. But over the last few weeks, the questioning voice in her head had got louder. What, exactly, was she going for?

She sat next to Jazz on the dusty floor, resting her elbows on her knees. 'I was in Bristol for three whole years.'

'Wow.' Jazz's eyes widened. 'A lifetime!'

Sophie laughed. 'I know. I was with this guy, Trent, for just over two of them, and I thought that was it – that I was staying. We had a good life together: he was a teacher at the local secondary school, I was working in a trendy, arty café, making my notebooks on the side, selling them at craft fairs and markets. I thought we were happy.'

'Uh oh,' Jazz said ominously.

'Then he asked me to move in with him,' Sophie said, 'and I felt instantly claustrophobic. Even though I'd have been giving up a grotty little flat to move into his beautiful town house. He'd been saving for a house deposit since university – talk about being prepared.' She shook her head.

Jazz laughed, then said, 'But the flat was your safety net?'

Sophie nodded, the lump back in her throat as she remembered how it had fallen apart. Slowly, at first, with Trent's frustration showing as snippy remarks and periods of silence, everything awkward when before it had been so comfortable between them. And then, how quickly the momentum had gathered; that race downhill to rock bottom. 'I told him I needed more time, and he said that I was *never* going to be ready, so what was the point?'

'He had no patience?' Jazz asked.

'He had been so patient with me – really, more than I deserved. I knew it was my fault, that we'd been together long enough, so I decided I could do it; that I could be braver. But then he told me I couldn't make notebooks and work in cafés for the rest of my life, that I was always going to be treading water, that I was incapable of committing to anything important.'

'Shit,' Jazz murmured.

Sophie rubbed her hands together. 'We need to make sure the heating's put on early on festival days – and that it's also on the week before, when people come to make decorations. This place needs time to heat up.'

Jazz nodded. 'What happened next? With Trent?'

Sophie closed her eyes for a moment. 'I felt like he'd betrayed me. I thought that, even if I gave up my flat and moved in with him, I couldn't trust him any more: not if that was what he really thought about me. It was as if, while things were good between us, he hadn't bothered to say anything, almost as if he was humouring me. But how could I be with someone who thought the way I lived my life wasn't worthwhile? I couldn't trust him, he didn't believe in me, so it was over.' She shrugged and wrapped her arms around her knees.

'I get that,' Jazz said. 'All the people who say they can get you things, provide this or that, who offer false promises and give you hope, only to take it away again. I guess what you have to decide is . . .' Jazz drew a pattern in the dust with the end of a cable. 'You have to decide to let go of that distrust. If you're happy, you can't sit around waiting for people to let you down. You have to . . . I guess you have to let yourself believe that they won't. You have to be braver, otherwise you'll never feel settled. You'll always keep running.'

That, in a nutshell, was how Sophie had lived her life. She was a few years off forty, and she still acted as if nobody was trustworthy, as if everyone would let her down in the end. It was, she conceded, a ridiculous way to exist.

She tipped her head back and groaned, then stood up and took the mic off its stand, turned the amp on. 'Jazz . . .?' she said, her voice booming.

'Ambrose,' Jazz said, grinning. 'My surname is Ambrose.'

'Great surname,' Sophie said into the mic, her words echoing off the walls. 'Jazz Ambrose, you are half my age and twice as wise. From now on, I am going to be more like you: I'm going to take chances and be braver. I'm going to live, rather than exist.' What she'd been doing recently – with the festival, with Harry – felt like living, and she wanted more of it.

Jazz smiled up at her, wincing whenever feedback whined through the amplifier like a petulant child.

'I won't just think about myself any more,' Sophie went on, then had to swallow. 'Mistingham is . . . it's my home, I suppose.' Her words faded, uncertain, at the end, but Jazz either didn't notice or chose to ignore it.

'You're really staying?' she asked.

Sophie closed her eyes. She remembered Harry leaning in to kiss her, laughing in bed while they ate cold toast together; she pictured the way the summer sea faded from blue-green close to the shore, out to a deep navy on the horizon, the gunmetal grey and ferocious white horses of winter; she thought of the chunky flint houses with hollyhocks outside on hot, dusty days, the twinkling decorations adorning windows and roofs right now. Dexter and Lucy, Fiona and Ermin, May and Jazz.

She opened her eyes, returned Jazz's infectious grin and said, 'Yes. I'm really staying.'

She waited for the panic, for her heart to try and beat out of its chest, leading the way to the exit, but there was only a gentle thrumming, a sizzle in her blood and a skip in her pulse that wasn't terror, but anticipation. She was here, in Mistingham, and it was time for her to stop running.

Chapter Twenty-Four

Harry appeared in Hartley Country Apparel at five to five on Tuesday afternoon, and was greeted by Sophie's warm smile and Fiona's raised eyebrows.

Sophie was already buoyed up, because a customer had come in earlier and bought ten notebooks, then spent half an hour with her, commissioning three bespoke designs that she would have to squeeze in somehow, but was adamant she could get done in time. The drip of Christmas enthusiasm was turning into a flood, and Fiona's sales of hats, scarves and gloves had been near record-breaking for a Tuesday.

'Hi, Fiona,' Harry said. 'Sophie.'

'Hey,' Sophie said. 'Your place or mine?'

Harry's smile widened. 'Yours. Ready to go?'

'More than.' Sophie put on her coat and joined him at the door. They said goodbye to Fiona, and Clifton gave her a farewell bark as Sophie slipped her arm through Harry's and they walked to her flat.

'I was thinking we could have bacon sandwiches,' she

said, hurrying into the living room ahead of him, tidying the coffee table, moving her notebook and the copy of *Jane Eyre* to a low bookshelf.

'You don't have to do anything, you know.' Harry took off his coat and hung it on the hook by the door. 'But it's very hard for me to turn down a bacon sandwich.'

'We need fuel while we work.' She busied herself in the kitchen, getting out a pan, bacon, bread. With only the oven light on, she could see a couple of twinkling lights on the dark sea, tankers or fishing boats, just as Harry had talked about.

'Are you OK?' He slipped his arms around her waist, pressing up against her back. 'Is *this* OK?'

Sophie swallowed. Now would be the perfect time to tell him she was staying. But instead, she said, 'We've got all the decoration materials ready for the hall, and Jazz and I checked the mic and amplifier yesterday. We should go through our checklist, see what's left.'

She turned in his arms, and when his lips found hers, when he pushed her gently against the counter, so she could feel him, strong and solid against her, it seemed as if there were more important things than checking they had enough bunting or working out how to run their Scrabble tournament.

'I don't think we need to spend the entire evening on it,' Harry whispered. 'We're sensible enough to sort it out.'

'Sensible?' Sophie echoed. 'Is that how you're selling yourself to me?'

'I thought I'd already sold myself to you quite well,' he said against her throat, and Sophie tipped her head back and agreed that yes, he had done that quite well already, actually.

* * *

The following day, she met Harry and Dexter on the village green in her lunch break. The sun was attempting to peek through the clouds, and the green looked welcoming despite the whorls of muddy ground visible through the grass, the recent rain having had an impact. She'd brought her larger handbag, the copy of *Jane Eyre* stowed safely inside.

'Are we going to need some kind of flooring?' she asked, after her foot had skidded in the mud.

'It obviously wasn't an issue last year,' Harry said sheepishly. 'No idea what happened before that.'

Dexter shrugged. 'People wore boots, got a bit muddy, but didn't mind because it was Christmas.'

'Right.' Harry blew out a breath. 'Good to know. We need to plan the layout; where we're going to put everyone.'

'And you needed my ladder as well as yours, because . . .?' Dexter asked.

'Because we're putting the lights up.' Harry pointed at the boxes he'd brought from the manor, the sets of lights they'd bought in Norwich. Inside the biggest box, Sophie thought gleefully, was the light-up goat.

'And we need two of us to do it,' she added.

Dexter tipped his head back, looking at the top of the statuesque oak tree. 'Great.'

'You sound thrilled,' Sophie said with a laugh.

'I'm not a huge fan of heights.'

'Why do you have a ladder then?' Harry asked.

'Because sometimes you need a ladder, and you just have to get over your fears.' Dexter sighed. 'Anyway, this is going to be much better than a street festival.'

Harry glanced at Sophie. 'I know. I'm glad I was made to see sense.'

'Don't worry Dex,' she said, 'you can be our man on the ground. I'll go up with Harry.'

Dexter's shoulders dropped. 'You sure?'

'Of course. Can I show you something, though?'

'Go ahead.'

'I'll get the lights ready.' Harry strode to the other side of the green, and Sophie couldn't help watching him go. He'd had that same certainty, that confidence, under the sheets with her the night before.

'Sophie?' Dexter prompted with a laugh.

'Oh! Yes. Right.' She took the copy of *Jane Eyre* out of her bag and handed it to him. She had wrapped the brown paper loosely back around it, wanting to keep it pristine.

'What's this?' He turned it over slowly.

'Someone left it for me at the shop. It had a postcard addressed to me, a message about how I needed to look closer to home to find what I was missing, but I have no idea who's behind it. Winnie's been given a book too, and I just wondered if . . .'

'I remember you telling me about this ages ago. And now Winnie's had one? Where's mine?' he said with a grin. 'I'm afraid I haven't got a clue who sent it to you. It's a beautiful edition, but I don't remember even Bernie selling copies this nice in the bookshop.'

Sophie sighed. 'I'd be able to understand the message more if I knew who was behind it – I'd like to thank them.'

Dexter shrugged. 'Maybe they don't want thanks: maybe you're just supposed to enjoy it.'

They stared down at it, and Sophie realized she'd already got a lot out of it. Rereading the story, having a mystery to try – and so far fail – to solve. It was the reason she'd volunteered for the Oak Fest, which had thrown her together with Harry. Her life had changed a lot because of this book.

'Thanks Dex.' She put it back in her bag and they went to join Harry, who looked as though a Christmas tree had exploded all over him, one set of lights draped over his shoulders and another tangled round his arm.

'How has this happened?' he asked. 'I've been here *five* minutes.'

Sophie grinned. 'You're not used to sparkly, joyful things?'

He narrowed his eyes at her. 'Take that back, Sophie Stevens. The lights clearly have it in for me.'

'I take it all back.' She found the end of the dinky, book-shaped lights, and began to unwind them from round his arm. 'It can't be *that* difficult to get you out of this.'

'Let's see, shall we?' Harry raised an imperious eyebrow, and Sophie got so distracted by his expression that she made the tangle worse, and Dexter had to take charge of the situation.

Half an hour later they were having the same issue, but Sophie and Harry were now twenty feet up, their ladders leaning against the trunk on opposite sides of the oak tree.

'How the fuck did Winnie do this for so many years?' Harry called, as he leant forward and tried to drape his lights over a particularly thick branch.

'She got a helicopter in,' Dexter shouted from the safety of the ground.

Harry stared down at him. 'Fuck off.'

Dexter grinned. 'Yeah, I'm joking. I have no idea. One day the tree was bare, the next it was decorated. You didn't think to ask her?'

Sophie and Harry exchanged a look, and she saw her own frustration mirrored in his eyes. 'Don't you dare lean out too far,' Harry called to her.

'Or you,' she shot back. 'How the hell are we going to do this?'

Harry rested his forehead against the trunk. 'Ask Winnie? Hope it isn't actually a helicopter?'

There was a commotion from below and Sophie looked down, getting a sudden sway of vertigo as Simon and Jason appeared, each carrying ladders.

'You've been trying to get the lights up just the two of you?' Jason called up.

'We thought it would be fine,' Sophie shouted.

Jason shook his head, said something that sounded like *amateurs*, then Simon called, 'We'll come and help you!'

'That would be amazing!'

'Yes, thank you,' Harry added grumpily. She shot him a knowing look, and his returned gaze was incendiary. 'No risks, Sophie. I mean it. I'm not enjoying this a whole lot, and I'm usually fine with heights.'

'It's my least favourite bit of festival wrangling so far,' she agreed.

'We'll have to come up with a way to burn off the adrenaline later,' he said, against the metal clank of two more ladders finding purchase on the oak tree's sturdy trunk.

'I wonder what,' she replied with a smile, as the married couple came to join them and, it turned out, make the job of draping the oak tree in its festive cloak a hundred times easier.

Soon, their centrepiece was festooned with trails of lights: rainbow-coloured globe bulbs nestled among the branches, next to the dangling book lights Sophie had picked out, and little gold acorns that added a touch of twinkling glamour to the ends of the smaller twigs.

'Is it too much?' Harry leaned back on his ladder, and Sophie's stomach twisted unpleasantly.

'Nah.' Jason shook his head. 'You can't have too much where this festival is concerned. You might get complaints that it's too subtle.'

'Don't listen to him,' Simon said, 'it looks great. Just the right side of gaudy.'

'Brilliant.' Sophie sighed. 'And we still have our pièce de résistance.'

'What's that?' Jason asked, as he started his descent.

Sophie felt a wave of relief when her feet found the firm-ish ground of the green. She wobbled, and Harry was beside her in an instant, his hand on her waist.

'I thought you would have forgotten about that,' he said in a low murmur.

'Never.' She grinned up at him.

'What are we missing?' Dexter asked.

'The goat!' Sophie said triumphantly.

'*Goat?*' Simon, Jason and Dexter echoed in unison.

Harry rolled his eyes. 'I take absolutely none of the credit.'

Together, he and Sophie opened the large cardboard box and lifted the goat out. Sophie had forgotten how cute it was, how much attention had been given to the ears, the little horns, the hooves. Harry unwound the cable and went to plug it into their outdoor extension box, and Sophie positioned it below the tree, so it looked like part of a nativity scene, waiting for its farmyard friends.

'That,' Jason said, standing in front of it and crossing his arms, 'is a great goat.'

'I love him,' Simon added. 'What does he do?'

'Do?' Sophie frowned.

'What colours does he turn?'

'Oh! Loads of different ones, I think. Harry?'

'Hang on,' he called. 'Just taking a look. It's got about a hundred different settings.'

'Let me see.' Dexter joined him, crouching alongside the wall of the village hall, where the weatherproof electrical box had been fixed.

With Dexter and Harry occupied, Sophie turned to Jason and Simon. 'Can I show you something?' She took *Jane Eyre* out of her bag and showed it to them both, telling the story all over again.

They exchanged a glance, their expressions puzzled.

'What is it?' Sophie asked.

'We got one of these,' Jason said.

Sophie's heart thudded. 'Really?'

'*Moby Dick*,' Simon said with a laugh. 'It looks a lot like this, except the cover's blue, with silver fish. I wondered if it was because of Batter Days.'

'Did it come with a postcard?'

'Yeah,' Jason said. 'A tacky one of the prom and the cliffs. On the back it said something like, "For the hardest-working couple in Mistingham. Happy Christmas from The Secret Bookshop." No idea what that is, but it was pushed through our letter box, hand-delivered because it didn't have our address on.'

'It's someone local.' Sophie tapped her fingers against her lips. 'Winnie got one too, so maybe they're going to work their way around everyone before Christmas?'

'Maybe,' Simon said with a shrug.

'The more people who get one,' Sophie mused, 'the more it narrows down who could have sent it.'

'Unless they send one to themselves,' Jason pointed out. 'If I was doing this and wanted to stay anonymous, that's how I'd throw people off the scent.'

'*Is* that what you're doing?' Sophie asked, sliding *Jane Eyre* back into her bag.

'No way.' Jason laughed. 'I'm far too busy concocting baked Alaska recipes for the Oak Fest to go round being secret fucking book Santa. Besides, where would I get them from? They must cost a fortune.'

Sophie sighed. 'You're right, so what—?'

'We've got it working!' Dexter called.

At the base of the oak tree, the little goat was shimmering a bright, pillar-box red. It pulsed purple, then pink, then orange and green. It was the perfect accompaniment to the lights twinkling in the branches above.

Sophie glanced up as Harry came to join her, her breath catching when she saw his grin. He looked proud, even though he'd grumbled about the goat from the beginning.

'We'll have to bring Felix here to show him,' she said. 'He'll love it.'

Harry wrapped his arm around her shoulder and planted a kiss on the top of her head. 'He'll probably want us to bring it home once the festival is over. You'd better start thinking of a name.'

He'd said it casually enough, probably by accident, but the words lanced through her like a spear. *Want us to bring it home.* She'd only spent one night at the manor, and he'd spent one night at her flat, but maybe it had slipped out because he felt the same as her: that what they had together had all the fun and thrill, the heady desire of a new relationship, but also felt solid and safe, as if they'd known each other for years. As if they belonged together.

Sophie leaned into Harry's chest, noticing the surprised looks from Dexter, Simon and Jason, and knew that this bit of news would be all over Mistingham before the end of the day. She couldn't find out who had sent her a beautiful, unusual gift – though not for want of trying – but a man kissing a woman on the head: well, that would be front-page news. She felt ridiculously happy that Harry must also have known that, and decided to do it anyway.

Chapter Twenty-Five

'How are you and lover-boy, then?' These were the first words that greeted Sophie when she stepped into the village hall on Thursday. It was nine days until the festival, and they'd agreed to have the hall open every evening, for people to come and make decorations, to drink tea and play board games. Jazz had called it a soft launch, and Sophie supposed it was.

She smiled at old Mr Carsdale. 'Excuse me?'

'You and Lord of the Manor,' he said. He was wearing a royal blue scarf over a green and yellow Pringle jumper, even though they'd given the heating enough time to get going and it was toasty warm inside. 'Everyone's heard about the stir you caused when the lights went up.' He gestured to the window, where the twinkling oak tree cast Mistingham Green in a beautiful rainbow glow. 'Could have been done for indecent exposure, from what they were saying.'

Sophie narrowed her eyes. 'He kissed me on the head and put his arm around me.'

'You know what Mistingham's like.' Mr Carsdale had a gleam in his eye.

'Good to see you're abreast of everything in the village,' Sophie said evenly. She had known she wouldn't be able to keep her and Harry a secret, but they hadn't been ripping each other's clothes off on the front steps of the hotel. Maybe they should – that would give everyone some *real* gossip. 'Have you got everything you need?'

'I'm going to teach the others to play bridge.' He gestured to several of the older villagers sitting patiently around a table. 'I don't have the dexterity for all that fiddly crafting any more, but it'll be good to get a bridge tournament up and running again.' His smile was small and content, and Sophie's irritation faded.

'That sounds lovely.'

'And I've been practising for the open mic.'

'I have your name down,' Sophie said, 'but not what you're doing. A bit of Frank Sinatra, maybe?'

'*The Odyssey*,' Mr Carsdale said. 'By Homer, you know.'

Sophie tried to hide her panic. 'The whole thing? Isn't it several books' worth?'

He chuckled. 'We'll see how we go.'

'We will indeed,' she said, wondering how she could cut him off politely. *The Odyssey* would take up an entire night of the festival – maybe two – and they only had four nights in total.

'Tea's on the way, Frank,' Jazz told him. 'It doesn't look too bad, does it?' she said to Sophie.

They'd been working hard in their spare moments this week, and Sophie took in the finished effect. Sets of gold waterfall lights hung over two of the walls, and there were new, plum-coloured cushions on the plastic chairs. The trestle tables had been decorated with red and green tablecloths, and each one had a bud vase with a spring of holly in, and a couple of battery-operated tea lights.

They had lowered the screen, and Ermin's laptop was projecting an image of a glowing fireplace, the wall-mounted speakers sending a low crackle through the hall. A real Christmas tree stood in the corner, its silver star brushing the ceiling, its mirrored baubles reflecting the twinkling silver lights, giving it a disco ball effect.

'It looks amazing,' Sophie said. 'We've knocked it out of the park.'

Jazz beamed. 'I'll go and get the teas.'

The door pushed open, and Sophie went to greet the newcomers. 'Hello,' she said. 'Come in and sit down.'

A man with a shock of grey hair was supporting a woman on crutches, a shorter, rounder man leading a crocodile of three small children, all under ten. Their excited giggles and wide eyes were all the confirmation Sophie needed that the hall looked the part.

'Let me show you to the Decoration Station,' she said to the excited group. Jazz had named it, a flash of inspiration so pleasing that Sophie smiled whenever she said it.

Indigo waved as they approached. He was wearing a green elf hat with a red bauble on the end, and he'd taken out some of his many face piercings. Sophie felt a rush of affection for him, especially when he opened his arms wide and greeted the children with a squeaky rendition of 'Jingle Bells' that had them in fits of giggles.

She grinned at him, then went into the kitchen, where Fiona was preparing plates of Dexter's mince pies and cranberry sausage rolls. 'I didn't know if anyone would come to these decoration sessions,' she said. 'But it's busy out there already.'

'It's a chance for people to get together on cold winter evenings,' Fiona replied. 'And I'm sure with the children—' she gestured with a mince pie '—their parents and grand-parents are glad to have somewhere they can come that will exhaust all their pre-Christmas energy.'

'Birdie's bringing Lucy in a bit,' Sophie said. 'Dexter's working flat out, and I don't think we're the only ones who have commissioned things from him.'

'Birdie's really taken a shine to that girl.'

'And Lucy must be in heaven, with all her witchy books and potions.'

'I'm sure their friendship is based on more than that,' Fiona said with a chuckle. 'It's lovely to see, though. And Dexter's working as hard as he can so he can take a whole week off over Christmas to spend with her.'

Sophie opened one of the large Tupperware boxes, and started putting sausage rolls on the willow-patterned serving dish that Fiona must have brought with her. 'He'll need the break,' she said. 'These look so delicious.'

'I did wonder if we'd see you tonight,' Fiona went on. 'Or if you'd be ensconced in your love cocoon.'

'My *love cocoon*.' Sophie laughed.

'How's it going with handsome Harry?'

'It's good,' Sophie said, her cheeks warming. 'Actually, it's great.' She had gone back to the manor last night and, in between other activities, he'd shown her the finished bunting. She'd been incredulous: not just at the amount, but the quality of it.

I told you, I'm good with my hands.

Well, I know that now.

Predictably, after that, they'd got distracted all over again.

But she felt guilty, because she still hadn't told him she'd decided to stay in Mistingham. Jazz knew, and that probably meant Fiona did too, but the person Sophie had got closest to, the person who had changed her mind, was still in the dark. Her stomach churned with nerves every time she thought about telling him, because it felt like the biggest step of all, but she knew she needed to do it soon.

'He's in London today,' she told Fiona. 'He's got a meeting with the people he consults for. He should be on his way back now – I think the train gets in at eight.'

'I bet London's a nightmare this close to Christmas,' Fiona said. 'I heard from Dexter that you've been asking around about the book, too. It seems like quite a few things have changed for you.'

Sophie thought how plausible it was that Fiona was behind The Secret Bookshop, even though she'd always denied it. Until she'd got to know Harry, May and Jazz, Fiona had probably been the only person who cared whether or not Sophie stayed in Mistingham. She thought of all the times her friend had bemoaned the loss of The Book Ends, and wondered if it had been a way for her to bring back the spirit of the bookshop, while also encouraging Sophie not to leave.

'Fiona?' She put the last sausage roll on the plate, checked the counters for paper napkins.

'What is it?' Fiona paused, her hands hovering over the plate of mince pies.

'I need to ask you something.' She looked at the woman who, almost as soon as Sophie had arrived in Mistingham, had appointed herself a friend and colleague, had given her

272

business a fighting chance with a permanent corner in her shop. Fiona was as straightforward as they came. 'It's OK,' she said. 'Forget about it.'

'Come on,' Fiona said jovially. 'We don't have secrets from each other, do we?'

'No.' Sophie looked at her boots. 'No, we don't.'

'Then tell me what's on your mind.'

Sophie didn't think it *could* be Fiona, but she needed to know for sure. She wanted to start this new phase of her life with complete honesty.

'Sophie?'

'Did you leave that book for me?' she asked in a rush, and watched Fiona's eyebrows lift in surprise. 'Did you give one to Winnie, and one to Simon and Jason too?'

'I told you I didn't.'

'It was left in the shop – how could you not have seen who did it?'

'I was out in the back room,' Fiona said calmly, 'making tea or checking stock, answering the phone. You know what it's like.'

'Yes, but—'

'I'm really all you have?' Her tone was harder, now. 'Out of everyone in the village? Birdie and Dexter, Harry and May. Natasha? What if it was a mistake? What if they meant to say more on the postcard, sign their name, then got distracted and forgot? What if this was never meant to be a mystery, Sophie?'

Sophie flung her arms up, exasperated. 'So then why has nobody come to see me, to say, "Hey Sophie, what did you think about the book?" Why don't Simon or Winnie have any idea who it is either?'

273

'Perhaps it wasn't meant for you. Perhaps the postcard was left inside it ages ago, and it's all a huge coincidence?'

'You're clutching at straws.'

'And *you're* clutching too, if you think I would do it and then lie to you.'

Sophie picked at a loose bit of edging on the counter. 'But is it really lying, if it's this elaborate secret? A game, almost.'

'It's a lie,' Fiona said flatly. 'I would never lie to you, Sophie.'

Sophie nodded, but didn't look up. Her friend wasn't furious, but she knew from her tone, from the way she kept saying *Sophie*, that she was disappointed. 'I'm sorry—'

'We need to get these snacks out to our ravenous elves,' Fiona said. 'Help me carry them?'

Sophie picked up her platter and tried to put her conundrum to the back of her mind.

The hall was busy all night with villagers coming to make decorations, write secret wishes or messages of gratitude, play board games and talk about *Jane Eyre*. Sophie started the discussion off, spent half an hour talking about the themes, before the conversation inevitably turned to other books, then other things. It was the nature of a book club, she knew, that it would stray off topic, the original story acting as a springboard, a much-needed ice-breaker.

She hadn't seen a glint of knowing or amusement in anyone's eye when she'd held up her beautifully bound edition, a hint that she was the butt of their Secret Bookshop joke, but then she didn't know any of these people, had met most of them for the first time that evening. And, after her chat with Fiona, she wasn't feeling enthusiastic about investigating anyway.

She had moved over to the Decoration Station, her fingers soon covered in glue and purple Sharpie, while Frank Carsdale ran his bridge sessions with enthusiasm, swapping people in and out and keeping the energy high.

At the end of the night, once they'd said goodbye to the last guests, Fiona tidied the tables while Jazz and Sophie cleared up in the kitchen.

'You OK?' Jazz asked, as she passed her a stack of plates. The dishwasher had left everything clean but soapy, its rinse function clearly worn out, but this was still easier than a sink full of suds and a scrubbing brush.

'I'm fine.' Sophie couldn't help replaying her conversation with Fiona, the crackle of tension it had left between them, her friend's *I would never lie to you*. She couldn't stop thinking about the monumental decision she was keeping from both her and Harry. She needed to be braver, just like Jazz had said, because was she really committing to staying if she hadn't told the most important people in her life?

'Sophie, you've put that plate in the saucepan cupboard,' Jazz said with a laugh. 'Something is fucking with your brain.'

'Oh shit.' Sophie's own laugh was hollow. She moved the plate to its rightful place. 'I'm thinking about what I told you the other day.'

Jazz's eyebrows went skywards. 'You're not having second thoughts, are you?'

'No.' She rubbed her forehead. 'Not at all. I just . . . need to tell people.'

Jazz laughed. 'So tell them. Is it really that difficult? What are you expecting them to do?'

Sophie didn't know. She didn't understand how, after everything Jazz had faced, she was able to accept the

275

kindness that people offered her, all the promises, and not question them. But Sophie had lived her short-term life-style for decades longer than Jazz; it was all so ingrained. 'It's not easy,' she admitted, reaching into the bottom cupboard to put the baking tray away, trying not to think about the spiders that might be lurking inside.

'Harry,' Jazz said.

'Yes, of *course* Harry,' she replied, her head half inside the cupboard. 'He's been so lovely. *Too* lovely, if anything.'

'That sounds like a backhanded compliment.'

Sophie whacked her head on the roof of the cupboard, her heart thundering. That was *not* Jazz's voice.

Jazz laughed. 'I wasn't asking if he was one of the people you needed to tell,' she said. 'I was saying hello to him.'

Sophie backed out of the cupboard, gave herself a second to breathe in relatively fresh air, then looked up. Harry was wearing the black wool coat, dark trousers and shiny black shoes he'd put on that morning, before he'd left for his train. His cheeks were pink from the cold.

'Hey,' she said. 'How was London?'

'Not much fun, but pretty productive.' He made no more allusions to what she and Jazz had been talking about, and she thought he probably wanted to wait until they were alone. She didn't know how much he'd overhead. 'How has tonight been? Can I walk you home?'

'It's gone really well – it's been so busy. My flat is only two minutes away, you know.'

'My place is further.' He held out a hand and, when she took it, he pulled her to her feet. The momentum brought them close, so she could see the flecks of green and brown in his eyes, the individual bristles of his stubble, turned pale under the florescent lights. His lips, slightly cracked, were angled up, ever so slightly, at one side.

'Trying to work out if I'm too lovely?' he whispered.

'I know you are.' She matched his smile, and he seemed to relax. 'Give me five more minutes to finish up here, and we can go.'

'Give me a job, and it'll only take two.'

They finished clearing up together, then Sophie went round and switched all the lights off.

'Hello, Harry.' She heard Fiona greeting him at the main door. 'And your lovely dogs. What are they called again?'

Sophie paused, could hear the reluctance in his voice as he told them, then Jazz's high laughter as it reached near hysteria.

'Darkness and Terror!' she screeched, and Sophie grinned to herself.

Outside, she locked the door and handed the key to Ermin. Jazz was leaning on Fiona's shoulder, her whole body shaking.

Harry gave Sophie a pained look, and she wrapped her arms around him.

'Darkness and Terror,' Jazz said again, her voice muffled, and the two dogs, which Harry had tied up outside along with Clifton, looked up at her.

'They're very stately dogs,' Sophie said soothingly.

'Thank you for trying to rescue the situation.' Harry slipped an arm around her waist.

'Right. We'll be off, then,' Fiona said. 'See you in the shop tomorrow, Sophie?'

'Of course.' She swallowed. Her friend still sounded chilly, and she knew she needed to rebuild that bridge as soon as possible.

'Cheerio,' Ermin said.

'Bye Harry, Sophie.' Jazz's eyes were glittering. 'Bye Clifton. Bye, *Darkness and Terror*.'

The two larger dogs surged forward, accepting strokes and licking Jazz's palms, oblivious to the fuss their names had caused. Then Fiona, Ermin and Jazz strode off in the direction of home, and Harry, Sophie and the dogs turned towards the manor, walking on roads slippery with frost, the air so cold it felt like icy breaths against Sophie's skin.

Their footsteps echoed in the quiet, and a tawny owl hooted from somewhere close by. If she really concentrated, she could hear the shush of the sea, and she wondered how many fishermen's lights were dotting the invisible horizon, dark sky bleeding into dark water.

'What do you need to tell me?' Harry asked eventually.

Sophie's sigh turned to mist in front of her. Could she do it? It would mean no going back, relinquishing some of her control.

'Soph?' Harry prompted. 'Are you OK?'

'I'm good,' she said. 'Relieved how well tonight has gone, that people are embracing our new and improved festival. We have a lot of handmade decorations already, and there's still over a week to go.'

'You must be tired,' Harry said. 'Working all day, making more stock, and now you'll be spending your evenings in the hall, as well as finalizing things for next week.'

'You've been in London,' Sophie pointed out. 'You're not exactly putting your feet up.' She stopped, facing him. 'I'm glad I get to see you now, though. That I'm not going home to my flat, alone.' The word hung in the air between them, the moonlight fractured by the trees overhead. She could

278

only see Harry's features in patches, but she knew he was looking at her, perhaps trying to read her expression.

'I'm glad you're here too,' he said. 'Actually, let's take it up a couple of notches from glad.' He leaned forward, his lips close to her ear, gusting warmth onto her chilled flesh. 'I am delighted you're here. Want me to show you how much?'

'When we're inside in the warm, if that's OK?'

'Come on, then.' He picked up his pace and Sophie hurried to keep up with him, the dogs barking into the darkness, thinking it was a game.

He'd lit a fire in his room. It was a much smaller fireplace, more modern than the huge caverns on the ground floor, but the glow and crackle were instantly soothing, shadows dancing across the walls.

Harry stood in the firelight, his smart blue shirt showing off his lean torso. Sophie shivered and put her bag on the floor under the window. When she opened it to take out her phone, she saw *Jane Eyre* nestled inside, the talking point of tonight's book club chat. She'd left the brown paper at home, so its beautiful cloth cover was visible, the gold foil details dulled in the shadowy interior of her handbag.

'Soph?' Harry came up behind her and slid his hands down her arms. 'Are you sure you're OK?' He bent his head, kissed the sensitive spot where her neck met her shoulder.

She leaned into him. This was what she wanted. His touch and the low rumble of his voice settling over her like a blanket, turning her into heat and sensation, obliterating all other thoughts. 'I am now.'

He put his chin on her shoulder, his hands on her waist. 'Can you tell me . . .?' He stopped, his grip tightening, his body frozen behind hers. It lasted a second, maybe less, then he softened, and she heard him swallow. 'Can you tell me what you and Jazz were talking about?' he said, but he sounded different. Flatter, somehow.

Sophie turned in his arms, and his gaze snagged hers, a slight furrow between his brows. She tried to think how to start; how she could possibly change the course of her life with a few, simple words. But then, before she'd uttered a single one, Harry kissed her. He lifted her into his arms and carried her over to his bed, lowered her onto it and then followed, his knees on either side of her hips, his hands cupping her face as he kept kissing her, over and over.

Sophie let him claim her, let him take her breaths until she felt as if she had none left. She leant up on her elbows, then higher when he pulled the hem of her jumper, lifting it over her head.

'Harry,' she gasped, tugging at his shirt, roughly undoing the buttons, sliding it off his wide shoulders.

'Shh.' He hovered over her, feathering light kisses across her jaw and neck, down to her collarbone.

'I don't—'

'Forget I asked,' he urged. 'Don't say anything at all.'

Sophie nodded and looked into his eyes, saw the heat in them, a fervour he'd never shown her before. She gave herself up to her desire and his, let him kiss and touch her, overwhelm her with every part of him, and wondered if he'd been saying those words for her alone, or if he'd been saying them to himself, too.

Chapter Twenty-Six

The final days before the festival opening were a whirl-wind of bunting and lights, logistics and measurements, worries about too-soft grass and dramas with people signing up for then dropping out of the open mic; questions about whether the Rudolph Hoopla would be too loud, concerns over the visit from Santa Claus.

'It has a hole in the leg, look.' Harry held up the Santa suit, which was made of thick red wool and had a musty scent that made Sophie wrinkle her nose.

'That's what you get for going to the hire shop on the twentieth of December.' But she got up to examine it with him. It was unusual to see Harry panic: he was normally so steadfast, so certain about everything. 'Harry,' she said with a laugh, 'this hole is tiny. You sewed about ten miles of bunting not long ago.'

'I can fix it,' Harry said, 'that's not the point.'

'What is the point?' She looked up at him, her breath catching as it seemed to do every time their gazes held.

'The point is that the shop shouldn't rent something out in this condition, and it's the first night of the festival tomorrow, and we have a hundred other things to do. Plus—' he flung his arm at the study window, and the wind flung sleet back against the pane '—we didn't get a grotto.'

'We can rig something up in the village hall if we need to. There's already a tree and fancy lights in there.' Sophie slid her hand down his arm, hoping it would soothe him.

'And your Decoration Station, and the bridge tournament, and space for the pot-luck dishes people are going to bring. There won't be room for Santa Claus and his presents.' He threw the trousers in the direction of his desk, and they knocked the leather pen pot onto the floor. Darkness, Terror, Clifton and Felix looked up from the rug in front of the fire, but it was only the goat that stayed interested, the others going back to their snoozing.

'Harry, come on.' Sophie dragged him over to the armchairs and pushed him gently into one. He went without resistance, and she climbed onto his lap, then tipped his chin up so he couldn't help but look at her.

'You're going to tell me I'm being melodramatic,' he grumbled. 'I have never been accused of being melodramatic in my life.'

'I'm *going* to tell you it will all be OK. We have mulled wine, Jason's baked Alaska, Simon's fish and chips and mince pies from Dex – not to mention the pot-luck dishes. So the refreshments are sorted, and when you've got food and alcohol, that's half the battle won.

'The oak tree is looking twinkly and festive, and we have the outdoor games from Annie and Jim, the open mic, which has been a *lot* more popular than I anticipated, and the activities in the hall. Also, Birdie wants to do a candle-light blessing around the oak on Christmas Eve.'

'What?' Harry tensed, and Sophie put a hand on his chest.

'I think it'll be beautiful. It's completely non-religious, and it ties in perfectly with our wish and gratitude decorations. The candles will be tiny, and it's far too damp for the tree to be at risk, anyway.'

'That's one good thing about this shit weather,' Harry said.

'*Exactly*.' She kissed the tip of his nose. 'It'll be a wonderful way to end four incredible days. Everyone in the village is coming every evening from what I can tell—'

'They are?'

'Of course they are,' Sophie said. 'This is the Oak Fest. Hasn't it always been the biggest Christmas tradition in Mistingham?'

'It has,' Harry agreed.

'And, what?' Sophie laughed gently. 'You thought, because *we've* organized it, that nobody would come?'

'It's more that, because I vetoed the green and the oak last year, people might . . .'

'Veto you?' she finished.

He nodded.

'Not a chance, Harry Anderly. Everyone loves you now, and this year's going to be the best one ever.'

'Even if Frank Carsdale recites *The Odyssey* on the open-mic stage and nobody else gets a look-in?'

Sophie grinned. 'Now he's got the bridge tournament to oversee, I've convinced him to pick a couple of his favourite verses. I told him the tournament is crucial to the community spirit of the event – which it is – and that he can't let us down. He likes being important.'

Harry laughed and squeezed her hips. 'You're a genius.'

'*We're* geniuses,' she corrected. 'Genii? Anyway. As long as we're together, we'll be fine.' She leant towards him, until her face was inches from his.

'Together,' he whispered it, almost as if it was a new word and he wanted to see how it sounded.

Something shifted in Sophie's heart. She still hadn't told him that she'd decided to stay, and so far Jazz had kept her secret. There was a tiny part of her that was worried the moment she declared it, the whole thing – her growing happiness, everything with Harry – would dissolve in a puff of smoke, as if it had been a temporary Christmas spell, transient and ethereal, not set to last.

'Penny for them?' Harry said quietly.

'All three games are working fine,' Sophie confirmed. 'Annie's been testing them regularly, and I know she won't let us down.'

'No,' Harry pushed a strand of hair off her forehead, 'I mean, a penny for your thoughts. What's going on back there? Behind those eyes I can't stop staring at?'

'Oh.' Sophie's heart squeezed harder. 'I was just thinking about how much has changed.'

'Do you know what that means?' He sounded hesitant, so unlike him. 'For . . . for after Christmas?'

At that moment, with their pets gathered around the crackling fire like an approximation of a nativity scene, and with this man who had let her into his life, who had opened up to her even when it wasn't easy for him, Sophie wondered why she was finding it so hard to admit it: to say that one, simple sentence.

'I . . . I think so,' she said cautiously. 'I think . . . that I'm going to stay.' She could hardly hear herself over the beating of her heart.

Harry froze, his lips parted in surprise. Then he ran his warm palm up her jean-clad thigh. 'You are?' He said it lightly, as if he didn't want to startle her.

'I would like to stay,' she said, trying the words out for size. 'But could we . . . let's get the festival out of the way, then we can talk about it properly. Would that be OK?'

The tenderness in his expression made it hard for her to breathe. 'Of course, Soph,' he said. 'Of *course*. You know how much I want you to stay – I hope you've realized that by now. But let's talk about it then. And, actually, there's been something I've been meaning to say to you too, because I saw . . . Fuck!' He jolted, grabbing Sophie's hips to stop her falling off his lap as they were joined by a small, fluffy goat, who had jumped up and somehow managed to land in between them, on a very sensitive area.

When Sophie was steady, Harry let go of her and lifted Felix up, so he was dangling, bleating happily, revelling in his *Lion King* moment.

Harry glared at him, his breathing slightly elevated. 'Felix,' he said seriously, 'that is not on, OK? We men, we have to stick together, and jumping on a man's . . . *intimate parts* is tantamount to betrayal.'

Felix bleated, and Sophie lost it, dissolving into laughter at Harry's stern tone.

'OK, Felix?' he repeated.

'Didn't Felix get castrated?' Sophie asked. 'Male goats who aren't smelly or aggressive have usually had their bits snipped, and Felix might be a lot of things, but he isn't either of those.'

285

'I got him castrated when I rescued him,' Harry said. 'That's not the point.'

'It isn't?'

Harry leaned over and, very gently, put Felix on the floor. 'I don't know why you're finding this so amusing,' he said to her. 'The state of what's in my boxers affects you too.' He raised an eyebrow, and Sophie's laughter faded. She found herself dissolving for an entirely different reason, and had to go and get her notebook from Harry's desk – the sleet and wind still battering against the window – so they could run through what they had to do before kick-off without getting waylaid by other things.

The next day, Saturday the twenty-first of December, was the opening night of the festival. The sky was grey and the wind was whipping the sea into a fervour, sending herds of white horses galloping towards the shore and shaking the bare branches of the trees. But the lights had stayed put, and the green was relatively sheltered, both by the oak tree and the village hall, and at least the rain and sleet had stayed away – so far, anyway.

'Yes!' Sophie fist-bumped the air.

'What is it?' Harry stood in the doorway of her bedroom, wearing the – now mended – Santa trousers, and a slim-fitting white T-shirt that hugged his torso.

Sophie got lost for a moment, enjoying the sight of him looking so good in her flat. They'd decided to get ready here, as it was so much closer to the green, and if it *did* start raining, they wouldn't get too soaked before they arrived.

'Um.' She blinked herself back to the present. 'Mary and

Winnie are going to kick off the open mic with "Santa Baby" and "Fairytale of New York". They wanted to do "Carol of the Bells", but as it's just the two of them I was worried it would sound a bit sad – haunting, rather than uplifting. Winnie's message says they're prepared to compromise on this occasion.'

Harry rolled his eyes. 'As if singing some fun Christmas songs is a compromise. Mistingham's not Norwich Cathedral, for God's sake! I'm going to set up my own choir next year.'

'Oh you are, are you?' Sophie walked towards him. 'You've finally caught the community bug, after spending all your time up until now as the Dark Demon Lord of Mistingham?'

He stared her down. 'I take it back. And I wouldn't be doing any of this if it wasn't for you.'

Sophie laughed. 'Don't you mean May?'

'No, I mean you. I hope we can do it together next year, too. Build on our success.'

She busied herself finding Harry's hat and beard. 'We have to see if this year *is* a success first.'

He didn't reply, and when she finally looked up, he was watching her intently from the doorway.

'Golly, it looks magical!' Fiona said when she, Ermin, Jazz and Poppet stepped onto the green. The bar had just opened, and Sophie was helping Jason with the awning of his hired food truck. He was selling miniature baked Alaskas to be eaten then and there, and some full-sized ones for customers to take home for Christmas Day.

Relief shot through her like a lightning bolt, because Fiona was right.

It *did* look magical, with all Harry's bunting up around

287

the edge of the green, flapping gaily in the strong wind. The stalls were bright and enticing, the Hook the Duck and Christmas Tree Carnival Toss glossy and bright, the Rudolph Hoopla drawing attention with its flashing lights and blaring soundtrack. They'd put that in the corner farthest from the oak tree, which had the open mic stage beneath it, so that everyone who had bravely agreed to perform wouldn't be drowned out.

'I'm so glad you think so,' she said.

'The tree looks wonderful.' Ermin laughed and rocked back on his heels. 'The little goat!'

'A homage to Felix,' Sophie explained, as Jason grunted and yanked the awning so that it finally slid up, revealing his neat counter. 'And we'll be hanging the homemade decorations, with wishes and gratitude notes, throughout the evening.'

'Where's Harry?' Fiona asked.

'He's in the hall, getting all set up for Santa Claus.' Sophie mouthed the last two words, realizing there were a few families here already and not wanting to ruin anyone's Christmas before it had even started. 'We've set his grotto up behind the village hall, a little bit out of the way, but if the weather gets too bad we can move him inside.'

'I helped May make the grotto last minute,' Jazz said proudly. She was wearing a pair of holly deely boppers, her soft silver jumper and warm-looking coat clearly from Hartley Country Apparel. 'It's a tent and some paper chains, but – even if I do say so myself – it is totally banging.'

'Banging what?' Ermin looked alarmed.

Jazz laughed and pulled him over to the Carnival Toss, saying something about a wager.

Then it was just Fiona and Sophie, and Jason setting up his display of peaked desserts that looked like mini snow-covered mountains.

'You've done a wonderful job, Sophie,' Fiona said.

Sophie smiled even as her spirits sank, because her friend still sounded frosty, which was appropriate for the time of year but so unlike her.

'I'm so sorry,' she said in a rush. 'I'm sorry I accused you of lying to me. I was just desperate to—' She stopped herself. 'No excuses. It was wrong of me.'

Fiona smiled. 'I know you're sorry, and it's OK. I understand why you thought I might be behind the books. Any luck finding the culprit?'

She shook her head. She could hear Natasha calling her, knew she needed to go.

'What about Cornwall?' Fiona asked. 'What about everyone here? The old sweet shop? Harry?'

'I . . .' Sophie didn't want to tell her now. Fiona had been so kind to her, she deserved more than a hurried explanation in the middle of the festival. 'Can we talk about it later?'

Fiona nodded, but there was a barrier between them that hadn't been there before. Sophie hoped that, once she told her she was staying, they would be able to knock it down. 'I hope you make the right decision for *you*, Sophie,' she said. 'Natasha's calling you, I think.'

'She is.' Sophie hurried over to the bar truck, leaving her friend behind.

Soon the green was teeming with people young and old, strolling and running, laughing and chatting. A queue was forming in front of Christmas Hook the Duck, proving that traditions were hard to break, but there was also a steady stream of people going into the village hall, coming out with handmade decorations and paper plates heaped with pot-luck lasagne and mini turkey pies, salads and pigs in blankets. Mary and Winnie were first in a long list of people preparing for their open-mic performances, and Sophie was triumphant – their blend of new and old was working perfectly.

So far, she had been a one-woman whirlwind; trouble-shooting problems, directing Vea, Birdie and Dexter to their stalls, showing children how to play Rudolph Hoopla and helping them hang their felt Christmas puddings, tiny leather bells and glittering cardboard candy canes on the lower branches of the oak tree.

She got a thrill seeing the villagers enjoying themselves, wandering the craft stalls, eating fish and chips, squealing as they got a foam ball in a hole in the Christmas Tree Carnival Toss. Birdie beamed from behind her gleaming jars of jam and chutney – Sophie had checked there were no little packets of mushrooms – and Vea was selling friendship brace-lets and homemade stocking kits, gift sets for embroidery, crochet and jewellery making. Sophie made sure that when anyone complimented the bunting, she referred them to Vea's stall, while also crediting Harry's hard work.

And that was the only problem with tonight: Harry was round the back of the hall, in the camping tent grotto, being Mistingham's Santa Claus. It was an important role, of course, but it meant he wasn't outside, sneaking sips of mulled wine or challenging Lucy to a game of Rudolph Hoopla. But he was doing a good job, judging by the squealing and happy grins as families came out of the tent, with prettily wrapped gifts clutched to their chests. And Sophie had heard the compliments, too:

'Such a stern-looking Santa, but he was so sweet to my Amy.'

'That deep voice, the *ho ho ho* set something off inside me, I swear!'

'Did you see his eyes? That is one *hot* Santa under the curly white beard.'

OK, so most of the compliments had come from mums, but Sophie couldn't blame them, and Harry would be glad he'd been well received (though probably uncomfortable with being lusted after, so she might not tell him *everything* she'd overheard). She did think he needed to see the rest of it, though, so when Ermin sidled over to her, a half-eaten baked Alaska in his hand, and said, 'You and Harry need to do a speech,' she didn't recoil at the idea.

'We'll have to get Harry to change,' she said. 'He can't come out dressed as Santa and spoil it for the children.'

'Leave it to me.' Ermin tapped his nose. 'Meet us at the stage in ten.'

'Sure.' Sophie was confident that Harry would take the reins, and that all she would have to do would be to stand next to him and smile.

True to his word, Ermin appeared a few minutes later with Harry, who was dressed in jeans, a green jumper with gold Christmas trees around the collar, and a black jacket that he needed because the wind was ramping up. The oak tree created its own melody as globe, book and acorn lights jangled in the branches.

291

'Hey.' Sophie rubbed the red line along Harry's jaw, where the Santa beard elastic had clearly dug in. 'How are you doing, Sexy Santa?'

'Please don't call me that,' Harry murmured. 'I'm better now I'm in the fresh air. That tent is on the stifling side.'

'Out in the winter chill, you mean.'

'You'd find it refreshing if you'd spent hours in an itchy wig.'

'The mums loved you,' Sophie said, deciding a little bit of teasing was OK. 'I heard them pining. Desperate to know what you'd got in your sack.'

Harry's eyes danced with amusement. '*Sophie*.'

'They were telling each other how much they wanted you up their chimneys.'

'Santa goes *down* chimneys.'

'Going *down*?' Sophie tapped her lips. 'I *think* I heard one of them say—'

'Good evening, everyone!' Ermin's voice boomed across the green, the mic squealing with feedback.

Visitors turned towards the stage, their chatter and laughter dying down, leaving only the glitzy soundtrack of the Rudolph Hoopla. But it was in the furthest corner from the tree, and Sophie had almost managed to tune it out.

'Good evening everyone,' Ermin said again. 'I trust you're all having a wonderful evening?'

There were whoops and cheers and someone shouted 'Baked Alaska!' followed by lots of tittering. Sophie thought the mulled wine must be flowing well.

'I'm going to hand you over to the organizers of tonight's festival, who I think we can all agree have done a marvellous job. This is the first of four nights of fun and festivities, put on seamlessly by our much-loved villagers, Harry Anderly and Sophie Stevens!' He gestured towards them as the applause got louder.

Much-loved? Harry mouthed with a frown, but Ermin was thrusting a microphone into his hand, pushing him forward on the stage.

'Hello,' he said, as a huge gust of wind tinkled the lights above him. 'Thank you all for coming.'

There were more whoops and cheers.

'I think Ermin's said it all, if I'm honest. We have taken over the reins from Winnie, who had done a lot of the groundwork for us.' He cleared his throat and shot Sophie a glance. She could tell he was nervous, but he sounded – and looked – great, fitting the lord of the manor role perfectly.

'I also wanted to say,' he went on, 'that I owe you all an apology.' His cheeks reddened, and there was a moment's pause, when it seemed that the crowd, even the wind, held their collective breath. Then something new kindled in his gaze.

'Last year I stopped the festival from taking place here, on Mistingham Green. I was over-protective of the oak, and I was . . . basically, I was being selfish – wallowing in the past. A Christmas Day Grinch.' He was louder now, more confident, and a few people laughed. 'Someone told me I needed to let it go, let the green be enjoyed, used as it was meant to be, by the whole village.

'And now, standing here, seeing you all tonight, and knowing the effort that's been put in by Simon and Jason, Annie and Jim and their Christmas Hook the Duck, Vea and Birdie and Dexter, Natasha and Indigo, May, who volunteered me for this role, together with Fiona and Ermin, of course, and everyone brave enough to perform as part of the open mic . . . Now I can say, with complete confidence, that I'm glad I was persuaded, and that I've been a small part of the festivities we're bringing you over the next four nights.'

There was more applause.

'I won't take up too much more of your time,' Harry said with a smile. 'There's just one, final thing, one more person I need to mention: the person who changed my mind about the oak tree, who has been my partner – who has led the way, really.' His eyes dropped to his feet, then he looked up again. 'I have been back in Mistingham a while, as most of you know, but I haven't really been . . . *back*, if you see what I mean. But for the first time in years, I feel a real part of this village: I know I'm where I'm supposed to be, and that's down to Sophie Stevens. She, more than anyone, has made tonight what it is, and she's made it . . .' He glanced at her, then turned back to the crowd. 'She's made this all worthwhile, for me. I wouldn't have wanted to do it without her.'

As cheers filled the air, he stepped back and handed her the microphone, in the one moment she couldn't have said anything even if she'd wanted to. Harry Anderly was a private person, he didn't like airing his clean – let alone his dirty – laundry in public, so what was that? What had he just done? Sophie took the mic, took a step forward, and tried to remember how to breathe, and then how to speak.

Chapter Twenty-Seven

The next morning, Sophie was sitting on the kitchen counter in the manor, reading a book she'd found shoved unceremoniously on the end of a bookshelf in Harry's study: *The Art of Being a Consultant Who Cares*. Harry was frying bacon, slicing a seeded sourdough from Dexter's bakery, and the radio was playing festive songs, 'Fairytale of New York' following 'Last Christmas' in the background.

'Listen to this,' Sophie said, swinging her legs.

'Do I have to?' Harry took four eggs out of a box and put them next to the hob.

'*Being a truly caring consultant,*' she read aloud, '*means thinking like your client, bringing yourself to their level. You will never understand how best to help them unless you identify with them in some way. See what colours they like, match your tie to their jumper. Bring them their favourite coffee when you meet. Take an interest in their children's lives. Harry!*' she laughed.

'It was my leaving present when I left the job in London – a tongue-in-cheek one.'

'It's a real book, though,' Sophie said in wonder. 'It has a publisher and everything. But it's incredibly nuts. Is the writer a real human, do you think?'

'He's probably a psychopath. You get a lot of them in high-stakes business.'

She leaned back on the counter. 'Are *you* a psychopath?'

'I don't think so.' Harry turned the bacon over, and the sizzling ratcheted up a notch.

'You said nice things last night.' She put the book down. 'About Mistingham, and about me.'

'And you returned the favour.' He put down the spatula and stood in front of her. She widened her legs, caging his hips between them.

'I didn't,' she said. 'I mumbled something pathetic up on that stage. But that was *your* fault, because you caught me off guard.'

'I think you said . . .' He closed his eyes, as if he was trying to remember. '*Working with Harry has been great*.' He opened them again, and gave her what could only be described as a cheeky smile. It entirely warranted her flicking a tea towel at his arm.

'Hey!' He rubbed the spot where she'd landed her weapon. 'You are way too good at the tea-towel flick.'

'A boy in one of my foster homes did it constantly, so I had to up my game.'

Harry squeezed her waist. 'No need to up your game here,' he said. 'You don't have to change anything about yourself; you don't need to try at anything. Just be you.' He kissed her nose, then went back to his pan.

'OK,' Sophie managed around the lump in her throat. 'Except I think we'll have to try hard to rustle up some visitors for tonight.' She gestured to the window, the blur of rain against the glass, the tap-tap-tap from the sleet that was mixed up with it. The trees were swaying chaotically, like a backing group that had all been given a different dance routine for the same song.

'Some of the hardier villagers will still come,' Harry said. 'And if it gets too awful, we can move most of it into the hall. The open mic, the Rudolph Hoopla. The bridge tournament and the Decoration Station will just have to be squeezed a bit.'

Sophie slid off the counter and got out plates and cutlery. 'It's going to fuck everything up, though. We can't possibly fit all of it in the hall, and the craft stands and food trucks won't survive a monsoon.'

'We'll play it by ear,' Harry said calmly. 'Take every challenge as it comes.'

It was this, Sophie thought: his certainty, his confidence, that she loved so much. One of the things, anyway. It made her feel safe, it made *her* feel certain. Her brain was stuttering over the word that had come so easily to her, the *L* word, when he said, 'You remember that book you mentioned? You said you'd been given one as an anonymous gift?'

Sophie stilled, clutching two forks. 'So I *did* tell you, then.'

'You mentioned something about it.' Harry cracked eggs into the pan. 'Any luck finding out where it came from?'

'No,' Sophie admitted. After accusing Fiona, it felt tainted, somehow. Not the book itself, but her desperate need to find out the source. It was as if it was telling her to stay well away, enjoy it for what it was – like Winnie and Simon were doing with theirs – and stop digging. 'I didn't find out, but I don't mind, really.'

'No?' Harry asked.

'It was a generous gift, a story I love, so what else do I need to know? Sometimes, these things find their way to you exactly when you need them. I think it's best if I leave it at that.'

'Right,' Harry said quietly, and when she glanced at him, he was staring at the frying eggs, as if they held within them all the mysteries of the universe.

'This is a disaster,' Sophie said loudly, as she and Harry reached the green that evening. Puddles covered the grassy surface, and the bunting was dancing frantically, one end looking perilously close to coming untied.

'What?!' Harry shouted, and she turned to him and repeated it. They were soaked already, their waterproof coats shielding them from the worst of it, but nobody would want to play Hook the Duck or eat baked Alaska in this.

'It might ease off,' Harry said, as Jason ran to his truck, carrying a box of supplies wrapped in a large plastic bag.

'See you've not wangled the weather in our favour!' he called over, grinning.

'We're trying,' Harry called back. 'Leave it with us!'

'Maybe we should get Birdie to perform a spell,' Sophie said, staring at the oak tree. 'Some kind of anti-rain dance.'

'I'd happily ask her if I thought it would make a difference. I need to check that the waterproof box for the electrics has stayed waterproof.'

Sophie's stomach clenched. 'Can't someone else do that?'

'What?' He looked at her, his eyes gleaming beneath his hood.

'Someone . . .' she wanted to say *more expendable*, but that would sound beyond callous. 'Just be careful, OK?'

'Yes, boss.' Harry gave her a reassuring smile, then strode over to the outside wall of the village hall, where the electrics for the lights, sound system and Rudolph Hoopla were plugged into a sturdy-looking box. It promised it was waterproof, and Sophie hoped that, even in the face of such a horrible storm, that was a promise it would keep.

An hour later, both the wind and rain had faded, and Harry had posted an update on the Mistingham Facebook group that wellies were the preferred footwear, but that there was more fun to be had at the Festive Oak Fest.

'It felt strange, writing those words,' he admitted, as he and Sophie sheltered under the awning of Natasha's bar with cups of steaming mulled wine.

'Using the words "more fun to be had" ?' Sophie grinned at him.

'Exactly.'

'I've had quite a lot of fun with you, recently,' she pointed out.

'Let's not perform *that* on the stage tonight,' Harry said, in the low growl that did funny things to her. 'I'm not sure we'll be invited to organize any more events if we do.' His lips were inches from hers.

She swallowed. 'It would be talked about for a hundred years, at least. But I didn't just mean that. I meant all of it – buying lights together, late-night paddling, goat rescuing.'

'You enjoyed the goat rescue?'

'I enjoyed your shower afterwards. And I enjoyed Felix being safe.'

'Felix is a menace.'

'You love him.'

'For my sins.'

'You're the best goat dad.'

'*Goat dad?* Sophie Stevens, you are just about—'

'Just about what?' She smiled up at him, and he glared at her. He was trying, but mostly failing, to keep a straight face.

'Come on,' he said. 'Let's go and whip up some festive cheer amongst the people who have bothered to turn out tonight.'

Apart from the puddles, the evening got off to a good start, a four-piece band of teenagers starting off the open mic with a rousing rendition of 'Santa Claus Is Coming to Town' that got everyone singing along.

'Sorry about the puddles,' Sophie heard Harry say as the young saxophonist picked his way across the grass afterwards. 'You were great, by the way.'

'We've got more songs if you want,' the young man said with a cocky grin. 'We can do Rihanna's "Umbrella".'

Harry laughed. 'Definitely do that. I'll find you space in the schedule.'

Half an hour later, Sophie had let go of most of her concerns. The villagers didn't seem to care about the bad weather – seemed to thrive on it, in fact – and Simon's fish and chips and Natasha's mulled wine were both popular on such a cold night. The Decoration Station was also getting a lot of interest, and it swelled Sophie's heart to

300

know that each one of the little handmade decorations had a Christmas wish or a message of gratitude inside: that the oak tree – at the heart of the village where it belonged – was also carrying their heartfelt messages.

She was showing one of Lucy's friends, Sabina, how to stand and throw to have the best chance of scoring big on the Carnival Toss, when she saw a familiar figure meandering through the crowd.

'Thanks, Aunty Sophie,' Lucy said with a grin, her reindeer antlers jiggling in the wind. 'We're good now.'

'You sure? OK, then.' She said goodbye and chased the dark ponytail across the green. She hadn't seen May properly for a few days, and she wanted to ask her about Christmas presents for Harry. They hadn't talked about what they were doing on Christmas Day, which seemed ridiculous when it was only three days away, but she thought that was probably because Harry didn't want to pressure her into committing to anything she wasn't ready for. She felt guilty, and she wanted to show him how much he meant to her.

'May!' she called. She had to raise her voice to be heard over the Rudolph Hoopla and someone singing 'Mack the Knife', and over the wind that had returned with full force, whistling between the food trucks and craft stalls, sending the oak tree's decked-out limbs into a discordant frenzy.

May clearly hadn't heard her, but Sophie persisted, pausing when there was a shriek from somewhere, making sure it was a happy shriek, not one signifying disaster. When she was confident it was a patron enjoying themselves, she hurried on. She saw May turn towards the row of craft stalls, and then, as she got close, someone shouted her name, their voice rising above the other festival sounds.

Sophie peered over the tops of heads to see who wanted her. It hadn't sounded like Harry. Ermin, maybe? Was it . . .? There was a huge crack of thunder, followed by a long, loud rumble, as if a giant had taken the break on a huge pool table in the sky, and the balls were rolling, rolling, rolling above them. She instinctively ducked down, and now there *were* some unhappy squeals in the crowd, because with the thunder came the rain. It fell all of a sudden, like an icy sheet.

'Shit!' She scanned the green again and saw Harry standing by the oak tree, his hand raised, waving frantically, his expression telling her that she needed to get over there.

She raised her arm, hoping he'd seen her, and began to cross the green towards him, weaving through people who had their heads down, looking for shelter. Then the whole scene lit up in a huge flash, a second of complete whiteout, and the thunder crashed again. There were shrieks and people running, pelting rain and the howl of the wind. Sophie stood for a moment, frozen to the spot, and then, just as she was about to get going again, a deafening BANG obliterated all the other sounds, making her jump and plunging everything into darkness. No more Rudolph and his soundtrack, no more Frank Sinatra renditions, no more glimmering lights in the trees or glow through the hall windows. No more streetlights.

The whole of Mistingham faded to black, and then, all hell broke loose.

Chapter Twenty-Eight

The shouts and squeals and screaming wind made it hard for Sophie to think. There was no moon because of the storm clouds, which meant that everything was truly dark.

Voices called around her, high and panicked.

'Beth! Beth, where are you?'

'What happened?'

'Is everyone OK?'

'Jesus, what a storm.'

A few phone torches flicked on, but they were will-o'-the-wisps, not lighting enough to make sense of anything other than the obvious reality that people were panicking and hurrying, as if the green itself was dangerous.

A hand gripped Sophie's arm, making her jump again. 'Are you OK?' It was Dexter.

'Oh, Dexter, I'm fine. Are you OK? Where's Lucy?'

'Hopefully with Sabina and her parents, but I need to find her.' He put his phone light on, highlighting them both.

'I should take control of this,' she said. 'I'm supposed to be in charge.' What she really wanted to do was find Harry, check that he was all right. The wind was still raging, but the crowd felt thinner, as if people had decided to head for home, where they at least knew where things were, even if they couldn't see them.

A large, bright spotlight shone over the green, and for a moment Sophie thought the power had come back on, but then Ermin called out, 'If you all want to make your way to the hall, we can shelter there until we decide what to do. If you want to go home, and you're safe getting there, that's fine, too!'

There was agitated chatter and a swell of movement, Ermin shining his torch on the door of the village hall. Above them, Sophie could just make out the rolling storm clouds, and around her, flickers of people finding each other with their phones, but that was all. The edges of the green were nothing but different shades of black.

'I've seen Lucy,' Dexter said, sounding relieved. 'I'm going to make sure she's OK, then I'll find you, help wherever I can.'

'Great. Thank you, Dex, but stay with Lucy if she needs you.'

He disappeared into the melee, and Sophie found her own phone, put on the torch and went to check on the food trucks. Natasha had a Maglite angled across her mobile bar, and was rapidly tidying everything away.

'Are you all right?' Sophie asked.

'I need to get back to the Blossom Bough. I've left a couple of my part-timers in charge, and they'll be having kittens not knowing what to do in a power cut.'

'Go,' Sophie said. 'I'll lock up your stand.'

'Sure?'

'Sure.' She took the keys from Natasha, used her light to make sure everything was tidied away, then pulled down the shutter and locked it. Everything was so much more difficult with limited light and a thrashing wind. She gave one final pull on the door, checking it was secure.

'Sophie!' Her body recognized the voice before her brain did, and she whipped round, saw a torch beam heading towards her.

'Harry!' He was walking awkwardly, his long strides off-kilter over the uneven ground. 'Are you all right?'

'I'm fine,' he said. 'Are *you*? I didn't know where you were.'

He brought his right arm around her, pulling her against him, and she buried her nose in his neck. His skin was chilled and damp, but she felt calmer immediately. She reached her hands behind his neck and he flinched.

'Harry?' she took a tiny step back.

'I'm fine.'

'What happened?' She held her phone up and to the side, so she could see his face without blinding him.

'I'm not sure the village hall is the best place for everyone right now,' he said. 'A lot of people have gone home, but there's Frank and his bridge players. Dexter and Lucy are still here, and Birdie, Jazz, Fiona and Ermin. There's no comfort; it's just cold and dark.'

'Harry?'

'I've got a generator at the manor. I installed it a while ago, so . . .'

'*Harry.*' She touched his cheek, turned his head so he was facing her. 'Why did you flinch when I put my arms around you?'

'It's nothing.'

'*What's* nothing?'

He clenched his jaw, irritated. 'Something fell on me when that lightning flared. I was standing next to the village hall and something fell off – a bit of the roof, I think – but it didn't hit anyone else.'

'Oh, that's OK then,' Sophie gritted out. 'As long as it's only *you* who got injured. Where does it hurt?' She felt sick all of a sudden, desperate to check he wasn't bleeding, that he hadn't broken anything.

'My shoulder, but I'll be fine. Let's get everyone to the manor, wait out the storm there.'

Sophie was shivering, the icy rain hitting her skin in shards, and Harry had his hood down, his hair plastered to the top of his head.

'Are you sure you're happy to have everyone at the manor? The power might come back on in a minute.' But the thunder and lightning were relentless, and Sophie reasoned that it wouldn't be fun sitting it out with no possibility of light except candles, no heat except blankets. The manor, with all its fireplaces, was a much more welcome prospect. Add in a generator, and it was positively palatial.

'I think we should go there and see what happens,' Harry said. 'Everyone's put so much effort into this event, and I know it might be ruined now – we'll have to wait until it's light to see the damage – but this is the least I can do for them.'

'OK.' Sophie squeezed his right arm, frowning when he tried to rotate his left, then winced. 'And I can have a look at your shoulder.'

'It's fine,' he said again.

'Except it's obviously not. Come on, let's get out of the deluge.'

Harry was right: the village hall was cold and inhospitable, with the rain drumming against the glass, the hard wooden floor and the meagre flickers from the battery-operated tea lights. In the light of Ermin's torch, Sophie was met with a sea of anxious, unhappy faces.

'OK everyone,' Harry said, managing to sound both direct and soothing, 'anyone who wants to can come back to the manor. I've got a generator there, so we should be able to get some light, and at the very least I've got fireplaces.'

'Ooh lovely,' said a voice.

'Mistingham Manor? It's like bloody Narnia, that place. Not sure it even exists.' Sophie was sure that was Valerie, one of Frank's more forthright friends.

'How will we get there?' someone else asked.

'I've got my car,' Ermin said.

'I can get the Land Rover,' Harry added. 'If you're happy to wait fifteen minutes.'

'I can go.' May stood up and put a hand on Harry's arm. 'You rally the troops.'

She gave Sophie a quick smile, her features shadowy, then she was gone, out into the cold night, the door banging behind her.

'Will Felix be there?' piped up a young voice that Sophie thought must be Lucy.

'Yes,' Harry said. 'And the dogs.'

'Darkness and Terror!' Lucy shouted, jubilant.

'Fuck's sake,' Harry murmured, so only Sophie could hear. 'I am never going to live that down, am I?'

She slid her hand around his waist. 'Never in a million years.'

'I'm glad you're here,' he said simply.

'Me, too.' There was something about the exchange that made her chest ache, the drastic turn the night had taken knocking her off-kilter, somehow. She wanted to fast-forward half an hour, until they were all safely at Mistingham Manor, with proper light to see by and a fire crackling in at least one of the rooms. She wanted, more than anything, to make sure Harry was OK.

Against the backdrop of the storm, the pelting rain and howling wind, the thunder an intense, constant rumble and lightning taking bleak, intermittent snapshots, Mistingham Manor looked like the starring attraction in a 1950s horror film.

It was still in darkness when Sophie clambered out of the Land Rover and helped Frank, then his friend Valerie, then Birdie, down from the high vehicle, and she could just make out their apprehensive looks.

'I'll get the generator going,' Harry called over the rain, hurrying to the side of the house. 'Take everyone into the lounge.'

'OK!' Sophie called, but it was May who led the small, bedraggled group through the large hall, everyone murmuring excitedly as they went, and Sophie realized that she'd never been in the lounge, because Harry had always taken her to his study.

It was at the back of the house, May's sweep of the torch revealing a huge room with two floor-to-ceiling windows. It faced away from the sea, and Sophie wondered why that was, but she didn't have time to ponder the architectural anomaly, instead helping Frank, Valerie and Birdie to the sofas arranged around the fireplace. May knelt in front of the hearth, trying to get a fire started.

'Let's get settled here,' Sophie said. 'I'm sure Harry will have the power working in a moment.'

'This is a bloody castle,' Valerie announced. 'This room alone is bigger than my bungalow.'

'Harry's family have owned it for generations,' Frank told them. He sounded sad, and Sophie wondered if he'd been friends with Bernie Anderly.

'Here we go!' May sounded as cheerful as always, much brighter than the situation warranted, but then a whoosh of flames filled the fireplace, the light and warmth softening the shadows. It made the raging storm seem less sinister, and Sophie felt some of her tension slipping away.

'Does Harry need help with the generator?' she asked.

'My dad's helping him,' Lucy piped up from one of the sofas. Darkness and Terror had found her, Clifton was already scooting onto her lap, and Sophie wondered where Felix was.

'We could do with some more wood,' May said, poking at the fire.

'There'll be some in Harry's office.' Sophie squeezed the other woman's shoulder. 'You're incredibly calm about all this.'

May shrugged. 'A little bit of drama never hurt anyone. It's sometimes when the best things happen – as long as nobody gets hurt.'

'Harry's hurt his shoulder,' Sophie said, a flutter of concern in her chest.

'I'm sure once he's got the power back on, he'll let you play nurse.'

Sophie didn't miss the amusement in May's voice, and she hoped the other woman saw her scowl before she turned on her heel and, using her phone to guide her, left the lounge and went back into the hall, then through to Harry's study.

She felt better in here, because it was such a familiar room to her now. But it was freezing, and the sound of heavy rain hitting the windows, the wind screaming through the trees outside, was overwhelming. She tried not to think about what the sea might look like right now; how big and terrifying the waves must be.

She padded over to the fireplace and crouched next to the log basket. She picked out a couple of the larger logs, and was about to stand up when there was another noise. It sounded as if it was inside the room, a creak, followed by a rat-tat-tat. Sophie shivered. She knew there were rumours of a ghost at the manor, but she'd been here so many times now, and had never felt anything remotely eerie. *That's because you've always been with Harry*, said a little voice in her head.

She glanced over to the far corner of the room, but she couldn't see anything except shades of grey and black, shapes that looked like they were moving, but couldn't be. She returned to her task, choosing a couple more logs. The noise came again, louder than before. A long, slow creaking, as if something was gradually ripping open. All the hairs prickled up on the back of her neck, and goosebumps covered her skin.

Sophie put the logs down and raised her phone to

illuminate the far side of the room, where there were floor-to-ceiling bookshelves. Was there a mouse, or some other small creature? Was this room falling apart? Harry had told her it wasn't finished, but she thought he meant it needed new furniture. It had always seemed structurally sound when she'd been in here.

She panned her light over the bookshelves, and froze. There was a gap, right in the corner of the room. Shining the light on it, she could see a black, impenetrable void. It made no sense, but there was a *gap* between the bookshelves. The rat-tat-tat came again, followed by another creak, and Sophie swallowed her fear and got to her feet.

She tiptoed across the room, holding her phone up in front of her. She got closer, closer . . . and then she saw what was going on. Part of the bookshelf was also a door. The shelves were real, the books arranged on them were real, but a portion of it was on a hinge, and the door was ajar, revealing a void behind it.

Sophie pressed her palm against the books and pushed, and the door moved slowly inwards. She was hit with a waft of cold, damp air that was nothing like the air in the study.

She blinked, her brain trying to make sense of what she was seeing, and then there was a flash, and all the lights came on: the side lights in the study lit her from behind, and in this new, hidden space there was one large standing lamp and a smaller lamp, both of which were now glowing, illuminating everything.

The first thing Sophie saw was that this was an annex, a single-storey room bolted onto the side of the house, and that it had been damaged in the storm. A thick branch must have snapped off a tree in the high winds and crashed through the roof, landing in the centre of the space. Rain fell through the gap, swirling to the floor, drenching everything inside. The next thing she noticed was Felix, standing frozen next to the fallen branch, as if unsure how he'd ended up there. Sophie swallowed, wondering how close he'd come to being hit by the bit of tree. He was wearing a blue jumper covered in silver snowflakes, and when he saw her he let out a plaintive bleat.

Sophie held out her hand to him, but her attention was snagged by the walls, all of which were lined with books, rows and rows of them, on built-in shelves. Some looked new but a lot of them were old, tatty, falling apart. Some didn't have covers, their spines visible, glue covering the pale lines of the sewn signatures.

Her eyes fell on the wall to her right, and the pine desk that looked like a workstation. It was covered in tools that Sophie was so, so familiar with. There was a carpenter's square and an awl, a cutting board, a ruler, and a sharp-looking craft knife. She could see a wooden book press and a roll of mull, the fabric used to strengthen the spines of books, fixing the adhesive but leaving them flexible so they could open properly. These were all things she used to create her casebound leather journals, and seeing them here, in a secret room in Harry's house, made her brain stutter.

And then, right in the middle of the desk, spot-lit by the lamp sitting on a shelf above it, there was a single, beautiful book.

Sophie's breath stalled.

It was bound in a rich blue cloth, and had bronze foil details – they looked like dandelions – scattered over the cover. The colours were different, but it was so similar to her copy of *Jane Eyre*, to Winnie's *Mrs Palfrey at the Claremont*. On the front was written, in bronze foil to match the dandelions: *Northanger Abbey* by Jane Austen.

Her heart in her mouth, Sophie stepped forwards and picked it up, tipping it so she could see the spine. The title and author were printed down the side and then, at the very bottom, there was the same logo she'd puzzled over on her own book, wondering what it meant.

Suddenly, it was obvious. The little house with two chimneys, its roof a perfect, symmetrical triangle, was an H laid over an A. H for Harry. A for Anderly. Her book had come from him: he had lied to her. She gently placed *Northanger Abbey* back on the desk, her thoughts scrambling as she turned away from it.

Harry was standing in the doorway, holding his shoulder, his expression a confusing mix of pain and panic.

'Sophie.'

In that moment, all her hopes of staying in Mistingham with him fell away, leaving behind anger, and hurt, and sad resignation.

'What is this?' she asked, emotion clogging her throat.

She stood there, with Felix's warm, damp body pressed against her leg, and waited for Harry to somehow explain all this away, so she didn't have to give up on the future she had only just found the courage to hope for.

Chapter Twenty-Nine

'It isn't what you think it is.' The moment he said it, Harry made a face, as if realizing that was the least promising start to his defence.

'Right.' Sophie's voice sounded so flat, she almost didn't recognize it.

A crash of thunder made them both jump, and Harry held his hand out. 'Let's go into my study. I don't think it's safe here.'

'What about your precious books?' Sophie flung her arm out behind her.

She saw him waver for a split-second, his gaze flicking over her shoulder, then he shook his head. 'Come on.' She let him pull her out of the annex and into the study. He shut the door firmly, then went straight to the fireplace, even though the lights – and so presumably the heating – were working again.

'You got the generator going, then,' Sophie said, because even though she was angry and confused, she hated the silence between them: hated that he'd been out in the rain with an injured shoulder.

'It took me and Dex longer than we'd like, but we did it.' He arranged paper around the wood, nestled the fire-lighter in the middle and lit it, staying on his knees until it was flaming. Then he hauled himself up and dragged one of the armchairs across the rug, so they were closer. He gestured for her to sit down, then sat right in front of her.

'How's your shoulder?' she asked.

'I think we have more important things to talk about, don't you?'

'If you're injured, you need to let someone look at it.'

'I will, but not now. I didn't mean for you to discover . . .' He glanced behind him. 'To discover that. I was going to tell you about it.'

'Your Secret Book Lair?' She folded her arms.

Felix, set free from his watery cave – although he had never actually been trapped – was warming himself in front of the fire, his ears pricked up.

'It's not a secret,' Harry said. 'It's . . . when Dad couldn't run The Book Ends any more, there was a lot of stock left. Some of it went back to the wholesaler's, some of it we passed on – to charity shops and the library in Dad's care home – but there were still all these books, a lot of them really old, just . . . sitting there. And they were there for too long, because I was still in London and I didn't make enough time, but I finally hauled them all here. When I moved back, one of the first things I did was build the annex to store them in.' He rubbed his forehead. 'Clearly, I didn't make it stormproof.'

315

Sophie didn't know what to say. All of that made sense, but it didn't come close to explaining *her* book, or Winnie or Simon's, or why he hadn't told her he bound books in his spare time; that they had that in common.

'And then?' she prompted. The fire crackled encouragingly, and Sophie wondered how the others were coping. Was May looking after Frank, Valerie and Birdie? Was Lucy OK?

'I told you, I think, that I started to find my work in London soulless?' Harry said, and she nodded. 'I was in a pub one night, and there was this sign on the wall for evening courses: develop a hobby, find your passion, that sort of thing. I was feeling completely hollowed-out, really unhappy, so I looked at the website. I didn't even know if the company existed any more. Who puts flyers up on pub walls these days?'

'People who accidentally add an extra couple of zeros to their flyer order?' Sophie suggested. 'End up with twenty thousand instead of two?'

Harry looked at her, surprised. But she had to find some levity, or she'd drown in her disappointment before he got to the end of his story.

'I did it with some expensive leather sheets,' she explained. 'I ordered two hundred instead of twenty. I didn't realize until the bank called me to tell me I'd gone over my over-draft limit, and by then they were already on their way. It was four years ago, and I still have a lot left. They do make beautiful notebook covers though,' she added pointedly, and Harry closed his eyes.

'One of the courses they were offering was bookbinding,' he went on. 'It sounded archaic, so old-fashioned, but . . . I guess I was thinking about Dad, feeling guilty. I couldn't

come home because then we'd have lost this place, so I just
. . . I went to the first night. It was a small group, and I
was the youngest there by a long way – apart from a girl
called Destiny who was setting up an Etsy shop, who wanted
to rebind romance books.

'I didn't really have any aims, except to lose myself in
something that wasn't about ambition or greed. And I loved
it. I kept going with the sessions. Then, when I moved back
here, I decided that all those old books that had been in
Dad's shop, some of which were damaged, the covers ruined
– I would try and rebind them. I got the tools and the
materials, set up that desk in the annex. I didn't want to
tell anyone, not until I'd seen whether I could really do it.'

'Then what were you going to do?' It was both heartwarming and heart-*breaking* that he'd done this: felt so
miserable and trapped in London, found something good
that made him think of his dad. If she hadn't been so angry,
so upended by her discovery, she would have wrapped her
arms around him.

'I don't know.' Harry shrugged a shoulder. 'I thought . . .
maybe reopen The Book Ends, eventually. But it's not quick
work, I'm still pretty amateur, and the house repairs had
to take priority. Clearly, I still have a long way to go with
those. But I didn't . . . I never meant for that copy of *Jane
Eyre* to end up with you.' He frowned.

Sophie's heart thudded. 'You didn't?'

'I didn't know you had it, not at first.'

'I told you . . .' Sophie thought back, trying to remember
what she'd told him about it and when. She knew she'd
mentioned it, but had she given him all the details? 'What
do you mean, Harry? I don't understand.'

'I didn't leave that book for you at the shop. You mentioned you'd been given a book, that you didn't know where it had come from, but I had no idea it was one of mine. Not until . . .'

'When?' Sophie asked quietly.

'The night I came to meet you at the village hall, the day I'd been in London. Your bag was open in my bedroom and I saw it.'

'But you didn't say anything?' Sophie stood up. She had too much nervous energy to sit still any longer. She heard barking in another part of the house, and Felix's head turned, but he didn't leave his spot on the rug. 'Do you know how it ended up with me? How Winnie and Simon ended up with your books too, if you're claiming it wasn't you?'

'It *wasn't* me,' Harry said. 'I promise you. And, at the time, I was pretty sure I knew what had happened, but I didn't want to say anything until I was certain.'

'And do you know, now?'

He nodded.

Sophie waited, her fingers tingling with tension. 'Who was it?' she asked, when he didn't offer up the information.

Harry swallowed. 'It was May.'

Sophie blinked. 'What? Why?'

'May left it for you, but she didn't tell me. I didn't know she'd done it until the day I saw it in your bag. She's the only other person who knows what I've been doing, who had access to that room and the books I'd bound.'

'But . . . but it makes no sense! *Why* would she do it?'

Harry sat forward, put his elbows on his knees, then immediately sprang back, pain twisting his features. Sophie needed to look at his shoulder, but she had to make sense of what had happened, first.

'May is a hopeless romantic,' Harry said.

Sophie laughed. 'She's a tech wizard. She went to Silicon Valley. She spends her days working with bits and bots and . . . whatever they're called.'

'She's technically brilliant, but she is also as sentimental as they come,' Harry explained. 'She's known me for a long time; we stayed in touch when we were miserable on opposite sides of the world. She knew about the bookbinding and, once we'd both moved back here, she said we had to do something special with the books I'd rescued. She knew I wanted to reopen the bookshop at some point, but she said there were other ways of being creative, of making magic out of what I was doing.

'I thought she meant when I'd finished a good number of them; when the house was done and I'd spent some time bringing my skills up to scratch. I didn't realize she'd taken that copy of *Jane Eyre*, or the others. I didn't notice they were gone, because that room is full of books and I tend to focus on the one I'm working on, and lately, with the festival, I've been too busy to spend any time in there anyway.'

'So she took them without your permission?' Sophie couldn't help sounding sceptical.

'She did.'

'And you didn't *notice*?' She walked over to Harry's desk and pulled back the curtain. The floodlights lit up the driveway and the still pelting rain. It was dark and miserable, and she turned back to the cosy room.

'I didn't notice,' Harry repeated. 'If I'd asked you more

about *your* book, if I'd seen it earlier, I would have known it was one of mine.'

Sophie shook her head. She'd instantly dismissed Harry as her anonymous giver. She hadn't properly asked him about it, had never shown him the – *his* – beautifully bound book. 'But you *did* know,' she said. 'Ten days ago.'

'I wanted to make sure I'd got it right before I said anything to you.'

'You knew May was the only person it *could* be,' Sophie said. 'You could have told me. You could have trusted me.' He'd chosen May over her; had wanted to protect his friend, rather than be honest with Sophie.

'It wasn't about *not trusting* you,' Harry said. 'I didn't want to come to you with half the facts.'

'And what facts are you still waiting for? Because you *didn't* tell me. I found out by discovering your Secret Book Lair.'

'Secret Book Lair,' he muttered. He looked up at her, and he suddenly seemed exhausted. 'I wanted to find out from May *why* she'd taken one of my books and left it for you. And she has told me, but I suppose I was . . .' He swallowed. 'I suppose it was an uncomfortable thing, telling you the truth.'

Sophie sat back down, the armchairs so close that their knees were touching.

'Why was it uncomfortable?'

'Because May had realized I liked you.'

Sophie frowned. 'We didn't know each other. We'd seen each other a few times in the village, but hardly ever spoken. I got the book the day after our run-in on the cliff path.'

Harry closed his eyes. 'I didn't know exactly when you got it.'

'Why does that matter?'

He met her gaze. 'I'd mentioned you to May a few times, asked her about the woman selling notebooks in Fiona's shop, told her when I'd seen you out running. I'd done that thing of bringing you up whenever I could, because even though I didn't know you, I'd noticed you. I thought you were attractive, your smile was warm, and you were focused – determined. I had a . . . crush on you.' He grimaced. 'May understood immediately, because we've been friends for three decades. I wanted to speak to you, but it turned out I wasn't very good at it.'

Sophie remembered bumping into him outside Fiona's shop, when he'd spilt his coffee, and their run-in at the post office. This was another moment when she should have had her arms around him, laughing delightedly at the idea of forty-two-year-old mega grump Harry Anderly having a crush on her, being so rusty with his communication skills that she thought he hated her instead.

'She was matchmaking us?'

Harry nodded. 'She thought she could bring us together, somehow. She saw how much I messed up in the post office. When I confronted her, she said she thought she could do a better job.'

'With an anonymous book? How was that supposed to help?'

'She told me that you'd figure it out: that having the book would, at the very least, send you in my direction, because of Dad and the bookshop. She thought it would be a kind of treasure hunt, and that when you got talking to me, something was bound to happen between us.'

'It sounds like a fairy tale.'

'Soph,' Harry said quietly. 'She wasn't wrong, was she?'

'We got talking because of the Oak Fest.'

'Which she encouraged me to get involved in.'

Sophie thought back to that night in the village hall, how it was the mystery of the book that had made her put her hand up and volunteer: she wanted to get to know the villagers so she could find out who had sent it to her.

'She's been manipulating us.'

'She likes you,' Harry said. 'A lot.'

Sophie stood up again. 'So why not just tell me? Why not say: *I like you, Sophie, and I think you'd be great for my grumpy friend Harry?*' She flung her arms wide. 'This is ridiculous – all of it. And you've known for ten days, and you didn't tell me.'

Harry pushed himself to standing. 'I wanted to tell you. I was going to do it on Christmas Eve, once the festival was out of the way. I didn't want you to think we'd been conspiring against you. It's my book, and it sounds crazy – I *know* it sounds crazy that I didn't know about this, but I promise you I didn't. And I should be mad with May for going about things the way she did, but I can't be mad with her.'

'Because she's your friend,' Sophie said. 'That's where your loyalty lies.'

'No! I mean, of course I'm loyal to her. But the reason I can't be mad,' he said, taking a step towards her, 'is because it worked. Because it *did* bring us together, and it's been the best thing that's happened to me in years. I wouldn't wish us back to being strangers for anything.' He held his hands out.

Sophie stared at them. Her thoughts wouldn't slow down. 'You didn't tell me,' she said. 'For ten whole days, you knew May had done this, and you didn't tell me. You've been binding books – I make notebooks. It's something we've got in common, but you didn't want to share it?'

'I was shocked when I found out you made your own notebooks; that what we were doing was so similar. But my bookbinding . . . It's supposed to just be a hobby, my own thing, and I'm still such an amateur. I wasn't confident enough about it to tell you, I wanted to wait until I was better at it, and my books weren't supposed to leave the annex.'

'They're beautiful,' she said quietly.

'It was never about intentionally keeping anything from you.' Harry's eyes were gleaming in the firelight. 'It's hard for me to open up to people, but I've been more honest with you than I have with anyone in a long time.'

'Not about this.'

She needed time to think. She'd been desperate to know who had given her the book, and it had been May all along. She thought of all the times they'd had coffee and cake together and talked about Harry. Were her feelings even real? May had wanted her and Harry to be together, so she'd engineered it. Suddenly, Sophie couldn't breathe.

She was in charge of her future. Only her. She couldn't let anyone else decide, steer her in the direction *they* wanted. Trent had tried to do that, and when she didn't live up to his expectations, he'd discarded her as easily as if he'd been closing a door.

'Sophie?' Harry put his hands on her shoulders, looking at her with concern. 'Soph, are you OK? I'm so sorry. I'm sorry this happened, I'm sorry I didn't tell you the moment I knew. May's intentions are always good, but she got carried away. I don't think she realized—'

'This is *my* life,' Sophie said. 'I didn't . . . what if it isn't real? What if none of this is real?'

He squeezed her shoulders. His touch was usually so reassuring, but now she just felt trapped. 'It *is* real,' he said. 'My feelings for you are real. The book – it's just like the initial meeting, the *meet cute*. Nothing more.'

'I-I don't know!' She stepped back, extricating herself from his grip. 'I don't know any more. I need to go.'

'Please don't.'

'No. You lied to me, Harry. I don't – I mean, the book, May . . . You haven't been honest with me, so how do I know that *this* is true, what you're saying? What if you did it together?'

He held his hands out in front of him, as if she was a frightened animal and he didn't want to startle her. 'I didn't,' he said. 'I promise you, I didn't know. But I do want a future with you. I want us to have a future together here, in Mistingham.'

Panic rose inside her. It hadn't happened the way she'd thought; she hadn't been in control of any of it. 'I'm going.'

Harry hesitated. 'Now? Back home?'

'I'm leaving Mistingham,' she said in a rush. It was what she always did. It was how she stayed in control.

'What?'

'I told you that I was planning on leaving after Christmas. You *knew* that, Harry.'

'But I thought – you told me you were going to stay. You wanted to talk about it after the festival, but you said you'd changed your mind.'

'It's easier this way.'

'I thought we cared about each other.'

324

The panic was a tide now, rising higher. A distress alarm sounded somewhere inside her head, warning her that she was getting it wrong; that, for once, this wasn't what she was supposed to do. 'It's better if I go. For both of us.'

'You can't mean that. Soph—'

'This is *better*, OK?'

Harry stared at her, a deer caught in the shotgun's sights. He didn't say anything else.

'I'm going now,' she said. And, without kissing Harry, without squeezing his hand or looking at his injured shoulder, she turned away from him and hurried out of his study. She raced through the glowing house to the lounge, where Clifton was playing with Darkness and Terror on the rug, and she scooped him up.

She didn't meet anyone's eye, didn't say goodbye, she just took her dog and ran out into the storm. She was desperate to get away from Mistingham Manor, from the things she'd found out and the man inside, to have a chance to think things through without anyone interfering. She was always so much better on her own.

She couldn't help thinking of the words she'd read in *Jane Eyre*. The line that had stuck with her, that came back to her now: *'Farewell!' was the cry of my heart as I left him. Despair added, 'Farewell for ever!'*

Chapter Thirty

It was two days until Christmas, and Sophie was packing frantically, while the blue sky and sparkling sea mocked her from outside the window. They mocked everything that had happened the night before: the storm, her discovery, Harry's explanation. It was as if none of it had happened, as if she had invented it all.

She grabbed her few treasured paperbacks off the bookshelf and put them in the box waiting at her feet – she always held on to a few flat-pack boxes – and her fingers grazed the cover of *Jane Eyre*. The tiny Christmas tree she'd bought when everything had been a lot more hopeful – with its battery-powered lights and its shiny red baubles – wavered slightly but didn't fall from the shelf.

Sophie put the other books in the box, including the special edition of *Beach Read* by Emily Henry that had, up until a couple of months ago, been the most beautiful book she owned, and took *Jane Eyre* off the shelf.

She trailed her finger over the logo on the spine – Harry

Anderly, not a little house after all – and imagined him working away in that hidden room, performing the same actions she did at her own workstation. Clifton barked from the sofa. He didn't understand what was happening, why she was so upset. He didn't realize he was going to have to find new pathways to get used to in a new place, that he wasn't going to see Darkness, Terror or Felix again.

Sophie sat heavily on the sofa and opened *Jane Eyre*. She had nearly finished her reread, was almost at the point where Jane would find out the truth about Rochester and make her way back to him, confident that the love she'd never stopped feeling for him meant that they could start again. And yet, there were other, earlier parts of the book she couldn't help returning to: *That a greater fool than Jane Eyre had never breathed the breath of life, that a more fantastic idiot had never surfeited herself on sweet lies and swallowed poison as if it were nectar.*

The doorbell rang, and Sophie's immediate reaction was to put the book under the cushion. But there was no point, now. There was no mystery any more; no need for discretion. The bell rang again, and Sophie hurried down the stairs and opened the door.

'The day before Christmas Eve is prime present-selling time.' Fiona walked past Sophie and up the stairs without waiting for an invite. 'You should know that.'

'If that's the case,' Sophie said, following her up to her flat, 'why are you here and not there?'

Fiona's smile was sad. 'Because I have Ermin. He and Poppet are at the shop anyway. The storm damaged the front door and the carpet is soaked.'

Sophie winced. 'Is it fixable?'

'Completely,' Fiona said. 'Most things are, if you put some effort in.' Her gaze fell to the box on the floor. 'Stand your ground and repair whatever is broken. Running away is rarely the best option.'

'What if the problem is me, and the only way I can fix it is by leaving?'

'Darling,' Fiona said, surprising her with the endearment, 'if you keep having to leave, then how can you possibly know it's what you need? Isn't it possible, *probable* even, that it isn't the solution? That it's time to try something different?'

Sophie didn't know what to say to that, so she picked up *Jane Eyre*. 'I know who it was. I'm sorry I accused you.'

Fiona just nodded.

'Don't you want to know who left it for me?'

'I went to Mistingham Manor before I came here,' Fiona said calmly. 'I thought you'd have stayed there overnight, especially with the storm still raging.'

Sophie stared at the carpet. 'I found his Secret Book Lair.'

Fiona sat on the sofa and lifted Clifton gently into her lap. 'You know that there have been rumours about the Anderly family for as long as I can remember,' she said. 'There were rumours that Bernie was losing control of his finances, struggling to keep the manor and bookshop afloat, especially when Harriet got ill and he had to care for her too. Then he was a widower, and there were rumours that Harry and his sister Daisy were going off the rails, being entitled and badly behaved without anyone giving them proper guidance. The manor has always had a ghost – the bookshop too. And yet, everyone loved The Book Ends. It was a safe space in this village, and Bernie was the sweetest man – to his customers, at least. Then he got sick, and it was time to level all those rumours, those accusations, at the absent children. Daisy got off lightly, because Harry was the oldest. And when he got back . . . well, we didn't hold off, did we?'

'Why are you telling me this?' It was painful, thinking about everything he'd been through; how much of it he'd kept to himself so as not to taint his father's reputation in the village.

'You've been the exception,' Fiona said, 'until now. You've seen him for who he really is, I think. But you're telling me he's got a Secret Book Lair?'

'He built an annex to store all the books that were left in his dad's bookshop after it shut down. He's been rebinding them.' She gestured to *Jane Eyre*.

'I know all that now.'

'He told you?'

'May answered the door when I went to the manor.' Fiona was watching her closely. 'She feels awful. She had no idea that, when you'd discovered where the book came from, you'd be angry with Harry.'

'He's known for ten days, and he didn't tell me.'

'From what May said, you hadn't really spoken to him about the book – not in great detail. He didn't realize how much it mattered to you: how invested you were in it.'

'I *was* though,' Sophie said. 'It's . . . changed things.'

'All Harry knew was that one of his books had ended up in your bag, and then he confronted May, and she told him what she'd done. And perhaps, Sophie, the reason you didn't talk it through with Harry, that it became less of a pressing issue in his presence, was because he mattered more than a mysterious gift someone had given you.'

329

Sophie went into the kitchen and started pulling crockery out of the cupboard. 'He didn't tell me he's been rebinding books – we have basically the same workspace. And May was trying to force us together. They both lied to me.'

'May gave you a gift and did a bit of matchmaking, but hardly in a harmful way. Harry has a hobby he feels self-conscious about and, from what you've told me, has been nothing but a gentleman.'

'It's all got so complicated.'

'Has it? Or have you realized that you care about these people, that you're invested in the relationships, and it's scary because now you have something to lose?'

Sophie looked at Fiona. Clifton had his head nestled under her chin, no problem with showing his affection. 'I care about *you*. You and Ermin and Jazz. Of course I'll miss you when I go, but it's easier for everyone.'

'I saw Harry too,' Fiona said. 'This morning, at the manor. He was moving books from the annex into his study. He looked like he was in a lot of pain.'

Sophie huffed out a breath. 'He needs to get his shoulder checked by a doctor. Something fell on him at the festival, when the storm hit.'

Fiona nodded. 'It wasn't just physical pain.'

Sophie piled her crockery on the counter. 'We've only known each other a couple of months, and we're already arguing.'

Fiona laughed. 'Sophie, all couples argue. It's healthy, because it means you're not holding any resentment or irritation inside. May told me Harry cares about you a great deal, that he thought you were abandoning your Cornwall plans. Jazz said you'd decided to stay here.'

330

'Well, now I'm not. I'm driving down tomorrow.'

'Do you have somewhere to go?'

'There's this hotel,' Sophie told her. 'It's right on the cliffs, overlooking the sea.' It was the only one she'd found that had a room at such short notice, and it was only because – the receptionist had told her – they'd had a cancellation. Two nights there wasn't cheap, and she wasn't holding out much hope that she could find a rental that quickly; she didn't think letting agents would be eager to help her between Christmas and New Year. It was a terrible plan, but at least it was familiar, the muscle memory of packing, of choosing the route, had been soothing when she'd felt so off-kilter since last night.

'Sophie,' Fiona said, much more gently. 'Why can't you just talk to Harry? Talk to them both? Tell them why you're upset, and let them explain. Give them a chance – give *Mistingham* a chance. Ermin and I don't want you to go, and I'd bet the shop on us not being the only ones.'

'It's become such a tangle,' Sophie said. 'It's too messy to sort through. If I leave now, I get a fresh slate.'

Fiona nodded. 'Your life has been a procession of new front doors, beds and people, and you've struggled to find somewhere you think of as home. And I know that – when you have been comfortable – you've been let down.'

'What do you mean?' Sophie couldn't stay still, so she put the kettle on, took two mugs out of the cluster on the counter and put teabags in them.

'Mrs Fairweather, who gave you the notebook that started everything off, retired and couldn't keep you.'

'That's just the nature of foster families.'

'But you wanted her to choose you.'

331

Sophie got the milk out of the fridge. 'She couldn't do that. I knew that.'

'And then Trent – who you loved, who you trusted – discarded you when you couldn't live up to his standards.'

'I couldn't commit to him as much as he wanted me to, but he didn't *discard* me.'

'No?' Fiona said quietly. 'You've told me snippets here and there, and I know you better than you think. And Jazz hasn't been shy about telling me what she's been through, what it's like to be on your own: how isolating it can be, how you cling onto any affection that comes your way, but can't always trust it. You think May and Harry have broken your trust, and that's the worst thing they could have done.'

Sophie squished the teabags against the sides of the mugs, then added milk and brought them over to the sofa. 'Here you go.'

'Thank you.' Fiona took a sip. 'Just take some time to think about it. I know your independence is important, but has what's happened really put that in jeopardy? Think what you'll lose by moving on.'

Sophie had done nothing but think about it since the night before, but every time she'd gone through it, the thing she'd come back to – her default position – was that it was better to start again. The first chapter of a new story; that crisp, white page in a notebook, with nothing hanging over her or weighing her down. Just her and Clifton and the green-blue of the Atlantic ahead of her.

She looked out at the deep, shimmering navy of the North Sea beyond her window. She thought of the runs she'd taken along the cliff path, the unbeatable views, and how, even in the summer when it was bursting with tourists, she could find pockets of quiet beauty and calm in Mistingham. She would never forget the evening she'd come across Harry fixing his fence, or that he'd been doing it for a tiny goat in a paisley jumper. Her heart squeezed.

'Think about never seeing us again,' Fiona said softly, 'because I doubt that once you leave you'll be paying us a visit.'

'We can call each other.'

'Of course. But what about Dexter – and Lucy, who calls you Aunty Sophie? What about the old sweet shop, the opportunity to have a proper place to run your business from? Will you go back to selling at fairs and markets, days in the cold, hauling everything out of your car boot, having to work in cafés and bars again?'

'I did that for years until you let me have your concession stand.'

'And here you could have a permanent shop, a proper studio to make new stock, build up your reputation and your customer base, increase your profits. People would know where you were, and they'd come back to you again and again.'

It was a tantalizing thought. It offered her more stability, less anxiety: the chance to live a life without the restlessness that had become a part of her. Could she leave *that* behind, instead of Mistingham?

'You wouldn't see Darkness or Terror again. You'd miss out on Felix's jumpers.'

'And his escapades,' Sophie added.

She expected her friend to jump on her agreement, to push her point home, but instead the silence stretched between them, and the panic welled up inside her. This was what she did, she reminded herself. This was how she kept everything safe, didn't get her heart stomped on again, like it had been with Mrs Fairweather, with Trent.

'Think of never seeing Harry again,' Fiona said into the quiet. 'Think how much he means to you, and then imagine him disappearing from your life, without a backward glance.'

Sophie swallowed and rubbed at her throat, which felt thick with the urge to sob or scream. But he hadn't told her about the book, even when he knew May had sent it: he had kept *her* secret, instead of revealing the truth to Sophie. How could she trust him after that?

Fiona put her mug on the coffee table and lowered Clifton gently to the floor. 'Think about what it would do to you, if he was suddenly gone – after everything you've shared, all the ways you've let yourself care for him. Because that's what you're doing to him by leaving.' She walked to the door. 'Come by whenever you want to pack up your note-books. We're open late today.'

Fiona stepped through the door of Sophie's flat, then closed it quietly behind her, leaving her alone with too many thoughts, and a plan that – far from being the simple escape she had always intended – was looking more and more complicated by the minute.

Chapter Thirty-One

Mistingham on Christmas Eve was a twinkling snow globe of festive cheer.

Almost every building was adorned with lights, and while most of them displayed a soft, elegant gold, a few – like Penny For Them and Two Scoops – were draped in shimmying rainbow bulbs, candy colours that couldn't fail to make you smile.

When Sophie stepped outside with Clifton, wrapping her scarf tightly around her neck because it was bright but extra cold, she heard the melodic tones of 'Silent Night', too rich to be coming from a speaker. She walked up the street and saw that, outside the hotel, a Salvation Army band were performing, the shine of the brass instruments as enticing as the music.

After Fiona had left the day before, Sophie had spent the afternoon packing, flinging things into bags and boxes. Then she'd stood forlornly in her sparse flat, her notebook tools and materials the last things left to tidy away, so similar to the ones she'd seen in Harry's secret room. It was something they had in common, and it should have brought them closer, but he'd kept it from her.

She'd stood there, looking at what little her life was made up of, the central heating no match for the chill she was feeling. Then she'd phoned the hotel and changed her booking, the receptionist at Crystal Waters pleasant but with an understandable note of irritation, as Sophie had explained she would be arriving on Christmas Day instead of Christmas Eve.

She reasoned that it would give her a bit of extra time, and the roads would be clearer on Christmas Day anyway, while everyone was ensconced with their loved ones, opening presents and popping champagne corks, the aroma of roasting turkey wafting through houses and flats, hugs exchanged.

Sophie walked through the village, smiling at people she passed, wondering how many of them knew, now, that she was going. A niggling voice in her head asked what she needed extra time for. She was packed – she'd waited until evening to clear her notebooks from Hartley Country Apparel, using her set of keys when she was sure Fiona and Ermin had left for the day. There was nothing left to do. She could get in her car and leave right now.

She stopped in front of Ye Olde Abandonede Sweete Shoppe, that and the bookshop next door conspicuous by their lack of Christmas cheer. Their reflections stared back at her, Clifton bright-eyed and fluffy, her looking tired and pale and bundled up against the cold, her boots crusted with mud.

She peered inside, trying to imagine the space decked out with her notebooks, other lines of beautiful stationery that she'd always imagined adding to her stock one day. *One day when what?* the niggling voice said. She was going back to fairs and markets, boxes in the boot of her rusty old car, another makeweight job in a café or restaurant. She wouldn't have the time, the funds or the room to expand her business.

Another figure joined her reflection, and it took her a moment to realize who it was.

'Sophie,' May said, their eyes meeting in the glass. 'How are you?'

Sophie couldn't put everything she was feeling into words, so she shrugged.

'I am so, so sorry,' May rushed out. 'I never meant for things to turn out like this. I wish I'd pressed pause at the festival, before the storm hit and you found out the way you did.'

Sophie turned, wanting to face her properly, and saw that some of May's eternal optimism had faded. She had dark smudges under her eyes, and her usually glossy brown hair was tied up in a messy bun, strands escaping in every direction.

'Why did you do it?' It was the one thing Sophie couldn't get her head around. Before November, they had been little more than casual acquaintances.

'Can we go somewhere? It's so cold today.'

They sat at a window table in the hotel lounge, the sound of the band muffled through the glass, so they could still hear each other over the festive tunes. Sophie loved this view, the hotel on a slight hill so she could see Mistingham Green and the village hall, the lights on the oak tree twinkling, showing that they, at least, had survived the storm. Perpendicular Street ran down to the sea, with Hartley Country Apparel on the right and then, further down, Batter Days and her flat, the blue of the sea visible in the gaps between buildings. *She loved this view.*

'The green doesn't look completely destroyed,' she said, while they waited for their miniature Christmas puddings, neither of them able to avoid the novelty item on the menu, the sticky sweetness and brandy cream it promised.

'A few of us patched it up yesterday afternoon,' May said. 'We put some sand down, a bit of gravel in places, once Harry and I had moved the books out of the annex. The tent grotto didn't survive, but everything else is fine.'

'Right.' Sophie swallowed. 'The festival went ahead yesterday?' She hadn't turned up, hadn't wanted to face anyone. What did it matter anyway, when she wouldn't be here after tomorrow?

'It was really well attended,' May told her. 'I think because people felt cheated out of it on storm night. Tonight's the last night,' she added, a hopeful note in her voice – although of course Sophie knew that.

'Why did you send me the book?' she asked. 'Leave it for me, I mean?'

'I love Harry.' May unfolded her napkin, then looked up. 'As a friend. He's my best friend. He's always been there for me, and he had an awful time those last few years in London, doing a job he hated, trying to save the estate from afar, then his dad getting ill. He came back here and threw himself into repairing the manor, but it was in such a bad way and he only ever seemed happy when he was working on those books – rebinding the damaged ones; giving them

338

new covers. It's meticulous work, it requires so much concentration – you know that, of course.' She shook her head. 'It was as if he was carrying on his dad's legacy.'

'They're really beautiful,' Sophie said truthfully.

May nodded. 'I know. But he didn't want to *do* anything with them. He just wanted to keep them in that hidden room, hoarding them away, and books – books are *magical*. Even when they've been read a hundred times and the cover is falling off, or they've got stained pages, or they've got an ill-advised, ugly cover from the Seventies.'

'Some modern covers are ugly too,' Sophie said.

'Oh, I know.' May rolled her eyes. 'Some are *so* ugly. Anyway. I didn't think he should spend all that time and effort on them, only for them to sit there, forgotten. He'd told me how he'd been sent that book by his dad – *North and South*, the old copy that Bernie had once upon a time given to his mum – and how it changed everything. It had made him realize he needed to come home. So I thought – why couldn't I do the same? Why couldn't I give someone this beautiful, special book, and see what happened?' She was animated, her eyes bright, and Sophie could see that she believed wholeheartedly in the magic of books, the power of what she'd done, even if it hadn't worked out how she'd expected.

'Why did you pick me?' She sat back when Jazz brought their tray over, with a pot of tea and two of the mini Christmas puddings.

'Fiona says you're leaving,' Jazz said without preamble, her eyes hard, like shiny black buttons.

Sophie picked up her fork. 'It's time to move on. You know what it's like.'

But Jazz was already shaking her head. 'From *here*? From Fiona and Ermin and Dex? From that shop, just waiting for you to fill it with all your fancy notebooks? What about Harry? You can't let her do this.' She stared imploringly at May.

'It's not my decision,' May said. 'I probably have the least sway of anyone right now.'

'I am here, you know,' Sophie said with a laugh.

'Not for long though,' Jazz replied. 'So why you do you give a shit if we talk about you?'

'Jazz—'

'No,' Jazz cut in. 'Don't you realize what you've got here? *Who* you've got? I thought you did – I thought we talked about this and you had decided you were staying.' She swallowed. 'I didn't expect to find anything but a dry place to sleep and some chips before I got booted out and had to move on again, to the next place I didn't belong. But nobody here has made me feel like I don't belong. You're totally nuts.' She spun on her heel and disappeared into the kitchen, and Sophie saw Mary, standing next to the door with her arms folded, doing absolutely nothing to reprimand her staff member for the outburst.

'Why me?' she asked May again, trying not to show how flustered Jazz had made her.

'Because you seemed so nice, even though we'd only talked a few times. I knew a bit about your background from Fiona, and then . . .' She laughed. 'It was so obvious Harry liked you. He kept bringing you up in conversation, but he was so hopeless whenever he saw you. I think he felt self-conscious, so he blundered, then he was angry with himself and that made him angry with everyone and . . .'

340

She sighed. 'He'd just finished binding *Jane Eyre*, and it was stunning. He put it on the shelf, alongside the others, and I thought . . . I thought it was special. The story, of course, but also the care he'd put into every aspect of it. The foil details, the bookmark, the logo on the spine. I thought if I left it for you, and wrote a puzzle of a note, you'd go looking.'

'I *did* go looking.'

'And I convinced Harry that, after making the village change their entire set-up for the festival, the least he could do was offer to help out.' She shrugged. 'I thought you'd find out it was his book a lot sooner, that the mystery would be solved quickly, you'd laugh about it, get to know each other, and that it would just be one tiny part of how you met.'

'But I didn't . . .' Sophie stuck her fork in her pudding, swept up some cream with her spoon, and combined the two. 'I dismissed him straight away. Harry was so upfront about everything, and we didn't even know each other until we started working on the festival. It just seemed impossible that it was him. Then Winnie and Simon got books, too.'

May nibbled an icing holly leaf. 'I should have come clean sooner. I was going to, but then Harry told me you were leaving Mistingham, and I realized my gift hadn't worked, that you felt singled out rather than included. And your changes to the festival, getting the whole community involved, gave me the idea of giving books to other people. I thought, that way, you'd feel a part of the village, instead of separate from it.' She dropped her head into her hands, her next words muffled. 'I should have trusted that you and Harry would be fine without it, and now the thing I did to bring you together – it's broken you apart.' She looked up. 'Don't blame Harry, Sophie. Hate me if you want to, but don't leave because you think Harry doesn't care about you.'

'He kept it from me for ten days,' she said, but it was a weak protest. Fiona had reminded her that Harry hadn't known what a big thing the book had become for her: he hadn't realized she'd been searching so hard, or that him not telling her would feel like a betrayal.

May nodded. 'He wanted all the facts before he came to you. But Sophie . . .' She put her hand on the table, fingers outstretched. 'He cares about you. *So* much.'

Sophie sipped her tea. '*Jane Eyre* leaves when things get complicated.'

May made an exasperated sound. 'It's a bit more than *complicated* with Jane and Rochester. Harry doesn't have a wife locked up in his attic, I promise you. He has a wayward goat he's too fond of, but that should send you *into* his arms, not out of them.'

'It *is* complicated though,' Sophie said. 'For me.'

'Why?'

She sliced her pudding with her fork, working out how best to put it. She realized she wasn't angry with May any more, or with Harry. She wasn't sure she'd been angry with either of them for very long at all. It was panic, more than anything. 'Because,' she said, 'whenever I let my guard down, it goes wrong.'

'So you're going to leave us all behind because you'd rather be alone on your own terms than trust that people love you and will always be there for you? Sounds pretty self-defeating to me.' May gave her a gentle smile.

Sophie couldn't be drawn in. 'It's what's best for me.'

342

May nodded, her shoulders dropping. Sophie waited for her to argue, to tell her how selfish she was being, like Fiona had done. Instead she just took small, methodical bites of her pudding.

'How's Harry?' she asked, when she couldn't bear it any longer. 'His shoulder, I mean.'

'It's bruised,' May said. 'Nothing's broken, according to the doctor, but I know it's painful. And I got my brother to check the roof is safe, that nothing else was dislodged in the storm. Harry did a good job as Santa last night, and he's going to do it again tonight.'

Sophie felt a pang at the thought of missing Harry dressed as Santa on the last night of the festival. She put her fork down. 'I'm really glad it's not broken. I should get going, though. I've got a lot to do before I leave. Thank you for explaining. I'll leave the book with Fiona – Harry should have it back.'

May looked shocked. 'Don't do that. I know Harry wants you to have it – take it with you. Please.'

Sophie could only nod. 'Bye, May. Say goodbye to Harry for me.'

She didn't wait for the other woman to respond, but put a twenty-pound note on the table and then, with Clifton hurrying to keep up, with her emotions a choppy sea of hardened resolve combined with despair, she left Mistingham Hotel as the band started to play 'In the Bleak Midwinter'.

Sophie put her empty glass on the table and looked accusingly at the wine bottle. She would have to pour the rest of it down the sink. She had a long drive tomorrow, and she wanted to set off early, with a clear head.

The flat was packed up, all her boxes stacked by the door. Her hat and scarf were on the hook next to her coat, both in a soft, rose-pink wool. She'd bought them when she'd arrived in Mistingham and first met Fiona – ever the brilliant salesperson – and she'd been giddy at the thought of this new, promising place to start over in: a place she'd heard someone talking about on a train that sounded so romantic, so magical. *It is*, the voice in her head whispered. *More than you ever imagined.*

She couldn't spend the whole evening in her echoey flat, looking up fairs and markets in Cornwall to contact in the new year. Usually by now she would be bubbling with excitement at all the possibility.

'Come on, Clifton.' She put his harness on, then slipped into her coat, scarf and hat, and left the flat.

It was just after seven, and the air was crisp and cold, with a bite that made her think of rubbery wellington boots and noses made out of carrots, of the cold splash of a snowball sliding down inside her collar. The sea air was unmistakable, but so was the telltale hint of snow. Would it really snow now, just before Christmas?

She could hear the Oak Fest from her front door: the jivy, over-the-top Rudolph Hoopla soundtrack, mingling with shouts and laughter, the high-pitched scream of an over-excited child. It was louder than the other nights, and Sophie knew that was down to the added giddiness of Christmas Eve. It was still early, so families could come out for a baked Alaska and a round of Christmas Hook the Duck, take part in Birdie's candlelit blessing before heading home to their Christmas traditions: stories read and stockings hung in fireplaces, milk and cookies or

344

whisky and mince pies laid out in preparation for their late-night visitor.

Sophie's chest ached. She had her own traditions, the little things she did, just for her: she made herself a beautiful new notebook, a brand-new design for a fresh year, then wrote a list of all her wishes, setting herself challenges that she wanted to fulfil over the next twelve months. She allowed herself a bottle of champagne – if she could afford it, and had a glass on Christmas Eve then put a teaspoon in the neck, keeping it fizzy for the following day. This year, she had forgotten to buy one.

Mrs Fairweather had cooked pancakes for Christmas breakfast, with a variety of toppings, and Sophie had carried that over into her life with Trent. His favourite topping was berries and yoghurt, so she'd always gone with that instead of what she wanted, hoping it would make him happy. She had pictured having pancakes with Harry this year, making them in Mistingham Manor's building-site kitchen, May, the dogs and Felix there too, eating breakfast together on Christmas morning.

'Not joining the party tonight?'

Sophie jumped. It was Dexter, standing with his hands in his pockets, giving her a curious look.

'No, I . . .'

'This is your thing, though.' His frown didn't last long. 'Though it is Christmas Eve, and everyone's got stuff to do. I've been paranoid about having all Lucy's presents ready, and I'd forgotten where I'd put that scarf I bought her. I remembered where it was just now, so I thought I'd nip home and arrange it with everything else.'

Sophie opened her mouth.

'It's OK, Birdie's with her,' Dexter said. 'Probably buying my daughter her third ice-cream dessert of the evening.'

'She must be excited.'

'Oh yeah, she's off the scale. Extra sugar is not necessary, but what can you do?' He laughed, and Sophie thought how lucky Lucy was to have such a warm, loving father, who worked so hard to make her life as good as possible.

'I hope you have a lovely Christmas,' she said.

'What are you up to?' Dexter glanced towards the green when there was a raucous shout.

'Oh, I'm . . . travelling.'

'To see friends?' The furrow appeared between Dexter's eyebrows again, because surely it was common knowledge that Sophie had no family to go and see. But at least it seemed that news of her departure hadn't made its way around the whole of Mistingham.

'Sure,' she said, not wanting to lie, wishing she hadn't walked the minefield of coming out into the village one final time. 'Have a wonderful Christmas, Dex.' She squeezed his arm. 'Say Happy Christmas to Lucy for me.'

'Come round when you're back, if you like? We'll be at home – Birdie's coming, and who knows who else? It's always a bit of a free-for-all round here, and you'd be very welcome.'

'I'll . . . I'll see. Thank you.'

'Merry Christmas, Sophie.' He strode off in the direction of his house.

She waited until he'd gone, and then she took the narrow, less-trodden road that branched off Perpendicular Street, walking up it and emerging at the side of the village hall. She was careful to keep to the shadows, not wanting the lit windows to give her away.

The noise got louder as she got closer, and she felt camou-flaged by it, everyone's attention on the games, stalls and food. Jason and Simon stood together at the mobile bar, cheers-ing each other with plastic pint glasses, clearly having relinquished the running of their food stands to their staff. Vea was holding up beautiful felt baubles, offering them as last-minute additions to Christmas trees, and Jazz was standing with Natasha's son, Indigo, at the Carnival Toss, laughing over his attempts to get two balls into the holes at once.

Then Sophie heard a familiar, joyful sound, a happy bleat, and Clifton strained on his lead towards it. She stayed where she was, holding him back, pressed against the outside wall of the village hall so the darkness hid her from view, and felt her heart ache in a way it never had before.

Because there was Santa Claus, without a grotto because it had been destroyed in the storm, but commanding all the attention anyway. He was tall and wide-shouldered, his black boots impossibly shiny, his eyes hazel – though she couldn't actually tell that from where she was; she just knew it was true. She knew every little bit of him. She could see how his left arm was hanging limply at his side, and how tired he was, despite his deep 'ho ho ho' and the way he was engaging with the children around him. And there were a lot of children around him tonight, because he had an assistant with him: a small, furry assistant with floppy ears and tiny horns, and a green and red jumper with little gold bells that jingled when he moved. He was wearing a harness underneath it, tethered to his master by a lead.

'Who's that?' a little boy pointed.

Santa crouched down and encouraged the boy forward to stroke the furry nose of the goat, who was, for once, being entirely compliant. 'This is my elf,' Santa said. 'He's called Felix.'

'And that one,' a girl asked, pointing to the plastic, glowing goat that Sophie had insisted on getting the day they went to Norwich.

'This is . . .' his voice trailed off. 'He doesn't have a name. What do you think he should be called?'

The suggestions came thick and fast.

'Pudding!'

'Elfy!'

'Flora.'

'Poo head!'

And then an older voice, one Sophie recognized, said, 'How about Sophie?' and Fiona stepped into view, looking down at Santa and the two goats, the cluster of excited children.

'Sophie,' Santa repeated. 'She said Felix would love it, and look.' He gestured to where Felix was butting his head against his plastic counterpart, bleating gently. 'She was right,' he said with a laugh. It sounded sad, defeated.

'She might have been right about a plastic goat,' Fiona said, managing to sound sensitive and stern all at once, 'but there were other things, much more important things, that she got completely wrong.'

'Can I touch the goat?' a boy shouted, and Santa beckoned him over.

'Gentle now,' he said to the blond-haired boy, and then to Fiona, 'She has to make her own decisions. I could have begged her to stay, but what good would that have done?

She had to *want* to stay here, to choose it on her own, and she didn't.'

'You're as scared as she was,' Fiona said. 'She should have realized what she had, and you should have stepped out of your comfort zone and flung yourself at her feet. If you love someone, then you have to be prepared to risk your pride for them.'

Santa spread his arms wide. 'I have no pride left, Fiona, and I don't even care. I did all of this for her and, even though she's gone, I'm not going to put my feelings in a box. I'm going to be the best damn Santa I can be, and then I'm going to finish the manor, and then I'm going to—'

'What's *best damn Santa* mean?' one of the children shouted. 'Are there *more* Santas?'

Santa and Fiona stared at each other, exchanging panicked looks, and Sophie's cheeks bunched in a smile.

'Of course not, darling,' Fiona said smoothly. 'This is Santa Claus. He has magic words, you know, to communicate with Felix and Sophie. Isn't that right, Santa?'

'Right,' Santa said in a low voice. 'Let's see if I've got any presents left, shall we?'

There was a chorus of yes-es, little feet stamping happily, and Sophie felt the relief of a disaster averted. She watched as Santa turned round, angling his body towards her hiding place to pick up the large red sack that was on the ground behind him. He paused, glancing up, and she could see his eyes now, so perfectly Harry, clear and beautiful and with so much warmth and generosity in them: so much love, if you were lucky enough to be chosen by him. And she had been.

She realized she was holding her breath, but after a moment his attention was drawn back to the children, to where Felix had started to nibble one of the little girl's sleeves, because that goat couldn't go anywhere without causing a scene.

'Bye, Harry,' Sophie whispered. She turned away, wondering if her words would be carried to him on the last, dying gusts of the storm that had almost worn itself out, or if they would dissolve into nothing before they reached him. She strode back to her flat, Clifton padding at her side, leaving the Mistingham Festive Oak Fest, and all the people she'd got to know over the last year, behind.

Chapter Thirty-Two

Sophie was woken by her alarm blaring into the darkness, and it took her a few moments to remember where she was. It was Christmas Day, and she was still in Mistingham. She lay on her back, listening to Clifton stirring in his bed under the window, and rubbed a hand over her chest. She thought about what she was doing today, what she *had* to do today. It felt bigger, more monumental, than any decision she could remember making in the past.

She made herself a cup of coffee with only the oven light to guide her. The kettle wasn't hers, but the mug was, the grooves of the handmade ceramic fitting her fingers perfectly as she wrapped them around it. At this time of day, just before the winter dawn, she could see the little fireflies of fishing boats out on the inky water, and she wondered what kind of Christmas they would be having when they returned: taking their fresh catches to their families; local pubs and restaurants waiting for hauls, fish starters for their Christmas Day menus.

Would any service stations be open today, offering turkey sandwiches in spongy white bread, the furthest thing possible from Dexter's roast chicken doorstops? She let herself have a few more minutes of stillness, before she dragged herself into action mode, getting showered and dressed in her comfiest jeans and a green knitted jumper.

She put on her coat, hat and scarf, then dressed Clifton in the tartan jacket she'd bought him last winter but hadn't been brave enough to use before now. When she stepped outside, it was so cold that her first inhale was almost painful, and as the sun started to rise, intent on banishing the darkness, she could see wisps of pale pinkish clouds above. She felt the solid weight and sharp corners of *Jane Eyre* tucked against her chest, and tightened her arm around it.

'You need your jacket today,' she said to Clifton. He barked up at her, excited by this walk, so early in the morning.

Sophie set off, her feet crunching through the quiet village streets, all the Christmas lights twinkling and dancing, giddily announcing that the day was finally here, even though the shops and arcade, the chippy and ice-cream parlour, would remain firmly locked up today.

Seagulls wheeled above her, cawing plaintively as she took the familiar alley that passed through two buildings, then walked past the row of town houses, past old Mr Carsdale's, still in darkness and with the curtains drawn. The cold air expanded her lungs, and the sunrise over the sea mocked the LED bulbs with all their fancy colours. The sun was an orb of amber fire, the silver-blue water lit with a pathway of gold that reached the sandy shore, shimmering pearlescent in the dawn light.

'Look at that,' Sophie whispered, tears in her eyes as she stopped on the cliff path, facing the water. She picked Clifton up and hugged him tightly, shifting the book so she could keep hold of them both. 'Just look at it.' She wondered, fleetingly, if she could stay there forever.

She pulled her gaze away from the rising sun and put Clifton down, determined to reach the highest point of the path, her boots easily finding the right divots to step in, because she'd walked and run this route so many times over the last year. She strode forwards with her little dog at her side, and when she had the lookout in her sights, she saw something else, too: a figure coming towards her. Her breath caught and she stumbled, and she saw his steps falter, too. And then everything was pounding, her feet on the path and her heart in her chest, her pulse racing as if it was desperate to catch up to him.

As they got closer, she drank him in. How tall he was, his shoulders wide in the familiar black jacket, the side of his face kissed by the sun, hair tousled by the breeze. His long legs in dark jeans, his brown, sturdy boots. She tried to picture which soft jumper was under his coat, which one he would have picked for Christmas Day, and swallowed.

'Merry Christmas,' she said, when they were a couple of feet apart.

'Merry Christmas.' Harry sounded stunned, incredulous. 'You're . . . here.'

She nodded. 'It's a beautiful sunrise.'

He glanced at it, then turned back to her. 'Are you walking Clifton before you set off?' He gestured to *Jane Eyre*. 'May said you were going to give that back, but honestly, Sophie – keep it.'

353

Sophie took a long, slow breath. This was the hardest thing for her. She summoned all her courage. 'No, I . . . That's not what I was doing.'

'I was coming to see you.' He took a step towards her. 'I thought you'd gone already, but I messaged Dexter this morning and he said he'd seen you last night; that you weren't leaving until today. I didn't dare to hope. Everything was such a rush yesterday, because—'

'Santa and his goat elf are kept pretty busy on Christmas Eve?' She realized her mistake as soon as the words were out of her mouth.

'You were there?'

'I saw you,' she admitted. Clifton put his paws on Harry's shins, and Sophie felt her panic fade just a little. 'I was coming to see you, too.'

Harry paused, then lifted her dog up, cradling him against his chest. 'This isn't a last walk before you leave for Cornwall?'

'No,' she said. 'I've . . . done a lot of thinking. Talked to a few people. I realize that I . . . I'm not very good at this.'

'At what?' Harry asked quietly.

'At . . . *being*. Staying. At trusting.'

'I know that,' he said carefully. 'And I should have told you, as soon as I knew May was behind the book. It felt like laying myself on the line, admitting how long I'd liked you for, how miserably I'd failed at being a normal, communicative human. I was scared, I think.' He put Clifton down and held out his hand. Sophie took it. 'I didn't expect you to come into my life, but you did. And now you're here, and I *know* you don't think you can stay, but . . . I love you.' His gaze softened. 'I love you, and I'm not saying it as emotional blackmail, but because it's the truth. I didn't think I'd get this chance, but you're still here so I have to say it. I love you, Sophie Stevens. At least you know, now, before you go. You are loved. Completely. By me.'

Sophie felt the burn of tears in her eyes and nose. She squeezed Harry's hand and tried to remember how to breathe. 'I love you, too,' she said. 'I think that's what frightened me the most. It's why I overreacted, why part of me wanted to run – because it's easier; there's less to lose. But I saw you at the festival last night, and heard you talking to Fiona. I realized then that, if I went, then I'd lost anyway, because my feelings are already here, and I'm pretty sure they're not going anywhere. I'm so sorry, Harry.'

His fingers tightened around hers. '*If* you went? You mean . . . you feel the same, and you . . .? Soph, what's happening?' He rubbed his face with his free hand.

For the first time, happiness sneaked in, diluting Sophie's anxiety. She had thought he would dismiss her, tell her that it was too late – that he'd already put her out of his thoughts, begun to move on. But this moment felt like hope, with the sun rising and the air fresh and clear, Christmas Day starting in houses everywhere – quiet and content or large and messy; everything in between.

'You want me to stay?' she asked.

There was a moment of stunned silence, then Harry said, 'More than anything.'

Sophie squeezed her eyes shut, trying to ward off the tears, but it only made things worse. 'I'm staying,' she said. 'I decided last night, but after everything I said to you, I didn't know if you still—'

'I do still,' he said urgently, his hands coming to her waist.

'I do. You're staying? Seriously? And not just for another week, or a little while, or—'

'I want to stay here permanently,' she said. 'I want to be with you, Harry.'

He looked down at her, and she felt a soft puff of warm air on her cheeks as he exhaled. 'I want to be with you,' he said. 'I've never wanted anyone in my life the way I want you.' He brought his hand to her face, his thumb icy-cold as he wiped a tear from her cheek.

'Not even Felix?' she asked.

His mouth kicked up into a smile. 'I like having him around, but no. I don't want to hold hooves with him as we walk along this path, and I don't want to go to the Blossom Bough with him in the evenings. I can't imagine watching him open a successful stationery shop in the village, and I definitely don't want him under the duvet with me every night.'

Sophie grinned. 'Fair enough.'

'Also, I'm fairly sure I don't have to plan for a lake swim or rescue mission with you in my near future.'

'Not right now, no,' she assured him. 'But have you ever gone skinny-dipping in the lake in summer, when there isn't a risk of hypothermia?'

Harry tipped his face towards hers. 'Do I have to remind you of the mud? The weeds? The sea is much better for skinny-dipping.'

She sucked in a gasp. 'The *sea*? Harry, have you—'

'Just down here,' he gestured with his head, 'where hardly anyone goes. It's so difficult getting down that path, and—'

'It's not that difficult,' Sophie said, laughter bubbling up inside her. 'Loads of hikers and walkers go on that part of the beach.'

Harry's eyes widened. 'Tell me you're joking. Nobody used that part of the beach when I was growing up. *Ever.* The path to get onto it is so steep.'

'There's another, easier cut-through. Haven't you found it?' She pressed her hand against his chest. 'Now I can see where some of the rumours about you originate. The Beast, for example?'

'Sophie,' Harry said solemnly.

'Can I tell everyone?'

He shook his head. 'I'm just starting to be accepted again.'

'Secret skinny-dipping isn't going to change that: you'll just end up with a bigger audience.'

Harry closed his eyes and groaned. 'Have I told you, Sophie, how glad I am that you're staying here?'

'No,' she said, her smile fading. 'But if it's anywhere near as glad as I am that I decided to stay, and that you hadn't given up on me, then I'm guessing it's *pretty* glad.'

'Monumentally glad,' Harry murmured. 'I can't believe you're here.'

'I'm right in front of you,' Sophie whispered, and then he was kissing her, his arms wrapped tightly around her, bringing them as close as possible while the sun rose higher in the sky, and a thick bank of peach-hued clouds chased it down. She slid her hands around his neck and threaded her fingers through his hair, letting the last slivers of uncertainty melt away. His kiss claimed her, rewarded her, told her he was confident that she was here for good, and that they belonged together.

He pulled back, glancing in the direction of the manor. 'We should go. I promised May I'd make pancakes for breakfast.'

Sophie's breath hitched, her heart pounding for an entirely new reason. 'Bacon and maple syrup?'

'You can have whatever toppings you want. Are you staying all day?' He lifted Clifton over the fence, settling him gently on the other side, then held his hand out for Sophie. She passed him *Jane Eyre*, then put her hand in his.

'I would love to stay, if you'll have me.'

His eyes were soft, his smile gentle when he said, 'Always.' He squeezed her hand. 'Come on, you can use this as leverage.' He put his boot on the bottom line of wire, and Sophie put her foot on his, then hesitated.

'How's your shoulder?' she asked.

'Better. I promise.'

'OK.' She used his weight to spring herself up and over. 'How will you get over?'

'Like I did on the way here,' he said. 'Very carefully.' He grinned, then gingerly stepped over the fence, the barbed wire catching on the inside of his denim-clad thighs. With her gloved hands, Sophie prised him off.

'Why didn't you come through the village to my flat?' she asked, taking his hand again as they started walking.

Harry huffed out a breath. 'I didn't want to wake the dogs or Felix, and they were asleep in the hall because it was so cold I left the fire going last night. I came out of the side door and then, well, I was on the right side of the estate, and the sun was rising, and it looked so peaceful, so I thought I'd go along the cliff path. You were coming to see me too?'

Sophie nodded. 'I wanted to come this way. It made me think of that day we met on the path, and that gave me a bit of confidence that you wouldn't turn me away.'

He tightened his grip on her fingers. 'I wouldn't have. Not ever. What made you change your mind? You said you spoke to some people.'

Sophie laughed. 'I did. I spoke to Fiona, who didn't hold back; May, who apologized and told me why she'd done it. Jazz, who gave me both barrels.'

'Three strong women, changing the mind of a fourth.'

'No.' Sophie shook her head. 'They had things to say to me – things that made a whole lot of sense – but you were the one who changed my mind.'

'Me?'

Sophie's throat tightened, and she had to clear it so she could continue. 'I realized that I loved you, I trusted you. I didn't want to live my life without you.'

Harry stopped, bringing her to a halt, too. 'This is real, isn't it?' His laugh was low and rumbly and perfect. 'It's like something out of a book.'

She smiled up at him, happiness flooding through her. 'I want a book-worthy kiss then, please.'

'Happy to oblige.' He lifted her off her feet with his good arm, spinning her around and then, when she'd stopped squealing, he kissed her, holding her tightly against him. Sophie wrapped her legs around his waist, held onto him and kissed him back as if her life depended on it.

When they pulled apart and her feet were back on the ground, Sophie realized they had an audience, standing on the front steps of the manor. May was in her pyjamas and dressing gown, Fiona and Jazz next to her, and Ermin was waving a ribboned bottle of champagne in the air. Dexter had his arms folded and a grin on his face, and Lucy was jumping up and down, Birdie standing alongside her wearing a long, purple cloak that did nothing to dispel the rumour that she might actually be a witch. They were all cheering and whooping, and Sophie resisted the urge to bow.

'What is this?' she asked.

Harry shrugged. 'I thought I'd invite a few people round for Christmas. We have enough room, enough food. I've realized, over the last couple of months, that this is a good village full of great people, and I wanted them in my life again – if they'd have me. It turns out they did, and now – though I hadn't dared to hope – I've also got the holly on top of the pudding, the angel on top of the tree.'

Sophie waved at her friends. 'I'd rather be a star on top of the tree.'

'Angel a bit too pious?'

'A bit,' Sophie agreed, 'especially considering all the ways I'm planning on celebrating our reunion.'

'Give me half an hour,' Harry rushed out. 'I'll send everyone back to their own homes. Fuck being community-minded on Christmas Day.'

Sophie laughed and leaned into him. 'It'll be worth the wait.'

'God.' Harry exhaled a harsh breath. 'Today is going to be torture, isn't it?'

'Uncle Harry!' Lucy squealed. 'Aunty Sophie! Come and see what Santa bought me. It's my favourite Romantasy trilogy – the special editions! Dad says I can read you all the first chapter before champagne.'

'I said we'd ask everyone what they thought,' Dexter corrected. 'I didn't say it was a done deal.'

'But they'd *love* it,' Lucy protested. 'That wasn't just a

friendly kiss, was it, with Harry and Sophie? It was a *romantic* kiss, and these books are *full* of romance.'

Dexter's eyes went wide. 'They are YA though, right? You told me they were YA.'

Lucy shrugged and looked away.

Fiona chortled. 'Should have checked the small print.'

'Where do you find small print on a *book*?' Dexter ran an anxious hand through his hair.

'I'll skim through them,' Jazz said. 'Tell you how bad the sex scenes are.'

Dexter groaned, and Ermin patted his shoulder. 'Looks like I should open this bottle right about now.'

'It's not even nine o'clock in the morning,' Fiona chided, but without much heat.

Sophie felt a rush of giddiness, of *rightness*, so intense it almost knocked her backwards. She caught May's eye and saw the same emotion reflected back at her. They swapped smiles, and Sophie mouthed, 'Thank you.' She would say it properly later, along with an apology for how she'd reacted over her gift: the gift that, if she was honest, had changed everything.

'Sophie,' Fiona said, 'good to see you.'

'It's good to see you too. I have a whole lot to say to you, to apologize for.'

Fiona waved a dismissive hand. 'Not now. All that matters is that you're here, and it's Christmas.'

'Happy Christmas!' Jazz shouted, flinging her arms to the sky, and a few rooks lifted out of the nearest tree, cawing as they flew off.

'Happy Christmas,' Sophie said, and was about to hug Fiona, when she felt a tug on her jeans. It was Felix, nibbling the denim, wearing a blue and red knitted jumper with silver Christmas trees all over it.

'Felix,' Harry said wearily, 'please at least wait until after the turkey before you start eating everyone's clothes.'

'Yes,' Lucy added. 'It's not very nice to chew your guests' trousers.' She wagged her finger at the goat, who remained oblivious, nibbling away contentedly. Sophie didn't have the heart to extract him.

Harry put his arm around Sophie's shoulders and pulled her against him. 'Sophie's not a guest,' he said, and it might have been her imagination, but she thought his eyes were a little too bright, his voice rough in a way it wasn't usually. He gave her a slow, gentle smile that warmed her to her core and added, 'she's family.'

Chapter Thirty-Three

The fire was humming happily in the grate, four dogs laid out in front of it, along with a very sleepy goat, sated by a Christmas lunch of sprouts and potatoes, and the pocket of Fiona's coat which he'd somehow got to without anyone noticing.

Christmas carols played quietly in the background, the beautiful strains of 'Silent Night' accompanying their post-lunch chatter, after Lucy's request to play the Michael Bublé Christmas album for the eighth time in a row had been vetoed. Now she sat on the sofa, the first book in her new trilogy open on her lap. Jazz had told Dexter that, from what she could see, it was definitely YA and the romance was firmly closed door.

Sophie was snuggled up against Harry, her socked feet on the coffee table, happily full of turkey, Christmas pudding and champagne, feeling more content than she could remember. Harry had told her he had a present to give her later, when everyone had gone, ('Not *that* kind of present,' he'd whispered, 'or, not *only* that kind of present.') and she had a wrapped parcel in her coat pocket: a pair of the beautiful gloves in buttery caramel suede from Fiona's shop. She wanted to get Harry more than just that, but – she realized disbelievingly – she would have a whole lot of time, now, to buy him gifts.

Everyone had been delighted that she was staying, but none of Harry's guests had seemed that surprised – certainly nowhere near as surprised as Harry – as if they'd all known something she didn't about the power of Mistingham, or were simply confident that she'd realize, in time, that she was in the best place she could possibly be.

'What are you doing with your notebooks?' Birdie asked, cradling her cup of tea. She also had her feet on the table, and was wearing festive socks with little gold crackers on. Before she'd taken them off, Sophie had almost choked on her champagne when the older woman had swept back her purple witchy cloak to reveal a pair of luminous green Crocs.

'I'm going to keep making and selling them,' Sophie told her. 'I did well in the run-up to Christmas, and now that I have a permanent home for them—'

'And for you,' Jazz pointed out.

'And for me,' she smiled, 'I'm going to branch out. Look into *widening my stationery offer*,' she added, in a faux-businesslike voice.

'And the shop?' Fiona asked. 'I could be wrong, but it's possible we might be able to convince the owner of the vacant shops on Perpendicular Street to do you a good deal.'

Sophie looked up at Harry, only to discover he was already gazing at her, a dazed smile on his lips.

'I'm sure we could sort something out,' he said. 'I can't

think of anything better for the old sweet shop than to become a high-end, artisan notebook shop.'

'Ye Olde Sweete Shoppe.' Jazz elongated all the e's.

'Luckily, it isn't ever going to be called that again,' he said.

'No,' Sophie agreed, on the verge of laughter. 'It's going to be called Ye Olde Notebooke Emporiume.'

'You are not,' Harry said.

'I am. You told me I could, when we were on the way back from our midnight paddle – you said you'd be more than happy with that name.'

Harry winced. 'I did, didn't I?'

Sophie laughed. 'It has a lovely ring to it. Ye Olde Notebooke Emporiume. Or, if I'm branching out, Ye Olde Stationeree Emporiume.'

'Fuck's sake.' Harry raised his eyes to the ceiling. 'Will I never be free of stupidly quaint shop names?'

'Small ears,' Fiona said.

'Not that small!' Lucy piped up, without looking up from the pages.

'If the sweet shop is getting a new lease of life,' Dexter said, 'does that mean the bookshop might be, too?'

The silence that followed was loaded. Sophie glanced at May, who gave a tiny shake of her head, then turned her gaze on Fiona, widening her eyes. Her friend seemed to get the message, giving Sophie a short, sharp nod. May had told her earlier that she didn't want anyone else knowing who was responsible for the freshly bound books, about Harry's secret hobby and what she had done with it. She said she'd admitted it to Fiona, but was sure she could swear her to secrecy.

'Why don't you want anyone knowing?' Sophie had asked her.

'Because Harry's self-conscious about the books, and he's only finished a few – hardly enough to do anything with – so it's best if we keep it between us. If that's OK?'

'Of course it is,' Sophie said, then added, 'and do you have more projects planned, in your self-appointed role as Secret Bookshop Fairy Godmother?'

May had given her a serene smile, which Sophie thought was answer enough.

She had wondered if, now she and Harry were together, and that she was staying, May hadn't completely given up on the idea of gifting Harry's beautifully bound books to people, and now she was convinced she was right. May fully believed in the magic of her Secret Bookshop, and, despite her initial surprise, and her disproportionate reaction when she'd discovered the truth, Sophie couldn't help believing in it a little bit now, too.

She would keep their secret, and she would always treasure *Jane Eyre*, which right now was upstairs in Harry's bedroom, a floor above where he had transformed it from an old, tatty edition into something special. Nobody else had asked Sophie if she'd unmasked her mystery gifter, and she thought that it had mostly been forgotten in the face of festivals and storms, and the all-consuming nature of Christmas. Neither Winnie nor Simon had seemed intent on solving the conundrum, so she thought that May would be free to do whatever she wanted to – as long as Harry was happy – without anyone else realizing it was her.

'I'm a long way from resurrecting the bookshop,' Harry admitted. 'I've got to get this place in order first.' Sophie knew the annex roof patch-up was a big job, that all the books were temporarily piled up in his study to protect them, as the secret room was now exposed to the elements.

'It's beautiful,' Fiona said, indicating the lounge, 'even if it's still a work in progress.'

'Bernie would have loved what you've done so far,' Ermin added.

Sophie felt Harry stiffen beside her. 'I hope so,' he said. 'I really hope that, after everything, I'm not letting him down. I want the estate to be part of the village again. I'm done hiding.'

'Well, good,' Fiona said firmly, but Sophie thought she sounded slightly choked.

'He'd have loved this, most of all.' Ermin waved his hand between Sophie and Harry.

'Yes,' Jazz added with a smirk, 'she's the best thing Harry's done, for sure.'

'Jazz!' Fiona sounded outraged, and Sophie felt her cheeks burn. Harry's hand slipped to her waist, his fingers sliding under the hem of her jumper to find her bare skin.

'I didn't mean that,' Ermin blustered. 'I just meant—'

'Don't listen to her.' Fiona patted her husband's arm. 'She's run rings around you since she arrived, and I doubt it's going to change any time soon.'

'Not a chance,' Jazz said with a grin.

'I wouldn't have it any other way.' Ermin looked over at the young woman, and Sophie's heart squeezed at his tender expression.

There was a loud bang from outside, and all four dogs pricked their ears up.

'What's that?' Sophie asked. 'Not another storm?'

Harry slid his arm out from around her and stood up. He held his hand out, and she took it and let him pull her to her feet. 'Jason and Simon said they were going to do this.'

'Do what?'

'Fireworks on the green. If we go outside, we should see some of them above the treeline.'

'Let's go, then.' Fiona pulled Ermin up, and Dexter waited for Lucy to put her book down, sighing heavily as she abandoned her fictional world for the temporary delights of the real one. Jazz helped Birdie up and everyone followed Harry onto the front steps.

The fireworks were louder out here, and Sophie saw a bright spark, a pink flash followed by a bang and the sound of scattering rain. Everyone stared up, waiting for the next mini explosion, and Harry stood behind her, wrapping his arms around her waist, pulling her against his chest.

'I never imagined I'd end Christmas Day like this, with my arms around you,' he said into her ear. 'I never imagined my Christmases would be this good again: that my life could be this good.'

'It's only been a day,' Sophie said, but only because it was easier to be flippant than serious. She didn't know how to tell him that this day, this Christmas, had outstripped her previous ones by an almost incalculable amount. She promised herself she would find the words, embrace the emotion that would no doubt accompany them, when they were alone together, later. 'Anyway, there's more to come. It's not over yet.'

'I haven't forgotten,' Harry said, sliding his hand under her jumper again. 'I don't think I'll ever forget what you said to me out there on the lawn.'

'Which bit? About how we're going to celebrate, or that I realized I loved you?'

'That one,' he murmured.

'Harry!'

'All of it,' he said, his fingers drifting round to her belly button while everyone was focused on the fireworks. 'Everything you said to me, Soph. But mostly the part where you said you didn't want to live your life without me.'

'I don't,' she said, simply. 'Not ever.'

The last firework filled the night sky over Mistingham with the glamour of festive lights set to twinkle mode, and Sophie felt something cold land gently on her nose. As she looked up into a dizzying swirl of snowflakes, and realized her perfect Christmas Day had one more trick up its sleeve, she leaned back into the arms of the man she loved, and knew that she was here to stay for good.

In Harry's bedroom on the first floor of Mistingham Manor, a gust of wind slipped through the cracked-open window and ruffled the pages of *Jane Eyre*. The section it fell open on proved, perhaps, that May was right to believe in the magic of the books he'd given a new lease of life to.

'Thank you, Mr Rochester, for your great kindness. I am strangely glad to get back again to you; and wherever you are is my home – my only home.'

The End

Acknowledgements

Writing and publishing a book takes a whole village and, like Mistingham in this book, the publishing village around me is full of wonderful people I couldn't do without.

Thank you, first and foremost, to my editor Kate Bradley, who helps make my books immeasurably better, from concept through to edits, and all the insight and support she gives me along the way.

Thank you to Agent Extraordinaire Alice Lutyens. I am still overjoyed that she picked me to be one of her authors, and now I can't imagine doing this without her (and really wouldn't want to). Thank you to the whole team at Curtis Brown who support me so brilliantly, including rights agent Emma Jamison and Rakhi Kholi.

I am so lucky that I get to work with the HarperFiction team, who do so much to make sure my books find readers. Thank you especially to Lynne Drew, Susanna Peden, Sian Richefond, Meg Le Huquet and Katelyn Wood.

I dread to think what state my books would be in without Penelope Isaac, my copy editor. I wonder how many fictional timeline issues she's had to fix during her career. Thank you to Penny, and also to Kati Nicholl for the essential proofreading.

Every time I see the cover for my latest book, I decide it is my favourite. I love this cover so much! The colours, the snowflakes, the little houses surrounding the harbour, Sophie and Harry depicted so perfectly going for an evening stroll. Thank you to designer Emily Langford and illustrator Camila Gray for creating something so special.

I first read *Jane Eyre* by Charlotte Brontë when I was about fifteen and remember being overwhelmed by its magic and emotion; how it took me from desolation to hope, everything in between, and then to that beautiful ending. I have so enjoyed rereading it, taking little snippets of it that fit in with Sophie and Harry's story. The edition my quotes are from is the *Penguin Classics* edition, and if you haven't read it then I highly recommend it: I think it's one of the most romantic books ever written.

Fellow author friends are the best, for general book chat, for commiserating and celebrating, laughing and inspiration and encouraging productivity. A big thanks to Kirsty Greenwood for all the Zoom sessions while I was writing this book – I would have been so unproductive without you! Huge thanks also to Sheila Crighton, Sarra Manning, Jane Casey, Pernille Hughes, Katy Marsh, Isabelle Broom and Sam Holland.

David is the best husband an author could have (anyone could have, in my incredibly biased opinion). I wouldn't be writing these books without his love and support, his way of effortlessly providing me with romantic hero inspiration. He makes it all worthwhile.

I am lucky to have a hugely supportive mum and dad who understand the book world, are happy to let me talk endlessly about my characters and books, my sales and future plans. Thank you, Mum and Dad, and thank you to Lee, too.

Releasing a new book into the world is always nerve-wracking, so my last thank you has to go to readers, booksellers, reviewers and librarians; the people who read my books, shout about them and push them into other people's hands. I really hope you love Sophie and Harry, Mistingham and all its inhabitants, and thank you for still picking up my books and immersing yourself in the pages.

Cosy up with more delightful stories

from Cressida McLaughlin

All available now.